THE TROJAN PROJECT

Other books by the author:
THE MANIFESTO OF INDIVIDUALISM (1968)
MAKERS AND TAKERS (1997)

The TROJAN PROJECT
A Novel of Intrigue about Reshaping America

Edmund Contoski

American Liberty Publishers
Minneapolis, Minnesota

Copyright © 1997 by Edmund Contoski.

All rights reserved. No part of this book may be reproduced or transmitted in any form or by any means, electronic or mechanical, including photocopying, recording, or by information storage and retrieval systems, without permission in writing from the publisher except in the case of brief quotations in critical essays and reviews.

American Liberty Publishers
P.O. Box 18296
Minneapolis, MN 55418

Cover Design: Paul Kielb

ISBN 0-9655007-5-6
Library of Congress Catalog Card Number 96-78788
Printed and bound in the United States of America.

THE TROJAN PROJECT

Chapter One

Don Emerson was startled to realize that someone must have driven his car. It was Monday morning, and he was about to leave for work. He had entered the garage from the house and walked toward the overhead garage door to unlock and open it. But as he approached, he saw the car was parked so close to the door that he couldn't squeeze between the two to reach the lock and handle, which were in the middle of the door. He knew he couldn't have left it that way because there was no way he could have closed that door except from the outside, which he knew he hadn't done. He always closed it from the inside, then entered the house from the garage.

He immediately thought that his wife, Jan, must have used his car. He had no objection to that; it was just that she very seldom did so, preferring instead to drive her own car. He thought something must have been wrong with her car. But if that were the case, it was funny she hadn't mentioned it to him. He looked her car over quickly. No flat tires. Nothing obviously wrong. He tried to think where she might have gone over the weekend that she might have used his car and where he had been that he hadn't realized when she had gone. She hadn't said anything to him.

Suddenly, he looked at his watch and thought *I'd better get moving; I'll talk to Jan about this tonight.* He opened the overhead door to Jan's stall, went out and opened the door to his garage from the outside. Then he backed his car out, closed both garages and drove off.

On his way to the office he puzzled over what could have happened. The car was so close to the door that even Jan, who was smaller and thinner than he, would have had difficulty squeezing into that space. And even if she were able to do so, it would have been so uncomfortable that she probably wouldn't have done it. Would she instead have closed the door from the outside, then opened the door to her stall and reentered the garage that way—the reverse of his procedure this morning? But why would she have gone through that roundabout operation? It didn't make sense. Maybe, he thought, she closed his garage door from the outside because she was going to stay outside. Why would she do that? He immediately said to himself *I'll bet the children were outside. She probably closed the garage door from the outside so that she would be with them. Then later, when they were ready to go in, they probably entered the house directly through the side door, rather than by going back through the garage.* He concluded there might well be other explanations, too, and in any case the matter was so trivial that he wouldn't even mention it to Jan after all.

    Don Emerson was a computer consultant. He was an electronics engineer who, after college, had worked for two years for an electronic instrument company in San Diego which made certain types of military instruments. Then he moved to Silicon Valley, where for the next five years he worked for two computer companies in various positions.

    He had always liked the idea of having his own business, and he liked the idea of going back to live in the Minneapolis area. One day he decided that if he was ever going to make the move, this was as good a time as any.

    A few months after moving back to Minneapolis, he got reacquainted with Jan. He had known her all her life because their parents were friends; but since she was eight years younger than he, he had paid no attention to her as a child. They became reacquainted as a result of one of Don's mother's many parties, to which Jan's parents had been invited.

    In the course of conversation at that party Don had asked about Jan. He was surprised when her parents told him that she would be graduating from the university in June with a degree in computer science and would be looking for a job. He still thought of her as a little girl. He remarked that his new business was growing and that he was thinking of hiring an assistant and that if she was interested, she should give him a call. She called the next day and was hired. A year later they were married. Now they had two children, Jason, who was four and a half, and Kathie, three and a half.

    Jan worked full time until the children came. Since then, she had worked only part time, preferring to spend much time with her small children. But she also liked her work and wanted to stay involved in the business. Conveniently, a lot of the work she did could be done at home. If it was necessary for her to go to the office, she knew she could always drop the children off at her sister Delores' for a few hours. Delores loved children—she had five of her own—and was always willing to look after one or two more.

    Jan's flexible work pattern was a valuable asset for the couple's consulting business. She could work more or fewer hours depending on the workload. And her knowledge and ability to run the day-to-day operations of the business left Don free to spend additional time on promotion and exploring ways of expanding the business. Their little company provided a good income and had now grown to include five full-time employees.

Don and Jan were not only successful in their business but made a very attractive couple: he, an inch over six feet, with rugged good looks and a fit body from regular tennis; she, a slim brunette, attractive enough to be a model, which she had been part-time while in college. The two were happy with their business, their lives, each other and often said they couldn't imagine being married to anyone else. They often wondered why so many other couples had so many problems, such troubled marriages, when everything seemed so idyllic for them. They weren't rich in material goods, but they had what they needed and through hard work could see themselves getting ahead little by little.

They had bought an older house to which they were gradually making improvements. Their next project was to get new flooring and new cabinets in the kitchen. The contractor was scheduled to begin the work on Wednesday, and Don and Jan were going to spend a few days at Don's mother's house, about twenty minutes from theirs, while this work was being done.

Monday evening, after the children were in bed, Don and Jan talked about their going to his mother's house after work the next day. Don reminded her that she would be fixing supper over there and that his mother, Helen, would not be eating with them since she was going out for the evening. He said she would be leaving fairly early because she was going to pick up some other ladies.

"She shouldn't be driving any more," Jan said.

"That's what they always say about older people, but my mother's never had an accident," he replied. "She's a good driver. You've ridden with her."

"I know, but..."

"And how about all the other people who ride with her when she goes to her three bridge clubs, her hobby club, her church group, or when she goes to the theatre or the symphony? None of her friends seems to be afraid to ride with her. Most of those women she goes with are younger than she is. Don't you think they would say, 'Helen, we'll pick you up' if they were afraid of her driving? And how about her sister, Cecily? She's seven years younger than my mother. Don't you think she would say, 'Helen, I'll drive' if she had any qualms about mother driving?"

"I've never been afraid to ride with your mother," said Jan. "It's just that after that incident two months ago where her car was found one morning parked a half a block down the street and she didn't remember where she went or how it got there, you have to wonder. I mean, after all, as people get older their minds often start to go. Usually it starts with just being a little forgetful, then progresses to something worse, like Alzheimer's or senility. I worry about something happening to her, her mind failing at a critical moment in traffic when she could have a serious accident."

"Well," said Don, "when have you seen mother's mind or memory fail? When she comes back from one of her bridge clubs, she can tell you every interesting hand she played, trick by trick. Few people of any age could do that. Besides, both of her parents lived into their nineties, and they were both mentally sharp to the very end. Mother is only 71. That's not so old nowadays. Lots of people who are older than that manage to drive safely for many years, people who don't have my mother's vitality and apparent good health. Heck, she doesn't even need glasses, not even for reading. How many people her age can boast that? She really is in very good condition and very capable."

"Then how do you explain her car being a half block down the street that time and her not knowing anything about it?"

"I can't explain it. No one can. Not even her doctor," said Don, shaking his head. "After that incident I finally got her to go in for a checkup. You know how hard that was! She always says, 'Why waste time—and money—going to a doctor when you're not sick?' She hadn't even been to a doctor in fourteen years, not since her gall bladder operation. And you know what Dr. Zacharais said. He said she's in remarkably good health, that if everyone were as healthy as she, he'd be out of business. I told him about the car incident, and he said he couldn't explain it but that he could find no medical reason mother shouldn't drive."

"But why wait until she has an accident? Don't you think she should stop driving, just as a precaution?"

"Just as a precaution? Has our society become so protective that people have to stop living *just as a precaution?* I..."

"I didn't say she had to 'stop living,' just stop driving," interrupted Jan. "You're exaggerating. You know very well that if your mother didn't drive, in most cases her friends would be glad to pick her up. Your mother's crowd does that now for some of their less able members.

Surely they'd do so for your mother. They all love her company. She certainly wouldn't miss out on much."

"All right. It wouldn't mean she'd have to stop living, but it would certainly diminish her lifestyle as well as her independence and probably her self esteem. Do you or I, or society for that matter, have the right to cut back another person's lifestyle—to limit that person's freedom of action and enjoyment of life—*just as a precaution* when that person has done no wrong or injured no one? What happened to the old principle that a person is innocent until proved guilty? You can't take away a person's freedom of action—put them in jail—just as a precaution. And what is it that she's supposed to be guilty of in this case? It's no crime to park one's car a half block down the street from one's house—there were no 'No Parking' signs—and it's no crime to forget where you parked your car or where you went yesterday. And no one was injured—or even endangered—by any of those things," said Don.

"I suppose you're right, but I was just thinking it would be for her own good."

"Well, you're still saying that *some* people should be deciding what's good for someone *else*. My point is that one ought to be free to decide that for one's self. I grant you that my mother's friends would be glad to cart her around—they're all such sweet ladies—but my mother would be too proud and too independent to ask them; they'd have to offer. Besides, how would she shop for groceries? Again, she'd have to be dependent upon others for transportation or she couldn't live in that big house by herself. And mother wouldn't be happy being dependent upon anyone, nor would she be as happy living anywhere else."

"I've never been able to understand why your mother continues to live in that big house all by herself. Why doesn't Cecily move in with her? She only lives five blocks away, and she's over at your mother's house half the time anyway. It doesn't make sense to me for the two of them to maintain separate residences when their lives are so close."

"It makes sense to them, and that's what counts," said Don. "They're not only sisters; they're best friends. On days when they're not together they can still talk for an hour or two on the phone, even though they just saw each other the day before. But they do have their differences. They like to be together, but they also need time to be away from each other. The present arrangement works out fine. Mother says Cess isn't neat and orderly enough, and Aunt Cess says mother is too finicky and fussy. So I think if they lived together they wouldn't get along as well as they do now. Besides, mother belongs to clubs and entertains groups to which Cecily doesn't belong. So it would be awkward for both of them if Cecily were there all the time. Occasionally, as you know, Aunt Cess stays over night, if they've been watching a movie together on TV late into the night, or if it's raining or she just doesn't feel like going home. But she still wants to have her own place, even though it's far smaller than mother's. As long as they can afford it and that's what they want to do, that's their business, their choice."

"But don't you worry that your mother could have an accident, say, fall down the stairs or have a heart attack, and she'd just lie there with no one to help her?"

"Of course I worry about it. That's why I installed a phone by her bedside three years ago, so it would be easier for her to call 911 or us or Cecily if she needed to. Not that that would solve every possible emergency, but that's about all we can do consistent with where and how she wants to live. After all, you can't make life totally risk free—at least if you want a life worth living. She's aware of the risk, and this is how she chooses to live. Doesn't she have a right to that choice, even if it turns out badly? Granted she'd be more secure in some senior citizens' complex where they have a staff to watch over everyone, but to her that wouldn't be living. I'd rather see her have a shorter life living the way she wants to live—even if it ends tragically for her—than see her live many years longer in some secure institution where she would be unhappy. Isn't that the same choice you would make if you were in her shoes? Here she entertains her friends—sometimes twelve or fifteen people, as you know—for lunch or dinner in her familiar surroundings of forty years. She has and does what she wants, she's no threat to anyone, and I wouldn't take any of that away from her."

"I wouldn't either," Jan said. Smiling, she added, "You know I'm very fond of your mother. I couldn't ask for a better mother-in-law."

Don nodded appreciatively. He was glad Jan and his mother got along so well.

"I really do admire her in so many ways," Jan continued. "She has more energy than I do. Honestly, darling, I don't know how she does it! All those clubs, all the entertaining, the concerts and everything else. She never ceases to amaze me," said Jan, getting to her feet. "I'm just concerned about her, that's all."

Jan bent over and kissed Don and said, "I'm going to bed, Honey. The children get me up so early." Then as she straightened up she added,

"You usually have a little snack before going to bed. Maybe you'll have a little more than usual tonight. I'm afraid the supper was rather meager. When I made that casserole a few days ago, I thought there would be plenty for two meals. But when I heated it up tonight, there seemed to be less than I remembered so the portions were rather skimpy. Did you have enough?"

"Yes, I had enough," he said. "I really wasn't very hungry this evening. I'll have a couple of your good cookies before I turn in—if there are any left."

"The kids got into them pretty good, but, yes, there are a few left—just a few."

Don went into the kitchen but couldn't find the cookies. Figuring the kids had finished them off, he settled for a couple of crackers with peanut butter and half of a banana. Then he went to bed.

On Tuesday Don awoke well before the alarm clock rang. This happened to him occasionally, perhaps once a month. When it did, he would try to get up without waking Jan, go downstairs and leisurely read the morning newspaper, usually with a cup of coffee.

There was no definite pattern to these early risings though often they seemed to be associated with the anticipation of an unusually busy day or some change of his usual routine. This morning, he speculated, it might have been because the workmen were to start on the kitchen tomorrow and he and his family would be going to Helen's today.

This morning he picked up the newspaper at the front door and then went to the kitchen for his coffee. As he entered the room and headed for the coffeemaker, he looked out the window and could see the top of Jan's garage stall—and the door was open! As he stepped closer to the window, his field of vision expanded—and now he could see that the rear of her car was protruding about two feet out of the garage!

At first he thought that Jan might have forgotten to close the garage door. But when he saw the car sticking out of the garage, he knew that explanation was inadequate. He thought of a break-in, a robbery, but he could see the portable TV set in the kitchen. He thought that was one of the first things a robber would grab. Immediately he thought of the safety of the children, but now he could hear their voices and Jan's voice upstairs. There was no indication of alarm in their voices, so they were all right. He looked back into the living room. The stereo components and the VCR were still there, untouched.

He thought about calling the police, but he couldn't report a robbery if nothing was missing. And he wasn't even sure there had been a break-in. If the police came out, they might just say he or Jan had parked the car poorly and left the door open.

He stood at the window for several minutes, watching the rear of Jan's car. Nothing was happening. There was no sound except that of his family's voices upstairs. He concluded that whatever happened had taken place during the night. It was over now; it was broad daylight. Whoever had done this was probably no longer around. Cautiously he walked toward the garage, the path he took every morning for work. He opened the door but didn't go in. He stood silently by the side of the door for perhaps 30 seconds, listening carefully. Everything was quiet inside. Looking into the garage, he could see nothing disturbed. So he slowly walked in. There were tools—including power tools—laying right where he had left them. There was the battery charger, Jan's bicycle, everything just where it should be. He looked at the car; there appeared to be no damage. He peered in the car windows—half expecting to see a body there. Nothing.

He walked back into the house. Jan and the kids were coming down the stairs. He met her at the bottom of the stairs.

"Jan," he said, "was there anything unusual about the way you parked your car in the garage yesterday?"

"No, of course not," she said, a quizzical expression on her face. "Why?"

"Something's happened. I don't know just what, but we're all okay. We're safe; that's the important thing, and nothing is missing as far as I can tell," Don said.

"What do you mean? What are you talking about?"

"C'mon into the kitchen, and I'll show you. And you kids stay close to us."

He didn't need to say anything further. As Jan entered the kitchen, she gasped, "Aaagh! Who would have done this?"

"I haven't any idea. Nor can I see why. Nothing is missing, as far as I can tell. It couldn't have been the children. They're too small even to be able to lift that big garage door, let alone move the car."

"Shouldn't we call the police?"

"I've thought of that, but what would we tell them? Nothing is missing. There's no evidence of a break-in. Would the police conclude there has been a crime—or would they say we parked the car poorly and didn't close the garage door, or—worse—would they say we fabricated the whole thing and called in a false alarm?"

"I don't know. What should we do?"

"Where are your car keys?"

"They're always in my purse," she said. "I'll go check."

"Good," he said. "I'll check on that extra set of keys in that little drawer in the desk."

"My keys are here," she called out. "And my money's here, too. At least I think it's all here. I don't remember exactly how much I had, but it doesn't appear that anything is missing."

"The other keys are here in the desk, too, right where they're supposed to be," he called back. "I don't know what to make of this, but I have to ask you about something else."

"What's that?" she said coming over to him and still rummaging through her purse.

"Did you drive my car over the weekend?"

"No, of course not. I haven't driven your car for months. It's been so long I can't even remember the last time."

"Then someone has been driving *both* our cars," he said. He explained his experience the previous morning, when his own car was parked so close to the door he couldn't open the garage from inside.

"What are we going to do?" she asked.

"The first thing I'm going to do," he said, "is have all the locks on the house and the garages changed."

"That sounds like a good idea," said Jan. "I'm not superstitious, and I know you're not. I don't believe this house is haunted or anything like that, but it will be good to get away from here for a few days and stay at your mother's while the kitchen is being remodeled."

THE TROJAN PROJECT

Chapter Two

It was nearly five-thirty that afternoon when Don and his family arrived at Helen's. She was just getting ready to leave for supper and an evening of bridge with some of her friends.

"I hate to leave just when you get here and not have supper with you tonight," she said. "But I'm eating at Eleanor's, and I have to pick up Irene and Lucille. It's my turn to drive."

Helen suddenly smiled broadly as Jason and Kathie walked toward her. "How about a kiss for your Grandma?"

Don kissed her, too, and said, "Have fun, Mom."

"Don't worry about that," she said. "We always have fun. And Eleanor is such a good cook. I always look forward to going over there. I hope you'll all make yourselves at home while I'm gone. I don't feel like a very good hostess running off like this; but as you know, this evening was planned a long time ago, and I can't disappoint the other girls. Jan, you know where everything is. Just help yourself to whatever you need. See you all later."

After she left, Don remarked how tired he was. "That's not surprising," said Jan. "After all, you did get up extra early this morning. And if that wasn't enough, you've had the strain of worrying about someone driving our cars. Why don't you stretch out on the davenport for a little while until I get supper together? I'll call you when the hamburgers are ready."

"Sounds good to me," he said.

Jan was right. He had been worrying about what had happened with the cars. But now he felt a sense of security in his mother's house, the house where he grew up. He relaxed. In only a few minutes he was sound asleep on the davenport.

In the kitchen Jan busied herself with preparing supper. She had the hamburgers frying and was thinking about what else she would serve. She was familiar with Helen's kitchen, but it wasn't the same as operating in her own. She had to think twice about where things were. Everything seemed to be taking a little longer. The children were excited about their different surroundings, and she had a hard time getting them to settle down. She set the table and then poured each of them a glass of milk. Then Kathie spilled her milk. As it spread over the table, some fell onto Kathie's lap and some on the floor.

Jan moved to clean up the mess. Preoccupied with that, she forgot about the hamburgers—until she smelled them burning. Quickly she ran to the stove to remove the frying pan from the fire, just as she would have done in her own kitchen. But her cookware had insulated handles; here she was using Helen's old-fashioned cast iron frying pan. Her action was automatic: she grabbed the frying pan as she would one of her own—barehanded—and cried out in pain as she felt the hot handle and dropped the frying pan, which hit the floor with a loud clang.

In the next room Don awoke with a shriek of terror.

"Don't worry, dear," Jan called out. "I just dropped the frying pan and burned myself a little bit. Nothing serious. Sorry to awaken you."

"It's not that," he said. "There's a body in here. I woke up as this man was rushing at me. And just as he got to the foot of the davenport, he suddenly seemed to become paralyzed, like he had a stroke or something. His mouth was open, his expression frozen. He was rigid for a moment, then keeled over, and I knew he was dead."

"What are you talking about?" said Jan, entering the room.

"Right there, at the foot of the davenport. Isn't there a body there?" he asked.

"No, of course not," she said. "I can see that whole area right from where I'm standing. See for yourself. You just had a bad dream."

He got up and looked. He couldn't believe it, but there was nothing there. Puzzled, he sat down again and shook his head.

"I could've sworn…" he said. "It was so vivid, so real. But I guess it must have been just a dream."

"Sure," she continued. "You know when something bad is about to happen to you in a dream, you always wake up."

"Yes," he said. "Your consciousness won't let you sleep through your own destruction in a dream. But what was really weird about this dream was that the person who was rushing at me looked just like *me*."

"Well, it's over now, and I've got a mess to clean up in the kitchen," she said, turning to leave.

Just then the phone rang. Being closer to it, Jan said, "I'll get it."

Don watched as she picked up the phone and said "Hello." Then in horror he saw her mouth drop open and the expression on her face freeze as though she had become paralyzed—just like the person in his dream! He jumped up from the davenport and slapped the phone from her hand.

She recovered quickly and asked, "What happened?" He told her, and she said she didn't remember anything except answering the phone.

Slowly Don picked up the phone. The caller had already hung up. Slowly he moved the phone toward his ear. As it came within two or three inches of his head, he was aware of a strange sensation, a kind of faint numbing that was coming over him. He moved the phone back, and the sensation disappeared. He repeated the procedure with the same results. Then slowly he tried it on Jan. She could feel the sensation when the phone was still about eighteen inches from her head. When he tried to move the phone slightly closer, she began to get that paralyzed look again. He quickly took the phone away.

Don thought it was odd that his mother had never said anything about this strange phenomenon occurring with her phone, but then he thought that maybe she wasn't aware of it. He already knew that Jan was far more sensitive to it that he was. Maybe his mother wasn't sensitive to it at all.

As he was puzzling over the mystery of his mother's phone, he thought suddenly and unexpectedly about another mystery concerning his mother: the time her car was found parked half a block down the street. He wondered if there was any connection between the two. *Of course not,* he told himself. *That would be absurd.*

But then his mind made another unexpected connection: he thought about his and Jan's cars being moved, too. He couldn't help but wonder whether those mysterious movements were somehow related to what had happened months earlier to his mother's car. His mind was trying to piece things together, to connect these unexplained happenings in a way that would make sense. Still, even if there was a connection between his mother's phone and that unexplained relocation of her car, could there be a similar cause behind the nighttime movements of his and Jan's cars—even though they couldn't feel the strange sensation on the phones in their own house?

Then he thought of the phone in his mother's bedroom and said to Jan, "Come upstairs and let's see if we can feel the same thing on the newer phone in mother's bedroom."

"Look," she said. "You worry about that. I've got kids to feed and a mess to clean up in the kitchen."

"No," he said, grabbing her gently by the arm. "This is important, and it'll only take a minute."

They went upstairs. First Don picked up the phone and held it to his ear. He could hear the dial tone but felt nothing. Then it was Jan's turn. She couldn't feel anything either.

"That's what I wanted to find out," he said. "Most phones probably don't give any indication of what's happening. That old relic of a phone downstairs is telling us something."

They went downstairs, Jan to the kitchen, Don back to the old telephone. He repeated the earlier experiment, moving the phone slowly closer to his head, then away from it. The result was the same as before. When the phone was close to his head, he could feel that strange, faint numbing sensation. His puzzling over the mystery was interrupted by Jan's call to supper.

During the meal Don said very little, but Jan knew he was thinking about what had just happened. When they were through eating, he said, "You know, dear, I've been thinking. When my mother's car was found a half block down the street, we assume she must have driven it there. But when our cars are moved, we assume somebody else drove them. Yet that would mean that somebody not only had the keys to our cars but also the key to the garage, because there was no evidence of a break-in. It's possible, of course, to start a car without the ignition key, by manually connecting the ignition wires under the dash or the hood. It's called 'hot-wiring.' But I saw no evidence of that on either of our cars. Whoever moved your car, or mine, had the key. Who besides us could have the keys to our cars?

"Suppose some attendant at a parking lot where we may have parked our cars had duplicates made of the car keys and also of the garage key. That was the first thing I thought of, that some kid had keys made to go 'joy riding.' But when kids steal a car to go 'joy riding,' they don't bring it back. They run it till it's out of gas, and then they abandon it. It would make no sense for them to return it because doing so would increase their chance of being apprehended."

"So you think we moved our own cars?" asked Jan with astonishment. "Why would we do that."

"That's what I've been trying to figure out," he said. "What if there's something coming through the phone lines, not a biological entity but something transmitted by an electronic signal, something like a computer virus. Let's call it a telephone virus. But instead of affecting computers, it affects people. Suppose it makes them get up at night and do things they don't remember—like drive their cars around. After you answered that phone before supper, you didn't remember what happened to you before I slapped the phone out of your hand. If whatever is coming over the phone leads people to drive their cars, they probably wouldn't remember that either. Even ordinary sleepwalkers don't remember what they've done. Why should it be any different if an electronic signal coming over their phone causes people to do some kind of sleepwalking?"

Jan looked at him skeptically and said, "That might be a plausible explanation for your mother's car being found a half block down the street one morning, but it wouldn't explain what happened with our cars. We were nowhere near your mother's phone, and we haven't experienced this numbing sensation, or whatever you want to call it, on the phones in our house."

He countered: "But maybe what happened here is happening with all phone lines; it's just not as obvious as it is here with this particular old telephone. Remember that neither of us could feel anything on the phone in mother's bedroom. Yet that's the same phone line.

"Now, as I was thinking about all this, I started to wonder if the dream I had before supper wasn't what I thought it was. That image of myself rushing toward the davenport seemed so real! Maybe what I thought was the dream and what I thought was reality were reversed. Maybe that person lying on the davenport was the dream and the person rushing back was the real me! Of course, if that were the case, the reclining image should have vanished when I woke up, and I should have been standing there where the rushing image keeled over and disappeared. So I know that can't be the explanation. But I think there's some connection between whatever is coming over the phone lines and the mysterious movements of our cars."

"Look," said Jan, "dreams are sometimes very realistic. You just had a bad dream. That's all. I don't think you should be trying to make too much of it."

But Don continued: "Since I woke up on the davenport, that image of me had to be real. But maybe the other image was real, too. Maybe they were *both* real. Maybe that's how the cars are moved while people are asleep—maybe the form or image of the person lies there while the real person moves cars or does other things like a sleepwalker. And then the image and the reality recombine when the person wakes up—which is why I saw that image of myself rushing at me as I woke up. Maybe that 'dream' I had seemed so real because it *was* real."

"You don't really expect me to believe that, do you?" she said. "Sounds like a science fiction story."

"I expected you to say that, but it would explain a lot of things. It would explain how our cars could be moved and yet our car keys were never missing; we would know where the keys were and would put them back. And we would never remember what we had done. So we would think someone else had used our cars. It would even explain why there wasn't as much of that leftover casserole on Monday as you thought there should be. It would explain why the cookies were all gone when you thought there were a few left."

"You're jumping to conclusions," said Jan. "I probably just misjudged the amount of that casserole. That's a lot more sensible explanation than you've come up with. And as for the cookies, the kids probably ate them. That, too, is a lot more rational and believable than your theory. I can see that you're serious about this, but the whole idea is so preposterous! I don't see how you can expect anyone to take it seriously."

Don had no answer to that. If he couldn't convince Jan, whom could he convince? "I know it sounds ridiculous," he admitted. "I don't know what the explanation is, but I feel sure that all these strange happenings are related somehow."

At the sound of his mother's garage being opened, Don put down his magazine and glanced up at the clock on the mantel, whose hands showed a little past eleven. "It's rather late," he said when Helen entered the room. "You must have had a good time."

"Oh, yes, a wonderful time," she said. "The food was elegant. That Eleanor is such a good cook. And I was the big winner at the card table. There was one particularly interesting hand. I made a little slam. Irene, who was my partner, dealt and opened with one heart. I had 19 points and a six-card diamond suit headed by the ace, king, queen. So I jumped to 3 diamonds. We ended up at six diamonds. The opening lead was the king of clubs. I played low from the board and…"

"I'm sorry to interrupt, mother," said Don. "I'm glad you had a good time and won, but we haven't got time for all the details. It's late and I want to talk to you about your telephone." He described the earlier experience with the phone, but he didn't tell her about his "dream" or about his "explanation."

"What on earth are you talking about?" said Helen as she strode over to the telephone. "There's nothing wrong with my telephone." She picked up the phone and held it to her ear. "See? Everything's fine."

"You don't feel any kind of a strange sensation, a kind of numbing effect?" he asked.

"No, of course not," she replied. "Is this some kind of joke? Or are you trying to get me to buy a new phone? This old phone is just fine. It's a waste of money to buy a new phone when this old one works just fine."

Don took the phone from her and slowly moved it closer to his head. Again the numbing sensation returned. So whatever it was was still there, but Helen wasn't sensitive to it. He hung up the phone and said, "It's all right, mom. If you don't feel anything, I guess there's nothing for you to worry about."

During the night Jan was awakened by a noise in the hall. She thought it was probably one of the children, perhaps a little disoriented by being in new surroundings and sleeping in a strange bed. She got up and moved to the doorway, but then she stopped as she saw that the noise had not been caused by one of her children but by Helen, who was now descending the staircase. Jan was glad her children were sleeping soundly; but after Helen disappeared from view, she thought she would check on them anyway, as long as she was up. As she walked down the hall to the room where they were sleeping, she passed Helen's room. The door was open about an inch. She stopped and glanced in—and there she saw Helen fast asleep in her bed!

She hurried quietly back to her room, gently woke Don and whispered what had happened. He quickly got up, whispered to her to go to the doorway to his mother's room and watch her sleeping while he would go downstairs and try to find the "other" Helen.

He returned in a few minutes to say he couldn't find her. He had also checked the garage, but her car was there and didn't look as though it had been moved. A light rain was falling, and her car was dry.

Jan whispered, "What should we do now? Should we wake her?"

Don thought for a moment, then shook his head negatively and motioned for her to follow him back to their room. After quietly closing the door behind them, he turned to Jan and said, "I'm not sure what would've happened if we had awakened her. I *think* she would probably have had the same experience I had, of this other person rushing to get back before she fully woke up, but I'm not sure. Maybe it would have ended differently for her. Maybe in her case the person sleeping would have perished instead of the one returning. Or maybe they both would have perished. With my own mother I couldn't take a chance."

"I guess your theory about your 'dream' being real isn't so ridiculous after all. But I never would have believed it if I hadn't seen what I've just seen with my own eyes," Jan said.

Don and Jan crawled back into bed, but it took a long time for them to fall asleep again.

When Don left for work in the morning, Helen was still sleeping. She came down just as Jan was finishing breakfast with the children.

"How did you all sleep last night," Helen asked.

"Oh, just fine. How about you?" Jan replied.

"Marvelous! I had the best night's sleep I've had in a long time. As I get older, like most people I don't always sleep so well; I wake up often. But last night I slept soundly the whole night through. Maybe I sleep better just knowing my family is here with me."

Jan knew there was no point in pressing the issue. Helen wouldn't remember a thing about last night.

THE TROJAN PROJECT

Chapter Three

When Don arrived at the office that morning, he checked the status of the various projects under way and made sure his employees had their work lined up for the day. He satisfied himself that there were no problems or decisions that would require his attention for at least the next several hours. Then he headed for the phone company.

He had thought about simply calling but decided instead to go in person. In view of the story he was going to tell, he wanted to be sure he was talking to the right person. And he wanted that person to see that he was a responsible-looking businessman, not some kook, and to believe that this was a very serious matter, not some college prank phoned in by some fraternity house.

The receptionist greeted him with a warm smile and a very polite, "Good Morning. How can we help you today?"

"I need to talk to one of your technical people."

"Fine. Would you like to talk to one of our servicemen?"

"No. I need to talk to someone higher up."

"Would you like to talk to our Customer Relations Manager, Roger Garcia?"

"I really need to talk to a technical person."

"I think you should talk to Mr. Garcia. If he thinks you should see a technical person, I'm sure he'll arrange for the appropriate person."

"All right."

"Fine. Just have a seat over there, and I'll tell Mr. Garcia you're here to see him."

In a few minutes Mr. Garcia came out, introduced himself and ushered Don into his office. "Would you like a cup of coffee?" he asked. "Make yourself comfortable," he continued, pointing to one of the plush chairs in his office, "and tell me how I can help you."

Don observed that he was a perfect customer relations person: smiling, courteous and seemingly concerned about his visitor. Don began his story. He watched as Roger Garcia raised his eyebrows and several times seemed to be trying to suppress a smile or even a snicker. Finally he spoke.

"What you've been saying is hard to believe. It's fantastic. I don't even think it's possible, but I'm not a technical person. I'd like to have you talk to one of our technical people. Wait right here, and I'll see if I can get someone."

Garcia walked a few doors down the hall and stopped at the office of Walt Eilers. He stuck his head in the door and said, "Have you got a few minutes, Walt? There's a guy in my office I'd like to have you talk to. I think he's just plain goofy, but I'd like the opinion of someone with your expertise. It'll only take a couple of minutes."

Eilers looked at his watch. "Okay, I can spare a few minutes."

The two men returned to Roger Garcia's office, and Roger said to Don, "Mr. Emerson, this is Walt Eilers. He's one of our top technical people. I'd like to have you tell him what you just told me."

Walt Eilers had none of Roger Garcia's public relations skills. He laughed out loud at Don's story. Garcia tried to smooth things over:

"Now, now, Walt. Mr. Emerson has a problem, and we shouldn't be laughing at his problem. We should be trying to help." Then, turning to Don, he said, "It's just that I don't think we can help you. I don't think it's a phone company problem."

"Look," said Eilers, recovering from his laughter. "If there's something the matter with your mother's phone, buy her a new phone. The phone company is only responsible for bringing service to the residence. You say the phone in her bedroom works perfectly, so that proves you have adequate service to the residence. The phones are the customer's responsibility. Years ago it didn't use to be that way; the phone company owned the phones and leased them to the users. But that's not the way it is now. As for all the other stuff, the cars being moved and your wife's cookies and casserole being eaten, I don't see how you can pin that on the phone company."

"I'm not trying to 'pin' anything on the phone company," said Don. "I just think something is coming over the phone lines that causes people to do these things, which later they don't remember. And I think this is a matter of concern for your company and for the public, because if this spreads—or has already spread—throughout society, then we've all got a huge and very serious problem."

"I think you've been reading too many science fiction stories," said Eilers.

Don saw he was getting nowhere. He thanked them for their time and got up to leave.

Roger Garcia extended his hand and said, "Thanks for stopping by. Why don't you do as Walt suggested and buy your mother another phone? If that doesn't take care of it, come back and see me again, and we'll see if there's anything else we can suggest."

Don shook hands and left. After he was gone, Roger turned to Walt and said, "Well?…."

"You were right the first time," said Eilers, "He's goofy as hell."

"If he comes back, I'll try to subtly suggest that maybe he should see a doctor," said Garcia. "Someone with those kind of delusions really ought to see a psychiatrist."

Don headed next for the offices of the city's newspaper, *The Minneapolis Journal American.* He had often driven by this large old masonry building but never had an occasion to go in. Now he paused outside and looked at the massive stone arch over the main entrance. There, over the doors, was the address, 1021. He read these numerals as "10, 2, 1," which sounded like "10 to 1." *Those,* he thought, *are probably the odds against anyone in this building believing anything I'm going to tell him.* Well, there was only one way to find out. He took a deep breath and walked through the doors. Inside he told the receptionist he would like to speak to the science editor, Jim Phillips. After a short wait, he was allowed to see him.

Phillips had the most cluttered office Don had ever seen. There were stacks of paper, file folders and books everywhere. These were crammed—with no apparent order—into every square inch of shelf space or heaped in untidy piles on the floor along the walls. Phillips removed a foot-high stack of papers from a chair and placed it on the floor so Don would have a place to sit.

Don couldn't help but think that the office was a reflection of the man. Phillips' clothes were rumpled enough to have been slept in, and his hair was as disheveled as the papers strewn all over his desk. But he was willing to hear Don out. He listened carefully, didn't interrupt and didn't laugh. When Don finished, however, Phillips hit him with a barrage of questions without waiting for an answer to any of them:

"Do you have any *scientific* proof? Can you name anyone outside your own family who can verify what you say? Has there been any actual research conducted on this phenomenon? Is there any scientifically-accepted theory which would explain or support your conclusions?"

"I don't have the kind of proof you're looking for yet," said Don, "but I had hoped you would find my story convincing enough to alert the public. I think the public has a right to know and deserves to be warned."

Phillips frowned and shook his head. "The public has already been 'warned' by too many scare stories that later turned out to have no factual or scientific basis. Remember when microwave ovens were new on the market and those scare stories were floated around that you could get cancer from them? Turned out that microwave ovens are the *safest* form of cooking; they produce fewer carcinogens than broiling, boiling, frying or roasting.

"Going back even further, there were the same health scares when television first came out. It was said to cause leukemia or other forms of cancer or to damage one's eyesight, none of which turned out to be true. So there's nothing new about saying that home appliances are dangerous to your health. You've just come up with a new twist for a different appliance, the telephone. But don't expect me to write an article about it unless you can come up with some concrete evidence that what you're talking about is really true.

"And it's not just appliances that have been the subject of unsubstantiated scare articles. Remember the asbestos scare? We were all told that asbestos insulation in buildings could cause cancer. The nation spent $35 *billion* for removal of asbestos just from schools. Then even the Environmental Protection Agency—the outfit that started the whole ruckus in the first place—said the asbestos wasn't a problem after all. In fact, the removal made things worse. Research showed that breathing air in buildings where the asbestos is sealed in the structure is the same as breathing outside air. But when the asbestos is disturbed, as in the removal process, loose fibers lodge in the buildings' ventilation systems and can result in higher levels of asbestos in the inside air for years. Furthermore, the asbestos used in building insulation is a totally different kind of asbestos from that which caused cancer in shipyard workers in World War II, which was supposed to be the reason for removing it from schools.

"In recent years there have been a whole string of scare stories that have alarmed the public without any scientific evidence. There's been acid rain, global warming, chlorofluorocarbons destroying the ozone layer..."

"You mean those aren't true?" interrupted Don.

"They haven't been proven to be true. Take acid rain, for instance. The theory was passed off on the public that this is a product of our industrialized society. Well-meaning people, such as yourself, felt they had to 'warn' the public of this 'new' danger. But borings into the

Antarctic and Greenland ice sheets show that rain was just as acid tens of thousands of years ago as it is today. Furthermore, rain more acid than tomatoes has been found in such remote locations as Samoa, the jungles of South America, the arctic coast of Alaska, and islands in the middle of the Indian Ocean. How can that be due to industry? The public was told that the primary culprit was coal-fired burners, principally from electric utilities, which discharged large amounts of sulfur dioxide. Carried eastward by normal weather patterns, this type of air pollution from the heavily-industrialized Great Lakes states was said to be the cause of acid rain in the Northeast. But the theory doesn't fit the facts. Hurricanes that originate in the Atlantic Ocean bring rain to the East Coast that is even more acid—and there are no industries out in the Atlantic. Furthermore, California has an acid rain problem, but it has no coal-fired utilities. Does its acid rain come from industries in the Pacific Ocean?"

"What about global warming?" asked Don. "Didn't we have the warmest years on record in the 1980s? Doesn't that prove the 'greenhouse theory' that we're warming up the earth's climate?"

"Not at all," answered Phillips. As he spoke, he stood up and began to rummage through piles of papers and folders on one of the many cluttered shelves in his office.

"Here, this is what I'm looking for," he said, pulling a large folder from underneath one of the piles. "I've got several more like this, just on global warming. Keeping abreast of such issues is part of my job. My office may be a little messy, but I can usually find things when I need them."

Opening the folder, he continued, "These contain scientific articles and references to scientific studies. They all refute the idea of global warming. You mentioned that we had the warmest years on record in the 1980s, but that was just in the United States—or, more accurately, just in *parts* of the United States. That doesn't mean *global* warming. Here's an article carried by the Associated Press on March 30, 1990, reporting on a decade of global temperature measurement made by satellites, which everyone concedes is the most accurate way of measuring global temperature. Yet this article states: 'No long-term warming.... The net effect for the globe is basically zero.... The data cannot be used to say we've got an enhanced greenhouse effect.' The press quietly reported this, and then everyone—including most of the news media—continued to talk about global warming as though it were a reality! Everyone still talks about the 1980s as 'the hottest decade in history' in spite of a decade of satellite measurements to the contrary!

"And even within the United States," he went on, picking out another paper from the folder, "there's no convincing evidence of long-term warming. This paper refers to a National Oceanic and Atmospheric Administration study of temperature records spanning a century, which concluded that there has been no global warming since 1895."

Picking up another paper, he continued, "Here's an article by climatologist Patrick Michaels which says the northern hemisphere oceans have been gradually cooling since the 1940s. Oceans cover seventy-three percent of the earth's surface, Mr. Emerson. You tell me how we are experiencing global warming while these vast northern oceans have been *cooling!*

"Here's a later article from *Technology Review* summarizing a study by three MIT scientists of ocean temperatures taken all over the world by mariners since the mid-19th century. It states: 'One of the most striking results suggested by the data is that there appears to have been little or no global warming over the past century.'

"And this is from a study by the prestigious George Marshall Institute in 1992: 'The predictions of the greenhouse theory are contradicted by the temperature record to such a degree as to indicate that the...greenhouse effect has not had any significant impact on global climate in the last 100 years.... Nearly the entire observed rise of 0.5 degrees Centigrade occurred before 1940. However, most of the man-made carbon dioxide entered the atmosphere after 1940. The greenhouse gases cannot explain a temperature rise that occurred before these gases existed. Furthermore, from 1940 to 1970, carbon dioxide built up rapidly in the atmosphere. According to greenhouse calculation, the temperature of the earth should have risen rapidly. Instead...the temperature actually *dropped.*'"

Picking up another paper, he continued nonstop, "Here's an article by Andrew R. Solow of the Woods Hole Oceanographic Institution: 'Existing data show no evidence of the greenhouse effect.... Some will say that the scientific establishment demands an unreasonable degree of certainty before accepting a new idea. But in the case of climate change, and particularly with regard to detecting change with existing data, it is not a question of evidence being tenuous. *It is a question of there being no evidence at all.'"*

"But," said Don, "if there's no evidence, how come we keep hearing projections of disaster scenarios? Aren't those projections based on factual trends?"

"Not at all. They're based on computer models. Those models are based on *theory*—not facts. People have accepted the projections because they've accepted the theory—even if it contradicts the facts! According to the best computer models, the most likely place to first observe global warming is in the Arctic. Yet here," he said, holding up another article from the folder, "is a study by J. D. Kahl and others. The title says it all: 'Absence of Evidence for Greenhouse Warming over the Arctic Ocean in the Past 40 Years.' This was published in the prestigious British scientific journal *Nature* on January 28, 1993."

"What about the chlorofluorocarbons?" asked Don. "Surely it's an accepted fact that CFCs destroy the ozone layer and pose a threat to the environment? What about the ozone hole over Antarctica that we've all heard so much about? Surely that's a reality."

"The so-called ozone 'hole,'" replied Phillips, "is, in reality, not a hole at all. It's only a thinning of the ozone layer that takes place for about four to six weeks a year over Antarctica. But there's no proof that CFCs are responsible for even that. For one thing, the ozone 'hole' was discovered in 1956—before aerosol spray cans were even invented and before there were any significant industrial releases of CFCs into the atmosphere. For another, it's happening in the wrong hemisphere. The vast majority of CFCs are used in the *northern* hemisphere, but the ozone 'hole' is over the *South* Pole. Furthermore, it seems ridiculous to blame the destruction of ozone over Antarctica on chlorine from CFCs thousands of miles away while ignoring an active volcano, Mt. Erebus, that discharges 1000 tons of chlorine per day into the air just 15 kilometers upwind from the Antarctic observation station at McMurdo Sound. This is the station whose measurements supposedly 'prove' the connection to CFCs."

As he spoke, Phillips opened one of his desk drawers and was looking for something. "I keep files on CFCs, too," he explained, "just like on global warming." Pulling out a bulging folder and opening it on his desktop, he said, "Ah! This is what I'm looking for."

He picked out a paper and said, "Here's an article by John E. Kinney, Diplomate of the American Academy of Environmental Engineers, that says chlorine levels at the ozone 'hole' are 50 to 60 times higher than predicted from CFCs. So the chlorine has to be coming from some other source," he said, scratching his head with one hand and further disheveling his hair.

Hauling out another item from the folder, he said, "Here's an article by Petr Beckmann, Professor Emeritus at the University of Colorado, that states that ocean spray from storms is an even greater source of atmospheric chlorine than volcanoes. A single hurricane—with the force of 10,000 hydrogen bombs—sends so much ocean chlorine skyward that it's absurd to be concerned about spray cans of CFCs or man-made refrigerants. They're trivial by comparison.

"This folder is full of articles with explanations other than CFCs for the ozone 'hole.' Here's an article that says the 'hole' is due to natural oscillations of the weather system. Here's another that says NASA scientists attribute it to small climatic shifts in the upper atmosphere. Here's one by Robert Pease, Professor Emeritus of Physical Climatology at the University of California that argues the 'hole' is due to the long Antarctic night in which there is no sunlight to create ozone. Here's another article by Professor Pease in which he says that the theory that CFCs are destroying atmospheric ozone is *'incompatible'* with 'what we *know*' about the ozone layer.' Here's an article that says scientist Linwood Callis of NASA's Atmospheric Sciences Division at Langley Research Center studied a whole list of things which could cause ozone destruction, including volcanic eruptions, the sunspot cycle, changing tropical wind patterns, and highly energetic electrons. He concluded: 'CFCs come in a very poor last as the cause for lower levels of global ozone.'

"Furthermore," continued Phillips, "if you look at ozone measurements at places other than Antarctica, you find that the ozone layer has been *increasing*—not decreasing as it should have been if CFCs were depleting it. Here's an article that says, 'Measurements by the National Oceanic and Atmospheric Administration indicate that the total amount of ozone above the U.S. is actually increasing.' Similarly, measurements since the late 1970s have shown that ultraviolet radiation reaching the earth from the sun has actually been *decreasing* just the opposite of what should have happened if CFCs were depleting the ozone layer.

"So here we have one more example of a theory that simply doesn't fit the facts. You, too, have a theory, Mr. Emerson, but you have yet to show me any facts to validate it."

"But," said Don, "if the stories about CFCs and global warming and acid rain aren't true, why are these kinds of stories being written and published?"

"Oh, a lot of reasons, actually. Sometimes it's a matter of ideology. Sometimes it's political. Sometimes it's simply a desire to be sensational in order to sell newspapers or magazines or TV viewership. A few years ago Charles Alexander, science editor for *Time,* freely admitted that on the issue of environmentalism 'we have crossed the boundary from news reporting to advocacy.' And Senator Tim Wirth stated: 'We've got to ride the global warming issue. Even if the theory of global warming is wrong, we will be doing the right thing, in terms of economic policy and environmental policy.' What it all comes down to—whether for ideological or political reasons or any other—is a willingness to accept and publicize theories without facts, even in contradiction to known facts. The motive is to achieve some 'higher purpose' than to convey the truth to the public. Ideological and political goals are just such 'higher purposes.' But you see, Mr. Emerson, I have no 'higher purpose.' My *only* purpose is to tell the truth to my readers.

"Truth is the only thing that interests me. That's why my office is such a mess. I'm not interested in neatness or appearances or anything else. *Image* means nothing to me; the *truth,* everything. I'll tell anyone who'll read my columns—or anyone who'll listen to me personally, as you have—the truth about all sorts of scientific issues. And I'm always looking for the truth. That's why I was willing to hear you out. You told me about a theory you have, but you have no facts to show that your theory is *true.* If you get those facts, then I'll write the story and do my best to alert the public. But in the meantime I'm not going to write a sensationalistic scare story to alarm the public over yet another unfounded, unproved theory. I'm sure you can find other journalists who will, but I'm not one of them."

As he spoke, Jim Phillips got up from his chair and began moving slowly toward the door, indicating that the meeting was over. Don thanked him for his time and said, "I'll be back when I have some proof."

"Fine. I'll be willing to listen—and to write—if you do," said Phillips.

As Don Emerson walked to his car, he reflected that Jim Phillips was right, that he didn't have any concrete proof that people would find convincing. He was sure his theory was correct, but how could he persuade others? He couldn't think of a way. Nevertheless, believing the problem was real, he still thought the public should be warned. He decided to make one more try. He got in his car and drove to the studios of KPXL-TV.

Inside the studio he asked to speak to the station's news director. After a few preliminary questions and a short wait, he was escorted into the office of Vicki Adams.

Her office was a striking contrast to that of Jim Phillips. It was immaculate. The room's color scheme, the style of the furniture, the paintings on the wall, the draperies and other furnishings all reflected either a professional decorator or at least someone very concerned with and skilled in interior design. Nothing seemed out of place or lacking. Many of the shelves were half empty, as if by design to accentuate whatever the shelves did contain or perhaps to make the room appear more spacious. Everything looked as though it was positioned consciously for effect.

The same was true of Vicki Adams. She sat behind her desk as though she were posing for a portrait. Or perhaps expecting to be on TV. She was stylishly dressed, meticulously made up, and seemed very self-conscious about the positioning of her well-manicured hands. Not a strand of her carefully-arranged hair was out of place.

She listened to Don's story with a mixture of fascination and skepticism. When he finished, she said, "The first requirement of a television news story, Mr. Emerson, is that it be timely. Yet you're talking about something that happened to your cars several days ago, and to your mother's car several months ago."

"But my point," said Don, "is that this is happening all the time. I just happened to notice it on those occasions days or months ago."

"If it's happening all the time," she said, "we should be able to get a picture of it. I'll send a camera crew out tonight if you can assure me your car will be moved in the manner you describe—or is even *likely* to be moved that way. But I can't justify sending a camera crew out there every night for weeks if nothing happens. If what you say happens really happens, it would make a spectacular TV story for our viewers if recorded on videotape. But it would make for very dull television viewing, and very poor news reporting, if all we can show is a parked car which we explain was driven in some mysterious way. It would be the same thing if we show a picture of a telephone and tell people something mysterious is happening through it which they cannot see or hear. It would also be the same thing if we show people a blank wall which has been painted and then tell them that the paint is drying. Our viewers would quickly switch to another channel. Television is an *action* medium, Mr. Emerson. We can't always be there right at the scene of the action as it is happening, but we look for visual stories. And in your case I don't see how we would have a story at all without visual evidence of the action itself. You have a theory, and theories don't make for interesting television viewing. We deal in *images,* not theories. *The image is everything.* We need an image of an event, something visual, an actual happening."

The conversation had come to a dead end. Vicki Adams was interested but unconvinced, and Don could offer nothing further. He thanked her for her time and left.

When he got home, Don explained to Jan the frustrations of his day. "Nobody believed me. Not the phone company, not the newspaper, not the TV station. I don't know what more I could have said or how I could have been more convincing, but it wasn't enough."

"Don't be too hard on yourself," said Jan. "It's something so fantastic that it's really hard for people to believe. After all, I didn't believe it myself until I had that experience with Helen in the hallway last night."

"The public ought to be warned, but I don't know how I can warn people when nobody believes me," he lamented.

"Maybe instead of trying to convince the news media," said Jan, "we should be trying to convince medical authorities that this is a public health problem. Maybe we should write a letter to the National Centers for Disease Control in Atlanta."

"I hadn't thought of that. It's certainly worth a try."

"Good. I thought you'd say that. So I got the address from the library and even typed a rough draft. I'll get it for you."

Don looked over the letter and complimented her on it. They discussed it and made a few minor changes. He mailed the revised letter in the morning.

THE TROJAN PROJECT

Chapter Four

In the next few weeks Don tried to think of some way he could prove his theory about the telephone virus. He looked his car over very carefully every morning for any evidence that it had been moved during the night. A few times there appeared to be minor differences in the positioning of the car—an inch or two this way or that—but the differences were so slight he couldn't be sure without actual measurements. Was he merely imagining that it had been moved? He thought about measuring the position of his car every night and then again in the morning, but what would that prove? It would prove his car had been moved, but he didn't need to be convinced of that. He needed to convince other people, and taking measurements and then telling people the results wouldn't accomplish that.

He thought about rigging up a camera to take a picture of his car if it was moved during the night. But what would that prove? The most he could hope for is that he would get a picture of himself taking his car out of his garage. Big deal. How would that convince anyone that something mysterious was happening? He would feel like a fool showing such a picture to people and telling them that it was more significant than simply a picture of him backing his car out of his garage during the night. Even if he had another camera take a picture of himself sleeping at the same time, how would he convince anyone that the two photos had been taken simultaneously?

One day he decided to call his old physics professor, Dr. Sorenson, to see if he might be able to offer some help. Don had been an excellent student, and the two had been in touch occasionally since Don's graduation. Don decided not to tell him about his theory of a person sleeping in one place and being somewhere else at the same time. Instead, he asked simply, "Is there anything you know of that could explain how something coming over a phone line could affect a person's behavior? I know, obviously, that germs and viruses can't be transmitted over phone lines, but I'm thinking of something electronic rather than biological, sort of like a computer virus."

Professor Sorenson replied, "A computer virus that affects people? Offhand, I don't see how that would be possible. I can't think of a known physical mechanism that would support that idea. And telephones have been used for over a century, hundreds of millions of them worldwide, without any evidence of such a phenomenon."

"But," said Don, "phones haven't been used for very long in conjunction with computers."

"No, that's true. But I still don't see how it could happen."

"I don't either, but recently I had some experiences with a phone at my mother's house which led me to think along that line. I was hoping you might be able to help."

"I can't offer a scientific explanation for that kind of an idea, and I really don't have the time or interest to investigate the matter," said the professor, " but I'll tell you who might. Your old college pal Bobby Bednarz. I know the two of you used to hang around together."

"Bobby! I haven't heard from him in years. What's he doing now? Is he back in town?"

"He stopped into my office the other day just to say hello, and we ended up having a long visit. He's between jobs right now and is taking a month or so off to visit his folks and just relax until he decides what to do next."

"Tell me more. We haven't stayed in touch, so you'll have to fill me in."

"He had a position at some eastern university, but he really didn't do much there," said the professor. "Basically, he was on loan to the Defense Department whenever they had a problem no one else could solve. They would give the problem to him, and he would coop himself up with it for a few weeks or a few months until he solved it. For this he would receive what he says were 'enormous amounts of money' from the Defense Department. Then he would go back to the university and wait for the next problem. With the collapse of the Soviet Union, however, and the cutback in our defense spending, the government no longer needed him for that kind of work. The university wanted him to stay on the faculty and teach. He tried that for a while, but it wasn't challenging enough. So he quit. He doesn't know what he wants to do next, but he's in no hurry. He has plenty of money, more, he says, than he ever thought he'd make in a lifetime; and someone with his qualifications and extraordinary abilities can always get a job anytime he wants, anywhere in the world.

"Why don't you give him a call? He's staying at his folks. They still live in the same house. You know where that is. If he wants to work on your problem, tell him I'll arrange for him to use the laboratory facilities here at the university if he needs a lab."

"Thanks, Professor. I'll do that."

Bobby Bednarz was a true genius. He had won the state chess championship when he was only eleven. The man he defeated for the title was the head of the physics department at the University of Minnesota, Professor Sorenson. When he enrolled at the university—at age 14—he quickly became Prof. Sorenson's prize pupil. The professor had said on a number of occasions that Bobby had the most brilliant mind of anyone he had ever met, student or faculty.

Bobby and Don hadn't really gotten to know each other until their junior year at the university. Though Don was a straight-A student, he was not Bobby's equal intellectually; but the difference in their ages largely compensated for that. Then, too, Don had a special talent that contributed to their intellectual relationship. He had an extraordinary memory. He could effortlessly remember most of what he read and could even recall class lectures with remarkable completeness. Bobby, who was at times rather absentminded, admired this talent and found the range of Don's knowledge stimulating. Don, in turn, was fascinated by the originality of the insights and inferences that Bobby would draw from information tossed to him, the way he would ingeniously connect seeming unrelated facts or ideas supplied by Don.

Don and Bobby also played a lot of tennis together, and here Don had a slight edge. Although they usually played singles matches, they found they made a very effective doubles team. Their differing styles were complementary in the way that makes for successful doubles play. Bobby had a big serve and a great overhead smash. Don was better in volleying at the net and had a far better backhand than Bobby.

The two also shared a couple of other interests that brought them closer. They were both interested in classical piano music, each having studied for a number of years. At one point Don had even considered making it a career. He decided, however, that he didn't have quite enough talent to be a world-class pianist and that the only other career in that field would be teaching, which didn't interest him. (At one point Don had also considered majoring in history, but the only thing one could do with a history major was teach, which again didn't interest him.) Don's mother, herself a fine amateur pianist, had a large collection of recordings of old master pianists, such as Rachmaninoff, Paderewski, Josef Hofmann, Leopold Godowsky, Moritz Rosenthal, Artur Rubinstein and Vladimir Horowitz. Bobby and Don spent many hours together at Helen's home listening to these. Bobby was so interested in these old recordings that he copied many of them onto audiotape cassettes for himself.

The other interest which the two shared was science fiction. They devoured every science fiction novel and magazine they could find, discussed them, and went together to every science fiction movie that came to town.

Bobby and Don had gotten to be very close in their final two years at the university. But, as so often happens, after graduation their lives diverged and they lost track of each other. Now Don was looking forward to renewing their friendship.

"Hello, Bobby."

"Don Emerson! I'd recognize that voice anywhere, even after all these years! Geez! It's good to hear from you!" They both laughed with joy at the recognition of each other's voices over the phone. Then Bobby said, "How'd you know I was here?"

"I just talked to Professor Sorenson."

They had a lot to catch up on. They talked about their work and their families. Bobby said he was still single and that his parents were fine. Don told about Jan and the kids, said his father had died a few years ago but that his mother was fine and still lived in the same house. Then he said, "That brings me to the reason I called Professor Sorenson and why I need your help." Then he told about his experience with the phone at his mother's house, about Jan's experience with Helen in the hallway, and about the cars being moved.

"Sounds like some of those science fiction stories we used to read."

"I know, but you know me well enough to know I'm not making this up. Are you interested in investigating this? Professor Sorenson says if you are that he'll make the lab at the university available to you."

"Yeah. It'll be a challenge. It'll be interesting to discover the explanation behind those strange happenings you describe. Besides, if it turns out that there's a real problem in the nation's phone system, I could make a lot of money by solving it. To begin with, I'll need your mother's phone."

"I'll probably have to wrestle her for it, but I'll get it for you one way or another."

Helen picked up the phone. "Hello."

"Hello, Mother. Do you remember Bobby Bednarz?"

"That cute Bobby Bednarz? Of course I remember him. How could I ever forget that impish grin with those adorable dimples, those soft brown eyes and all that wavy black hair? What's he doing now? Did he ever get married?"

"No, but…"

"Listen, you tell him I've got just the girl for him. My friend Beverly Graham has the loveliest daughter, really gorgeous, and she's smart, too, got a Ph.D. in something or other, and I…"

"Mother, Bobby never needed any help getting dates. He doesn't want you to get him a girl; he wants you to give him your phone."

"My phone? Of all things! What on earth for?"

"Well, I told him about our experience with your phone when we were staying at your place while our kitchen was being remodeled. He wants to make some tests."

"But there's nothing wrong with my phone."

"That's beside the point. This is a matter of scientific research. You wouldn't want to stand in the way of scientific progress, would you?"

"Well, I suppose not, but I need my phone…"

"I'll get you another one. I'll pay for it. It won't cost you a thing, and you can have the old one back when Bobby's through with it. How about it, Mom?—in the interests of *science!*"

"Well, if it's for a good purpose, as you say, I suppose so. Just don't throw it away. It's a perfectly good phone, and I want it back when he's through with the tests."

"Fine. I'll be out this evening to bring you a new phone and pick up the old one. Will that be okay?"

"Yes, that's okay. And don't forget to tell Bobby I've got a nice girl all picked out for him.'"

"All right. Thanks, Mom."

THE TROJAN PROJECT

Chapter Five

When Don returned home that evening after taking Helen's phone over to Bobby, Jan said, "Someone just phoned for you. I didn't recognize the voice. He didn't leave a message or say who he was. In fact, he seemed unsure whether or not he had the right number. I told him you'd be back in a little while, and he thanked me and said he'd call back."

A little while later the phone rang. Don picked it up, "Hello."

"Is this Mr. Don Emerson?"

"Yes."

"I'm not sure if I've got the right person, but I'm trying to locate someone who came into our offices at the phone company a few weeks ago. I think his name was Don Emerson. My name is Walt Eilers. Do I have the right person, Mr. Emerson?"

"Yes, you do," said Don, greatly surprised.

"I'm afraid I owe you an apology, Mr. Emerson, for laughing at you that day. Recently I've had a couple of experiences which made me change my mind about what you said. If you've got a few minutes, I'll tell you about them."

"Sure. Go ahead."

"Well, Friday night is my poker night. Naturally, I was out quite late. When I came home, my wife was in the kitchen in her nightgown snacking on some leftover chicken. She said she couldn't sleep and decided she was hungry. Then she went back upstairs to bed, and I followed a few minutes later.

"The next day just about suppertime she came into the living room and announced that supper was going to be delayed. She said that because *I* had eaten the leftover chicken which she was planning on serving for supper, she would have to prepare something else, which would take a little longer. Of course, I told her that she had eaten the chicken and asked why she was blaming me. She said she wasn't 'blaming' me and didn't care if I did eat the chicken; she just wanted me to know why supper was delayed. I asked her why she was saying that when we both knew she had eaten it, because she was eating it right in front of me when I came home from poker. She didn't believe me! She thought I was kidding because I had eaten it. At first I thought she was the one who was kidding. We almost had a fight over it. Then I realized she really didn't remember what had happened.

"That got me thinking about some of the things you were telling us in the office that day. But the real clincher came this afternoon. I stopped at a gas station to fill up my car on the way home from work and ran into our neighbor Harriet Martens there. She said she had just seen my wife in front of Sampson's Supermarket about an hour ago. I mentioned this to my wife when I got home, and she said she hadn't been to Sampson's today. She said she didn't feel well and had gone to bed and slept all afternoon. She had just gotten up shortly before I came home. Now, Harriet Martens is our next-door neighbor. She sees my wife practically every day. She couldn't possibly have gotten her mixed up with someone else. If she says she saw my wife there, she must have actually seen her there. Your theory—crazy as it sounds—is the only thing that could explain these events.

"I checked our phone line and can't find anything wrong with it, but part of the problem is that I don't know what to look for. I remember what you said about your mother's phone, and I'm wondering if I could do some tests on it at our company laboratory."

"I'm sorry," said Don, "but I got my mother a new phone, just as you suggested."

"What happened to the old one?"

"I gave it to a scientist who's a friend of mine, who's going to run some tests of his own."

"Well, if he needs any help, you tell him I'll place the phone company lab at his disposal and assist him in any way I can. And if there is anything else I can do to be of assistance to you on this problem, don't hesitate to call on me. I know this probably sounds strange to you after my reaction at our meeting a few weeks ago, but I really mean it. I'll do anything I can to help."

"Thanks," said Don. "I can't think of anything at the moment, but I'll keep your offer in mind. Thanks for calling."

A few days later Jan called Don at work to say that he had a letter from the National Centers for Disease Control in Atlanta. He said, "Open it and read it to me."

She read:

"Dear Mr. Emerson:

"Regarding your suggestion that we investigate what you call a 'telephone virus,' I am sorry to say that we are unable to devote any of our limited resources to this issue. Our budget is stretched thin as it is. Furthermore, even if our budget were much larger, it is unlikely that we would be able to devote any of our financial and manpower resources to this matter when there are so many higher priorities.

"Communicable diseases are known to be caused by bacteria and viruses. This is an established scientific fact. Thousands of people die every year from widely-recognized diseases with these scientifically-accepted causes. To date, we have not received a report of a single death—or even an injury—from the phenomenon you describe. I am sure you can appreciate that we cannot expend any effort in this direction when needs are so much greater elsewhere. For example, food-borne illnesses infect 6.5 million people every year in the United States and result in 9,000 deaths.

"I am sorry I can't be more helpful about this, but thank you for writing to us anyway.

"Wishing you good health!

Yours truly,

(signed)
Ward E. Peterson
Assistant Director"

"Looks like another dead end," said Don.
"I'm sorry, dear," Jan replied. "I was really hopeful that this letter would offer some encouragement."
"That's okay," he said. "Win some, lose some, I guess. If the Centers for Disease Control isn't going to be of any help, at least we've got Walt Eilers of the phone company on our side now. So that's some encouragement."
She knew he was discouraged but trying to sound upbeat.

That evening as Don and Jan were watching the news on TV there was a short item about Minnesota Senator Ray Stafford. He was a slim, erect man with silver hair and patrician bearing. Jan turned to Don and said, "Maybe we need to get a senator or congressman on our side. What would you think of trying to contact Senator Stafford?"

"I don't have a lot of confidence in politicians or the political process," said Don. "I don't think this problem has a political solution any more than a lot of other problems in our society. But we've tried everything else without really getting anywhere; we might as well try this, too. It can't hurt, and it might help. If we're going to take this approach, then I guess Senator Stafford would be as good a choice as any. He's always seemed like a sensible person and is well respected. I'll call his office in the morning and give it a try."

When Don called the senator's office in Washington, he was told that the senator was unavailable at present and would be returning to Minnesota in a few days. Don described in vague terms what he wanted to talk to the senator about and asked if it would be possible for the senator to meet with him and a representative of the phone company while he was in Minnesota. The person he was talking to said he would have to check with the senator and would call back. Later in the day he called back to say he would schedule an appointment for them the following week at a condo the senator maintained in downtown Minneapolis.

Don immediately called Walt Eilers to see if he could be at the meeting. "You bet I'll be there," said Eilers. "You can count on it."

THE TROJAN PROJECT

Chapter Six

When Don and Walt arrived for their scheduled appointment with the senator, he was very friendly but said he was having a busy day and asked them to make their presentation as brief as possible. Don began and did most of the talking. The senator didn't interrupt or rush them, nor did he laugh or seem to find their explanation ridiculous, as they had expected. Don noticed, however, that the senator seemed more intent on watching his visitors than on what they were saying.

When they had finished, Senator Stafford said, "I don't know what to make of what you've just told me. It seems hard to believe, but then I'm really not one who can evaluate these ideas. To tell the truth, I was never very good at science and math when I was in school. I actually don't know much more about electricity than that you plug in appliances and they work. So I really don't know if what you are saying is true or even possible. But I've watched you both very closely as you were talking, and I can see that you really believe in what you've been telling me. Given your professional backgrounds in electronics and with the phone company, if you think this is what's happening, I'm not going to dispute you. And if you sincerely think this is something that the public should be made aware of—as you have said—and which the government should get involved in, I'll go along with that. We have to do what's best for the public.

"The question is how we should proceed. If you were representing an institution, a university for example, I'd have no trouble saying we should go for a research grant to study this issue and make the findings public. The government makes hundreds of grants for research on issues which seem of far less importance to the nation than the subject you've raised. It's not that this issue isn't important or wouldn't justify such a grant; it's that you're not an institution. You're a couple of private citizens. The government doesn't make such grants to private citizens; it makes them to universities, hospitals, foundations, or in some cases to private companies engaging in scientific research. You're none of these.

"Furthermore, you don't even have a proposal. Before the government would spent any money—perhaps millions of dollars—on research on this issue, it would have to have a formal proposal detailing how the money would be spent, how the research would be carried out, what the total cost would be, etc. That's not an insurmountable problem, but it's one that would have to be addressed before we could get you any government research money.

"When I get back to Washington, I'll talk to Senator Billington about all this—he's the chairman of the Senate Appropriations Committee—and see if he has any suggestions. He might even know how we could incorporate this issue into some existing proposal or appropriation. Right now I don't see how we could do it, but Senator Billington might know of a way. He's certainly the expert on that sort of thing.

"Another thing we could do is contact various government agencies that might have an interest or jurisdiction in this area. The U. S. Department of Health is an obvious choice."

"I thought of the health issue myself," said Don "and already contacted the Centers for Disease Control in Atlanta. They said they weren't going to do anything about it."

"Well, that's only one agency. There are dozens of agencies within the Health Department alone whose activities might well encompass this issue. Plus there are all sorts of other agencies and departments. There's the Consumer Product Safety Commission and the Federal Communications Commission. There are a number of agencies within the Commerce Department—more than I can name offhand—which may be relevant.

"So you see, there are really a lot of options. I don't know offhand which agency or department we should contact first, and I really don't have time to examine the question further right now. As I said, I've got a very busy day. However, I'll give the matter further thought and talk it over with Senator Billington when I get back to Washington next week. He should be helpful not only on the possibility of a research grant but on which agencies would be the most likely ones to contact in the light of their currently-funded activities. I have your phone number, Mr. Emerson, and I or a member of my staff will call you after I've talked with Senator Billington."

The two visitors thanked the senator for hearing them out, and he thanked them for bringing the matter to his attention. They shook hands and parted.

As they walked away from the senator's condo, Walt asked Don how he thought it went. "Better than I expected," he replied. "Maybe we're finally going to get somewhere."

"I'm encouraged, too," said Eilers.

"Hello, Bobby," said Don. "Thought I'd phone and see if you're making any progress."

"There's definitely something there. I don't know just what it is, but it's intriguing," said Bobby.

"Good. I'm glad you've found it's for real—instead of telling me I'm nuts—but there's another reason for my call. Walt Eilers, the phone company guy I told you about earlier, and I just met with Senator Stafford, who is going to help us. He said if we make out a formal proposal and are affiliated with an institution such as a university we might get a government grant for a lot of money to research this issue. I don't know that that's the way to go—I'm leery of all these government programs—but I thought I'd see what you think. We'd probably have to formalize your relationship with the university, or else maybe we could get Professor Sorenson to sponsor the proposal. The senator said it's important that the proposal come from an institution such as a university. What do you think about the idea?"

"Geez," said Bobby, "now I *do* think you're nuts. I've seen some of those proposals that run hundreds of pages. The scientists of this country spend more time writing proposals than they do solving problems. What do we need a government grant for? We'll still have to do the work—only then the government will horn in on the credit and claim the political process brought about the solution. Everything would be more expensive, and we'd be taking other people's money to do it. I have everything I need right here; and if I didn't have this setup, Eilers said I could use the phone company lab. So there's no need for a government program.

"Furthermore, if we get a government grant, then we have to gear up for a big operation. We have to hire people for the paperwork and the accounting. That means we have to worry about whether our hiring practices meet federal equal opportunity standards, whatever they are. We'll have to worry about whether someone we refuse to hire will file a complaint that he or she was turned down because of being too old or too fat or some other ridiculous reason that constitutes violation of equal employment opportunities. So we'll have to document everything in case we have to defend ourselves. That means a lot of extra paperwork. We'll have to worry about whether we're complying with workplace regulations set by the Occupational Safety and Health Administration. That will mean hours of reading regulations. We'll have to take withholding tax from all our employees paychecks and make payments and reports to the government. We'll have to pay for unemployment insurance and health insurance. We'll need an accountant to keep track of all these expenditures plus all the expenditures for the actual study, an accounting that will be required by the research grant. All these things will require time and money and people—*and they will not contribute one single bit to solving the actual problem!* I will not spend any of my time screwing around with all that stuff. You can spend your time that way if you want to. Apply for that government grant if that's what you want to do, but I tell you this: I'll have this problem solved before you even get your proposal written—much less get it approved. And who is it that's going to have to approve your proposal? People who don't know any more about science than Senator Stafford?"

"Basically, I agree with you," said Don. "I guess I was temporarily swayed by the lure of government money, but I still think the senator can be useful to us in contacting various government agencies to alert the public."

"How did you plan to alert the public before you talked to the senator?"

"My plan was to go back to Jim Phillips, the science editor for the newspaper. He impressed me as fair minded and certainly dedicated to the truth. He said if I can prove what I told him is true, he'll write it up and alert the public. I think other media will pick up the story from there and spread it around the country. I still intend to contact Phillips, but I think that government agencies could help in getting the word out to people."

"I'll concentrate on the scientific end," Bobby said.

A little more than a week later Senator Stafford called Don to say, "I've been talking with Senator Billington. He's not only chairman of the Senate Appropriations Committee but chairman of the Senate Armed Services Committee. He thinks that what you discussed with me may have national security implications. He says he'd like to know if it would be possible for you to come to Washington for a few days to discuss this with him and with someone from the Defense Department. What do you say?"

"Why, yes. I can come"

"Good. I'll give you the number of Senator Billington's office, and you can call and arrange a time that will be convenient for both of you."

THE TROJAN PROJECT

Chapter Seven

Senator Billington sat alone in his office, deep in thought. He was a portly man with a large red face. His bushy white eyebrows were knit in a frown of concentration and concern. He was about to make a short phone call to someone he worked closely with, and the subject of that call and its ramifications disturbed him.

Theodore Billington was widely regarded as the most powerful man in the United States Senate, where he had been serving for twenty-seven years. He was the leader of the majority party, chairman of two of the most powerful Senate committees, and an influential member of more than half a dozen others. But it wasn't just his seniority and positions within the Senate that were responsible for his formidable reputation. He was even better known for his behind-the-scenes maneuvering. He had a well-deserved reputation as the biggest wheeler-dealer in Washington—a characterization that he viewed not as a disparagement but with the pride of an accomplishment. He knew how and when to twist arms and when to be conciliatory and compromising. His mind had a computer-like storage capacity for not only voluminous legislative details but for extensive information on his fellow senators. He kept meticulous mental accounts of favors owed and favors granted. People said he never forgot or overlooked even the smallest good turn—or the smallest slight. Fellow senators were often surprised to hear Senator Billington remind them of something trivial they had said or done way back that they themselves had long since forgotten. He delighted in such displays because he believed the adage "knowledge is power" and believed that the more knowledge he had of other people, the more he could exercise power over them. And he believed that making people aware of his knowledge of them maximized that power. He knew how everyone in the Senate had voted on previous bills and why, and he knew how such information could be used to influence their future votes. He also knew a great deal about his fellow senators' personal lives—and how that information could be used to influence their future votes. His opponents often accused him of ruthlessness and "dirty politics." He simply said he "knew how to get things done" and asked to be judged by his results. "My record," he often said, "speaks for itself." He had a phenomenal record for seeing his wishes determine whether a bill would be passed or voted down in the Senate.

The man he most admired, and patterned himself after, was Lyndon Johnson, whom he regarded as the greatest politician of the century. He never claimed Johnson was a great president—only that he understood and practiced the art of politics in its purest form better than anyone else.

There were many similarities between Lyndon Johnson and Theodore Billington. Johnson had been a school teacher. Billington had taught political science at a small, obscure Southern college. Both had begun their political careers in the House of Representatives with close elections amid charges of voting irregularities. Once there, they solidified their political bases with patronage, by currying favor with persons whose political connections could advance their careers, and by consistently managing to obtain an array of pork barrel projects for their districts in order to ensure voter loyalty. The successful practice of these policies carried them both to the Senate, where they developed an ever-greater mastery of their methods.

The man Senator Billington was about to call was Dr. Malcolm Steiner, head of an enormous research project at the Defense Department. Dr. Steiner had a reputation as a brilliant scientist. He had an impressive academic background including several honorary degrees. He had authored a large number of scientific articles in professional publications, articles which no one ever read on obscure subjects of no practical value. Secretly he envied other scientists—who he was sure were less intelligent than he—who had made practical inventions or discoveries that had made them rich and famous. He found it all the more frustrating that most such men had made their achievements at a younger age than his 59 years.

As the years advanced on him, Dr. Steiner consoled himself for his lack of singular achievement with the knowledge that he had a powerful and well-paying government position. He was financially secure; that was an important compensation, he told himself. Furthermore, he could control the destinies of brilliant scientists working under him; he could command obedience and respect. He would never admit, even to himself, that that was an important compensation, too, but it was.

Since the work Dr. Steiner was in charge of was top secret, he knew he could never expect to be famous. But the project to which he was now devoting all his time held the promise of compensation on a far greater scale than anything his career had ever given him before. That's why he was even more disturbed than Senator Billington when he picked up the phone and heard the senator say, "Someone's found the telephone virus."

It took a moment for the news to sink in. Then he said, "How much does he know?"

"I haven't any idea. I just got a call from Ray Stafford, the senator from Minnesota. He said somebody out in Minneapolis found this thing and thinks the public should be alerted."

"Well, we certainly can't have that. How do you think we should handle it?"

"I think we should talk to him first, find out how much he knows."

"Do you want to talk to him, or should I?" asked Dr. Steiner.

"I think we both should. I think you should talk to him first. You're better at the technical stuff. Pump him. Find out what he knows. Then I'll meet with him a couple of days later. Meanwhile, you and I will have had a chance to talk and to decide how we want to proceed before I meet with him. Stafford said this guy is going to call me about meeting with us. I'll pretend that, due to our prior commitments, the best we can do is schedule two appointments a couple of days apart. That will keep him in Washington here for a few days."

"Good. Good."

"How much do you think you'll have to tell him?" asked the senator.

"I think I ought to tell him everything—everything, that is, except about The Project itself. First of all, if he thinks I'm being candid and leveling with him, he's more likely to share with me what he knows. I'd like to know how he found out about this. Maybe there's something we can learn from him.

"Second, I want to impress him with how much we're doing on this so he'll be satisfied that everything is under control and just go back to Minneapolis and keep his mouth shut. I can't convince him of that if I'm going to be secretive. My best chance is to show him how *much* we're doing—as much as I can, anyway."

"I think you're right," said Billington.

"As we're talking," said Dr. Steiner, thinking out his plan as he spoke, "it occurs to me I should have my assistant, Monica Gunderson, at the meeting and then have her give him a guided tour of our facility. If beautiful women are used to sell everything from beer to automobiles, why shouldn't we use one to sell our program to this guy from Minneapolis?"

"Heh, heh. Great idea!" chuckled the senator. "If I had your Monica Gunderson on my staff, I'd never fail to get the Senate to pass a bill I favored."

When Don came home from work, he said to Jan, "Looks like I'll have to go to Washington for a few days next week. You'll have to keep an eye on things in the office while I'm gone."

"No problem," she said, "but what's happening in Washington?"

"I talked to Senator Billington's office, as Senator Stafford suggested, and they want me to meet with a Dr. Steiner from the Defense Department on Monday afternoon. Then they want me to meet with Senator Billington on Wednesday afternoon. They apologized for not being able to schedule the two meetings closer together but said that was the best that could be done due to existing commitments. I said that was okay.

"It turns out that I can't get a reservation on a direct flight back to Minneapolis Wednesday evening. So I'm staying over until midmorning on Thursday.

"I hate to be gone for four days on this, but maybe some good will come out of it."

"I think that's just great, honey!" said Jan. "At last somebody seems receptive and actually wants to hear what you have to say. That's real progress!"

"I'm encouraged," he said, "but I don't want to get my hopes up too high. Maybe those people in Washington won't believe me either."

"Hello, Bobby," said Don. "I have to go to Washington for a few days. Just thought I'd give you a call before I leave and see whether you've made any progress."

"Some," he said. "Ever hear of W. D. Gann?"

"Wasn't he that Wall Street guru that made millions in the stock market and died thirty or forty years ago?"

"That's the guy. Actually, he probably made even more money in the commodity markets than in the stock market. Back in 1908 he opened an account with $130—prices were lower in those days and you didn't need much money—and he ran it up to $12,000 in just thirty days. In 1923, starting with $973 in another account, he made $30,000 in two months trading just one commodity, cotton. In one year he made enough in another commodity, coffee, to buy a yacht, which he named 'The Coffee Bean.'

"One of his most amazing feats was in 1909, when he predicted that the September wheat contract would sell at $1.20. At that time wheat had never traded as high as one dollar, and price moves were generally smaller in those days, so that seemed like an extravagant prediction. At noon on September 30th—the last day on which his prediction could be fulfilled before the contract expired—the price was only $1.08. His friends came to him and said it looked like his prediction was going to be wrong. He said, 'I don't care what the price is now; it must go there.' In the final hour of trading the price rose to exactly $1.20—not one tick higher."

"That's all very interesting, but what's it got to do with our telephone problem?" asked Don.

"It may have a lot to do with it. Gann made all that money in stocks and commodities because he could predict what prices would do. He said he could make these predictions because prices obeyed what he called The Law of Vibration. He never told anybody what this law was—not even his own son, whom he was in business with—but he said it was applicable to everything.

"When you called, I was just reading a reprint of an article from *The Ticker and Investment Digest* of December 1909, in which Gann said: 'The Law of Vibration is the fundamental law upon which wireless telegraphy, wireless telephone and phonographs are based. Without the existence of this law the above inventions would have been impossible....

"'In going over the history of markets and the great mass of related statistics, it soon becomes apparent that certain laws govern the changes and variations in the value of stocks and there exists a periodic or cyclic law, which is at the back of all these movements.... The law which I have applied will not only give these long cycles or swings, but the daily and even hourly movements of stocks. By knowing the exact vibration of each individual stock I am able to determine at which point each will receive support and at what point the greatest resistance will be met....

"'Stocks are like electrons, atoms, and molecules, which hold persistently to their own individuality in response to the fundamental Law of Vibration. Science teaches that an original impulse of any kind finally resolves itself into periodic or rhythmical motion; also, just as the pendulum returns again in its swing, just as the moon returns in its orbit, just as the advancing year ever brings the rose of spring, so do the properties of the elements periodically recur as the weight of the atoms rises...

"'Thus, I affirm, every class of phenomena, whether in nature or in the stock market, must be subject to the universal law of causation and harmony.... Vibration is fundamental; nothing is exempt from this law; it is universal, therefore applicable to every class of phenomena on the globe.'

"Gann proved the universal nature of his Law of Vibration by applying it to a number of subjects other than the financial markets. For example, he made a huge war chart showing all the wars since 1588 and all major battles since 22 B.C. Applying his rules of vibration to this, he was able to predict with remarkable accuracy the end of World War I and the beginning and end of World War II and the Viet Nam War. Gann died in 1955, long before the Viet Nam War ended. The last war prediction he made was for 1982-83, which he marked on the chart with a large red arrow. That turned out to be when American soldiers were involved in the war in Grenada.

"Gann even applied his theories to lotteries and race tracks, where he was very successful. One of my favorite stories is about the time he was vacationing in Mexico and decided to bet on the dog races. He accumulated all the data he could on the dogs, their dates of birth, races they ran, where they finished in those races, dates of the races, etc. After studying this information, he concluded that a particular dog in a particular race, say the fifth dog in the fifth race, was going to be a big winner. Next day he went to the race track and bet heavily on that dog, which was a real long shot. It finished dead last! Gann couldn't believe it! He went back to his hotel and restudied his calculations. They still pointed to the fact that his dog should have won. He couldn't reconcile himself to what had happened at the race track.

"Next day he was reading the newspaper. He looked at the page that listed the previous day's dog races. There was the listing showing that his dog had finished dead last. But then in the next column was a listing for races at the *other* racetrack. It showed that there the fifth dog in the fifth race—which was an even greater long shot—had won! The payoff would have been astronomical. Gann had picked the right dog but gone to the wrong race track. He thought there was only one.

"I think Gann's long-lost Law of Vibration could hold the key to unlocking the secret of our telephone virus."

THE TROJAN PROJECT

Chapter Eight

When Don arrived at Washington's Dulles Airport, he took a taxi to the address he had been given for his meeting with Dr. Steiner of the Defense Department. The taxi took him to a sprawling complex of government buildings on the outskirts of Washington.

At the door he was required to register and was given a security badge which would enable him to proceed to Dr. Steiner's office on the ninth floor. Along the way he marveled at the number of security guards throughout the building. He wondered what was going on here that was so important and so secretive as to require such heavy security. He speculated that such a large complex of buildings probably had a great many programs and projects going on, not just the one which was the reason for his being here, whatever that was.

Upon reaching Dr. Steiner's office, he was greeted by a receptionist, who said, "Come in. Dr. Steiner's been expecting you." She escorted him to the inner office.

Dr. Steiner rose and came forward as they entered, his arm extended and a broad smile on his face as though he were greeting an old friend. "Well, I see you found us all right. I'm Malcolm Steiner. It's good to meet you. I'm glad you could make it," he said shaking Don's hand warmly and, it seemed to Don, almost too enthusiastically. "Senator Billington tells me you've found the telephone virus," he continued.

"You mean you already know that a telephone virus exists?" asked Don with astonishment. "I came to Washington thinking I was going to be telling you something new. I was wondering how I was going to convince you of something that I can't get other people to believe—and here you already know about it? You don't need to be convinced?"

"That's right," said Dr. Steiner with a smile of amusement at Don's reaction. "We've known about it for over a year. It got away from a laboratory in California that was under contract to us to work on artificial intelligence. It's no secret that the Defense Department has been interested in that subject for many years. There are a number of private companies exploring that field, some for us, some on their own…"

Just then the door opened and in walked the most beautiful creature Don had ever seen—a dazzling, shapely blonde. "Hi!" she said simply in a warm voice that was more than friendly; it was downright alluring. She flashed a kittenish smile that was at once both wholesome and seductive. She projected that mixture of sex and girlish innocence that men find so attractive, yet did so without any cunning or conscious effort, as though she was unaware of the effect she was producing. The sheer naturalness of her behavior made her all the more enticing. "I'm Monica Gunderson."

"This is my assistant," said Dr. Steiner. "I've asked her to sit in on our meeting, and afterward she'll give you a tour of our facility. Monica," he said, turning to her, "this is Don Emerson."

She came forward, and they shook hands. "Glad to meet you," she said.

"My pleasure," he replied—and his reply was not a mere formality! He had never experienced anything like this. He had never come face to face with such feminine perfection. He was smitten. He couldn't get over her beauty and the sexuality she was projecting so guilelessly. As they shook hands, he looked into her eyes. At that moment he would have been her slave for life if she had asked. She was more beautiful than any movie star he'd ever seen. He wondered why she wasn't world famous for her beauty instead of being hidden here in some secret office of the Defense Department. Her tantalizing smile revealed absolutely perfect teeth. Those eyes and that smile! He wondered if he hadn't seen them on the cover of some magazine somewhere. Or maybe in a toothpaste ad. Or maybe in the Miss America contest. Or was it the Miss Universe contest?

She turned, took a few steps, turned again and sat down in one of the chairs in Steiner's office. Don watched the movements of her body with aesthetic admiration and just plain lust. He was trying to remember which state she had represented in the Miss America contest or which country in the Miss Universe competition. Thinking about those beauty contests, he tried to visualize what she would look like in a swimsuit. Or without one. Had he ever seen her before?—on TV, in a magazine or movie—or only in his dreams?

Dr. Steiner observed Don's stunned reaction with satisfaction, but Don didn't notice. He couldn't take his eyes off Monica. Steiner continued, "As I was saying, this 'virus' got away from a contractor working on artificial intelligence for the Defense Department. They had a fire out there; the building was struck by lightning in a storm. About ninety percent of the computers and other equipment were destroyed..."

Steiner's talking brought back a sense of reality to Don. He was trying to follow what was being said to him, and he was trying not to stare at Monica though he found that difficult; his eyes kept wandering back to her.

Steiner went on: "Apparently in that ten percent or so of the computers that appeared to be undamaged by the lighting or the fire there was one computer—one of those with the artificial intelligence program—whose program was altered in some small but very significant way by the electrical charge or the heat from that accident. A mutation was created—perhaps, in somewhat the same way that many scientists believe life was first created by a charge of lightning passing through just the right mixture of chemicals and transforming them into living matter. In any case, what resulted here was a kind of computer virus—but one which affects people and can be transmitted to them through phone lines. All that was needed then was for someone in that contractor's office to connect that computer via a modem to a phone line for some routine operation, and, unwittingly, the damn virus got into the nation's phone system, where it has been spreading ever since. Every time someone makes a call to or from an 'infected' phone the virus is spread to another phone line…"

"Wow!" interrupted Don, grasping the enormity of what he had just been told. "It must be in practically every phone line in the nation by now, plus much of the rest of the world's phones, too."

"That's about the size of it."

"And all those people using those phones are now infected?"

"Well, not all," said Dr. Steiner. "There are many similarities between this telephone virus and true biological viruses. Just as is the case with biological viruses, some people seem to be immune to this virus. We don't know exactly how many. Our best estimate at this point is that somewhere around eighty percent of the population is affected; the other twenty percent is either immune or at least has not shown any symptoms as yet that we can identify as being caused by the virus. I'm speaking of the population of the United States, of course. We have no figures on what's happening in the rest of the world. So far as we know, nobody else is even aware of this phenomenon elsewhere in the world, much less studying it and compiling statistics on it."

"So probably eighty percent of the people of this country are already infected—and you're not doing anything about it, you're not even telling them!" said Don.

"We're not telling them—but that doesn't mean we're not doing anything about it," corrected Dr. Steiner. "On the contrary, we're doing everything we can. This whole complex of buildings is devoted entirely to this issue, to studying the problem and trying to come up with a solution. We have hundreds of scientists in a variety of disciplines working in laboratories right here…"

Don was not sure he heard correctly. He asked, "Did I understand you to say this *entire* huge building complex is occupied by scientists and laboratories working on just this one problem?"

"That's right," said Dr. Steiner. "And that's not all. In fact, what you see here is only a small part of the total effort. We have contracts with more than a dozen universities throughout the country to carry out research for us in their own laboratories. We have about an equal number of contracts with private companies doing computer research and medical research for us in their own facilities. Then there are a number of government agencies which are assisting us with research in their own institutions. These include the National Institutes of Health, the National Centers for Disease Control, the National…"

"Wait a minute," interrupted Don. "You just said the National Centers for Disease Control. But I wrote to them a few weeks ago, and they replied that they weren't going to investigate the telephone virus. They said they had higher priorities for their limited financial and manpower resources."

"Well, of *course* they told you they weren't going to investigate the telephone virus," said Dr. Steiner, somewhat condescendingly. "Do you think they would admit what they're doing and let the cat out of the bag? Their research and all the rest of our work on this is all being done under great secrecy."

"But why all this secrecy? If eighty percent of the people of this country are already infected, don't they have a right to know? How can you justify using the people of this country as unknowing subjects for your research—as human guinea pigs? That's irresponsible! It's morally wrong! In a democracy people are supposed to know what's going on in their government."

"Now, now," said Dr. Steiner, trying to calm his visitor. "It would be irresponsible not to maintain secrecy as we're doing. Consider how vital the telephone is to our lives, to our economy, to our society. Business couldn't function without it. If word got out about the telephone virus, society as we know it would no longer exist. Business would grind to a halt. People would be afraid to use the phones; they would be ripping out the phone lines. People couldn't do their jobs without phones. So there would be shortages of food and other essentials. And when people can't do their jobs, they don't get paychecks. The whole economy would spiral downward, and people would become desperate. We would have complete chaos. Without communications, law and order would break down—who would want to use a phone to call the police? And would the police want to answer? We would have *absolute panic,* and you know it. To tell the public about the telephone virus would be like shouting 'Fire' in a crowded theater. *That* would be irresponsible, Mr. Emerson. *That* would be morally wrong. We're doing the only responsible thing under the circumstances. We're working as hard as we can to solve the problem and meantime are maintaining the necessary secrecy. When we come up with a solution, then we'll tell the public about the virus and how they can counteract it or be protected from it. We're proceeding as rapidly as we can. That's why we have such a mammoth effort under way, to try to get a solution for the public just as quickly as it's humanly possible to do so.

"As for your comment about us using the public as guinea pigs, this isn't an experimental situation which we created—we didn't infect these people. This is a situation that's been thrust upon us, and we're doing the best we can to cope with it in an effective and responsible manner. Even in a democracy it's sometimes in the public interest to maintain secrecy. Remember the Manhattan Project, the secret project to develop the atom bomb during World War II? That was done under great secrecy, and obviously its success shortened the war and saved hundreds of thousands of lives on both sides. And consider what would've happened if the Nazis had learned we were working on an atom bomb and decided to develop one of their own and then beat us to it. Nazi Germany would rule the world, and you and I wouldn't be here arguing about this. So how can anyone say that the secrecy necessary for the Manhattan Project was a bad thing?

"Furthermore, secrecy has been necessary in certain issues from the earliest days of our country. I'm a scientist, not a student of government; but Senator Billington tells me that even the proceedings of the Constitutional Convention, which founded our government, were held in secret. So don't tell me that secrecy in government is unjustified or is some new evil or perversion of our government. We're just doing what has been done for 200 years in this country when it comes to serving the best interests of the public."

"I can agree with your point about not shouting 'Fire!' in a crowded theater and about the need for secrecy on the Manhattan

Project," said Don. "And, recalling my studies of American history, I have to admit Senator Billington is right about the Constitutional Convention maintaining secrecy about what went on there. But I still think people have a right to know if something such as this telephone virus is having an adverse physical effect on their bodies."

"That brings up another interesting aspect of this whole issue," said Dr. Steiner. "As far as we know—and we already know quite a bit about this virus—there really are no adverse effects. It's essentially harmless. Keeping that in mind, you can see that it would be even more irresponsible to create a panic in this country by alarming the public over something that isn't even dangerous to them."

Dr. Steiner sensed that he was allaying Don's skepticism over the government's program. He was most anxious to ask how Don had discovered the virus and to find out how much he knew about it, but he felt the time wasn't quite ripe for such questions. Not just yet. Hoping first to gain further confidence from his visitor, he said, "Let me tell you more about what we know about this virus.

"First of all, this virus manifests itself only when people are asleep. Then it seems to take control over their minds and bodies. It has no mind of its own and no sense organs. It can experience things only through the senses of its host. So it makes its victims do things for the sheer sensory experience. For example, when under the control of the virus, people love to sample foods. They love to play radios and television sets and stereo music. They're big on driving cars. We take driving an automobile for granted, but really it's a very sensual experience: the exhilaration of speed, the changing visual scene, the sense of power. I suppose the ultimate experience for this virus would be to be driving a car while listening to the car radio or cassette player and then stopping at a fast-food joint. And I'm sure you will agree that none of these things is inherently harmful to people.

"Furthermore, the virus utilizes the mind and tastes of its host. It has no skills of its own; if it's driving your car, for example, it'll drive it exactly the way you would, with the same skill, at exactly the same speed that you would under those conditions. It'll enjoy listening to exactly the same kind of music you enjoy, whether Beethoven or rock and roll or whatever. It knows exactly which foods are your favorites, and those are the ones it strives to experience. Since it's doing exactly what the people themselves would choose to do, how is it harmful to them? It can't make people do things they wouldn't otherwise do; it can't make them commit a criminal act, for example, unless, of course, they already have a criminal mind.

"And just as the virus has no mind or skills of its own, neither can it add to those of the people it inhabits. You can't remember anything that you did when controlled by the virus; for that would mean adding to your memory, which it cannot do. If you're out at night under the control of this virus and you meet someone you know, you'll recognize that person and be able to carry on a conversation just as if you didn't have the virus—so the other person will never recognize that you have the virus—but the next morning you won't remember this meeting, because the virus can't add to your memory. You can recall old friends but not make new ones; you simply will never remember having met them."

It all sounded familiar to Don. Everything fit: the cars, the food, how Walt Eiler's wife didn't remember conversing with him the night before while eating the chicken, how Helen didn't remember getting up at night when he and Jan were at her house. Don said, "Everything you're saying, Dr. Steiner, fits right in with my own experience."

Here was an opening. The time was ripe. Steiner said, "Tell me about your experience."

Don began to tell about his and Jan's cars being moved. Then he told about how his mother's car had been found half a block down the street some months earlier. As Don explained each incident, Dr. Steiner nodded knowingly.

When Dr. Steiner had been talking, Don kept his eyes primarily on him because he was the speaker, stealing only an occasional glance at Monica. But now that he was talking, he was addressing both of them so he turned alternately to one, then to the other. Even when he was facing Dr. Steiner, he knew Monica was watching him. He was pleased she seemed interested in what he had to say, and that fact stimulated his discourse.

Then Don told about how he had fallen asleep at his mother's house and how, when his wife dropped the hot frying pan in the kitchen, he awoke with this image of a man rushing at him—a man who looked just like himself—who then keeled over and vanished. As the words came out of his mouth, they sounded so incredible that he felt obliged to add, "Of course, it was probably just a dream, but at least it gave me a clue to what was happening."

"No, it wasn't a dream," said Dr. Steiner. "What you experienced is the most fantastic aspect of this whole story, but we've verified that sort of thing right here in our laboratories. Actually, we discovered it quite by accident. We had several cameras set up to videotape people as they slept. We were primarily interested in recording the motion of their eyelids. As you may know, when people fall into very deep sleep, they characteristically exhibit rapid eye movement. This is called 'REM sleep', for rapid-eye-movement sleep. We were interested in studying correlations between video tapes of the quivering eyelids and the sensors we had placed on the bodies of the subjects. Since the eyelid movements are small and very rapid, it was necessary to use high-speed cameras, so that we could play the pictures back in slow motion. We had cameras positioned at various angles. Well, one of the cameras was basically horizontal and pointed toward the subject from the side. It was, of course, focused on the eyelid. But when we played the tape back in slow motion, we were astounded to discover in the background an image of this same person suddenly advancing very rapidly from a wall about twenty feet beyond the sleeping subject. With great speed the moving image converged on the sleeping subject—and merged with it! It all happened very rapidly—so rapidly it couldn't be seen in real time. We were lucky we had the camera set to record the action in very slow motion. We were even luckier that that one camera happened to be right in line with the path of the virus-controlled image returning to the sleeping subject. Of course, since the camera was focused on the eyelid, the image of the advancing person was out of focus. That didn't matter. Once we knew what was happening, we set up other cameras, oriented them better, focused them properly, and repeated the experiment successfully with this subject and with others as well. Monica will show you some of these pictures later.

"The virus can only be active when the person it inhabits is asleep. It can't cope with or overcome a person's consciousness. Scientists have identified five levels of sleep. Usually the virus can escape from the person's body—along with that person's image—only during the deepest levels of sleep, levels four and five. There are some exceptions; if a person is sick or terribly fatigued, for example, the virus has an easier time getting out. And some people just seem to have less resistance, which allows the virus to escape and be active before sleep levels four or five are reached. In those cases level three may be sufficient, and in very rare cases only level two is required.

"In every case, however, the virus seeks to return before the host wakes up. Now, just as it usually takes a long time for people to attain the deeper levels of sleep—usually several hours—it normally takes quite some time for them to come out of them. They don't generally wake up instantly; they move gradually from sleep level five or four to level three, to level two, then level one and then, finally, they wake up. We don't know just how but somehow the virus-controlled image is able to keep in touch with the sleeping host and to know when that person is moving out of the deeper levels of sleep and beginning to wake up. This enables the virus to get back in time, at least in most cases. If something unexpected wakes up the host suddenly, then the virus is in trouble; it perishes—and vanishes—if it can't return in time. But it has to be something unexpected and sudden. It couldn't be an alarm clock, for example. That would be sudden but not unexpected; remember that the virus utilizes that person's mind and would know what time the alarm was set for and would be back well before the alarm went off. Your story about being awakened when your wife dropped a frying pan in the kitchen and yelled out in pain is a good example of the kind of unexpected event that is required to trap the virus outside the host before it can return."

"So that's the explanation!" said Don. "I had the right hunch. I just didn't know all the details."

"Yes," said Dr. Steiner. "I must say, however, that it was truly extraordinary that you woke up precisely as the virus image was returning. With the speed at which those images return, a fraction of a second earlier or later and you would have seen nothing. Your experience is one which we haven't seen in our experiments; in all our studies the virus either gets back before the person wakes up or is trapped some distance away and perishes before it gets close enough for the waking person to see it. It required incredibly fortunate split-second timing for you to see what you did.

"Now let's take the case you mentioned of your mother's car being found one morning a half block down the street. What undoubtedly happened is that the VCI—that's what we call the virus-controlled image—that was out driving her car sensed she was starting to wake up much sooner than expected. The VCI had to return quickly or perish. There wasn't enough time to drive the car back and put it in the garage. So it simply pulled over to the side of the road—and zipped back on its own. These VCIs, as I mentioned, travel very rapidly. Actually, they're ghostlike; they travel right through walls. I'm sure this one hoped that when it returned to your mother that she would then fall asleep again; then it could go back and retrieve the car. But it didn't work out that way.

One of two things happened: one, either your mother didn't go back to sleep before her car was discovered down the street; or two, the VCI didn't get back to her in time and perished. In that case, your mother would have been free of that virus and would have to pick up her phone again to be reinfected.

"It's curious," continued Dr. Steiner, "that these viruses have such an interest in driving cars, because it's very risky for them, far riskier than anything else they do. I'm sure they only do it if they believe the host will be asleep for quite some time, and I doubt that they ever travel very far. I'm sure they wouldn't drive a hundred miles, for example, because then it would take them a couple of hours to get the car back.

"Probably the things they do most often are watch TV or listen to stereo music, but these are the things that are hardest to catch them at. They simply turn off the sets and return to the hosts, who aren't far away. There's no way to tell if a TV or radio has been played after it has been turned off, so there's no evidence. And turning off a switch takes no time at all compared to bringing a car back. About the only evidence that might be left would be in cases of listening to recorded music; if a host started to wake up unexpectedly, there might not be time to rewind a tape cassette or put away a compact disc or LP recording. But would you notice if a cassette was not rewound to its previous position? And if you found your favorite CD or LP recording in your stereo player, wouldn't you think that you yourself had probably left it that way? Or that maybe some other member of your family had done so? Anyway, even that evidence probably doesn't occur very often because it takes so little time for the VCI to eliminate it—it's nothing like the amount of time needed to return a car.

"The other thing which the VCIs are fond of, sampling food, does leave evidence, but it's trivial. What's someone going to do?—call the police because half of a ham sandwich is missing? I'm sure this sort of thing has led to countless domestic arguments: husbands and wives accusing each other of eating something from the refrigerator, or throwing it away, or feeding it to the dog—or lying about what they did with it—but it's not the sort of thing that's going to make the newspapers. Nobody is going to attach any significance to such occurrences. Certainly nobody is going to think that these things happen because of something coming over a phone line. And if a VCI takes your car and drives to a nearby McDonald's and orders a hamburger and a Coke, would you realize that the small amount of money needed to pay for these things was missing from your pants pocket? And if you did, wouldn't you be more likely to think your wife had taken the money from your pocket? Or that maybe your kids had? Or that maybe you were simply in error about the amount of money you had in the first place? In any case, once again nobody is going to connect such a seemingly trivial event with something coming over a phone line."

Steiner figured he had given Don a lot of information, and now he wanted something in return. He had steered the conversation to where the question he wanted to ask would now flow smoothly and logically from his prior remarks. He said, "Which brings me to the point of asking how you discovered that the events you've described were due to something coming over the phone. How did you make that connection?"

Don replied, "Right after I awoke at my mother's house in time to see that VCI returning and perishing in front of me, the phone rang. My wife answered it—and she got that same kind of paralyzed, frozen expression on her face that the VCI had when it perished. I slapped the phone out of her hand, and she recovered; but that was the clue that led me to believe the culprit was something in the phone line." Then he told about how he could sense something from the phone when he picked it up but how his reaction was nowhere near as strong as Jan's. He told about how he and Jan had tried the newer phone in his mother's bedroom and felt nothing. He told about how Helen couldn't feel anything from the phone when she came home from her card playing. He knew what Dr. Steiner's next question would be, and it came:

"What happened to your mother's phone?"

Don didn't want to lie. He thought Dr. Steiner had been honest with him and had given him a lot of information—which was exactly what Steiner wanted him to think—and he wanted to be honest and helpful in return. But he was disturbed by the fact the government was not telling people about the virus which was infecting them, even though he knew that Dr. Steiner's explanation for the secrecy was entirely reasonable. He was even more disturbed that he had been deliberately lied to by the National Centers for Disease Control in response to his letter. So he said, "I don't have it any more. The phone company suggested I replace it so I did. My mother doesn't have it any more, and neither do I."

Don could have volunteered that he had given the phone to Bobby, but he didn't. He wanted Dr. Steiner to assume that he had simply disposed of it, which is what people usually do with a telephone that needs replacing. He was afraid he would now be asked if, in fact, he had thrown it away, or if he knew what happened to it. He didn't know how he would answer—whether he would lie or not—but he was very relieved when Dr. Steiner said simply, "Too bad you didn't hang onto it. It might have been useful to our research."

There was a moment of silence. Don wanted to change the subject before Dr. Steiner posed a follow-up question about the phone. The only thing he could think to say was, "Dr. Steiner, you said Monica would show me the videotapes of the VCIs returning to their hosts and also give me a tour of your research facilities. Would this be a good time to do that?"

Steiner hesitated a moment. He was reluctant to break off the conversation, but he quickly concluded he wasn't likely to get much more information from Don anyway, at least nothing that would be of any real value. "Yes," he said. "I suppose it's as good a time as any." Then as an afterthought, he added, "Unless there's something else you want to tell me."

"No," said Don. He had intended to tell Dr. Steiner about Walt Eilers' experiences. Eilers, however, was the one who suggested he replace his mother's phone. Don was now afraid that bringing up Eilers might lead to further questions about that phone. That he wished to avoid.

"Well, then Monica will show you around. She's extremely knowledgeable about our program and I'm sure will be able to answer any questions you may have."

Steiner wanted to ask Don to promise not to tell anyone about what he had learned that day, but he didn't want to seem overly anxious. He thought he had adequately dealt with the need for secrecy earlier in the conversation and decided to leave the rest of that issue for Senator Billington, whom he knew Don was meeting on Wednesday. He was sure Don wouldn't say anything to anyone before that meeting anyway. Just to verify the meeting, he said, "I understand you'll be meeting with Senator Billington in a few days."

"Yes," said Don. "We're meeting on Wednesday. The senator couldn't see me sooner, so I'm staying at the Kensington Hotel here for a couple of days."

"Ever been to Washington before?"

"No."

"Well, there's a lot to see here."

"I know," said Don. "I've always been interested in history. I'd like to see the Washington Monument, the Jefferson Memorial and some of the other historic landmarks."

Rising from his chair, Don continued, "Good luck with your program, and thanks for explaining your work to me. I really appreciate it."

"Thank you," said Dr. Steiner rising and smiling, "for coming here and sharing your experiences. Hope you enjoy your visit to Washington." They shook hands, and Monica and Don left the office.

Chapter Nine

Monica took Don to a projection room several floors below Dr. Steiner's office. She knew where to find the videotapes she wanted to show him, and she explained how the experiments were conducted and the technical details of how the pictures were taken. Don enjoyed watching her and listening to her and was surprised she was so knowledgeable about this aspect of the study.

When he saw the first example of a VCI leaving its host, Don said, "Why, it looks just like in the movies, those ghost films or science fiction movies where they use double-exposure photography to show a person's spirit or ghost leaving his body."

"Yes," said Monica. "It really does look that way, but I assure you that what you're seeing isn't double-exposure photography."

Next the videotape showed the VCI returning. Don said, "That's just like what I saw when I was waking up on the davenport at my mother's house!"

Monica showed several more tapes depicting the VCIs leaving and returning to their hosts. There were two examples of the VCIs perishing some distance away as the hosts were awakened, and the hosts failed to see them. Monica explained that these two incidents were the closest they had to what Don experienced. "Because we had these tapes," she said, "neither Dr. Steiner nor I were surprised by what you told us, but it was really unusual that you got to see what you did."

"Now," she said, "I'll take you around to some of our laboratories and explain their experiments to you."

As they left the projection room and proceeded down a long corridor, Monica explained how all the research fit together. She said that all the university laboratories, the private contractors and the government agencies carrying out research all worked on narrow aspects of the program. None of them knew what the other researchers were doing or how individual studies or projects fit into the overall program. She remarked that the function of this complex of laboratories here under Dr. Steiner was to tie together all the research being done by the laboratories across the country. She said that, for the most part, the work being done here was simply to bridge the gaps in the narrow, specific studies being conducted elsewhere and to explore correlations that the separate outlying laboratories were too specialized to investigate. She also mentioned that some studies were being conducted here because no one else was in a position to undertake them. "I'll show you an example of this next," she said. "We're going to one of the laboratories where they're trying to find out how the VCIs manage to stay in touch with their sleeping hosts and know when they are about to wake up."

By now they had reached a bank of elevators. As they waited for an elevator, Monica continued to explain what was being studied at the laboratory they were going to visit. She talked about brain waves, electrochemical processes in the brain, extrasensory perception and other parapsychic phenomena that were being studied here. Don was amazed at how much she knew about all this stuff. He was quickly discovering that Monica was as brilliant as she was beautiful, a fact which made her even more attractive to him.

They got off the elevator, and Monica continued her explanation as they walked down another corridor a short way to the laboratory. There Monica introduced Don to Dr. Czernikoff, who was in charge of the research. Monica asked him about his latest findings, about what he had done since he last briefed her on his progress. Don was amazed that her questions revealed such a thorough understanding of the work going on here. Monica then took him through the lab and explained what was going on at each station as though she herself had been working there.

Next she took him to another lab, where researchers were studying how the virus is transmitted from the phone line and accesses the brain of the host. She introduced him to neurologists, biochemists, acoustics experts, and electronic engineers and discussed their work with them as though she were one of them. She explained to Don that there were several theories about how the virus operates. The most promising one was that the virus reaches directly into the subconscious from the phone line via a frequency beyond the range of normal human hearing. Another theory was that the virus programs itself into the brain by signals that are within the range of human hearing but are in increments of such short duration that they are perceived only subliminally, not consciously. Another theory being explored was that the virus gains access to the brain through brain-wave messages that are somehow coded through the weak electromagnetic field generated by the current in the phone line. Still another theory was that the pulsing signal in the phone line sets up an interference pattern which blocks certain conscious functions of the brain while allowing the virus access to the memory, skills and tastes stored in the brain; then when that person falls asleep, the virus is able to utilize those faculties without triggering consciousness, that is, without that person awakening or later being able to remember what happened. There were other theories, too. Some of them Don didn't fully understand, but Monica certainly seemed to as she explained them.

She took him to other laboratories and introduced him to experts in computer science, particle physics, physiology and a number of other learned and specialized fields. Don marveled at the range of her knowledge as she discussed the work of these experts with them. He would have found it extraordinary for a man of Dr. Steiner's age and position to have such a range of knowledge, and here was a woman young enough to be his daughter with a mind like a scientific encyclopedia. The more Don saw and heard, the more unbelievable it all seemed to him. He started to wonder if it wasn't all going to turn out to be a dream and he was going to wake up.

But the tour came to an end, and he didn't wake up. Monica said, "Well, I guess that about covers everything unless you have any questions."

She smiled and he thought to himself that he was looking at that lovely smile and into those beautiful eyes for the last time. He had a lot of questions he wanted to ask her, but none of them was about the telephone virus or the work in progress at the laboratories here. He wanted to ask her about herself; he wanted to know all about her, how she got into this business, where she went to school, how old she was, had she ever been married or did she have a boyfriend. He noticed she wasn't wearing a wedding ring. He knew, however, that all of the questions he wanted to ask were inappropriate, so he said simply, "No, I think you've covered everything pretty thoroughly. I don't have any questions." They said good-bye, and she smiled again and turned away. He watched her as she walked away from him until she turned a corner in the hallway and was out of sight. Then he took a cab to his hotel.

As Don was riding in the cab he was thinking about Monica, what an extraordinarily talented and beautiful woman she was. But by the time he got to the hotel, his thoughts turned to the fact that he was going to call Jan that evening from his hotel after he had something to eat. He really loved his wife and kids. He would never do anything to hurt any of them. He was fascinated by Monica, but he was a happily married man. Besides, he knew it would be just plain wrong for him to get involved with Monica, and Don Emerson was the kind of person who always tried to do the right thing. Anyway, he knew he would never see her again.

He decided to dine at the restaurant in the hotel. Alone with his thoughts during the meal, he recalled meals that he and Jan had shared, then all the other things they had shared. The more he thought about it, the more he realized that Jan was the perfect wife for him, and the more guilty he felt about his feelings toward Monica. How could he have allowed himself even to think about Monica as he had? Besides, there was no reason to think Monica felt any attraction to him. Even if she did, he told himself, it would be wrong for him to get involved with her and he wouldn't allow himself to do so. And, once more, he told himself he would never see her again anyway.

When he got back to his room, he picked up the phone. For a moment he wondered if he would dial Monica if he knew her number. Then he dialed the familiar number of his own home. When Jan answered, he was surprised how sensuous her voice sounded. "It's good to hear your voice," he said.

"It's good to hear yours," she answered. "I miss you already. How did it go today?"

"Pretty good. The government already knows about the telephone virus, and there's an enormous program under way here to study and combat it. I can't go into all the details now, but I'll tell you more about it when I get home." He decided not to say anything about Monica. All he said was, "An assistant to Dr. Steiner gave me a tour of the facility and explained everything to me." Then he asked what was new with her and the kids.

She gave him some details of things that had happened at the office, and he was pleased that she'd handled those affairs so well. Then she told him about something silly that their son Jason had done. He laughed, enjoying Jan's description and her delight in telling about it as much as the event itself. It was good to hear Jan laugh, too.

When they said good-bye, Jan added, "I love you."

"I love you, too," he said.

A few minutes later Don heard the phone ring. He wasn't expecting any calls. Jan was the only one who might call him here, and he had just talked to her. He thought she must have forgotten something and was calling back.

He picked up the phone and was surprised to hear a *very* sensuous voice that he recognized immediately say, "Mr. Emerson, this is Monica Gunderson. I've got to see you right away."

"Monica! How did you know where to find me?"

"I heard you tell Dr. Steiner you were staying at the Kensington Hotel"

"Of course. But wouldn't it be simpler to say what you have to say over the phone."

"No," she said. "I can't talk here. I'm here in your hotel, downstairs in the lobby, and there are people all around me. May I come up to your room?"

Enticing as the prospect was, Don didn't want her coming to his hotel room. He was going to resist any temptation to be unfaithful to Jan. "I don't think that would be proper," he said. "Why don't I meet you in the bar downstairs or in the hotel coffee shop?"

"No," she said. "I don't want anyone to see us together. It's very important. You and I may not have a future if I don't get to see you now. Can't I come up?"

There was a pause. Don was weakening. Then she added, "Pu-leeezz?"

That did it. He could resist no longer. "All right." he said. "I'm in Room 804."

As soon as he hung up, he thought he'd made a mistake. He wanted to call her back and tell her not to come, but he couldn't. She was on her way, and he would have to face her. What in the hell was he getting into? His first day in Washington, he meets the most gorgeous woman he has ever seen, and now she wants to come up to his hotel room. Is this what life was like in the nation's capital? And what the hell did she mean by "you and I may not have a future if I don't get to see you?" He *couldn't* have a future with her. He was married and intended to stay married. True, he'd fantasized about her, but he'd never led her on, had never even said anything to let her know how he felt about her. He would have to say to her: "Look, Monica, I have to tell you something. I'm married. You're a marvelous woman. I'm impressed, truly astonished, by your beauty and your intelligence. If things were different, if I weren't married, then…"

There was a knock on the door. She was here already. He opened the door, and she stepped quickly inside.

He began his little speech: "Look, Monica, I have to tell you something. I…"

"Listen," she interrupted. "Just let me do the talking. I came here at great risk, and I can't stay long. I'm going to say what I have to say, and then I'm going to leave. Okay?"

Don was taken aback. He had expected this luscious woman would throw her arms around him, smother him with kisses, practically attack him. Clearly he had misunderstood her intentions in coming here. He gestured toward a chair and said, "Okay. Have a seat and tell me whatever it is you want to tell me."

"I came here to warn you. Your life is in danger."

"What?!!"

"Yes. Mine is, too. We both know too much."

So that was what she meant by "you and I may not have a future if I don't get to talk to you," thought Don.

Monica continued, "You're in danger because you're the only one outside of a few who are actually working on the program who knows about the telephone virus. Most of the people working on the research don't even know what's involved. Remember I told you how the work was divided up and farmed out to universities, private contractors and government agencies? Well, Dr. Steiner deliberately did it that way so that nobody could figure out how all this goes together and what his purpose really is. Most of the work being done in those outside laboratories is so narrow that even the researchers don't know that there already is an actual telephone virus out there affecting people. Instead they've been told that what they're doing will be used in an artificial intelligence program, or to protect against computer viruses in the national defense computer network, or to develop a defense against *potential* telephone viruses in the future. About the only ones who know about the real telephone virus are the ones working right here in Washington under Dr. Steiner. The most sensitive studies are under his direct control. He even has a secret lab in which he conducts all the experiments himself. I'm not even allowed in there."

"How do you know about it then?" said Don.

"I know about it because I had lunch with Paul Markowitz the day he was murdered…"

"What?! Murdered?" Don couldn't believe what he was hearing. "Who was Paul Markowitz?"

"He was Dr. Steiner's assistant when I came to work here. I didn't know him very long, and no one at work knew we were seeing each other, but we were lovers. Paul was the most brilliant man I ever met, more intelligent even than Dr. Steiner, brilliant as he is. Intelligence is the number one quality I look for in a man, and I quickly fell for Paul.

"Paul and I had lunch together the day he died. No one saw us leave the office, and we didn't come back together. During lunch Paul told me that he'd seen some of the papers on the research that Dr. Steiner conducts personally in his secret lab. He keeps them in a huge file cabinet in his office. The cabinet is always kept locked, and he's the only one who can open it. I've been in his office when the cabinet has been open—it's crammed full of documents—but I've never been allowed to read any of the contents. Well, at lunch that day Paul said that he'd come to the conclusion that all of this research is being undertaken for a very different purpose than all of us have been led to believe. He said he hadn't seen enough to have conclusive proof, but he was quite sure that Dr. Steiner's real purpose is not to cure or eliminate the telephone virus. That's just a front. The real purpose is to find out enough about how the telephone virus works so that it can be modified and used to one's advantage. You know how genetic engineering works?—how they modify a small genetic factor to produce a desired change in an organism? Well, that's the sort of thing Dr. Steiner hopes to do with the telephone virus, modify some small element just enough to produce the change he wants."

"And what sort of change does he want?" asked Don.

"Paul said Dr. Steiner wants to modify the virus so that it can alter a person's memory or change his behavior, at least in a small way. The goal is to have a virus out there that will affect people without them realizing it—but one which will tell them how to vote."

"My god!" exclaimed Don. "You're talking about the ultimate takeover of the United States government! A takeover that involves no bloodshed and in which the people will never even realize there has been a takeover!"

"That's it exactly," said Monica. "Everyone will still think the voters control the government. In reality they'll be controlled by two men in Washington who program everyone's subconscious through a computer program secretly carried by a telephone virus."

"You said 'two men.' Up to now we've just been talking about Dr. Steiner. Who is the other one?"

"Why, Senator Billington, of course. If things go the way they plan, he'll be our next president. It'll be a landslide. He should get right around eighty percent of the popular vote."

Don shook his head in disbelief. This was the weirdest day of his life.

Monica continued: "Paul said that after lunch he was going to confront Dr. Steiner and threaten to expose him and what this project is all about. I didn't talk to Paul again that day. That evening I was listening to the late news on TV and heard that he had been shot in front of his home. They said it was a 'random shooting.'"

"Well, maybe it was," said Don. "There are plenty of random shootings every year, especially in Washington. How do you know it was murder?"

"First of all, I was suspicious because I knew Paul had confronted Dr. Steiner that afternoon. Second, when I came to work the next morning, I was one of the first ones there—I got there well ahead of Dr. Steiner—and yet Paul's office had already been cleaned out. Everything was gone. Someone had been there during the night and removed everything, and I mean everything. I figure if it really was a 'random shooting,' the next morning his office would have looked just the way he had left it the night before."

"Did you tell the police about that?"

"Sure. They came around and interviewed all of us at the office. I told them, and they wrote it down, and that was the end of it. Their final report still said 'random shooting.' I didn't make any further protest to the police because I think Dr. Steiner and Senator Billington control the police in this city. If those two wanted this whole matter covered up and called a 'random shooting,' then that's the way it was going to be. And to whom could I protest if the police themselves were involved in the cover-up? Besides, if I tried to make a fuss, I might end up like Paul. I'm in greater danger than you or anyone else, because I'm the only one who knows what those two are really up to. I thought about quitting and moving out of town, but that in itself might look suspicious. With all their resources, Dr. Steiner and Senator Billington could find me if they wanted to. Besides, anywhere I might go to get a job, my employer would have to list my social security number for payroll deductions, so it would be easy for them to find me that way if nothing else. I decided my best course was to stay right where I was and go on with my job as though nothing had happened. I got promoted to Paul's position, but Dr. Steiner hasn't let me in on any of the secret research he shared with Paul. And I hope he doesn't."

"So you never brought this matter up with Dr. Steiner again or with the police. Have you ever told anyone else?"

"No, I've been afraid to, afraid for myself and for anyone I might talk to. If Dr. Steiner found out, we could all be in danger. But he already knows about you, so you're already in danger. I thought I should warn you. I don't want to see you end up like Paul."

"Thanks," he said. "I'll try to be careful."

She got up and started toward the door, saying, "I've got to get going."

As Don moved toward the door to open it for her, he thought not just about how beautiful she was but how frightened and vulnerable. He wanted to take her in his arms and protect her, to hold her and tell her everything would be all right and that she shouldn't be scared. Instead he just opened the door. She took one step into the hall, turned and paused. Was she waiting for him to take her in his arms? She stood there and looked as though she were waiting to be kissed. She looked up at him with those big, liquid eyes and said, "Don't tell anyone I was here and that I told you about any of this."

Just then a middle-aged couple, obviously intoxicated, came into view around a corner in the hallway. The man was staggering along the wall, having difficulty maintaining his balance. The woman appeared somewhat less inebriated and was fiddling with a very large purse.

The spell was broken. Monica said, "I've got to run" and hastened away. He closed the door and leaned against it for a long time wondering whether she really wanted to be kissed or whether it was just wishful thinking on his part.

THE TROJAN PROJECT

Chapter Ten

Senator Billington picked up the large manila envelope on his desk, opened it and removed its contents. He looked at the material, chuckled to himself and picked up the phone to call Dr. Steiner.

When he heard the familiar voice of Malcolm Steiner answer, he said, "Hello, Mal. I've got something very interesting here and thought you'd want to know about it. Yesterday I called Heffler at FBI. He owes me a few favors. So I asked him to keep Emerson under surveillance while he's here in Washington. Heffler sent a couple of agents who walked the halls at his hotel and, at the appropriate time, posed as a couple of drunks. Well, guess who they saw pay a visit to our friend Mr. Emerson last night—*your* Monica."

"Monica Gunderson? That's hard to believe. They just met yesterday afternoon. Are you sure it was Monica?"

"Very sure. As I'm talking to you, I'm looking at an 8 by 10-inch photograph of her leaving his hotel room. The two of them are standing in the doorway, and they look like they're about to kiss. She looks like she's puckering up for one. Either that or she's saying something; you can't tell for sure which. Anyway, it's a very compromising picture. There's no question that it's Monica. Also, the photo clearly shows the numerals "804" on the door, and I have a photostatic copy of the hotel registry showing Emerson registered for that room number. This information may be very influential in 'persuading' Mr. Emerson to cooperate with us.

"Heffler's men also combed the government's files for any information they could find on Emerson. Turns out he once worked for a company in California that made military instruments, so he has a security clearance. That clearance showed him to be an All-American-type guy: no character flaws, no skeletons in his background that we could use against him.

"He now has a small computer-consulting business in Minneapolis, is married and has two small children. Apparently he's a model citizen—just the type that is most vulnerable to the kind of 'persuasion' I alluded to, the kind of guys who are most anxious to preserve their good reputations, who don't want their wives to think they ever even look at another woman much less do anything wrong.

"His tax returns have been professionally prepared and show no obvious weaknesses. That doesn't mean, of course, that he wouldn't be vulnerable if we wanted to have the IRS give him a going over. As you know, tax laws are so complex that the IRS can find something wrong with just about anybody's tax return if they want to—or we want them to. And even if there's nothing wrong with his returns, the IRS can subject him to detailed audits, freeze his assets and harass him in a variety of other ways. So that's another weapon we can use if we have to."

"What we really need to know right now is how much he knows. How much do you think Monica told him?"

"I don't know if she told him anything. I don't know what she knows that she'd want to tell him in secret. I haven't shown her any of the special data that Markowitz had access to. Maybe it was a romantic thing. You just said the picture looks like they're going to kiss. Maybe she just went up there for a 'quickie'"

"Well, it would have had to be awfully quick," said the senator. "Heffler's agents said she was in there only a few minutes. That kind of thing doesn't seem very likely with someone she just met, does it?"

"No, especially knowing Monica. She doesn't seem like that sort of person. On the other hand, that Emerson is a good looking guy. Maybe she just simply fell for him."

"I'll concede he's good looking, but he's not *that* good looking," said the senator. "He's no young Robert Redford."

"Well, looks aren't everything to a woman, you know," said Steiner. "Maybe this guy Emerson has some kind of sex appeal that you and I just aren't able to appreciate. Besides, maybe she had to be somewhere else and therefore had to leave sooner than she would have liked. Where did she go after she left the hotel?"

"We don't know. Heffler's people hadn't been told to tail her. They're watching her now, for as long as Emerson is in town, but that's no help on last night."

Steiner was puzzled. "I still don't know what she could have told him. I don't think she could've told him anything that could be damaging to us."

"Maybe she told him about Markowitz," said Billington. "Or worse, maybe Markowitz told her what he knew before he died. Maybe that's what she told Emerson."

"I guess we have to face those possibilities," said Steiner, "but they don't seem very likely to me. First of all, what could she tell him about Markowitz? The police officially called it a 'random shooting,' so how could she make trouble for us about that? As to Markowitz telling her anything, he told me the day he died that no one else knew what he knew…"

"Maybe he said that just to protect her," interrupted the senator.

"Well, I have to admit that's possible, but, again, it doesn't seem very likely. If she knew anything, if she were suspicious, don't you think she'd have said something by now? I've watched her very closely at work for any sign that she's suspicious, and I've seen nothing, nothing at all, not a single clue in her behavior at the office. We've had her apartment phone tapped since the day Markowitz died, and she's never said one word over her phone to her friends or her family, the police or anyone about the circumstances of Markowitz's death or anything he may have told her. Don't you think she'd have said something to someone by now? How long has it been? More than five months. Even if she was being cautious at first, don't you think by now that she'd figure the coast was clear and have said something to someone? Or don't you think that by now that kind of information would be weighing on her mind and she'd feel the need to tell someone?"

"Listen," said Senator Billington. "This conversation is getting into areas I don't feel comfortable discussing over the phone. Why don't I come over to your office? Are you free right now?"

"I'll make the time available. Nothing is more important than this."

"Good. I'll be there in half an hour. Forty minutes at most."

The senator arrived promptly, and the two closeted themselves in Dr. Steiner's office. Billington was the first to speak: "On the way over here I was thinking that if romance was the reason Monica visited Emerson last night, then they'll try to see each other again, especially since their relationship is so new. Emerson has a free day today; he doesn't meet with me until tomorrow. Heffler's men will be watching him. We'll know by tomorrow morning whether or not he's had any further contact with Monica. If they don't make another attempt to see each other, then I think we can assume she went to his hotel for a different purpose, namely, to tell him something about Markowitz. And if as you say, she can't cause us any trouble about Markowitz's death—and I don't see how she could—then we have to assume Markowitz told her what he knew. We'll just have to assume that. We'll have to assume that's what she told Emerson. We'll have to plan for that and act accordingly."

"I agree. I was reluctant to believe Markowitz told her anything, but you're absolutely right. They'll try to meet again if there's a physical attraction between them. And if not, if she spilled the beans to Emerson and he now knows what Markowitz knew, then I suppose we have to consider the 'Markowitz solution' for him."

"For Chrissake, Mal! Don't talk like that! I don't want any part of it. Markowitz was your idea all the way. I was against it, and you know it. You were lucky you got away with it once, but don't push your luck. Murder was never part of our original agreement. Besides, even if you take care of Emerson, what'll you do about Monica?—bump her off, too?"

"We may not have to. If she's been too scared to tell what she knew for the past five months, think how scared she'll be if Emerson is knocked off. I'll bet she'll keep her mouth shut for at least another five months—if not permanently—and another five months is about all we'll need. We're making a lot of progress on the research, you know. But if we had to, yes, I'd silence her, too, beautiful as she is and much as I'd hate to."

"Goddammit, Mal! Don't even think along those lines! There have to be other ways. If not, then we have to close down the Trojan Project, cover our tracks and forget about it. I won't be a party to murder. I never agreed to that when we started all this, and I won't agree to it now."

"Why the hell are you so goddam sanctimonious?" said Steiner raising both his voice and his eyebrows. "Everything you politicians do is based on the power of a gun. That's what political power is, the power of a gun. Behind every one of those thousands of laws you pass lies a gun. That's the only thing that makes your laws mean anything…"

"We don't shoot people."

"Well, suppose some guy uses a gun to rob a bank but doesn't shoot anybody; he merely threatens to do so. Suppose another guy robs a bank and does shoot somebody in the process. Both obtain what they want by means of a gun. You politicians are like the first robber; you obtain what you want by threatening people. Only in your case people don't see the gun; it's hidden under all those legal papers and official procedures, and you leave the enforcement to the police. That way you can appear above the fray and pose as lofty, high-minded civic leaders; but you're the ones who write the threats into law. Threats of violence are the currency of your profession, the coin of your realm, the coin you trade for votes, for personal advantage, and for advancing your favorite causes, whatever they are. Picking a noble cause doesn't change the nature of how you get what you want. The number of laws you pass—which you always seem so proud of—are the number of ways you threaten people."

"You're getting carried away," said Billington. "Of course, laws have to threaten penalties and have to be enforced. Otherwise they wouldn't be obeyed. But we provide a lot of positive benefits, too. We pass laws providing for disaster relief for victims of floods and hurricanes; we pass laws giving benefits to the needy and the unemployed; we pass laws that create jobs, stimulate the economy, provide for medical care and education; and we don't write threats into those laws. And, I daresay, the people who participate in these programs and benefit from them don't feel threatened."

"No, but the people who pay for them are. All the benefits you dole out so magnanimously are paid for by other laws that threaten violence against people if they don't pay the taxes funding your 'generosity.' If they don't pay, the police will seize their property and/or throw them in jail, at the point of a gun if necessary. The only difference between you and the bank robber who uses the gun only as a threat and doesn't actually fire it is that he keeps the money and you give it away. So you get to feel good about yourselves for allocating tax money to your high-sounding causes, but morally you're equal. You both get what you want the same way."

"You're the last person who should be giving me a lecture on morality."

"Really? Let me tell you something. You may think I'm like the second robber I mentioned, the one who pulls the trigger when he has to, but at least I'm honest about it. I'm not a hypocrite. I don't hide the gun under a pile of laws and regulations and try to pretend it isn't there."

"Let's not argue. How the hell did we get into this argument anyway?" said Billington.

"There's nothing to argue about, really," said Steiner. "We're two of a kind. We both rely on the power of a gun to obtain our objectives. Just don't give me that holier-than-thou attitude simply because you deal only in threats. Sometimes the threat isn't enough; sometimes one has to pull the trigger. How else could we silence Markowitz? How else could we achieve our goal? There was no other way.

"Believe me, it's not something I wanted to do, and it's taken its toll on me. You can't imagine the tension I've been under ever since. The anxiety, the suspense of not knowing if I could really get away with it has been incredibly stressful, much worse than I thought it would be; but the Trojan Project is worth it. Markowitz had to be silenced—and instead of being sanctimonious and critical you ought to be thanking me for taking care of that dirty job and saving The Project."

"I'm not going to argue with you," said Billington. "We can't afford to argue. We've got a problem, and we've got to think this thing through. The 'Markowitz solution' is out, and it wouldn't work anyway. It's not practical. Emerson is only going to be here one more day. Then he goes back to Minneapolis. I doubt that the professionals you hired for Markowitz would be willing to take care of him in 24 hours. Wouldn't they need more time?"

"Yes, you're right about that," said Steiner. "Those guys had months to plan the Markowitz job so they'd be ready if needed. That's why it went so smoothly. I doubt they'd be willing to take care of Emerson here in 24 hours, especially since he's in a downtown hotel; that makes the job a little more complicated."

"Furthermore," said the senator, "Those professionals might not be willing to do a job in an unfamiliar territory like Minneapolis. And even if they are, it would take even more time to familiarize themselves there and set things up. By then who knows how many people Emerson may have told. When I talked to Ray Stafford, the Minnesota senator, he said he met with Emerson and some guy from the phone company. So there's somebody else who already knows about the telephone virus whom we have to worry about. He's probably the first person Emerson will tell when he goes back to Minneapolis. What are you going to do about him?—bump him off, too? And what about Ray Stafford? Don't you think he would get suspicious if those other two guys meet with 'accidents'?"

"He'd probably never hear about what happens to that guy from the phone company back in Minneapolis," said Steiner.

"No? How can you be sure of that? Suppose Emerson's wife goes to him and says it looks suspicious that both of these guys who know about this issue are killed, and she asks him to look into the matter. Then what are you going to do?— knock off his wife and Ray Stafford, too? You can't go knocking off a U.S. senator and expect to get that covered up the way you did the Markowitz incident."

"No," said Steiner. "I didn't know about the guy from the phone company. Emerson never mentioned anything about him. I wonder why. Anyway, that definitely changes the picture. That and the time factor needed for taking care of Emerson would make the 'Markowitz solution' impractical. We'll have to handle this some other way."

"Good. Now you're being sensible," said Billington.

"As I see it," he continued, "we've got two chances to keep him quiet without resorting to violence. One is based on fear; the other, upon greed. The first, we'll call it Plan A, will be to confront him with the photograph and a copy of the hotel registration and imply we'll show them to his wife unless he keeps his mouth shut. Whether or not anything ever happened between him and Monica in that hotel room is irrelevant. I'm sure he'd rather not have his wife see that picture and draw her own conclusion.

"If that fails, then we resort to Plan B, which will be to cut him in on the deal. We'll make him a partner. I'm sure he's bright enough to see that that's a very lucrative offer. He'll realize immediately that our scheme can provide him with a far richer and more rewarding life than he could ever attain with that little computer business he's got."

"Well, at least that would buy us some time," said Steiner. "Then if we did want to use the 'Markowitz solution,' we could."

"I thought we agreed that was out?"

"It wouldn't necessarily be out if we had enough time," said Steiner. "But relax; I just said *if* we wanted to. I didn't say we would. We'll have time to make that decision later. What concerns me right now is what we do if Emerson doesn't submit to either Plan A or Plan B. Then what do we do?"

"Then we have to call it quits," said Billington. "We have to terminate the Trojan Project and destroy every trace of it. When we started all this, I agreed to get you the funding for everything you needed. I've certainly fulfilled my end of the bargain. In return, you promised that it would be very easy to hide the Trojan Project behind legitimate research on the telephone virus. If necessary, you said, you could destroy the Trojan Project so no one could ever trace it to me."

"Or me," added Steiner. "The legitimate work on the telephone virus is the perfect front. I personally handle all the research on the Trojan Project. No one else has seen any of the data. Nobody has evidence of any kind that could indicate that Trojan even exists. I tried to ease Markowitz into the secret research to accelerate the program, because you were pressuring me for results…"

"Well, I'm entitled to some kind of results," interrupted Billington. "I got you all the money you said you needed, and I still haven't seen any results. When we started this, you said you thought you'd have the answer by now. I got you everything you wanted, and I expect something in return. That's the way things are done in this town. But so far you haven't given me anything."

"I know. Things have taken longer than I expected, but you have to understand that something like this can't be accomplished on a rigid timetable. I'm sure I'm very close, but no one can predict exactly when the breakthrough will come. Besides, things can only go so fast when I have to do everything myself. I'm driving myself as hard as I can. I'm really doing the work of two people, you know. Directing the legitimate research is a full-time job plus I have all the work on the Trojan Project. This double workload is very stressful, and you just can't expect me to work any harder or any faster. Your pressuring me doesn't help any; it just adds to the stress. It's just not humanly possible for one person to do any more than I'm doing. I wanted to have Markowitz help me, in order to accelerate things, and that was almost a disaster. Actually, I hadn't even involved him that much in the secret stuff. I didn't think he'd be able to figure out what I was up to from the little I let him in on, but he was a very bright guy. He jumped to conclusions. Fortunately, we were able to silence him, but ever since I've done all the secret work myself. So, yes, if we need to, I could still terminate the Trojan Project, and we'd both come out clean."

"Good," said Billington, "because if I can't persuade Emerson to keep quiet and the word gets out, I'll have to call publicly for an investigation."

"That's fine," said Steiner. "All I need is enough time to shred the contents of the filing cabinet in my office."

The next morning as Dr. Steiner was hard at work going over data on the Trojan Project, Senator Billington phoned.

"Hello, Mal. I just got a call from Heffler. His agents tailed Emerson all day, and he spent it sightseeing like a typical tourist. He visited the Washington Monument, the White House, the Lincoln Memorial, the Jefferson Memorial, all the things your average tourist wants to see. He never made any phone calls or met anyone during the day. He spent the evening alone in his hotel room.

"Heffler's people also kept an eye on Monica from the time she left work at your place. She stopped to pick up a few groceries on her way home, then spent the evening alone in her apartment. She had only two phone calls. One was to her mother, whom she talks to almost every day. The other was from a girlfriend she's known since college, whom she talks to about once a month. The content of both phone calls was routine, trivial stuff. Nothing of any interest to us.

"Since neither Monica nor Emerson attempted to contact each other, she must have told him what Markowitz knew. We've got to face that fact and be prepared to dump Trojan if I can't persuade Emerson to keep his mouth shut."

"I'd hate to have to dump the project when we're this far along and with all the effort I've invested," said Steiner. "Maybe there's another explanation why they didn't meet yesterday. Maybe they had a lovers' quarrel. Maybe she got angry; maybe that's why she left in such a hurry Monday night. Maybe things didn't go well for them the first time. Maybe he left her unsatisfied and she left in a huff."

"She didn't leave in a huff. For Pete's sake, the photo looks like they're about to kiss, and that was taken as she was leaving," said Billington. "Besides, Heffler's people didn't say she looked like she was angry when she left. No, there's no other explanation. We've got to face the fact that Emerson now knows what Markowitz knew. I would hate to have to dump this project just as much as you would, but we've got to be flexible; we've got to adapt to changing circumstances. There's no point in hanging on until it's too late."

"Of course. I just don't want to abandon all this unless we absolutely have to."

"Right. I just want to make sure you're prepared in case it comes to that. I still think I can persuade Emerson with either Plan A or Plan B when he comes to my office this afternoon. I'll call you right after our meeting."

THE TROJAN PROJECT

Chapter Eleven

Senator Billington wasn't scheduled to meet with Don until right after lunch. He, therefore, had several hours that morning to plan how he would handle the meeting. He always liked to plan his political battles by taking into account his opponents' personalities, their behavioral quirks, and the strengths and weaknesses of their character; but his opponent now was a stranger to him. Billington had the material Heffler had collected on Emerson, but he had no personal acquaintance. The two had never even spoken, their meeting having been arranged by the senator's staff.

The senator considered going slowly at first, not bringing up either Plan A or Plan B until he had a chance to feel out his opponent. He could temporize, ask about Don's meeting with Dr. Steiner, his sightseeing the previous day, his family and his business in order to give him a chance to observe and take the measure of this man before confronting him. He toyed briefly with the idea of bringing up Plan B first, but he rejected that because he didn't want to take in another partner unless it was absolutely necessary. It would be much simpler, he thought, if Plan A would work. In the end he decided the element of surprise would be maximized if he sprung that plan right away. The idea was to throw his opponent off balance almost as soon as he entered the room. There would be the introductory pleasantries, of course, but then he would immediately bring out the photograph. He found it difficult to plan beyond that, for he felt that how he would proceed from that point would be determined by his opponent's reaction to the photo, something he found difficult to envision with a man he had never met.

When Don entered the senator's walnut-paneled office, the first thing he saw was the floor-to-ceiling windows that occupied almost half of the opposite wall and offered a spectacular view of the Washington skyline. The wall to his left was covered with shelves of books, and along the far end, near the windows, was the senator's massive desk. On the opposite wall, to Don's right, was an oil portrait of Lyndon Johnson. It hung in the middle of a row of four photo enlargements of more recent presidents, each with Senator Billington by his side and autographed by the president.

The senator rose from his chair behind the desk, and Don advanced toward him across the most ornate and expensive-looking carpet he'd ever seen. He didn't know it had been imported from Italy and cost fifty-seven dollars per square foot. The two men exchanged greetings and shook hands. The senator smiled, seemed disarmingly gracious, gestured toward a chair across from his desk and asked Don to make himself comfortable.

Before he sat down, Don glanced back at the wall containing the door through which he had just entered. It contained pictures of George Washington, Madison, Jefferson and Hamilton. There was also a framed replica of a document which Don couldn't make out at that distance but was fairly certain was the Declaration of Independence. In one corner stood a leather-topped stand trimmed with gold leaf and holding a marble bust of Julius Caesar. On the wall behind it hung prints of two Piranesi engravings, one of the Roman Forum, the other of the Roman Coliseum. Scattered about the room were other pictures of foreign dignitaries, military leaders and movie stars, all with Senator Billington. Above the bookcases on the wall behind the senator's desk were some civil war scenes. Atop the bookcase in the far corner was a bust of Lincoln. In addition to the books the shelves directly behind the desk held pictures of members of the senator's family.

Don noticed that he and the senator were about the same height when they stood and shook hands; but when he sank into the plush chair that was offered, he was seated several inches below the level of Senator Billington in his chair behind the desk. That effect, of course, was by design, to give the senator visual dominance over a visitor, who would be looking up while the senator was looking down during conversation.

Then the senator asked, "How did your meeting go with Dr. Steiner?"

"Fine," said Don. "I told him about my experiences with the telephone virus, and he briefed me on what he'd learned from the research so far. Then his assistant gave me a tour of the laboratory facilities. It was all very interesting, and I really learned a lot."

"Good. Then I presume you also learned that it's vitally necessary for us to maintain secrecy on this project."

"Yes, Dr. Steiner and I discussed that."

"Then you'll understand why it's necessary for me to ask what Monica Gunderson told you when she came to your hotel room Monday evening." As he spoke, the senator watched Don very closely for his reaction.

Don was shocked. He immediately thought about what Monica said about both their lives being in danger. He thought the danger must be much greater now that the senator knew about their meeting. Obviously, they were under surveillance; he didn't think the senator was bluffing. He didn't know what to say but decided to bluff and play dumb, at least for the moment, just because he couldn't think of what else to say. "What do you mean?" he said, trying to sound as though he didn't know what Billington was talking about.

"You know very well what I mean," snapped the senator, jabbing the air with his forefinger in the direction of Don. "No use pretending you don't." If he thinks I'm bluffing, he thought, I'll show him that I'm not. With that he turned over the photograph that had been face down on his desk, rotated it so that it would be right-side up for Don, and placed it on the far edge of his desk where Don could see it. Then he watched closely for his visitor's reaction.

He didn't see what he was looking for. He saw Don lean over and look at the photo. Certainly the man was surprised, but the senator was disappointed that he saw no trace of what he wanted to see: fear. In fact, his visitor seemed almost unruffled and certainly less surprised by the picture than he had been a moment earlier by the question that revealed a knowledge of Monica being in his hotel room.

Don was caught off guard by the suddenness of the senator's question about Monica, but he was on the defensive now. He knew that his opponent was studying him; he would give him as little additional information as possible. Moreover, the realization that Billington knew Monica had been to his hotel made it difficult for anything to surprise him now. He had a fresh, firsthand awareness that he was dealing with a plot of enormous scope run by men with almost unlimited resources who he knew would stop at nothing, not even murder. Why should he be surprised that they had arranged to take a picture of him with a camera hidden in the purse of a woman posing as a drunk in a hotel hallway?

Billington was surprised that Don viewed the photo so calmly, but he pressed on: "So you see there is no point in denying she was there with you. Now are you going to tell me what she told you?"

Don had overcome his initial shock. His mind was now racing to solve the problem of how to respond. He wanted to find some reply that would protect Monica, if possible. Monica had asked him not to tell anyone about her visit or what she had told him. He didn't want to act counter to her request, but he quickly realized that that was the only way to protect her: if Billington and Steiner thought she hadn't yet told him, they would have an incentive to kill her before she did. But if she had already told him, that incentive would be gone; it would be too late. So he said, "She told me everything. I know all about what you and Dr. Steiner are up to. I know that the research on the telephone virus is just a front for a secret project to modify the virus so that you'll become the next president of the United States. And I know what happened to Paul Markowitz."

"I had nothing to do with Markowitz," said Billington. "Besides, the police ruled it a 'random shooting.'"

Billington thought: we were right; she did tell him. Now was the time to press Plan A. He was more than a little disappointed that presenting the photo didn't bring as strong a reaction from Don as he had hoped; but if there was any chance for Plan A, it would have to be now. He said, "What do you think your wife's reaction would be to that photo?"

Don wasn't surprised by this question because from the instant he saw the photo he was sure Billington intended to use it to try to blackmail him. Calmly he replied, "That's an interesting picture, and it was ingenious the way you got it. But it's not what it appears to be. I'm sure my wife would be surprised initially; but if I explained the situation to her, I'm sure she'd believe me. We have a very good relationship. We've always been honest with each other. She knows I always try to do the right thing and would never do anything like what you're implying that picture suggests. I'm sure she trusts me and would believe my explanation. So if you think you're going to blackmail me into silence, I can tell you it won't work. If you don't believe me, go ahead and show her the picture. You'll find out for yourself what her reaction will be, but you won't get what you want."

He's not bluffing, thought Billington. Plan A wasn't going to work. The senator prided himself on his ability to read people, and to him Don appeared composed, sincere and downright confident as he spoke. There was no visible evidence of the fear and uncertainty that he'd hoped to play upon. But Billington was, as always, flexible, adaptable. He decided to jettison Plan A immediately and proceed in another direction. He felt he couldn't go directly into Plan B; he would have to improvise instead, go wherever the conversation led for the time being, be patient until an appropriate opportunity developed. He laughed and said, "Who said anything about blackmail? Don't worry, my good man, nobody is going to blackmail you. I just showed you that picture because I wanted to show you that things aren't always what they appear to be. I'm sure you'll agree that people could easily get the wrong impression from that picture. Well, in the same way, you've probably got the wrong impression about what's going on here in Washington."

"Wrong impression!" said Don incredulously. "You're planning to steal the election of the highest office in the nation by manipulating the voters, and you think I may be getting the wrong impression?!"

"But elections are stolen all the time. Voters are always being manipulated," said the senator. "We're just into a more high-tech way of doing it. Other advances in technology have been used the same way. Remember when television was new, when it was the latest thing in technology? Well, remember the Nixon-Kennedy debates which were televised and were the crucial factor in Kennedy's election? Those staging the debate wanted Kennedy to win. So they told Nixon that both candidates were being asked to wear a light colored suit because there would be a dark background in the TV studio. That was a deliberate lie. When the two candidates arrived to debate, Kennedy was wearing a dark suit, which made him stand out nicely against the light-colored background. Nixon in his light suit just blended into the background. Television was quite new then, and many people still didn't have TV sets. Public opinion polls showed that people who listened to the debate on radio thought Nixon won, not Kennedy. But people who watched the event on TV thought Kennedy won by a big margin, and that margin was the difference in the election. It was a very close election, and contemporary analysts and historians are virtually unanimous in agreeing that that first debate was the deciding factor."

"It wasn't just the color of their suits that made the difference," said Don. "Another factor in that debate was that Nixon refused to wear makeup while Kennedy did."

"You're helping to prove my point," said Billington. "Nixon—of all people—wanted to be honest, wanted people to see him as he was, not as an image artificially enhanced by make-up. In the second debate he finally consented to wear make-up—after strenuous urging by his advisors—and he looked much better, but by then it was too late to overtake Kennedy. The important point is that what counted was the *image,* not the reality. It's just like that picture of you and Monica; it's the image that counts, not whether or not you and she ever did anything wrong. It's what people think that matters, even if what they think is wrong or artificial or based on false premises. That's the way democracy is; the only standard is what the majority think, not whether it's right or wrong or accurate or even real. Maybe the 'lesson' Nixon learned from that election is that if you're honest and play by the rules, then you'll lose to those who manipulate the rules and the images. Maybe that's why he was later willing to be dishonest and participate in Watergate."

"That's conjecture on your part," said Don.

"Of course it is, but what we do know is that honesty didn't pay for Nixon in 1960 and that make-up artists and the dishonesty of those who staged the debate swung the election. Now, does it really make any difference if voters are manipulated through their television sets, as they were with Kennedy, or are manipulated through their telephones, as Dr. Steiner and I hope to do?"

"I don't approve of either. They're both wrong," said Don. "But surely there were issues involved, too, in that election. It couldn't all have been 'manipulation' as you suggest."

"Oh, couldn't it?" said Billington. "You're probably too young to remember this, but the number one issue—virtually the only issue in that election—was the so-called 'missile gap.' That was a phony issue if there ever was one. Kennedy claimed that Russia had more nuclear missiles than we did and was threatening our security. Nixon, of course, was Eisenhower's vice president and was running on the record of the administration. Eisenhower was one of the finest generals of the century, the man who had led the Allied armies in World War II to the greatest military victory in history. He knew better than anyone else how to protect our national security. He obviously knew a helluva lot more about military capabilities than Kennedy. Surely Kennedy must have known that his charge was preposterous. In fact, shortly after the election he admitted that there never was a 'missile gap.' It didn't matter then. The election was over; the votes had been counted. Nobody suggested he should give back the election because the principal issue of his campaign was a fraudulent one.

"President Kennedy, one of the most esteemed presidents of this century, is just one example of how the highest office in the land was captured by deception. I could give you other, more recent examples. Remember how George Bush got elected by solemnly, unequivocally promising 'read my lips: no new taxes'? Once elected, he proceeded to raise taxes anyway. So he lied. So what? Nobody asked him to give back the presidency because he won it on false premises, by deceiving the voters. Politicians lie all the time, make promises they don't intend to keep or couldn't possibly keep even if they wanted to. It doesn't matter once the votes are counted.

"The examples I gave are of the presidency, but senators and congressmen obtain their offices the same way. Look how many of them have campaigned over the past half century on promises to cut government spending and reduce the federal deficit, but once elected they increased government spending. If they did what they promised, we wouldn't have a budget deficit and a multi-trillion dollar national debt that just keeps on soaring. Since 1950, Congress has voted to raise the national debt limit 87 times.

"And it's not just campaign promises to reduce spending that have been deceptive; it's actual laws. In 1978 Congress enacted into law a bill introduced by Senator Harry F. Byrd, Jr. that said: 'Beginning with fiscal year 1981, the total budget outlays of the Federal Government shall not exceed its receipts.' What happened? Congress ignored its own law. We're a long way from 1981, and the federal budget has never yet been balanced. Few people today even know there was such a law. Then there was the Gramm-Rudman-Hollings Act, which was supposed to balance the budget gradually over a six-year period through a series of spending reductions. But six years later the deficit was larger than before that act was passed. We're not talking here about deception by individuals; we're talking about deception by institution, by the collective action of Congress. It's nothing less than the failure of democracy. The laws that were passed to give the impression that Congress was dealing with the deficit were products of the democratic process of majority rule by the duly elected representatives of the people. They weren't aberrations of the system; they were the essence of the system. Every congressman could then hold up these laws to the voters back home and say, 'See, I voted to cut spending and reduce the deficit.' Just like I said about that picture of you and Monica, it's the image that counts. In a democracy that's what gets the votes, and that's all that matters. Congress knows that. Congress is only interested in such images. In reality it ignores the very laws it passes to create the image of dealing with the deficit. Tell me that whole process is not deception?"

"Of course it is," said Don. "It's not right, and I don't approve of it. But at least it's done legally, according to established parliamentary rules. What you and Dr. Steiner are trying to do is beyond the rules. Do you think you're above the standards that apply to everyone else? Do you think you're some kind of elite that's exempt from the rules that apply to the rest of society?"

Theodore Billington just laughed. "Mr. Emerson, Congress is already an elite that's exempt from the rules that apply to the rest of society. For decades we exempted ourselves from the laws we passed that set the standards for everyone else. We exempted ourselves from the Equal Employment Opportunity Act, the Occupational Safety and Health Act, the Ethics in Government Act, the Equal Pay Act, the Fair Labor Standards Act, the Age Discrimination Act and its later amendments, the Freedom of Information Act, the Civil Rights Act of 1964, the Civil Rights Restoration Act of 1988, and the Family Leave Act. We wrote our exemption right into the laws themselves. Does it make you feel any better to know that the double standard we established was accomplished democratically by observing all the legal niceties and parliamentary procedures?"

"No," said Don. "It makes me feel worse. That's not the way our government was supposed to work. It's not right. Madison said in *The Federalist* that representatives of the people should 'make no law which will not have its full operation on themselves and their friends, as well as on the great mass of society.' He said this would restrain lawmakers from passing oppressive measures and create a 'communion of interests and sympathy of sentiments...without which every government degenerates into tyranny.' Furthermore, he said that if the spirit of the American people 'ever be so far debased as to tolerate a law not obligatory on the legislature, as well as on the people, the people will be prepared to tolerate anything but liberty.' It's sad to think we reached that point, but didn't Congress in 1995 vote to remove its exemption from its own laws?"

"Of course, the party that had controlled the House for forty years was defeated in the election in 1994, and it lost control of the Senate as well," said the senator. "The newly-elected Congress, as part of its 'Contract with America,' in 1995 did indeed vote to have Congress comply with *most* of the laws—eleven to be exact—from which it had previously exempted itself. But it would be unrealistic to assume that the party that has controlled Congress for most of the last half-century will never again be the majority party. If it does regain power, it could simply change the rules again. Congress can't bind future Congresses by its rules or even its laws. That's why that law sponsored by Senator Byrd to balance the budget beginning in 1981 had no effect. That's why the Gramm-Rudman-Hollings Act wasn't able to balance the budget either. Both of those laws were the result of popular sentiment and gave the public the image that Congress was correcting the problem. But with passage of a few short years and some changes in Congress due to elections, things were right back where they were before. It would be unduly optimistic to think that the practice of Congress exempting itself from its own laws, which was observed regularly for more than thirty years, is gone forever. There's nothing to stop Congress from changing the rules again whenever it wishes. Congress doesn't even need to go through the formality of changing the law or repealing it. All the government needs to do is pass a bill that doesn't obey the law—and *that* then becomes the law. For example, in regard to the law requiring a balanced budget in 1981, all Congress and the president had to do was pass a law authorizing an unbalanced budget for 1981, and that became the law, superseding the balanced-budget law.

"Besides, that 1995 law that removed Congress' exemption from those eleven earlier laws isn't exactly what it appears to be. It created the image that we would comply with the laws just as everyone else does, but in reality it provided for some exceptions—and we've since created various other ways of exempting ourselves. To begin with, the law exempted this entire Congress from OSHA regulations, which won't apply until the next Congress. Even then, senators and congressmen can't be fined for OSHA violations, only cited. And we wrote it right into the law that congressional offices couldn't be audited, as private companies are, for violations of the Fair Labor Standards Act. As for new ways of exempting ourselves, Representative James Barcia, a Michigan Democrat, has simply declared he won't pay overtime, arguing that his staff is all too high-level to fall under the law. Representative Bill Thomas, a Republican from California and chairman of the Oversight Committee that's supposed to enforce the law, has exempted his whole staff. Other members of Congress have created exemptions for their offices by changing job descriptions or reclassifying employees as seasonal workers under contract."

"It's not right," said Don shaking his head.

Billington took note of the fact that Don was so concerned with what was right. He noticed that his visitor often responded with phrases such as, "It's not right," or "It's wrong, and I don't approve." If this guy is so moral, thought Billington, then he probably would refuse to go along with Plan B just because it wasn't morally acceptable to him, regardless of how that plan could benefit him personally. As the conversation was going, the senator had less and less confidence in Plan B. But there was no Plan C; if he brought up Plan B now and it didn't work, then the meeting would be over—and so would the Trojan Project. He didn't want that to happen. Instead of bringing up Plan B, he would try to keep the conversation going until he could improvise an alternative, a Plan C. He was already beginning to see how that might be possible.

"How come you know so much about history?" asked the senator. "I thought you were in the computer business."

"I am in the computer business. I also happen to be interested in history, which I studied a lot in college. And every time I think about Congress exempting itself from its own laws I think of that passage by Madison. What's happening in this country isn't right—and what you and Dr. Steiner are trying to do isn't right either."

There's that moral emphasis again, thought Billington.

"Stealing an election is just as bad as stealing anything else," continued Don. It's robbing people of something that's legitimately theirs, something they have every right to. It's worse than an individual act of theft, because you're stealing from the whole country, robbing every citizen of the United States."

"But the government is already stealing from the whole country," said the senator. "We're already robbing every citizen of the United States and have been doing so for a long time. We're even robbing future citizens, those who haven't even been born yet. When we collect taxes, we do so, in effect, by pointing a gun at the heads of the taxpayers. Only the gun is hidden under a pile of government paper. So we pretend it isn't there and hope the taxpayers won't realize they're being robbed, but isn't it the same issue? When government taxes people's earnings, aren't we really taking 'something they have every right to' at the point of a gun?"

"Of course you are," said Don. "That's a good argument for why the role of the government should be vastly reduced. If government wasn't doing so many things which it shouldn't be doing, and things which it can't do as well as the private sector, there would be no need to rob people, through taxes, to pay for those government activities."

"And taxes aren't the only way we rob people," continued Billington as Plan C was beginning to take shape in his mind. "We've robbed them of the value of their money. *Webster's New Twentieth Century Dictionary, Unabridged, Second Edition,* right over there on that shelf," he said, pointing to his right toward one of the bookshelves lining the wall behind his desk, "defines paper currency as 'paper issued as a *substitute* for money.' Notice that it doesn't say paper currency *is* money; it says *substitute* for money. Paper currency of the United States used to carry the phrase 'Redeemable in lawful money…' It was receipts for 'lawful money,' which meant gold or silver ever since the Coinage Act of 1792. But under Franklin Roosevelt the government ceased to honor its receipts; it said a receipt itself *was* money and gradually withdrew from circulation all the currency notes with the redeemable phrase printed on them. Imagine for a moment that you took your watch or a pair of shoes to be repaired and the repair service gave you a receipt. Then when you wanted to reclaim your watch or shoes, the repairman refused and told you that the receipt itself *was* the watch or shoes. It would be preposterous for him to suggest that you could wear the paper receipt and use it just as you would the watch or shoes, and the incident would be seen as a blatant attempt to steal those objects of value from you. But that's exactly what our government—democratically elected—did with respect to our money. It stole material value from the money of everyone in the country. It robbed everyone at the point of a gun through legal tender laws that forced people to accept the replacement currency without any material backing—or else the guns of government would confiscate their property or throw them in jail.

"That enormous theft would have been bad enough if it were just a one-time incident in our past. Instead, it provided the mechanism by which government could continue to steal from the people indefinitely. The government replaced redeemable currency with paper that had only the *image* of its predecessor. The government said that the image was all that mattered—just like I said about that picture of you and Monica. It said that the image was just as good as the real thing, but it wasn't. Paper currency unbacked by any tangible material value has inevitably lost its worth over time. It did so because there was no longer any restraint on the amount of money government could issue. When government has to be able to redeem its paper receipts in gold or silver, its money supply is limited by its holdings of those precious metals. When a currency is unredeemable, government can print an unlimited supply of it. And the more it prints, the less it's worth. The purchasing power of everyone's money drops because there's more of it around to bid for the goods and services available in the society. In short, there's more money chasing the same amount of goods and services. The result is higher prices.

Nowadays we speak of higher prices as 'inflation.' If you look in old economics textbooks or even old dictionaries, however, you'll find inflation defined as an increase in the money supply without a corresponding increase in precious metal."

"So what you're saying," said Don, "is that we've switched the definition of 'inflation' from the cause to the effect."

"That's it exactly," said Billington. "Higher prices are merely the effect, of which increasing the money supply is the cause. But by defining inflation as 'an increase in prices,' we obscure the fact that government itself is the cause, that government is stealing value from the people's money—through the loss of its purchasing power—by increasing the money supply.

"Furthermore, the money supply has to be increased to accommodate the debt of massive government spending. It's called 'monetizing the debt.' The Federal Reserve Act was passed by Congress 'to furnish an elastic currency'—those words are from the title of the act itself. The Fed is required to make loans available to the government in whatever amount is necessary to meet federal spending. When the U.S. Treasury wishes to borrow money, it issues U.S. Treasury bonds or similar government paper. These debt instruments become 'reserves' in the banking system, and the U.S. Treasury receives corresponding credits to its checking account in a Federal Reserve member bank—which means that the total money supply of the nation is increased; for as the Treasury writes checks to pay its bills, these new credit dollars are added to circulation. These are dollars which didn't exist before. The money supply becomes 'elastic' not by printing more paper currency but by expanding the amount of credit deposits in the banking system. The process has the effect of diluting the purchasing power of dollars already in circulation, just as it would if more paper dollars were printed. So once again government is robbing the people. Everyone knows that prices were lower ten or twenty or more years ago, but few people know why. Since the advent of the Federal Reserve System, the dollar has lost more than 99 percent of its purchasing power. The colossal magnitude of that theft dwarfs anything that Dr. Steiner and I could ever hope to steal. What we're doing is trivial by comparison."

The natural flow of the conversation was fitting precisely with Billington's new plan, and he was making the most of it. His new plan was to convince Don the country was worse off now than it would be if the Trojan Project succeeded. If this Emerson guy was so moral,

Billington would convince him to maintain secrecy about that project because that was the *right* thing to do for the country. The senator would use a moral weapon to defeat this moral man: the Truth. He would tell the truth about how bad things were in this country and where we were headed, and Emerson would see it as his moral duty to cooperate in order to bring about reforms that would save the nation. Billington would even solicit Don's ideas on reform and promise to effectuate them once he was president. Of course, the senator had no intention of ever keeping such promises; to him they would be simply like campaign promises. To him the truth was merely a means to an end, a moral means to an immoral end. He would employ the truth merely to achieve victory in a rigged election, because he felt this moral man would succumb to the truth. Once "elected," he would have no further need of the truth or of Emerson.

"If you want another example of government stealing on a colossal scale," continued Billington, "look at Social Security. We pay retirees benefits now by stealing from the next generation. After robbing children so that we can play the hero and give the money to their parents—so they'll vote for us—we tell them not to worry because they, in turn, can steal from their own children. Never mind that the parents and grandparents are already wealthier than the children. The children don't vote. The federal government spends eleven times more per capita on the elderly than it invests in children, and the poverty rate for those under age six is nearly three times that of those over age sixty-five. The over-sixty-five group is twelve percent of the population, pays twelve percent of federal tax receipts—but receives 67 percent of federal benefit dollars.

"When today's thirty-year-olds retire, the best statistical projections—by the Congressional Research Office and the Social Security Administration itself—say that they'll get back only 98 cents for every dollar they've been forced to pay into Social Security over all the intervening decades. They won't even get their principal back, much less anything for interest or the decline in purchasing power of their dollars due to inflation. Poor though that return is, they may not get even that. The government has said—and the Supreme Court has upheld this view—that people have no *right* to the money they pay into Social Security; they have a right only to such money as Congress may from time to time allocate for the classification into which they fall. So Congress could vote to reduce future benefits. Something will have to be done because the money won't be there to pay the benefits people have been led to expect. It won't be there because we've dished it out so lavishly to ingratiate ourselves with the voters, in order to win elections, that there's no way the system can meet its future obligations. In 1945 there were 41.9 workers for every beneficiary. Now there are only 3.2, and the situation is going to get worse. When the generation of baby boomers retires, there will be a huge increase in beneficiaries. But the generation following them—the generation we've promised the boomers they can rob to get *their* 'fair share'—is the relatively small 'birth-dearth' generation of the 1960s and beyond.

"The public has no idea how Social Security really works. Most people think that what they pay into Social Security goes toward their retirement benefits. It doesn't. *None* of the money they pay in is put aside for their retirement. It's all spent. In 1983 Congress raised the Social Security tax in hopes of building up a surplus against future baby-boomer demands, but there is no surplus money. The federal government has borrowed *all* of the money from the Social Security Trust Fund to pay its current expenses. That trust fund consists entirely of U.S. government bonds, $436 billion worth. A bond is an I.O.U. from the government saying it will repay the money at some future date with interest. To repay that money, the government will have to take it from today's children tomorrow or tomorrow's children when they enter the labor force. It's not a matter of paying future beneficiaries by *supplementing* what they have paid into the fund; there is nothing to 'supplement'—it's all been spent! The *entire* amount—plus interest—will have to be paid by those coming after us.

"If government doesn't reduce Social Security benefits and thus shortchange people even more, then we'll simply have to create vast amounts of additional dollars. We can certainly create an unlimited supply of paper dollars since they're unredeemable, but that will be robbing the people, too, because those dollars won't buy much: the resulting inflation will mean you'll probably have to have thousands of dollars to buy a loaf of bread. And it won't just be Social Security checks that lose purchasing power; it'll be all dollars. Private savings will be wiped out. Look at what the scale of *that* robbery will be! It will be far greater than the wealth government has stolen directly through the Social Security system. The only other possibility is that the entire system will collapse—and with it, perhaps, our very system of government. Every period of inflation throughout history has been followed by a period of deflation or depression if not the complete collapse of civil order and often the government itself. There are going to be an awful lot of angry voters who may no longer tolerate the government that has robbed and defrauded them and failed to provide the security that they were promised. And who can blame them? After all, they didn't have any choice in the matter. We forced them under the threat of government guns to pay into the system. In return we promised them security in their old age—security which we said they were unable or too stupid to provide for themselves voluntarily. Instead they will face the prospect of being less secure than if we'd left them alone and Social Security had never existed.

"Jefferson said that it should be 'among the fundamental principles of every government' that no representatives of a nation 'can validly engage in debts beyond what they may pay in their own time,' for otherwise the earth would ultimately belong to the dead and not to the living. But that's exactly what we've done—and someday the living may rise up and rebel against a system that leaves them indentured to the extravagances of the dead."

"I agree with you that Social Security is a mess," said Don. "There are plenty of examples of incredible inflation produced by government spending beyond its means. In 1993 the annual rate of inflation in Brazil, for example, was 2,600 percent. A lot of people think it can't happen here, but it happened twice before in our history when our nation had unredeemable paper currency. After the Revolutionary War the 'continental' became worthless, and the same thing happened to the 'greenback' after the Civil War. The dollar could suffer the same fate as its predecessors.

"Like a lot of people our age, my wife and I are concerned that we won't get the promised benefits of Social Security when it's our turn to retire. What I don't understand is why the government doesn't let people contract out of the Social Security system and buy private insurance instead. I've been reading about studies that say doing so could save the system by reducing its future debt load. Young people could get more than twice the benefits from private insurance, and they would have a *right* to money they invest in insurance, which they don't have now under Social Security. If Social Security were made voluntary, the government would honor anyone's wish to remain in the system and receive future benefits. If the baby boomers contract out of Social Security in sizable numbers, that would greatly reduce the strain on the system when that generation reaches retirement age, which is when the real problem will come; it would then be possible to put the remainder of the system on a sound actuarial basis. People now in their mid-forties or older would probably find it financially advantageous to remain in the system, and they would lose nothing by others dropping out because the system is producing a surplus at present and for the intermediate future. Certainly, allowing people to contract out of the system would be the only fair thing for those who now face the prospect of financial loss after paying into the system all their lives. It would also put an end to the grotesque practice of one generation robbing the next."

"You're right. When *I'm* president," said Billington, "that's exactly what I'm going to do, make Social Security voluntary. You see, once I'm president, Dr. Steiner and I can use the modified telephone virus to make Congress vote for anything we want, just the way we'll have used it to make the general population vote for me. What you're suggesting was actually discussed the last time we reformed Social Security. It failed to pass because its opponents claimed that 'tampering' with Social Security would 'destroy' it. It didn't matter that the charge was false; it was the image that counted. Enough people were frightened by that image to make it politically unwise for Congress to vote for that measure even if it was a good one.

"You have to understand, Mr. Emerson, that the way things are now we have to be responsive to the people; we have to do what *they* want, not necessarily what we want or what we think is good for the country. If not, they'll elect someone else. I mentioned Presidents John Kennedy and George Bush earlier, but I didn't mean to imply that they were necessarily bad people; they were just doing what was necessary to get elected. Both men actually wanted to do good things for the country; but if they didn't get elected, they wouldn't get a chance to do them. The same is true of the Congresses that voted the extravagant payouts of Social Security benefits which will ultimately bankrupt the system. If those senators and congressmen hadn't voted for those much-too-generous benefits, the voters would elect others who would. The real problem isn't that public officials are able to buy their offices by generously giving out benefits; it's that the people are willing to sell their votes in order to receive them. As long as the people are so willing to sell, the candidates who promise to dish out the biggest handouts will be the only ones who can get elected. Or, if not the only ones, at least they'll be in the majority; and in a democracy it's the majority that controls the government.

"Voters have always been willing to sell their votes, often for surprisingly small handouts. The Founding Fathers were all familiar with providing 'bumbo' to obtain votes. 'Bumbo'—that was the term they used—meant rum punch or liquor along with cookies, cake and sometimes a barbecued steer or hog. Though the practice was universal, Madison considered it a 'corrupting influence' and decided to set an example of moral purity. Running for the Virginia House of Delegates in 1777, he refused to supply the bumbo. And he lost the election—to a tavern keeper! So you see, the situation was the same then as now."

"Not quite," replied Don. "At least the Founders paid for the bumbo themselves; they didn't pay for it with tax money. You politicians today appropriate tax money even for your campaigns, let alone for the benefits you promise the voters after your election. You use money stolen from the people at gunpoint in order that you can get elected and steal still more money to reward the people who elected you. H. L. Mencken was right when he said that in a democracy 'every election is an advance auction sale of stolen goods.'"

"Is that any better than what Dr. Steiner and I plan to do? At least we won't be stealing hundreds of billions of dollars to put ourselves in office and reward our constituents with other people's money like politicians do now. Let's face it, they do what they have to do to get elected. Otherwise they'd be defeated just like Madison was. That's the nature of democracy. Democratic elections become contests to see who can promise to give the voters the most."

"Twenty centuries ago," said Don, "Cicero said that democracies usually choose a leader 'who curries favor with the people by promising them other men's property.'"

"That's right," said the senator, "because government can't give anything to anybody without taking something away from somebody else. Government can't create wealth. I don't know why that's true, but it is. If government could create wealth, taxes would be unnecessary. So would inflation. The more promises and attempts we make to enrich the voters, the more we must resort to taxes and inflation. Taking money away from people—taxes—or taking value away from their money—inflation—are the only ways the government can pay for the benefits it promises to the voters. Democracy simply redistributes men's property in response to the demands of the majority. Whether or not those demands are wise or just or, in cases resulting in inflation, even self-defeating is irrelevant. The successful democratic politician is neither wise nor just, merely popular—and the way to be popular is to promise to redistribute other people's property."

"That's the reason," said Don, "that our Founding Fathers feared and detested democracy and tried to protect us from it."

"You know *that?*" asked Billington in astonishment. "If you do, you must have really studied your history. There isn't one person in a hundred—no, make that one in a thousand—who knows that. We've done a remarkably thorough job of brainwashing the public into thinking our Founders intended to create a democracy and that it's the ideal form of government. The one thing that conservatives and liberals alike, academics and editorial writers, politicians and even religious leaders seem to agree on is that democracy is not only an unquestioned good but unquestionable. Whenever anything goes wrong politically, everyone blames the president or the Congress or some individual or some policy; and they call for new officials or new policies. They may even blame 'the system' in a vague, generalized manner, but no one will go so far as to blame democracy."

"I know," said Don. "Most people express disbelief when they hear what a low opinion the Founders had of democracy. Many refuse to accept it because they've been so conditioned to believe otherwise. Nevertheless, the men who wrote our Constitution had experienced firsthand the baneful effects of democracy in the state governments and the low caliber of men elected to state legislatures and were determined to avoid democracy in establishing a federal government. I don't know how their opinion of democracy can be denied or covered up as it has been when we have it so emphatically in their own words. Edmund Randolph, the governor of Virginia, was one of the more prominent figures at the Constitutional Convention and later became the nation's first attorney general and its second secretary of state. He was the one who presented the famous 'Virginia Plan' to the Convention. In an address early in the Convention he said that the 'general object' of the Convention was 'to provide a cure for the evils' traceable to 'the turbulence and follies of democracy.' Elbridge Gerry, a delegate from Massachusetts, said, 'The evils we experience flow from the excess of democracy.' On another occasion he called democracy 'the worst of all political evils.' Roger Sherman, a delegate from Connecticut, said the people should have as little to do as possible about government, that they lacked information and were constantly liable to be misled. John Rutledge of South Carolina made the point that the delegates to the Convention—an assembly of truly exceptional men—were not chosen by the people and that if they had been, such fine people would not have been selected. And Madison wrote that 'democracies have ever been spectacles of turbulence and contention; have ever been found incompatible with personal security or the rights of property; and have in general been as short in their lives as they have been violent in their deaths.'

"Even if one knew nothing of what the Founders said of democracy, a cursory look at the kind of government they established would show that they certainly didn't intend to create a democratic one. Of the three branches of government, the legislative, executive and the judicial, only one-half of one was to be elected by the people. Judges were to be appointed, for life—hardly democratic. The executive was to be chosen not by the people but by an electoral college; various other possibilities for selecting the executive were discussed at the Convention, including appointment by legislative branch, by the state legislatures or by the governors of the states, but popular election of the president was never a serious possibility. George Mason, for example, said it would be as 'unnatural' to refer the choice of a president to the people as it would be to refer a trial of colors to a blind man. Only one-half of the legislative branch, the House, was to be elected democratically. That was to be the only democratic element in the whole national government. It would give the people a voice in government without giving them control and would satisfy the need for obtaining the consent of the governed, which the Founders viewed as essential for supporting the government.

"The power of the democratic House was to be offset by an *undemocratic* Senate. Randolph said, 'The object of this second branch is to control the democratic branch of the national legislature.' The Senate was to be selected not by the people but by the state legislatures. Since all legislation had to be approved by both branches of the legislature, the Senate would serve as a brake on the democratic tendency of the House to vote away property and other rights of some people in order to achieve popularity with the majority of voters. An undemocratic Senate was regarded as *essential* to restrain the 'tyranny of the majority'—something the Founders clearly feared—which would express itself in democratic elections in the House."

"I know, I know," said Billington impatiently. "You don't need to lecture me; I used to teach political science, and I'm something of a history buff besides—though I must say most of my colleagues in the Senate could benefit from your remarks. What's important is that today—thanks to the Seventeenth Amendment to the Constitution—the Senate is democratically elected just the way the House is. That means there's no brake whatever on the democratic majority. Majorities in *both* branches of the legislature are now lawmakers who 'curry favor with the voters by promising them other men's property,' as Cicero put it. If those legislators didn't do so, the voters would elect others who would. So there's no way out of the present dilemma within the rules of the system as it has evolved. That's why we need to go outside the system, as Dr. Steiner and I intend to do, in order to achieve reform. Most people have no idea that originally the Senate was not elected by the voters—much less that that original system lasted for nearly two-thirds of our history, during which this nation grew to greatness. They're constantly told how great democracy is, and they assume the Senate should be democratic and always has been. They don't know any better, and they don't care. All they care about is 'what's in it for me' when they go into the voting booth. Given the attitude of the voters and the democratic nature of the system, it's not surprising that transfer payments have become the federal government's largest expenditure.

"Traditionally, national defense was the largest item in the federal budget. Forty years ago, for example, defense was 81 percent of the federal budget. Earlier it was an even higher percentage. In 1902 it was 87 percent. Now, however, federal expenditures for transfer payments, or so-called 'entitlements,' are twice as large as defense spending. Thus the principal function of the federal government is no longer national defense but the redistribution of wealth."

"That's not right," said Don. "It's not even Constitutional. The Constitution gives the federal government no authority whatever to engage in the redistribution of wealth, to play Robin Hood."

"You're absolutely correct," said the senator. "But the federal government is doing all sorts of things that are unconstitutional. There's no Constitutional authority for the federal government to involve itself in providing medical care, deciding what people should eat, establishing minimum wages, policing labor relations, granting subsidies, regulating prices, educating our children, restricting agricultural output, protecting the environment and a host of other activities in which federal action is now commonplace. And we keep adding to the list. Now we may even add health insurance. Several years ago there was a small book by Congressman Lawrence Patton McDonald which said that many congressmen privately admit that at least 80 percent of what the federal government is doing is illegal under the Constitution. Richard A. Epstein, a University of Chicago law professor, says much of the legislation since Franklin Roosevelt became president is unconstitutional.

"So you see, Mr. Emerson, we don't really have a Constitution any more; we have the *image* of a Constitution, but the reality is long gone. We have a piece of paper that's supposed to represent something, but it's not what it appears to be—just like that picture of you and Monica. Oh, there are a few Constitutional principles we've retained, such as freedom of speech and freedom of religion—just enough to make the image look real—but in the material world of economic reality in which people conduct their daily lives the Constitution has become essentially a meaningless piece of paper. People see the image, and they would like to believe they're still protected by what it represents; but they aren't because the federal government no longer respects any Constitutional limitations on its power. It has intruded itself into every aspect of our daily lives through outright usurpation, through the most outlandishly contorted interpretations of its powers, and by openly contradicting the intent and language of the Constitution. It's not just the Congress and the president but the Supreme Court, too, that have gutted that document.

"For example, in the case that upheld federal interference in agriculture, *Wickard v. Filburn* (1942), a man had been fined for growing 12 more acres of wheat than the federal government had allotted him. The government claimed its authority to regulate agriculture came from its Constitutional authority to regulate interstate commerce. But none of that farmer's wheat entered commerce at all, much less interstate commerce; it was consumed on his own land by his own farm animals. Nevertheless, the Court upheld the government's case by saying that if he hadn't used his own wheat for feed, he *might* have bought feed from someone else, and even though that feed wasn't transported interstate either, it *might* have affected the cost of other feed which was. It is hard to imagine a more ridiculously contorted justification for federal authority, but that Supreme Court decision has been the basis for the government's regulation of agriculture ever since.

"That would be bad enough even if the federal government had a legitimate role in controlling interstate commerce, but it doesn't. There's an ancient principle in law that 'the intent of the lawgiver is the law.' Without it laws would be meaningless; it would be hopeless for a populace to comply with a law which wasn't what it was intended to be, which was so variable and uncertain as to be lawless, and a constitution would be an absurdity. In some cases reasonable men may differ on exactly what a provision of a law was intended to mean, but in the case of the Constitution's commerce clause the meaning is absolutely crystal clear. We have it in Madison's own words that power over interstate commerce was not intended to be used for 'positive purposes' but only as 'a negative and preventive provision against injustice among the states themselves.' Many of the original states charged duties on goods crossing their borders. The commerce clause in the Constitution was the original NAFTA, or North American Free Trade Agreement. It was simply to prevent the states from taxing or otherwise impeding the flow of commerce across their borders. That this is the true meaning of this clause is indisputable; yet the government has claimed this clause authorizes it to regulate freight rates, hiring policies, working hours, wage rates, safety practices, and the licensing of transport and communications facilities, as well as deciding how much acreage farmers will be allowed to devote to which crops and establishing price support levels for those crops.

"The Constitution has become essentially meaningless in terms of its intended purpose of limiting government. The federal government can and does do anything it wants; it simply 'stretches' the meaning of that document by ever more twisted and far-fetched 'logic.' When even that isn't sufficient, it invents a new justification altogether—even if it contradicts the Constitution!

"For example, in 1964 the Supreme Court invented the one-man-one-vote doctrine and 'interpreted' it into the Constitution. Not only is this doctrine of equal voting power never mentioned or even implied in the Constitution, but it actually contradicts the Constitutional provisions for the Senate and the Electoral College. The Constitution says that every state shall have two senators, regardless of the obvious population differences among the states. The Constitution doesn't even mention, let alone require, dividing states into congressional districts. Clearly the Framers intended to leave that up to the states themselves. Nevertheless, the Warren Court ordered the states to reapportion their federal congressional districts in order to equalize the population of districts within each state and thus provide equality of voting power according to the one-man-one-vote doctrine it had just invented. Then it went even further and ordered the states to apply the same doctrine to the districts which elect the *state* legislatures! Nothing could be further outside federal jurisdiction."

"It's well known that by dividing the federal government into three distinct and equal branches the Founders hoped that each would act as a check on the other two and prevent any one branch from growing too powerful. It's less well known that under the Founders' plan the states would also serve as a check on the expansion of federal power through their power to select members of the Senate. But with the passage of the Seventeenth Amendment, the voters elected U.S. senators directly and the states lost the only power they had to protect themselves—and all of us—from the unbridled expansion of federal power. Naturally, the federal government has since grown astronomically, and the states have been reduced to mere departments of Big Government, doing only what Washington allows and in the manner Washington prescribes. There's now nothing to check the cancerous expansion of federal power. That's why Dr. Steiner and I have to do what we're going to do."

"What about the Bill of Rights?" asked Don. "Those first ten amendments to the Constitution, which are known as the Bill of Rights, have two in particular that are intended to prevent the expansion of federal power, the Ninth and Ten Amendments. The Ninth Amendment states, 'The enumeration in the Constitution of certain rights shall not be construed to deny or disparage others retained by the people.' The Tenth Amendment says that powers not otherwise mentioned in the Constitution 'are reserved to the States respectively, or to the people.'"

"You're right," said the senator. "Those amendments were intended to limit the growth of federal power, but they haven't been able to do so by themselves. There's no mechanism to carry them out now that the states have lost their representation in the Senate. The legislative and executive branches just ignore those amendments because there's no one to stop them. The Supreme Court, which should have been the defender of the Constitution, has actually bent over backwards to accommodate the expansion of federal power, as I mentioned in the example of the interstate commerce clause. Worse, in the case of *United States v. Darby* (1941) the Court by unanimous decision in effect *repealed* the Tenth Amendment by saying it 'states but a truism' and therefore has no force or effect in giving or withholding power."

"But," asked Don, "even so, isn't the federal government still supposed to be limited by the enumeration of its powers in the Constitution?"

"Not any more," answered the senator. "In 1936, the Supreme Court officially buried the doctrine of enumerated powers by asserting that 'the power of Congress to authorize appropriations of public money for public purposes is not limited by the direct grants of legislative power found in the Constitution.' By invalidating that aspect of the Constitution, the Court opened the door to spending for all sorts of 'good' purposes to please the voters and get ourselves elected. And since money was no longer backed by gold or silver but by government debt, there was no limit on the *amount* of money we could spend, just as there was now no longer any limit on the *kinds* of things we could spend it for.

"You must remember, too, that the federal judiciary has been an active participant in the expansion of federal power. I don't mean just through its decisions affecting the other branches of government but through its own role. Federal judges now assume authority: to act as administrators of prisons, hospitals, school systems and private businesses; to select routes for highways and sites for power plants, apartments and shopping centers; to establish rules for playing intercollegiate football games; and to establish rules for 'smoking' and 'nonsmoking' in public places. They have canceled school elections, set school tax rates, closed schools and forced districts to build new ones. They have required that billions of dollars be spent on tens of thousands of buses to transport children to distant schools in order to achieve racial balance instead of allowing them to walk to their neighborhood schools—despite the fact that the Civil Rights Act of 1964, which they claim to be enforcing, states that nothing in that act 'shall empower any official or court of the United States to issue any order seeking to achieve a racial balance in any school by requiring the transportation of pupils or students from one school to another…in order to achieve such racial balance.' They have ignored similar prohibitions on school busing in numerous appropriation bills. They have arrogated to themselves the powers of the legislative and executive branches as well as powers that *no* branch of government should have. The Founders would be shocked by the kinds of activities federal judges engage in and their disregard of the intent of the Constitution and the Congress.

"There are roughly 1200 school districts currently under federal court desegregation orders. One federal judge in Missouri is supervising the spending of $1.2 *billion* in Kansas City schools—in addition to the normal school budget. The expenditures go far beyond assuring that minority children are treated equitably. Judge Russell Clark decided the taxpayers should buy an Olympic-size swimming pool, a $32 million high school, a 25-acre farm, an assembly hall modeled after the United

Nations General Assembly, and more. He ordered a 25-percent income tax and doubling of the property tax to pay for these things. A subsequent Supreme Court ruling that federal courts could not raise taxes directly has been no deterrent since they can simply order a school board to provide the necessary finances or face contempt charges.

"If you wonder why the Supreme Court no longer interprets the Constitution literally, as it should, and why federal judges have expanded their own role far beyond anything intended by the Founders, recall how these judges obtain their offices. They're nominated by the president and must be approved by the Senate. Now that the Senate is democratically elected, it tends to approve the nominations of persons who are most likely to reflect democratic demands—as the Senate itself does—for enlarging the role of government, for social and economic equality, rather than for accurately interpreting the Constitution. The very last thing the Senate wants to do is approve the Supreme Court nominations of those who would blow the whistle on its own expansion of power and that of the rest of the federal government.

"Do you remember what happened when Judge Robert Bork was nominated for the Supreme Court a few years ago? Here was a man of impeccable legal credentials, who had a brilliant record in his writing of over 400 carefully-crafted legal opinions—far more than most other nominees have ever had—and who had been Solicitor General of the United States, the highest prosecutor in the U.S. Justice Department. He also was a man who said that if you don't interpret the Constitution literally then you're making it up. That view should have been a reason *for* approving his nomination—but in a democratically elected Senate it became the reason for rejecting him. The same thing happened some years earlier to the nomination of Clement Haynesworth, another extremely well-qualified individual. Such rejections may have been infrequent, but they've influenced the choice of many other Supreme Court nominations. The message has been clear: if you don't nominate someone sufficiently to our liking, we in the Senate won't approve. So presidents have had to be very careful not to nominate people who would interpret the Constitution too accurately for Senate approval. Even a president who favors a strict interpretation of the Constitution would rather nominate someone less satisfactory who has a chance of being approved than a better candidate who doesn't. Of course, most of our presidents in recent decades haven't favored a strict interpretation of the Constitution anyway. After all, they've been elected by espousing the same governmental activism that has been regularly electing majorities in the House and the Senate.

"The legislative branch—often at the urging of the president—has shown disregard for the Constitution by passing retroactive laws and laws that violate previous Supreme Court decisions. The Constitution states that Congress shall pass no *ex post facto* laws, that is, laws that apply retroactively. Earlier in our history the Court held that this prohibition applies to tax laws. Subsequent Court decisions have softened this position somewhat by allowing tax increases that are retroactive to the date the tax bill was introduced in Congress, saying that that is sufficient notice to the taxpayers. But in August 1993 Congress, with prodding from the president, passed a tax bill that was retroactive to January 1, 1993—before the president or House members even took office! The bill back dated the increase not only for income taxes but for estate taxes—thus taxing even the dead retroactively! Neither the president nor Congress seemed to be the least bit concerned that what they were doing was unconstitutional.

"They didn't have to be, because the Supreme Court turned out to be no longer interested in defending the Constitution on this issue. In June of 1994 the Court overturned a Federal Appeals Court decision that had found retroactive taxation unconstitutional. Relying on long-established Supreme Court precedents, the Eighth U.S. Circuit Court of Appeals had held that a person who relies on a law in making a will is deprived of due process if that law is overturned after his death. But the Supreme Court, in Justice Blackmun's words, said that precedents from an earlier time carry no weight. He and Justices Rehnquist, Stevens, Kennedy, Souter and Ginsburg ruled that tax law may be arbitrary and capricious as long as it relates to 'legitimate legislative purposes,' such as raising taxes. Justice Scalia noted that the Court's reasoning 'guarantees that all retroactive tax laws will henceforth be valid.'

"In 1935 the Supreme Court said that a retroactive bill to fund retirement programs for workers who had already left their jobs was an unconstitutional 'naked appropriation of private property.' Ignoring this precedent, Congress, with the endorsement of the administration, passed a retroactive tax in 1992 to cover a projected shortfall in funds for union health benefits to retired coal miners. Companies that had been out of the mining business for decades—or were never even in it—were suddenly hit with retroactive taxes. Princeton Mining Co. of Terre Haute, which now produces popcorn, had been out of mining for nearly three decades; it now has to pay $164,000 annually in retroactive taxes. For Templeton Coal, which quit mining coal 37 years before, the bill is $92,000 annually. Lanzendorfer Trucking, which had been in business for 77 years, went bankrupt when presented with a retroactive tax bill roughly equal to 20 percent of it payroll. The company never was in the mining business; it merely used its trucks to haul coal to power plants. This retroactive tax is a good example of how democratically elected politicians curry favor with voters by redistributing other men's property. Incidentally, as things turned out, these unjust and unconstitutional taxes weren't even needed because the projected shortfall never materialized, thanks to economic reforms adopted by the managers of the union benefit funds. Of course, that didn't help Lanzendorfer and a number of other small companies that were forced out of business, nor did it mitigate the injustice against the others that are still paying that tax every year.

"While the legislative branch passes laws like that which have no constitutional basis, the nation's chief executive exercises powers not found anywhere in the Constitution or in any laws passed by the Congress. Neither the Constitution nor any law authorizes the president to practice *government by intimidation* as he did by publicly castigating the pharmaceutical industry for 'unconscionable profits.' There's no authority whatever for the president to attack and intimidate anyone for doing something that's perfectly legal. It's misuse of presidential power. Every corporation in America is in business to make a profit, and there's no statute or principle that says beyond a certain level profits become wicked. In the absence of any standard how could a company possibly know when it had stepped over the line from praiseworthy success to 'unconscionable profits'? The president simply used his own subjective whim to determine when profits become evil and to control them outside the framework of the law by public intimidation—with its implicit threat of government force unless his wishes are met. In the United States the president isn't supposed to govern like some all-powerful ruler who can run his kingdom according to his own subjective whims. That's why we have laws and a constitution.

"Of course, the majority of voters approve this sort of benevolent despotism because it's always presented as benefiting the poor at the expense of the rich, the Robin Hood policy. Politically, the important point is that it benefits—or appears to benefit—the many at the expense of the few. The voters who would benefit from lower drug prices far outnumber those who would benefit from higher profits in the drug industry. Similarly, transferring wealth to retired union miners means far more votes to a politician than are lost by taking the money from industry.

"Always with our eyes on votes, we try to benefit as many people as possible with more and more schemes to redistribute other people's wealth to them. Take the Americans with Disabilities Act, for example. There are fewer than three and one-half million Americans who are blind, deaf or in wheelchairs. Those are the ones we initially said we wanted to help, but by the time we finished that piece of legislation forty-four million people were eligible for benefits. Everything from asthma attacks to obesity can now qualify as a 'disability' entitling some people to benefits at other people's expense. A salesman who was fired because he couldn't follow verbal directions won a settlement under the ADA by claiming that, even though his problem wasn't considered a disability, his employer *acted* as if it were one. In 1994 a woman in California sued her former employer for $1.2 million under the ADA because she was fired for objectionable body odor. She claimed body odor was a 'disability.' She didn't win the lawsuit—probably because she didn't have a very good work record—but she wasted taxpayers money in three days of court hearings, and the jury foreman called the whole thing a waste of taxpayers' time.

"There are at least 78 federal welfare programs, not counting Medicare or Social Security, that dole out $180 billion a year. State and local government welfare programs push the annual total to over $300 billion. In the last 30 years the United States has spent $5 trillion on means-tested welfare. Adjusted for inflation, that's more than this country spent on World War II and equal to 40 Marshall Plans. Is it any wonder that the redistribution of wealth has become the largest activity of the federal government? But now that we've given the federal government the role of playing the outlaw of Sherwood Forest, this new Robin Hood robs not just the rich but everyone, gives some of the money to the poor but at least as much to the rich, and keeps a very large portion for himself.

"One-half of all government benefit dollars now go to families with incomes over $30,000, and one-half of *those* dollars go to families with incomes $50,000 to $200,000. If you look at some of the individual programs, the results are much worse. In agriculture, for example, the government embarked on massive subsidy programs for the stated purpose of helping the family farmer, the 'little guy.' The nation has 2.1

million farms, but only about 700,000 of the largest receive federal subsidies. About 80 percent of the government's $10 billion farm subsidies go to the top 20 percent of those 700,000. The U.S. Department of Agriculture has also given $500,000 of taxpayers' money to McDonald's to advertise Chicken McNuggets in Asia and $50,000 to Paul Newman to market salad dressing. It also subsidizes cheap electricity for ski lifts in Vail, Colorado and luxurious resort hotels in Hilton Head, South Carolina. Once the government has the power to subsidize the poor, it also has the power to subsidize the rich.

"As the government has expanded its powers far beyond those intended by the Constitution, so also have government agencies expanded their activities far beyond their original purposes. Today farm programs account for only 25 percent of the work force in the U.S. Department of Agriculture. The remaining employees are involved in such far-reaching activities as electric power production, telephone businesses, rent subsidies for housing projects, subsidized food and nutrition programs, forestry management, and research programs that determine such things as how long it takes the average American homemaker to cook breakfast. Based on the trend since 1950, in the year 2001 the Department of Agriculture will have more employees than there are farmers in the United States. Sixty percent of the employees of that department are now involved in programs that redistribute wealth to the poor through subsidized food and nutrition programs, such as food stamps and school lunch programs. In just fifteen years, from 1979 to 1994, the food stamp program went from $550 million to over $26 *billion* —an increase of 4800 percent! It's two and one-half times the size of federal agricultural subsidies. In short, the USDA has become a large and rapidly-growing welfare agency. So you can see where the Supreme Court's decision to allow the federal government to 'regulate' agriculture under the interstate commerce provision of the Constitution has led us.

"In Ancient Rome the emperors used 'bread and circuses'—'gifts from Caesar'—to keep the populace contented and perpetuate themselves in office. I don't know what the modern counterpart of circuses is, but we certainly supply plenty of bread—gifts from the Caesars in Washington.

"Another example is the summer feeding program the federal government created in 1970 to give free meals to poor children during the summer. The program has been *consistently* criticized by the General Accounting Office for wasting food and serving meals to people not eligible. Even President Carter—an individual not known for a lack of compassion—tried to eliminate the program altogether. He failed. And the program, which cost $6.5 million and fed one-half million in 1970, twenty-five years later was feeding four times as many—at *thirty* times the cost.

"The latest scheme for redistributing wealth is the president's plan for mandatory national health insurance. Some people will be forced to pay for other people's health insurance, just as they're now forced to pay for others' sustenance through food stamps and school lunch programs. Where in the Constitution can anyone find authority for the federal government to force people into a socialized health care system? I suppose the interstate commerce clause will be used, if necessary; but if so, and if the Court upholds such a preposterous stretch of creativity, then the Constitution has become totally meaningless. If people can be forced to buy health insurance under the interstate commerce clause, then *anything* can be 'justified' under that clause. At least in the *Wickard* case, in which the Court upheld the government's authority to regulate agriculture, someone was engaged in an activity—growing wheat—which was agricultural and then interpreted as relating to commerce. But if people who are doing *nothing,* who are engaged in no activity relating to either producing or buying or using health insurance, can be said to be engaged in interstate commerce relating to health insurance, then there's nothing the government can't do under that clause. It can't be said that people are being forced to belong to the government's health program because of their occupation, employment, or business activities—as is the case with Social Security—but merely because they *exist.*

"If government has the authority to regulate people because of their health, then obviously it can regulate any activity impacting upon health. It could make tobacco illegal. It could make it illegal for people to be overweight by more than a certain amount—particularly since being overweight can affect health care costs. And since exercise is universally acknowledged to be beneficial to health, the government could require exercise programs not only for those who are overweight but for everyone. It could set mandatory limits on the amount of vitamins, fat and other components of our diet. It could require mandatory testing for the AIDs virus.

"And what would be the penalties for eating too many french fries or not enough fruits and vegetables? Would we send people to jail or merely impose fines for violations? Remember that we have to have threats of force in order for laws to be obeyed. Or would we merely try to intimidate people into eating right by having the president publicly denounce them for their 'unconscionable' appetites?

"And it wouldn't be only food and exercise that would be regulated. What if the government decides that watching too much television is harmful to children's welfare? The government could set limits on television viewing and enforce them through a system of permits or licenses. That's not as far-fetched as it may sound. In Great Britain, a nation that we think of as being one of the freest on earth and from whom our own legal system was derived, it has long been necessary to buy a license to watch television. A constituent sent me a recent clipping from *The Wall Street Journal* on that subject. The license costs 125 dollars and must be purchased from the post office every year. Watching television without a license is a criminal offense. The law is enforced by the TV license police, who may knock on your door without warning or peer through your windows. More than 1000 arrests are made every day. The average fine is $300, and scores of people—including a severely disabled person and a single mother of five—have been sentenced to *jail*. A babysitter was caught watching an unlicensed TV set in the home where she was baby-sitting. Although she had a license to watch her own set at her home, she was fined $110. Even blind people have been fined for having a TV set without a license. A foreign family was fined $240 even though their TV set got no reception because it had no antenna. The family had no need of an antenna because they couldn't understand English and used the set only for videos in their native language, Pashto.

"You might say, as a lot of Americans would, 'Oh, that could never happen here,' but we're already sending people to jail for not having permits. Not permits for watching TV but for other things. Environmental permits, for example. Mind you I didn't say we send them to jail for destroying or even damaging the environment—in some cases they were actually improving the environment—but we send them to jail for simply not having the proper permit. Take the case of Bill Ellen, a marine engineer from Mathews, Virginia. He was no polluter. He used to be a state environmental engineer who regulated wetlands. He ran a nonprofit wildlife rescue center and had been hired to convert part of an estate into a 103-acre wildlife sanctuary when he ran afoul of permit regulations for preserving wetlands. But he wasn't draining or filling wetlands—he was building them! The sanctuary he was creating was adding 45 acres of duck ponds. The land being converted to them was so dry that a dust-suppressant had to be used when bulldozers built the ponds. And Ellen wasn't trying to evade government regulators but to cooperate with them; he'd already secured 38 permits for the work and thought he was doing everything properly. He was shocked when he was sentenced to six months in jail for dumping two loads of dirt on a portion of the property that the U.S. Soil Conservation Service had previously declared to be non-wetland. A U.S. Corps of Engineers official using an expanded definition of 'wetland' from a new government manual—so new it wasn't even in effect yet—declared that area a wetland and Ellen guilty of dumping dirt on it without federal permission. Ellen ended up in jail for violating a federal regulatory standard that didn't even exist at the time of his actions—another example of a retroactive law.

"There have been other cases, too, of throwing people in jail for dumping dirt on their own property. In Florida Ocie Mills and his son Carey served 21-month prison terms for dumping clean sand on two lots Mr. Mills owned on which they were trying to build a house. They thought their action was acceptable because they already had permission from the state of Florida and Florida officials had told them no federal permit was necessary. But the federal environmental police arrested them for not having a federal permit to dump a 'pollutant' into 'navigable waters of the United States' under the Clean Water Act of 1972. Twenty-one months in the slammer. In an appeal in 1993 after serving a full 21 months in jail, Mr. Mills failed to get his conviction overturned even though the federal district judge acknowledged the site of the dumping was dry land, clearly not even a wetland much less a 'navigable water.' Judge Roger Vinson deplored the twisting of wording 'worthy of Alice in Wonderland' to stretch the meaning of 'navigable water' to include dry land—just the way the interstate commerce clause has been stretched—but said the court had to apply the law as it exists and cannot change it and that the law had clearly given the regulatory agency the authority to make this determination.

"Then there's the case of John Pozsgai, a Hungarian immigrant with little schooling who bought an old industrial dump site, cleaned it up by removing 7,000 old tires—and then committed the crime of adding topsoil without a federal permit. There's no question that the environment was improved by his actions. That wasn't the point. The point was that he did so without a permit. Three years in federal prison.

That's longer than a lot of criminals serve for violent crimes. On average, a convicted murderer spends less than 27 months in prison, and only 1.7 percent of serious crimes ever results in a jail sentence. Pozsgai also had to pay a $202,000 fine—despite the fact he had a negative net worth and only a very meagre income, which was his ailing wife's sole source of support. Here was a guy who fled the tyranny of communism in his homeland. He comes to this supposedly free country and is thrown in jail for something he wouldn't have been jailed for under a communist dictatorship.

"In all of the cases just mentioned the violators were shown no mercy because government officials wanted to demonstrate their policy of 'getting tough on polluters.' All went to jail even though none of them had any prior criminal record and the 'pollutant' in every case was the basic material of the environment itself: common, everyday, ordinary *dirt*. There was no damage to the environment or to other persons or their property. What these cases really demonstrate is not 'getting tough on polluters' but getting tough on freedom and individual rights. In this country that used to be known as the 'land of the free' more than 800 people have been jailed since 1982 for violating environmental regulations.

"Of course, there are a great many more cases that are ridiculous and shocking even though the 'criminals' were not sent to jail. In the little town of Port Bolivar, Texas, for example, Marinus Van Leuzen, a 73-year old immigrant from Holland built a retirement home on property he had owned—and paid taxes on—for twenty years. The property is less than half an acre located 50 feet from a highway. It had been used as a bait camp, a cross between a fishing bait store and a campground, complete with outdoor latrines. Nearby residents regarded it as an eyesore rather than an ecological national treasure. It certainly wasn't a 'navigable water.' Nevertheless, Van Leuzen was hauled into court by the Environmental Protection Agency and the U.S. Army Corps of Engineers for violating the Clean Water Act by depositing illegal fill in a 'navigable water' without a permit when building his house. Now he must pay $350 per month into a special account for eight years. Then that accumulated money will be used to move his house. He must also spend a good portion of his savings to pay civil penalties and to 'restore' the land to its 'pre-adulterated' condition. And he has been charged with contempt of court for failing to consult the Corps of Engineers before replanting vegetation in his effort to meet the requirement for restoring the property. The Corps didn't like the plants he had chosen. So he could still end up in jail.

"You can hardly do anything any more in this country as a matter of *right;* you have to get permission for almost everything. In the Los Angeles area you may need as many as 200 federal, state, regional and local permits to start a light industry, even a small one.

"In August 1993 the McNeil-Lehrer news hour on public TV interviewed a group of high school students from Kazakhstan, in the former Soviet Union, who had spent a year in this country and were now heading home. The interviewer, Charles Krause, asked what was the greatest misconception about America that they'd held in their homeland and that had now been removed by their visit to this country. The response was unanimous: the lack of freedom in America. The first one to speak said that they'd all been told to come to America because America is free, but once here they discovered that we aren't free at all. The other students all nodded in agreement. Another said with great emphasis, 'There are so many regulations and restrictions.' Again, the other students all nodded. Another added, 'There's hardly *anything* that you're free to do in this country any more.' Others chimed in that they couldn't possibly have imagined how many laws we have, how unbelievably they limit us, and how disillusioning and disappointing it was to discover the truth about America in this regard.

"Those students were right. We don't have a free country any more. We have the *image* of a free country. That's the picture we present to the rest of the world, but the reality is quite different. Behind the facade of a handful of freedoms that remain, such as freedom of speech and of religion, and a few of the surviving attributes of a free country, such as free elections and trial by jury, we've become a police state. There's an army of 128,615 federal regulators watching over the rest of us. They're there to enforce more regulations than most Americans can even imagine. The Occupational Safety and Health Administration, for example—just one agency—churned out 100,000 safety standards in just the first year of its existence. Countless more have been added since, all with fines or jail sentences for violators. Then think about all the other federal agencies that put out thousands of other regulations. Between a thousand and two thousand regulations change every month, according to consultants who try to help businesses comply. This amounts to 200 pages of new regulations every day. The federal regulators who enforce these laws don't wear police uniforms so we don't think of them as police, but they perform a police function. They don't march the streets carrying weapons like Mussolini's 'blackshirts,' but that's only because they don't need to carry them when the mere *threat* is sufficient: every one of their laws and regulations is backed by the threat of guns. Naively, most Americans still think of themselves as living in a free country because they don't see uniforms and guns on the federal regulators. Everything *appears* be the same as it was before we had all these regulations. Outwardly we still appear to be free.

"We like to believe we don't have a police state because these new federal police don't drag people from their homes in the middle of the night and execute them or send them to Siberia without a trial, like in the Soviet Union. We give them a fair trial, a legitimate trial by jury—and then we send them to a modern jail. Bill Ellen had a jury trial. So did Ocie and Carey Mills. So did John Pozsgai. A jury can only decide whether or not a person violated a law, not whether that law or the regulation it authorizes is reasonable and fair or downright outrageous. In the cases of these gentlemen there was no question that they dumped dirt on their own properties without a permit. That was the only issue the juries were allowed to decide. Naturally they had to return verdicts of guilty. Similarly, judges such as Roger Vinson have to carry out the law even if they strongly disapprove of it, as he did. Neither trial by jury nor honest, impartial judges can protect the citizens from abuses by the law itself, from the tyranny of the laws of a police state.

"Nor can the mere fact of free elections protect us. We assume that democracy is protection against oppression. We think that a police state can come about only where those who make the laws aren't chosen by the people, but that's not true. We forget that Hitler rose to power through the democratic process. And in the first free election in Serbia after the breakup of communist Yugoslavia, the man who received the popular mandate from the voters was Slobodan Milosevic, the man who started the genocidal policy of 'ethnic cleansing' in Bosnia. Thus this century's two most prominent examples of genocide—the ultimate crime of violating human rights as a matter of official policy—were both from governments that came to power through free, democratic elections.

"Democracy is no better at selecting truly wise leaders than it is at avoiding disastrous ones. Take the case of Winston Churchill, one of the greatest political leaders in history. All through the 1930s he was warning about the danger that Hitler posed. Had his views been heeded, the world wouldn't have had to pay such an enormous cost in human lives later in order to stop Hitler. The voting public in Great Britain, however, didn't have the sense to listen to Churchill and instead preferred the disgraceful Neville Chamberlain. Churchill wasn't elected prime minister until the outbreak of World War II proved he had been right all along. Then after the vital and heroic role he played in that war, the voters turned him out of office almost as soon as the war was over. It's hard to imagine what more he could have done in World War II to be worthy of voter support, but the democratic majority rejected him in 1945. So much for the 'wisdom' of the majority.

"In our country democracy has led to the virtual destruction of the one thing that could protect people from a police state, the Constitution. Aside from the handful of freedoms still operative under the Bill of Rights—which give us the image or illusion that the Constitution is still intact—the Constitution no longer offers any protection against the intrusion of the federal government into every aspect of our daily affairs. It's a federal crime to sell peaches in California that are less than two and seven-sixteenths inches in diameter or nectarines that are less than two and three-eighths inches in diameter. The federal government now dictates how many oranges shall be packed in a crate and that there shall be exactly seven sizes of olives—no more, no fewer. Are these really issues that should be decided by the *police power* of government? What is the Constitutional authority for these issues to be determined by the federal government?—the interstate commerce clause? Do we really need to have the federal government dictate warning labels for balloons and marbles, enforced with threats of the police? Yet these and hundreds of thousands of other issues are decided by those in a position to say, 'It shall be the law,' and enforce their commands with the threat of guns, just like the kind of totalitarian regimes we decry. Do you see what I mean about this country being transformed into a police state? The most minute aspects of our lives—the food we buy, the products we build, where our children go to school, the dumping of dirt on one's own property—are controlled by the police power of the federal government. Now we're even adding the issue of health insurance. The Constitution, by *limiting* the role of the federal government, should have been our protection against a police state; but when none of the three branches of our federal government respects those limitations, we arrive where we are today, where freedom is an 'endangered species' and the Constitution practically extinct.

"Do you know what 'fascism' is, Mr. Emerson? There isn't one person in a thousand who really knows. Most people would probably say it's some kind of oppressive government, but their understanding is so vague that they wouldn't be able to tell you what distinguishes it from socialism or any other type of government. Everyone knows that socialism means government ownership of the means of production. A distinguishing characteristic of fascism is that it retains private ownership of the means of production *but under centralized government control.* That's what we have today, a new kind of fascism. We've even carried it a step further; we've put not only the means of production under centralized government control but every other form of private property as well, from peaches and nectarines to vacant lots. We regulate practically everything you can buy and sell, from automobiles to balloons and marbles, from the kind of gasoline you can buy for your car to the foods that are for sale at your supermarket, from bicycles to heart pacemakers, from minimum wage rates to cable TV rates, from swimming pool slides to health insurance, from the kind of pavement that goes into highways to those 'child-proof' bottles your medicines come out of—if you can get them open."

"But," said Don, "if you know what has been happening to this country, how could you be a party to it? You're one of the people who makes our laws. Why haven't you tried to do something about the mess this country is in instead of being one of those who votes for the laws that increase government spending, take away our freedom, and accelerate the trend toward a police state and national bankruptcy?"

The senator smiled. "I wouldn't be here if I didn't go along with the trend. I'm responsive to the wishes of the voters. I didn't make the rules for this game; I just play by them—and I do it very well. Either you play by the rules or you're out of the game. I want to be in the game. That's why I came to Washington. I didn't come here to commit political suicide for the sake of my ideals or principles. I never claimed to have any principles. I'm a pragmatist; I do what works, what's necessary to survive and succeed, just the way everyone else here does—I just do it better than most.

"The majority of my colleagues view the situation pretty much the same way. They're responsive to their voters. They believe it would be desirable to balance the budget—but not at the expense of being voted out of office. Do you think they're going to commit political suicide by reducing Social Security payouts? Of course not. The same is true of other government spending. So even those who arrive here in Washington with the noble ideal of slashing federal spending find they have to compromise and vote for various spending measures if they want to stay in office and accomplish anything at all.

"We all find it politically necessary at times to vote for bills or provisions we don't really want. When that happens, we tell ourselves that that's a small price to pay for the good we can do in other respects, such as voting for better schools, food for the needy, relief for victims of floods or earthquakes, more regulations to save the environment, or all sorts of other causes we deem worthy—not to mention taking care of ourselves with very generous salary increases and the most lucrative pension plan in the world. Everyone here has his favorite causes. We tell ourselves that we wouldn't get a chance to advance these good causes if we weren't in office. Politics is the art of compromise, of give and take; everything we do is a matter of weighing trade-offs. We have to vote for our colleagues' good causes so they'll support ours. Take the bill for aid to victims of the 1994 Southern California earthquake, for example; it included funds for the renovation of New York's Penn Station, development of two sugar cane mills in Hawaii, a joint Russia-U.S. space project, and an FBI finger-printing center in West Virginia. And the $30 billion anti-crime bill we passed with a lot of fanfare in 1994 included funding for Alzheimers research and a lot of other things that had nothing to do with fighting crime. And the 1994 *defense* budget included $4 million for the Olympics, $20 million for AIDS research, $25 million for Black Colleges and Universities, $106 million for conservation, and hundreds of millions more for paying fines to other government agencies, plus billions more for all sorts of other things having nothing to do with defense. So the national debt just keeps on growing. That's nobody's fault in particular; it's just the nature of the system. We all do the best we can. I'm sure we all feel that on balance some good has come from our being here. In my own case I've done well for my constituents, and I've had a good life here in Washington, a good salary, prestige, everything I could ask for. And by making compromises to stay in office, I've put myself in a position to accomplish real reform through my association with Dr. Steiner. That opportunity would never have happened if I weren't in office and in a position to arrange for financing his work.

"If you want to blame someone for what's happened in America, don't blame me—I want to reform the system—blame the voters. Or blame democracy for giving them the power to shape this country the way they have. I suppose we're all responsible in a way, all three branches of government, but the voters are the ones who are most responsible. After all, they wanted the kind of government we've given them. If we didn't deliver it, they would've voted for others who would have. Nobody wants to live in a police state, of course, but almost everyone wants to benefit from laws employing the power of the police against others. The regulations on the sizes of peaches and nectarines, for example, were favored by agricultural co-ops in California as a way of achieving higher prices for their products. Politicians quickly saw that by favoring these kinds of regulations they could buy farm votes to help get themselves elected, but in most cases they also thought these regulations were good for their constituents. Typically, the kind of politicians who succeed in our system are precisely those who favor using the police power in this way, who believe in achieving desirable goals by threatening people with the guns of government. So each of these attempts to do good and please the voters—and get ourselves elected—has moved us ever closer to a police state.

"The thousands of tariffs, duties and import restrictions we've imposed benefit some segments of the voting population and buy us their votes—by taking away other people's freedom, specifically, their right to free trade, to buy foreign products at market prices. In the same manner, there were a lot of environmental votes to be gained by regulations taking away other people's right to use their land. More recently, we realized there were votes to be gained by promising people universal health insurance and taking away other people's freedom in the matter, as well as their money to pay for it. We take away people's freedom in order to buy votes for ourselves in the same manner that we take away their money, through taxes and inflation, to buy our elections. But in all these cases politicians could claim—and even sincerely believe, as most of them did—that they were doing the right thing, that they were reshaping society for the better even though they were doing so by means of guns, that is, by laws backed by fines or jail sentences enforced at the point of a gun if necessary.

"The simple fact is that in a democracy the majority of people want elected officials who *give* them things, either other people's property or things that are at the expense of other people's freedom. And the only way we can do that is by the police power, by threatening people with guns. That's *all* we have to offer. That's the one thing that's distinctively different about government compared to the other elements of society. That's what political power really is, the power of a gun. That's the power that people really believe in and want us to exercise, and that's why they elect the people they do. So it should come as no surprise that those whom they elect come to Washington to enlarge the role of the federal government by pointing more guns at more people in more ways and yet sincerely believe they are doing the right thing and improving society by the process.

"Do you ever wonder why people turn to the government for solutions to practically every problem in society in spite of our abysmal record? Why do people have such faith in the political process despite our inefficiency, our waste, our endless examples of deception and corruption? We've had the House banking scandal—which involved over 200 members of the House—the House postal scandal and dozens of individual examples of crimes and immoral behavior. Since 1970 more than 30 members of Congress have been convicted of bribery, illegal kickbacks, racketeering, embezzlement, perjury, tax evasion, mail fraud, influence peddling and other felonies. In addition, there have been scandals that haven't been followed up with convictions. Such was the case with Congressman Jim Wright, the Speaker of the House—the next in line for succession to the presidency after the vice president—who was forced to resign a few years ago in disgrace even though he wasn't actually convicted of a crime. Democratic Majority Whip Tony Coelho is another example; he resigned rather than face an investigation of his financial affairs. And then there were the five senators connected with Charles Keating, the criminal who operated the nation's most notorious savings and loan institution. A Senate ethics committee slapped the wrists of two and reprimanded a third, but none of the senators was actually convicted of a crime. Public opinion polls show that Congress is held in very low esteem by the people of this country—and yet the public keeps demanding that government solve all the problems of society. Why?

"When the federal government is so notorious for busting its own budgets, why in the world would anyone think it can hold down medical costs? A government that made the news by buying $600 hammers and $1100 toilet seats is going to reduce medical costs? When Medicare was enacted in 1965, its cost was projected to be $2 to $3 billion in the first year and not to exceed $10 billion until the 1990s. Well, the first year it cost over $7 billion, and by 1992 the annual cost was over $140 billion. In 1994 it was $179 billion. So why would anyone think that the federal government can hold down health costs?

"In 1993, Charles Bowsher, comptroller general and head of the General Accounting Office, said the federal government does 'an abysmal job of rudimentary bookkeeping' and has tens of billions of dollars in hidden liabilities. He found 'widespread financial management weaknesses' throughout the government, in the State Department, Agriculture Department, the IRS, the Energy Department, and even the Health Care Financing Administration. He said the federal government wastes $180 billion annually. So, in spite of all these facts, why do people still believe the government can give them lower health costs? I'll tell you why: because people believe in the power of the gun. You can put all the facts, the numbers, past history, anything you want on one side and then put a gun on the other side, and the gun will win. That's what the people will vote for.

"The voters don't approve of government inefficiency, waste and corruption, of course, but they're willing to put up with them in order to get the guns of government on their side, either for their direct benefit or for causes they favor. The people make compromises or trade-offs to get what they want from government just the way politicians do. The fact that they put up with all the notorious shortcomings of government and still vote for more government 'solutions' shows how much appeal the gun has.

"The people, at least the majority, don't want freedom, Mr. Emerson. They want 'entitlements,' subsidies, government grants, low-cost government loans, protection from competition; they want artificially high wages for their labor, artificially high prices for products they sell, artificially low prices for everything they buy. In short, they want almost any benefit they can conceive of obtaining by laws that somehow point a gun at others.

"People have traveled this route before. In Italy, for example, the people traded freedom for government control, just as we've been doing. They did it willingly, even enthusiastically; Mussolini was enormously popular. He was the one who invented the concept of the 'corporate state,' a kind of collaboration of government and business, what we call today 'industrial policy.' Thomas DiLorenzo, a professor of economics at Loyola College, has made a shocking comparison of the president's health care plan with the Italian fascist system for reinventing government. In Italy for each industry or industry group there was a legally recognized alliance just like the president's regional health care alliances. There was also a National Council of Corporations, which served as a federal overseer of the regional alliances, just as the president's National Health Board will oversee the regional health alliances. The National Council could set prices and budgets and issue regulations just like the president's proposed National Health Board."

"But the Italian system was an economic disaster," said Don. "Furthermore, government intervention in health care has bombed everywhere it's been tried. All the national health insurance plans in all the Western democracies are in acute financial crises. A lot of people favor a system like the one in Canada, but 10,000 doctors have fled that country in recent years because of that system. Can't we learn from the experience of other countries? Or even from our own experience with the skyrocketing costs of Medicare? And look at the history of price controls in general. They've never worked anywhere. So why would anyone think they can now work in the area of medical costs?"

"The numbers don't matter anymore," said the senator. "History doesn't matter any more. I just told you that you can put all the facts and numbers and history on one side and the gun on the other, and the gun will win. If you can get elected to point the gun in a way that pleases the majority, that's all that matters. Many years ago our government itself did a study of wage and price controls and couldn't find a single successful example in 40 centuries. We had our own more recent experience in 1971-73, when we had price controls on everything, on hospitals, insurers, nurses, drug companies, physicians, and everybody else. And a lot of the people responsible for administering that program are still around and warn that it didn't work then and it won't work now. It failed not only in the medical field but in every other field. People don't advocate price controls because they've been successful. They advocate them because they approve of the method, of employing the police power in this way. As long as they do, there will always be voters and candidates who are willing to try again. So history repeats itself.

"You mentioned the skyrocketing costs of Medicare, but Medicare is also an example of how attempts at price controls have reduced quality. In 1988 a Department of Health and Human Services Inspector General's report estimated 540,000 Medicare patients received poor-quality hospital care, primarily due to Medicare's price controls. And a 1992 General Accounting Office study of health care in Germany, France and Japan warned about the side effects of price controls 'especially in the long run on the quality of care.' All that doesn't matter. What matters is the gun, people's expectations of what it can bring, and the number of votes involved."

"But those things can't make anything economic," protested Don. "They can't make something work that has never worked before. They can't change the facts of reality. Two plus two still has to equal four."

"You're speaking mathematically, of course," said the senator. "In politics the correct answer isn't necessarily four. It may be three or eight or perhaps 26 million. The correct answer is whatever the people vote for. When we know what the voters want or what they'll accept, we make the numbers come out accordingly. That's why budget estimates are always way off. We use all sorts of gimmicks, from false labeling to outright lies, to come up with numbers that don't mean anything but appear to justify what we propose, which we know is what will satisfy the public. For example, in 1993 the administration's economic plan labeled a substantial tax increase on well-to-do Social Security recipients as a 'spending cut' rather than a tax increase. It also called a huge increase in welfare spending for the working poor under the Earned Income Tax Credit a 'tax cut.' Everyone knows the voters would rather hear the words 'spending cut' or 'tax cut' rather than 'tax increase' or 'increase in welfare spending.' So we tell them what they want to hear. Of course, when you then add up the tax increases and spending cuts, the numbers don't mean anything.

"Another such gimmick was the president's idea that money 'saved' by raising taxes and cutting spending would be put into a trust fund to be used only to reduce the deficit. Of course, the federal government saves no money at all. That's why there's a deficit. Any money 'deposited' in the trust fund will instantly be borrowed back to pay expenses. The Committee for a Responsible Federal Budget called the whole idea of a deficit reduction trust fund 'silly.' It said, 'By the same logic, I could say: I don't have the money for a Cadillac, so I won't buy a Cadillac. But I'll buy a Chevrolet with the money I 'saved' by not buying the Cadillac—never mind that I didn't have that money in the first place.'"

"So what you're saying," said Don, "is that you give us 'substitute economics' just the way you've given us 'substitute money.'"

"That's a good way to put it. The numbers aren't real, but then neither is the money. What makes both of them 'real,' or at least accepted, is the power of the gun, which is validated and legitimized by the democratic process."

"You can fudge the numbers all you want to make your budgets and projections look good, but you can't evade reality forever," said Don. "I'm reminded that Bernard Baruch, the famous financier, once said that the stock market bubble of the 1920s, the crash of '29 and the ensuing depression would never have happened if people had just kept reminding themselves that two plus two has to equal four."

"I'm reminded," said the senator, "of the time two decades ago when veteran Congressman Jimmy Burke credited his longevity in office to voting for every spending bill and against every tax increase. A naive, young reporter asked if that wasn't a prescription for chaos, and Jimmy smiled and said, 'You think this place is on the level?'

"Everything we do is not 'on the level' in terms of the way other people think. We live in a different world. We do everything differently than other people. We don't have to balance our checkbooks as they do. They live in a world of microeconomics; we, in a world of macroeconomics—'substitute economics' if you want to call it that. We spend other people's money; they can spend only their own. They can't threaten people with guns—if they did, they'd be criminals and subject to arrest—but that's the very basis of the way we operate. Other people don't have to think about whether their actions will be popular with the voters; we have to think about it all the time. We don't even have to obey all the laws that they do; as I mentioned earlier, we can—and have—exempted ourselves from laws. We can even increase our salaries simply by voting to do so, which employees nowhere else can do. In a sense, we've created our own reality."

"So you think you're exempt from the laws of reality that apply to everyone else?" asked Don.

"I wouldn't put it quite that strongly. The overwhelming reality for most of us is satisfying the voters. I would say that the kind of reality you're talking about is secondary to political realities."

"So 'substitute money' and 'substitute economics' supersede the real things?"

"Well, they work politically, and that's what counts. They get us elected and give the people what they want. No one doubts that two plus two has to equal four eventually—but it doesn't necessarily have to do so in our term of office! So no one worries about what will happen to Social Security eventually; none of us will be around by then. Similarly, the budget will probably have to be balanced someday, but that's too far down the road for any of us to be concerned about."

"Look," said Don. "We live in a scientific age. We all enjoy the benefits of a standard of living undreamed of in earlier centuries, thanks to science and technology. Science is the study of reality, of what actually exists. An idea is true or it's not true; it's either in agreement with the facts of reality or it isn't. The knowledge of science is possible only because reality is absolute. There is no 'substitute reality,' and there is no 'substitute truth.'"

"Well, perhaps not," said the senator, chuckling, "but there is 'substitute science.'"

"What?! I can't believe you're saying this!"

"Of course, the public doesn't know it's 'substitute science.' They think it's the real thing. Just like they think 'substitute money' and 'substitute economics' are real. And in the same way that political realities supersede real money and real economics, they also supersede real science while posing as the genuine article.

"For example, we spent a whopping $537 million dollars of the taxpayers money on a mammoth ten-year study of acid rain. It was called the National Acid Precipitation Assessment Program. It was a true scientific program. But did we enact legislation based upon it? No, political realities took precedence. We ignored the findings and recommendations of that scientific study and did what we thought would please the voters. The study said that acid rain could not be blamed on industrial pollution, such as the emissions from coal-burning plants. It said that the tens of billions of dollars that had already been spent on cleaning coal emissions had no significant effect on acid rain. But we felt that a lot of voters thought otherwise, because they had been bombarded with so much publicity to that effect from the environmental special-interest groups. So we passed the 1990 Clean Air Act requiring the installation of limestone scrubbers—a 20-year old technology—on older coal-burning plants at a cost of billions. Will that cure acid rain? Of course not. In fact, Dr. J. Lawrence Kulp, who was director of research for the NAPAP study, was critical of the legislation and said it will *preclude* the installation of cleaner coal technologies. Were we interested in his scientific opinion? Hell no. We were interested in political realities. If the public wanted legislative action that would point the gun in the direction they favored, we were perfectly willing to throw additional billions of dollars of other people's money at the problem and pretend it was a scientific solution."

"But eventually," argued Don, "the truth will come out. Eventually people will learn that your legislation did nothing to cure the problem and just wasted billions of their dollars."

"Eventually," replied the senator, "Social Security will go bankrupt and people will learn that billions of their dollars have been wasted. Eventually, the federal budget will have to be balanced. But all those things are too far down the road to worry about now. We've taken care of the immediate interests of the voters, and done so to their satisfaction, and that's what counts.

"In addition to the regulations on coal-burning plants the Clean Air Act of 1990 also required reformulated gasolines for automobiles. But will these new gasolines actually make the air any cleaner? Many authorities and a great deal of scientific evidence say no—and, in fact, that they'll probably make the air worse. Tom Austin, a former executive officer for the California Air Resources Board says that burning the new gasolines will increase emissions of the oxides of nitrogen. Motorists, he says, will 'end up paying more for dirtier air.' The state of Arizona tested these new oxygenated gasolines for one million miles on state-owned vehicles and found they did not decrease emissions. In fact, in some cases carbon monoxide emissions actually increased. A big argument for these oxygenated gasolines—mainly those with ethanol—was that they would decrease carbon monoxide emissions, but the Arizona test, and others since, have found that not to be true. Even the Environmental Protection Agency admits that ethanol increases emissions of nitrogen oxides and hydrocarbons, which are components of smog. And a report by the National Academy of Sciences has stated that using ethanol in gasoline 'would not achieve significant air quality benefits, and in fact would likely be detrimental.' The big political push behind ethanol had nothing to do with the science of clean air. It had everything to do with the political realities of millions of farm votes in the corn-belt states, because ethanol is made from corn, and millions of dollars in campaign contributions from Archer Daniels Midland, the largest manufacturer of ethanol. Once again, I'm sure that those who favored this legislation thought they were doing what was best for their constituents, but it's absurd to think that the law on this scientific issue was decided on the basis of science. It was decided on the basis of good old-fashioned politics.

"How could anyone expect it to be otherwise? We are, after all, politicians not scientists, and we operate in a political system on the basis of politics, not science.

"And that's not all. Ethanol is twice as expensive to produce as gasoline. So we pay the producers such as ADM a subsidy about equal to the wholesale cost of a gallon of gasoline—and that's supplemented by an additional 10 to 50 cents per gallon by certain state governments—which comes out of the taxpayers' pockets, too. Thus an unscientific policy is sustained by an uneconomic support program."

"So 'substitute science' is sustained by 'substitute economics,'" said Don.

"Exactly," said Billington. "Old-fashioned economics could never do the job. A report by the U.S. Department of Agriculture has stated that the costs of ethanol from corn 'are so large that ethanol production cannot be justified on economic grounds even if existing producers could get by with present subsidies.' In the last decade ethanol has soaked up at least $4.6 billion in tax subsidies and is currently costing taxpayers $740 million annually—not to mention the higher prices at the gas pumps.

"This whole ethanol business reminds me of the federal government's synthetic fuels program that followed the Arab oil boycott back in the 1970s. We spent at least $16 billion of the taxpayers' money trying to come up with an alternative to gasoline. We took an idea that was uneconomic and tried to make it economic by pouring tons of government money into it. The program was a monument to the idea that government can do anything that's popular with the people if only it spends enough money on it. In the end we had to admit complete failure, write the whole thing off as a total loss, and get out of the synthetic fuels business entirely.

"A rational man such as you would think government and the public would have learned our lesson. But, as I said earlier, history doesn't mean anything any more, numbers don't mean anything. People still believe that government can do anything they vote for, because government means the power of the gun. So the economic lesson of synthetic fuels is being repeated with ethanol.

"Furthermore, the energy you get from burning ethanol is less than the energy it takes to produce it, that is, the energy for growing the corn (for running tractors, for fertilizer, etc.) and for distilling the ethanol from the corn. But the program is still good politics because thousands of jobs are created in the ethanol industry, and that means thousands of votes. Never mind that those jobs are producing a product that's more expensive and offers fewer miles per gallon than regular gasoline. All those negatives are offset by the promise of cleaner air—a promise that has no scientific basis but masquerades under the name of science. All that this false promise of 'substitute science' really accomplishes is the redistribution of wealth from the taxpayers to the corn growers and the ethanol manufacturers. And, of course, the redistribution of wealth is the primary function of government. The whole issue is a classic example of democracy in action."

"And because the fuel isn't as good," said Don, "you then have to pass a law forcing people to use it under the threat of fines or jail sentences if they don't."

"Certainly," acknowledged the senator. "The democratically-elected government decides what's best for the people and then takes away their freedom in the matter, forcing them to accept the government solution. Classic democracy in the twentieth century."

"Yes," said Don, "but your example shows that if people were allowed to choose freely in the marketplace, they would choose not only the most economical fuel but the one which also happens to be environmentally superior."

"Well, that may be true in this case," replied Billington. "I don't know that that's always true."

"There are plenty of similar examples," said Don. "The internal combustion engine reduced pollution when it replaced the old steam locomotives with their huge plumes of black smoke. And the automobile put an end to the huge quantities of horse manure and urine deposited daily in our cities in the horse-and-buggy days. And new autos with cleaner emissions have constantly replaced older, dirtier models—a process that went on for decades before there were any environmental laws to govern auto emissions. And when people heat their homes with gas or electricity from utility companies, those companies produce only a fraction of the pollution that occurred when homes had to have wood or coal fires in them for heat. Yet all these environmental improvements came about entirely for economic reasons. They were simply by-products of people being able to exercise choice for their own benefit in a free market. That's the way a free market works. Automobiles and utility companies haven't increased pollution; they've made it less than it otherwise would have been. Economic solutions turn out to be environmentally beneficial if you consider the overall context. Real environmental gains are sustained by real economics; they don't require 'substitute science' or 'substitute economics.'"

"You've cited some interesting examples," said the senator. "I'm not entirely convinced your conclusion is correct, but that's beside the point. The point is that, even if you're correct, politically we couldn't afford to vote other than we did on the Clean Air Act. *The Wall Street Journal* noted that many politicians privately admitted they voted for the 1990 Clean Air Act because they didn't want to vote against anything with the words 'clean air' in the title. Do you think anyone wants to be accused of favoring 'dirty air'? So we passed a so-called Clean Air Act that will actually make the air dirtier. Similarly, because no one wants to vote against any bill with the words 'civil rights' in the title, we've passed so-called civil rights bills that actually *took away* some of people's civil rights. And we passed a Bank Secrecy Act that actually *took away* bank secrecy. That was the law that required banks to microfilm everyone's checks and make them available to the government. What an outright lie it was to call it a 'Bank Secrecy Act'! Obviously, truth in labeling is just one more requirement that we exempt ourselves from while demanding it from everyone else. I told you that we live in a different world and operate differently from the rest of society. You say there is no substitute for the truth, but it's often good politics to do exactly that, to give a law a title that substitutes a meaning exactly the opposite of the law itself. What the public perceives about a law is always more important politically than its substance. As I said before, it's the *image* that counts, not the reality. Laws are titled to serve political ends, not to serve the truth."

"And this," said Don, shaking his head, "is the government that piously proclaims itself the watchdog of truth and enacts truth-in-labeling laws for the private sector!"

"Sure," said Billington, "and the public wants us to play that role. Not because we're so honest ourselves but because we have the gun. It just shows you how much the gun appeals to the public as a way of getting anything they want, even the truth.

"We, the democratically-elected representatives of the people, are responsible for determining what is truth itself, what's good for people intellectually, just like we're responsible for determining what's good for them physically, whether it be the environment, the foods they eat, the cars they drive or even children's toys such as balloons and marbles. We protect the public from bad ideas in the same way that we protect them from bad products.

"A 'bad idea' is any idea that interferes with government policy or is counter to the ideology driving that policy. For example, for many years a great deal of government regulation was based on the doctrine that industrial technology was responsible for as much as 75 to 90 percent of human cancers. The assumption was that pesticides, herbicides, chemical additives in our foods, and industrial pollution of our environment were the causes of all these cancers. Contrary ideas or evidence had to be suppressed in order not to interfere with government regulatory policies and the good intentions of the regulators.

"Cancer is a subject I've followed with great interest and read a great deal about because a tendency to cancer runs in my family. So it's something I have to be concerned about. Also, my first wife died from cancer when she was still quite young." As he spoke, the senator swiveled around in his chair and removed a book from the shelves behind his desk. Spinning around again on his chair, he showed the cover to Don so that he could read the title. It was *The Apocalyptics: Cancer and the Big Lie* by Edith Efron. "This," said the senator, "is the most thorough investigation ever done on this issue."

Flipping to a marker in the book, he read: "Serious falsehoods have been disseminated. Information crucial to issues has been deliberately withheld by government agencies, resulting in false implications. Finally, actual myths and distortions of scientific history have been systematically pumped into the culture. In each of these cases, government agencies and high officials in the scientific bureaucracies are implicated." Then, flipping to another marker in the book, he read: "The Biologist State was concocting a pseudo-science and regulating industry on the basis of a fairy tale, while it was manipulating theory and data the way a cardsharp shuffles cards."

Closing the book and placing it to one side on his desk, Billington continued, "By 1990 even the Food and Drug Administration had to admit its earlier policies were wrong and that up to 98 percent of the cancer risk in the human diet was due to natural chemicals, not man-made ones. Dr. Bruce Ames, a world famous authority on the subject, puts the figure even higher, at over 99.99 percent. It turns out that you get more carcinogens—natural carcinogens—in a single cup of coffee than in all the pesticide residues and other man-made chemicals in your food in an entire year.

"Of course, once the truth was out, the FDA could say, 'We erred on the side of human health.' Earlier you pointed out that eventually the truth will come out about acid rain and the phoniness of the Clean Air Act provisions. At that point, the EPA will simply say, 'We erred on the side of a clean environment' and claim to have acted responsibly just like the FDA claims it did.

"The EPA has been guilty of the same kind of suppression of truth and propagation of false theories as the FDA and for the same reason, namely, to protect the ideology justifying its regulations. Way back in 1978 the EPA suppressed a surprising scientific study showing that up to 80 percent of air pollution was due to plants and trees, rather than to cars and smokestacks as was commonly believed. EPA officials later told *Washington Star* reporter John Holusha that the study was suppressed because it 'possibly would confuse hydrocarbon control strategy.'

"Here's another example for you. When a federal court, in response to a suit by Kennecott Copper, ordered the EPA in 1971 to justify its standards for sulfur dioxide emissions, it couldn't. EPA had set those standards arbitrarily, without any real evidence of how sulfur dioxide affected human health or the ecology of the planet. So EPA ordered the agency's Dr. John Finklea to conduct research on sulfur dioxide as quickly as possible. His staff completed about 20 complex scientific papers in weeks. But the results didn't show what Finklea and EPA wanted them to show. So he rewrote some of the reports, deleted material that didn't show the desired connection between sulfur dioxide pollution and human health, threw out statistics that weakened or contradicted the government's case, and wrote in estimates of health effects that were either dubious or unsupportable. These reports then became the basis on which EPA ordered not only Kennecott but coal-fired utilities across the country, and other industrial plants as well, to install scrubbers at a cost of billions."

"That's incredible!" exclaimed Don. Recalling his meeting with Jim Phillips, the science editor at the *Minneapolis Journal American,* he continued, "Recently I happened to learn that a lot of what we've been told about pollution and the environment isn't true, but *I had no idea the situation was this bad.* Why hasn't the public been told these things? Why didn't the stories you've just told me appear in the press?"

"They did," said Billington, smiling as he noted the way Don had emphasized *"I had no idea the situation was this bad."* He felt he had succeeded in getting to Don. "The first story was carried in the *Washington Star,* and the one about Dr. Finklea was carried in the *Los Angeles Times.* Both stories were picked up by various other newspapers across the country. None of them mattered. The public had been sold on the method, so the facts didn't make any difference. It's just like when people are sold on the concept of government health care or wage-and-price controls. The past failures of such policies are looked upon as failures of individual administrators, not as failures of the policies themselves or of the method. The adherents of those policies still believe in them regardless of the actual record.

"It's the same thing with the members of Congress who were convicted of various crimes, as I mentioned earlier. All those crimes were noted by the news media, but all that publicity didn't shake the public's belief in government as the solution to all the problems of society. The voters simply choose a few new faces, but they vote for the same old policies. Even in the case of the House banking scandal, only a handful of the worst offenders weren't re-elected; and then the House, and the voters as well, carried on as though nothing had ever happened. Even a scandal of that magnitude hasn't affected people's willingness to regard government as the means to any end they desire, despite that scandal being plastered all over the newspapers and repeated in newscasts for months. By now everybody has forgotten about it as well as the fact that dozens of the worst offenders involved are still serving in Congress. So you see, we can't rely on the press or on publicity to reform this country. That hasn't worked. That's why we need to go the route that Dr. Steiner and I've chosen. There's no other way to bring about real reform and get this country back on track."

The senator paused for just a moment to see if Don would protest. He didn't. Several times now Billington had mentioned that he and Steiner were going to use their scheme for a good purpose, for positive political reform. Although Don had never expressed approval, neither had he shown disapproval; he had shown no reaction whatever. Nevertheless, Billington took it as a positive sign that at least Don had voiced no disapproval. He took it as another positive sign that Don seemed to be increasingly concerned about the state of affairs in this country as described by the senator.

The senator leaned forward resting his arms on the desk and now spoke in a softer voice, almost as though he were conveying a secret and didn't want anyone else to hear. "I see that you're concerned about your country, and you should be. The situation is much worse than you think. You don't know the half of it.

"Any scientist who dares to question the scientific basis of government policies is placing his career in jeopardy. He risks being smeared, intimidated, blackballed and financially penalized if not ruined. Ever heard of Dr. Edward C. Krug?"

"No, I haven't"

"He's a scientist who was willing to put scientific truth ahead of politics—and he paid for it. When the EPA and Congress ignored the NAPAP study and pushed ahead with the costly and unnecessary acid-rain provisions of the Clean Air Act, Krug pointed out that the legislation was counter to the scientific evidence—and he did it on national television. He appeared on CBS's *60 Minutes* in 1990.

"Krug's politically-incorrect views led to his being smeared and blackballed. Once when he applied for an EPA-advertised position and scored 99 out of 100 on the civil service exam, he was told the position had been canceled. Despite the fact that his studies had earned worldwide respect, despite the fact that he was listed in *Who's Who in Science and Engineering,* despite the fact that Erik Eriksson of Sweden (considered the father of acid-rain theories) sent the U.S. government an unsolicited letter commending Krug's work, and despite the fact that his mentor John Tedrow (a world-renowned scientist at Rutgers University) says Krug borders 'on genius,' he was so smeared by the EPA that for years he was unable to find a job. I don't know if he ever did get one, but in 1992 he was still unemployed. Within days of his appearance on *60 Minutes,* EPA issued a statement blasting him for 'outlandish statements' and said he had 'limited credibility' and was 'on the fringes of environmental science.' The producer of the TV show said EPA attempted to discredit Krug even before CBS aired the story. Though he continually applied for EPA research grants—virtually the only source of funding for his kind of work—Krug was continually turned down even though scientists with lesser qualifications received funding. Columnist Warren Brookes labeled EPA's treatment of Krug as 'Scientific McCarthyism.'

"EPA even organized a scathing 'secret review' of a Krug article that had already been published in a professional journal and drawn international acclaim. The accepted scientific practice is for professionals of differing opinions to review prospective manuscripts, but EPA hand-picked only scientists who disagreed with Krug. Other scientists denounced the process as a 'sham.' Since the article had already been peer-reviewed and published, obviously the only purpose of the 'secret review' was to attempt to discredit Krug.

"Of course, Krug was right about acid rain, and so was the NAPAP study. Participants at the International Conference on Acid Precipitation in 1988 agreed almost unanimously with NAPAP's conclusions, which were in accordance with Krug's views. If EPA had been interested in science, it would've accepted them, too, but 'substitute science' triumphed for political reasons. When NAPAP was ready to release its final report, EPA Administrator William Reilly refused to approve it. Reilly once said that the Clean Air Act is 'the environmental flagship of this administration' and 'we will do nothing to embarrass it.' Finally, *after much revision,* EPA allowed the NAPAP study to be released though I don't know that Reilly himself ever officially approved it.

"EPA eventually issued something of an apology to Dr. Krug, but the incident nevertheless had its effect on the scientific community. The message was clear: politics will dictate what is scientifically correct—and you may be punished if you don't go along. There have been other examples, too, of the same sort of thing. Professor Reginald Newell of the Massachusetts Institute of Technology, for instance, was warned that if he continued to disagree with the politically correct view of global warming, his funding would be reduced. An independent thinker and a man of integrity, Prof. Newell refused to subordinate science to politics—and his funding was indeed cut. Professor Richard Lindzen, also of MIT, has warned that the whole area of global warming has become a new kind of McCarthyism and if you don't jump on the environmental bandwagon on this issue, you're going to be ostracized. Patrick Michaels, Associate Professor of Environmental Science at the University of Virginia has said, 'People who have a point of view which may not be the politically acceptable point of view are going to have problems.' He's one of the people who experiences those problems because he asserts there's no evidence of global warming and that for 95 percent of the last 100 million years the earth has been warmer than it is now.

"Everyone knows the story of how the ancient Greek wise man Socrates was forced to drink the fatal hemlock, but few people remember what his offense was that led to that death sentence. His offense was teaching 'bad ideas,' corrupting his students with ideas that the government—a democratic one—considered unacceptable. Nowadays we don't force university professors and researchers to drink hemlock for their views, but we let them know that advocating 'bad ideas' can be poisonous to their careers and can result in financial suicide.

"The threat of a cut in federal funding can also lead to pressures from other scientists. Meteorologist Walter Komhyr of the National Oceanic and Atmospheric Administration knows what that's like. He published a study, based on 25 years of data, that showed that the ozone 'hole' over Antarctica as well as global ozone depletion were linked to sea-surface temperatures in part of the Pacific and the way they affect wind patterns. As a result, he was chewed out by a number of atmospheric chemists who were afraid his findings might hurt funding for their research on chlorofluorocarbons. So you can see how the process of government funding has corrupted the pursuit of truth.

"Pressure from one's professional colleagues is mild compared to that from the professional politicians. Here we see, once again, *government by intimidation.* A prime example is the way Al Gore, when he was in the Senate, used his chairmanship of a key Senate subcommittee to intimidate researchers who knew a helluva lot more about science than he did and disagreed with him. The scientific community still buzzes over the way he flayed Dr. Sherwood Idso, a distinguished physicist who has published hundreds of peer-reviewed research papers. Idso's research led him to the conclusion there's no cause for alarm from an increase in carbon dioxide in the atmosphere or from global warming. Another scientist who testified on the same day said, 'Actually the whole purpose of the hearing as far as I could tell was to hammer Idso.' A career scientist from the Department of Energy added: 'It was a setup.' It had the desired effect. Idso returned to Arizona and told a colleague, 'I'm going to cool it' on pursuing controversial research. Another scientist said the incident 'sure as hell had a chilling effect on me. I would be very reluctant to cross Gore.' Thus government by intimidation scored another victory for 'substitute science.'

"Politics scored another victory over science in the case of William Happer. He was the chief scientist for the Department of Energy when he was fired for disagreeing with Vice President Gore about chlorofluorocarbons destroying the ozone layer of the atmosphere. Commenting on his dismissal, Mr. Happer said, 'I was told that science was not going to intrude on policy.'

"Al Gore wrote a book on the environment, but he has no scientific credentials whatever. He revealed the depth of his ignorance in an 'Ask Al Gore' section of a *Newsweek* environmental supplement for children. In it a child asks, 'What are we going to do about burning fossil fuels?' Gore's response is that 'fossil fuels, such as oil' need to be displaced by 'alternative fuels like clean-burning natural gas.' Now, you don't have to be a scientist to know that natural gas is as much a fossil fuel as oil. Most high school students know that. Every educated layman ought to know it, but this self-proclaimed environmental 'expert' didn't.

Frankly, it disturbed me to see such fundamental ignorance in someone so powerful in environmental politics.

"Nor has Al Gore been the only politician to attempt to intimidate scientists who come up with truly scientific answers rather than politically correct ones. When the NAPAP study came out, Rep. James Scheuer—another non-scientist—called it 'intellectually dishonest' and badgered NAPAP witnesses before his House Subcommittee on Natural Resources, Agriculture Research, and the Environment.

"It would seem more appropriate to question whether Rep. Scheuer was 'intellectually dishonest.' It would seem even more appropriate to question whether Al Gore was. At a round-table discussion Professor Richard Lindzen, a critic of the global-warming scenarios, made a concession about his objections to the way computer models deal with water vapor. Al Gore had the transcript of those remarks read that Prof. Lindzen had recanted his views about how water vapor might regulate temperature—which he had not done—and sent a copy of the transcript to Tom Wicker, who published the account in *The New York Times*. Then, in his best-selling book *Earth in Balance*, Mr. Gore claimed Lindzen withdrew his hypothesis about how water vapor might regulate temperature—and cited *The New York Times* article as a reference! Thus Senator Gore fabricated a supporting reference for his book and simultaneously wiped his fingerprints from the whole affair.

"If you want a more recent example of the government 'manipulating theory and data the way a cardsharp shuffles cards,' look at the EPA's 1993 report that said second-hand tobacco smoke leads to 3,000 cancer deaths annually. In order to get the conclusion it wanted, EPA moved the goal posts, so to speak. The standard for these kinds of studies calls for there to be a 5 percent or less chance that the association between a risk factor and a disease occurred purely by chance. But in order to get the result it wanted, EPA doubled the chance factor, to 10 percent. Even with this broader standard EPA found a 'significant' correlation between second-hand tobacco smoke and lung cancer in only one of the eleven studies it analyzed. (There were none by the usual standard.) That still wasn't good enough. So EPA then combined the data for all eleven studies and re-analyzed them with a technique called 'meta-analysis,' a process of *very* questionable validity in this situation, given the variables among the different studies. EPA also had to ignore a large and very recent study sponsored by the National Cancer Institute that came to the opposite conclusion. That study found no statistically significant link between second-hand smoke and lung cancer. Had EPA included that study in its analysis, it would not have been able to claim second-hand smoke was a carcinogen. *The American Spectator* observed that this EPA report is 'another example of the EPA shaping scientific findings to support its own preconceived policies.' And the managing editor of *Reason* magazine noted that 'it is difficult to avoid the conclusion that policy has dictated science.' Even the government's own Congressional Research Service disavowed both the method and the results of this EPA finding. And Michael Gough, of the Office of Technology Assessment, who happens to be adamantly opposed to smoking, nevertheless says that EPA 'played very fast and loose with its own rules' in order to conclude that second-hand smoke is a carcinogen.

"The carcinogenic risk from second-hand tobacco smoke is so low that it's only half the risk of the ordinary tap water that tens of millions of Americans drink every day. And it's far less than the risk from the electromagnetic fields emitted by hair dryers, computers, electric blankets and cellular telephones. Those risks are, of course, negligible, too; but if the government can make its new standard stick for the issue of second-hand smoke, it can use the same standard to open all these other everyday products to government regulation.

"The furor over second-hand tobacco smoke reminds me of the asbestos scare a few years ago. EPA initially claimed that 67,000 Americans were dying every year from inhaling asbestos fibers from building insulation. Later it lowered the number to 3,300, then to 88, then finally to 20—and a great many in the scientific community think even that figure is greatly exaggerated.

"What has happened in science has also happened in education, and for the same reason. Government has politicized and corrupted education just as it has science. And the voters continue to support both not because of the results but because they believe in the method: the gun. The government makes school attendance compulsory, dictates which children must go to which schools—even if they must be bussed over long distances—decides who is qualified to teach and what will be taught and determines the funding of the educational system. And its only power to do all these things is the power of fines and jail sentences. Government control of science and education in this country are the ultimate examples of the public's belief in the power of the gun to give them intellectual benefits, just like material ones."

"Yes, and public education has been a disaster," said Don. "Scholastic achievement scores have been dropping steadily for decades. I'm concerned about education and have read a lot about it because my children will both be in school in a few short years. Schools have been teaching such things as 'life adjustment' and 'multiculturalism' and politically-correct—but scientifically unsupportable—theories about the environment instead of teaching pupils how to read and write. American children have been getting 'substitute education' instead of learning the basics. School bussing and all the other social theories that have been imposed on our educational system have done nothing to improve the quality of education. Children schooled at home usually test better than those at government schools, regardless of a parent's official qualifications to teach.

"It's incredible to me that people don't connect the decline in the quality of American education with the degree of federal involvement. Scores on the College Board Scholastic Aptitude test rose every year from 1946 to 1962. Then they declined eighteen years in a row and have declined almost continuously since. It seems like more than a coincidence that the decline began in the early 1960s with the Kennedy-Johnson era's much-publicized drive to 'improve' primary and secondary education and that, moreover, the decline accelerated as federal funding and federal controls increased."

"That's true," said the senator, "but it's also irrelevant. Past failures don't mean anything as long as people approve of the method. It's just like the examples of wage-and-price controls and government involvement in medical care. People want the government to give them something, if not outright then at least for less than its actual cost. People expect to pay only part of the cost of educating their children and have the government pay the rest with other people's taxes. Once again it's an issue of redistributing wealth, of having some people—those who can better afford it—pay for educating other people's children. The majority of voters, believing themselves to be less well off than those who pay higher taxes, envision themselves as getting something at other people's expense. Just like in a government health care system."

"I'm afraid," said Don, "that American health care will decline just the way American education has. I've been reading Thomas Sowell's *Inside American Education: the Decline, the Deception, the Dogmas,* and the picture he paints is very frightening. He documents that public education has meant using children as guinea pigs for social experiments and targets for propaganda. He reveals the brutal brainwashing agendas of the government schools and shows how affirmative-action admission policies promote racism. He calls for an end to compulsory school attendance laws, an end to the licensing of teachers—which loads our schools with dumb teachers—and he calls for allowing parents the freedom to choose the schools for their children.

"Government money has corrupted our colleges and universities just like it has corrupted primary and secondary education in this country. I've read about how George Roche, president of little Hillsdale College in Michigan has fought a heroic battle for years to keep his institution from government controls by refusing to accept government aid. Washington bureaucrats demanded that Hillsdale submit to federal control anyway, which Roche refused to do. After a decade-long legal battle, the Supreme Court ruled that, even though the college itself accepts no federal funds, if even a single student accepts a federal loan or grant the entire college would be subject to federal controls. So Hillsdale has a policy of not accepting any student with federal aid.

"The federal bureaucracies empowered to interfere with higher education include the cabinet-level departments of Agriculture, Commerce, Defense, Education, Health and Human Services, Interior, Justice, Labor, Treasury and Veterans Affairs. Give the federal government an inch and it will take a mile—just like it has done in the matter of regulating interstate commerce. All branches of the federal government interfere with hiring policies, student admissions, accounting practices, college athletics, campus security, sexual behavior, research projects, and course requirements. Roche says that Washington demands that teachers be hired on the basis of race and sex rather than merit and pressures institutions to 'dumb down' by enrolling kids who are poorly prepared for college.

"Government funds are the seeds that have sprouted into a harvest of corruption on our campuses. Officials at New York University, Eastern Kentucky University and Mississippi, to name a few, have embezzled government money. Carnegie Mellon, Cornell, Dartmouth, Harvard, Johns Hopkins, MIT, Stanford, Rutgers, the University of California, the University of Michigan and the University of Pennsylvania, among others, have all been found guilty of overbilling for government research projects. Harvard Medical School, the University of Michigan, the University of Pittsburgh and Rockefeller University have all been scenes of fraudulent scientific research tests bankrolled by government funds. Dozens of universities have been embroiled in scandals for funneling government money to athletes who never graduate. At Memphis State University there was a ten-year period in which not a single black varsity basketball player graduated. If higher education is to be retrieved from its cesspool of mediocrity and corruption, Roche, in his book *The Fall of the Ivory Tower,* says government money must be shut off."

"Well," said the senator, sensing an opportunity, "if you want to reduce government money for education or anything else, you'd probably like to see a Constitutional amendment to require a balanced budget. As you know, such a measure failed to get the required votes in Congress in 1994 and again in 1995, and similar measures failed in 1982, 1986 and 1990. But when Dr. Steiner completes his work on the telephone virus, we'll be able get the necessary votes to ensure its passage and also the votes needed in the state legislatures for ratification. Aren't you in favor of a balanced-budget amendment?"

"Actually, I'm not," said Don, "because the balanced-budget amendment, at least the version that came up in 1994 and again in 1995, is just a gimmick. It's a phony trophy that politicians would like to hold up to their constituents and say, 'See, I voted to balance the budget,' but it really wouldn't solve the problem. It wouldn't require a balanced budget for another seven years. If Congress were really serious about balancing the budget, it could do so right now instead of pushing the solution seven years into the future. Furthermore, in seven years Congress could still have an unbalanced budget if 60 percent of its members so vote. Any amendment requires a two-thirds vote of both houses of Congress. So it would take fewer votes to override the balanced-budget amendment than are required for its passage in the first place! Are we to believe such a toothless measure will cure the budget-deficit problem? Besides, how would such an amendment be enforced? I suppose the Court could step in, but the prospect of the judiciary dictating the federal budget is horrible to contemplate. That would be almost worse than the original problem.

"A better solution would be a Constitutional amendment to make the dollar convertible once again into gold. That would automatically put the brakes on the government's deficit spending, because the deficit couldn't be financed by an unlimited supply of paper credit as it is now. It would also preserve the value of people's savings instead of seeing that value disappear through inflation that results from the government financing its deficits at their expense. When we had a gold-backed dollar, the nation never needed to worry about inflation or running up huge deficits. Gold provided a necessary discipline without which the politicians have run wild. The Constitution prohibits the states from making anything but gold or silver legal tender. The same prohibition should have been applied to the federal government. My proposed amendment would correct that."

"Actually," said Billington, "the Founders never intended to give the federal government the power to issue paper money. They just didn't prohibit it with exactly the same language in the Constitution that they applied to the states…"

"But doesn't the Constitution give the federal government the power to 'regulate the value' of money, and isn't that the power to create unredeemable paper currency?" asked Don.

"No. The Constitution grants the power 'to coin money, regulate the value thereof, and of foreign coin.' By the phrase 'regulate the value thereof' the Founders didn't mean to grant the power to give monetary value to paper. That phrase meant the power to fix the denominations of coins, their metallic content and their value with respect to foreign coins. We know this from the debates at the Constitutional Convention and those that accompanied the ratification process which followed. Also, Madison's notes from the Convention state that an early draft of the Constitution would have given the government the power 'To borrow money and emit bills on the credit of the United States.' The phrase 'emit bills on credit' in the language of that time meant to issue paper currency. However, Gouverneur Morris moved to strike out that phrase, and the motion passed 9 to 2. Thus the Founders expressly rejected giving the federal government the power to issue paper currency. Oliver Ellsworth, a delegate from Connecticut, observed that 'this is a favorable moment to shut and bar the door against paper money.' In the years before the Constitution the Continental Congress, under the Articles of Confederation, had the power to emit bills on credit—the worthless 'continentals'—and 9 of the 13 original states did the same thing. Having experienced the inflationary effects of these paper currencies, the Founders chose not to grant either the federal government or the states the power to repeat the process.

"It was so widely understood that the federal government didn't have the authority to issue paper money that no attempts were made to do so for almost three-quarters of a century. But because of the high cost of the Civil War, Congress passed the Legal Tender Act of 1862, which authorized printing of the 'greenbacks' you mentioned earlier, as an easy way to pay for the war. The man who was Secretary of the Treasury when the 'greenbacks' were first issued, Salmon P. Chase, later became Chief Justice of the U.S. Supreme Court. It's significant that as a justice he thought what he had done as Secretary of the Treasury was unconstitutional! Nevertheless, the Court upheld the Legal Tender Act. That Court decision paved the way for Congress later to pass the Federal Reserve Act, which provided for an 'elastic' currency. So here's another illustration of Congress and the Court going off in a direction unauthorized by the Constitution and completely contrary to what the Founders intended that document to mean.

"You're right that gold provides a monetary discipline. But politicians don't want any discipline, especially in regard to their power to spend money. They claim they need 'flexibility' to solve the nation's problems. That's why they wouldn't vote even for that toothless balanced-budget amendment in 1994 and 1995 even though the discipline it provided was so small it was almost trivial. They certainly aren't going to vote for a gold-backed currency with all the discipline that would require. Now you can appreciate the value of the telephone virus, because with it we can achieve the kind of reform that simply wouldn't be possible otherwise. I think you'll agree that what you propose is something that Congress would never pass on its own." The senator smiled because he knew Don would have to concede this point.

"You're right that Congress on its own would never pass an amendment such as I suggested," said Don.

"Good. I'm glad we can agree. Now we're getting somewhere," said Billington, smiling and rubbing his hands together. "Can you think of any other reform measures that are needed to put this country back on the right track again?"

"Yes," said Don. "We need an amendment taking away the federal government's authority to regulate interstate commerce. The amendment should reaffirm, as Madison stated, that the Constitutional phrase about regulating commerce among the states shall apply only in the negative sense, to prevent the states from imposing regulatory barriers, not in the positive sense of empowering the federal government to impose them."

"I can understand why you'd say that," said the senator, "after all the examples I gave of the government abusing its power regarding interstate commerce, but don't we need some regulation? What about the airwaves? If we didn't have a Federal Communications Commission to license radio and TV stations, wouldn't anyone be free to start broadcasting over any frequency they wished and interfere with the broadcasts of established stations?"

"No," said Don. "Owners of established stations should have their property rights recognized and safeguarded."

"Property rights for airwaves?"

"That's right," Don said. "The federal government should register and protect these rights just as it does patents and copyrights, which have always been protected under the Constitution. People shouldn't be allowed to infringe on the broadcast frequencies of registered stations, just as they aren't allowed to infringe on registered patents or on copyrights. Perhaps another Constitutional amendment would be necessary to extend this same protection regarding the airwaves, but the federal government shouldn't be allowed to regulate broadcasting as it now does through licensing based on regulating commerce. Such licensing allows the government to control the content of programming by threatening to withhold a license and is a violation of the right of free speech. No one should need a license to exercise free speech. If a license is needed to do anything, then one doesn't have a right to do it; a *right* is something that can be exercised without anyone's permission."

"That's an interesting point. Anything else?"

"Yes," said Don. "We also need an amendment stating that Congress shall pass no law exempting itself from any provision applying to others and that any law which originally exempted Congress shall be null and void in its entirety."

"You don't have to go overboard, do you?" said the senator with surprise. "I can certainly sympathize with your desire to have the law apply equally to everyone, but isn't it sufficient simply to require members of Congress to comply basically with the standards we've set for everyone else, as we voted in 1995?"

"No, senator. You yourself pointed out that Congress can't bind future Congresses by its laws. Even though Congress has now decided to require its members to comply with the same standards as everyone else on the eleven laws you mentioned earlier, future Congresses could change that any time. Who knows what laws they might pass and exempt themselves from? There's no reason to leave that power laying there dormant until some future Congress decides to use it again. We need a

Constitutional amendment that takes that power away from Congress permanently and voids all the laws from which Congress previously exempted itself."

"But why throw out all those laws in their entirety? There are a lot of good features in those laws which would be trashed. We'd have to start all over again from scratch on a lot of those issues."

"That's exactly what should be done," said Don. "If Congress had to begin from scratch knowing it will have to comply with its own laws, it would think twice about all those onerous regulations and the burden of paperwork it has imposed upon everyone else and probably write the laws differently. If Congress is simply required to comply with existing laws as they apply to everyone else, most of the ridiculous and burdensome requirements won't be eliminated. Instead Congress will simply add more staff members and spend more of the taxpayers money to put itself in compliance. How many employees are there in the legislative branch of the federal government?"

"A little over 40,000, according to the best estimates. Nobody knows the exact number."

"40,000!" said Don in disbelief. "That's even worse that I thought. There are only 100 senators and 435 members of the House."

"Yes, but we all have large staffs to help us cope with all the laws we write."

"And if Congress had to comply with present laws in every respect the way the rest of us do, that number would probably rise to 80,000," said Don.

"It probably would," acknowledged the senator.

"That alone would be reason enough for throwing out all those laws and starting over, but my next suggested amendment will make it even more clear that that's necessary," said Don. "We need an amendment stating that Congress shall make no appropriation for any purpose except those in the legislative powers enumerated in the Constitution. That would put an end to federal interference in education, agriculture, health care, the environment and all the other fields where it has no Constitutional authority and never should have gotten involved in the first place. Its performance in these areas has been consistently ineffective, wasteful, fraudulent and destructive of human freedom."

"What you're proposing," said the senator, "probably wouldn't achieve what you expect. Congress could still legislate in all those areas without appropriating any money for its edicts. It does so now through what are called 'unfunded mandates.' The federal government decides on some desirable objective and then orders the states and local governments to comply and foot the bill. In the 1940s there were only 16 examples of this, but in the last twenty years Congress has passed 174 of these unfunded mandates, which now cost state and local governments about $40 billion annually. In January 1995 Congress voted to refrain from passing *additional* unfunded mandates, but the legislation provides for an override of that limitation by a simple majority vote; and existing mandates were left untouched. Thus there is no real protection from unfunded mandates, only the *image* of their elimination.

"Governor Voinovich of Ohio says the federal government, not content on bankrupting itself, is bankrupting the states as well with these unfunded mandates. He says these cost Ohio alone more than $1.74 billion in 1992-95. The situation is worse in New Jersey. The governor there, Christine Todd Whitman, who has been trying to cut state spending, says the state faces an *increase* of a billion dollars annually in spending for *existing* federal mandates. One of these mandates requires all fifty states to test water supplies for a pesticide used only on pineapples in Hawaii, where its use was discontinued in 1977. Another requires that shredded tires be added to asphalt for highway paving even though this increases the cost of paving 200 to 300 percent and there are serious doubts about the durability and environmental effects of this rubberized asphalt. The federal government has no concern whatever that these requirements are uneconomic, because no federal money is involved. What you propose will simply make the federal government even more irresponsible: all its legislation in the fields you want to prohibit it from funding would shift the financial burden to the states. We would simply see new unfunded mandates.

"Furthermore, these unfunded mandates pre-empt the states and local governments from using their tax funds in ways that are more beneficial. All the money that's used to test for a pesticide in states where it has never even been used could obviously be put to better use. Likewise, the savings that could be made by using conventional paving instead of the mandated rubberized asphalt would mean a lot more money would be available for other, more urgent needs. Mayor Hal Conklin of Santa Barbara says the Americans with Disabilities Act required his community to spend $400,000 on new playground equipment—but that this money came right out of child care facilities and after-school programs for those with disabilities. Will the new playground equipment really be more beneficial to disadvantaged children than what they would have gotten without the federal mandate? If so, isn't it likely that the community would have appropriated the money for that purpose in the first place? Mayor Sharpe James of Newark says the average municipality spends as much on federal mandates as on public safety. He says if it weren't for federal mandates, the federal government wouldn't need to give municipalities more money for police officers, because they could hire them themselves. Chicago's Mayor Richard Daley has said that the money his city spends on federal mandates would pay the salaries of 3,200 additional policemen. So more federal mandates would simply divert more money from the ways state and local government can serve the needs of their own people."

"You're right," said Don, "but the unfunded mandates are an unfortunate by-product of the popular election of senators. If U.S. senators were elected by the state legislatures, as the Constitution originally provided, the Senate wouldn't be passing these laws that thrust financial burdens on the state legislatures and deprive them of the prerogatives of allocating their resources to solve their own problems. We need an amendment to repeal the Seventeenth Amendment and restore to the state legislatures the power to elect U.S. senators."

"But when the U.S. senators were chosen by the state legislatures," said Billington, "there was a lot of corruption. A lot of people felt that, given the quality of people elected to the state legislatures, the voters at large would do a better job of electing U.S. senators than the state legislatures."

"But if the voters aren't capable of selecting honest, competent people at the state level," said Don, "why should anyone think they could do so at the national level? Your objection is actually an argument against democracy—not one for giving it broader power. And the level of corruption we've seen in the U.S. Senate and House certainly shows that national legislators have no higher morality than those of the states, nor have they demonstrated superior wisdom. If the people are going to choose corrupt or incompetent representatives at either level of government, then it would be better to confine their choices wherever possible to the states, where they can do far less damage than at the national level.

"Madison believed that the best individuals for elective office would be obtained not through direct election by the populace but through indirect election. Here the voters would elect some people who, in turn, would elect others to various public offices. In this two-stage process those first elected would presumably be better informed, and probably better educated, than the general public and thus better able to make a wise selection. Madison referred to this as a process of 'filtration' that would refine the wishes of the public. He and the other Founding Fathers believed that, just as everyone wasn't equally qualified to run the government, neither was everyone equally qualified to determine who should run it. Except in the case of elections to the House, they deliberately tried to avoid a system where the less able and less qualified would have the same voting power as the wisest among them—which is the case with the one-man-one-vote doctrine you mentioned earlier. The Founders sought an electoral system that would maximize intelligent choice rather than popularity, quality rather than numerical superiority. Furthermore, *indirect election would remove the incentive for candidates to seek office by promising to redistribute other men's property in return for votes.* Indirect election was to be the method for selecting not only U.S. senators but the president as well since this was how the electoral college was supposed to function.

"As to your comment that limiting Congress' power to appropriate money would simply increase the unfunded mandates on the states," continued Don, "even now Congress has no valid authority to pass any legislation except for those grants of legislative power enumerated in the Constitution. But since Congress already ignores that limitation—and also the Tenth Amendment—we need to reassert these limitations. The amendment I suggested earlier about limiting federal appropriations should instead state: Congress shall make no appropriation for any purpose except those in the legislative powers enumerated in the Constitution; furthermore, since powers not delegated to the United States by the Constitution are reserved to the states or to the people, as specified in the Tenth Amendment, Congress shall make no law requiring states, local governments or private citizens to fund any purpose not included in its enumerated power in the Constitution; Congress shall make no law whatever for any purpose not specified in its enumerated powers, and any such laws as may now exist are hereby declared null and void.

"We simply have to cut back the cancerous growth of the federal government. The smallest excuses are used to expand its control. Even a single student accepting a federal loan or grant becomes a justification for bringing a whole institution under control of the federal government.

Any shortcoming in the private sector becomes the basis for bringing an entire industry under government regulation. The 'shortcoming' may not even be a criminal act by an individual or corporation; it may be as simple as a 'failure' to provide health insurance for 15 percent of the population or earning 'unconscionable' profits. Cries go up that freedom and private enterprise have failed and that now government must take over. But when government fails on a far more massive scale, there are no cries for turning its field of control over to the private sector. Public opinion polls have shown that 85 percent of the American people have some form of health insurance and that nearly 90 percent are satisfied with their health care. If this constitutes a 'failure' of an industry and is a justification for forcing everyone into a new, government system of health care, then the failure of public education should be a reason for getting the government out of that business and turning it over to private enterprise. Far more people are dissatisfied with education in this country than are dissatisfied with health care, and with good reason. Academic results have been in a persistent, well-documented decline for decades at the hands of the government. That's indisputable, as is the massive corruption that has followed the flow of federal dollars to education. It's time to shut off federal funds and get the federal government out of education.

"Similarly, it's also time to get the federal government out of the business of regulating the environment, because of the failure of its own performance as well as for Constitutional reasons. The government has lied to the American people about global warming, acid rain, the danger from asbestos, chlorofluorocarbons destroying the ozone layer and lots of other issues. It has wasted billions of dollars of their money on nonproblems and fraudulent studies, and has put people in jail for polluting their own private property with *dirt*. Furthermore, ABC News reported that the nation's largest polluter is—surprise!—the federal government. Well-known newscaster Peter Jennings reported that the federal government is polluting at twice the rate of private sources and that putting the government in charge of regulating the environment is like putting the fox in charge of the chicken coop. He said that the government's pollutants aren't just the products of the Defense Department's nuclear and chemical warfare projects but common industrial items such as fuels, lubricants, solvents and medical wastes—this from the government that puts its citizens in jail for dumping plain dirt! And Jennings cited the EPA itself as one of the offending agencies."

"But those things don't matter," said the senator. "I already told you that results don't matter as long as people approve of the method. The method that people find so attractive is the government's ability to threaten people with guns. That's why the people vote for government's role in education or the environment or anything else. When government fails, as it has in education and the environment, the voters want new administrators or new policies; and the administrators want more money and more employees. But nobody wants to abandon the *method*."

"That's why," said Don, "people need a Constitution that limits government's power to use that method only where it's appropriate, not wherever it's popular. The problems of education and science can have no political solutions because they're not political in nature; they can't be solved by threatening people with guns. That's why we need a Constitutional amendment that takes away government's power over these fields. Only then can true solutions be developed by the minds of free men acting voluntarily to solve these problems for themselves.

"It's the nature of reality that determines how problems can be solved. Reality isn't optional. Government isn't an optional or alternative method of solving problems of science, education, business and economics. It's very nature precludes it from providing true solutions. The solution to the problem of 2 plus 2 is to be found not by political action but by reference to physical reality. There's no alternative to the correct answer, and the method of obtaining it has nothing to do with democracy or writing laws or regulations that threaten people with fines or jail sentences. What's true of this simple example is true of all science, education and economics. The correct answers aren't arrived at through laws, and they don't need to be enforced by government. There's no need for a law telling us the correct answer to 2 plus 2 and threatening people with legal punishment for the wrong answer. Nature will provide sufficient penalty of its own for a wrong answer.

"Earlier, senator, you said, 'We do everything differently than other people. We don't have to balance our checkbooks as they do.... We spend other people's money; they can spend only their own. They can't threaten people with guns...but that's the very basis of the way we operate.' You were correct; you do indeed do everything differently—and that's precisely why government can never be an alternative to the private sector! Nature does not permit opposite methods to achieve the same results. You and your fellow politicians may intend to do good, but your method is fundamentally at odds with human nature and the nature of progress.

"The Founding Fathers were very concerned with the nature of man and the nature of government. Politicians today don't seem to be aware of either. But everything has a specific nature, and man is no exception. Neither is government.

"Nature has given every type of living organism the means of sustaining its life. Life is both the means and the purpose of its actions. A living thing can't exist if it doesn't act for itself. For man, the distinctive mode of his survival is his mind, which makes knowledge and a choice of actions possible. He can learn about his environment and his nature and choose appropriate ways to sustain and enhance his life. No other living creature has man's capability for choice. It's this unique capability that makes a truly human life possible. The more a man extends the range of his knowledge, the more he extends the range of his actions for sustaining and enhancing his life. The purpose of the human capability of choice is the individual's own life, not only his survival but the satisfaction of his own interests, the joy of living. Happiness is the reward for life, for successfully choosing the actions and values that sustain and enhance one's existence."

"But," said the senator, "isn't that selfish? As a practical man, I agree that a certain amount of selfishness is necessary. I'm certainly no saint, but isn't it more moral to act for the good of others than for one's self? Isn't that what morality is all about?"

"Not a morality of life," said Don. "A living creature has to act for itself or it will die. Is it the purpose of your stomach to digest food for your life or the lives of others?"

"But digestion is an involuntary action," said Billington. "Man has no choice about that."

"True, but man has a choice about what he puts into his mouth," said Don. "Do you put food into your mouth for your life or for others? Do you do so because the taste pleases you or satisfies your hunger—or because it pleases others or satisfies their hunger? The voluntary and involuntary actions of a living being must work in harmony, not at cross-purposes. They all have the same goal: the life of the individual. The survival of any living organism depends on all its faculties working together. Do your eyes guide your own hands and feet—or other people's? And don't your hands and feet move for purposes that *you* choose? When your mind tells you to run from danger, do your feet carry you away for the selfish purpose of saving your own life?—or for the benefit of society or the survival of the species? Individuals have to act for themselves. That's the nature of individual life. Other people, such as one's loved ones, the people one does business with, even humanity at large, may benefit as a consequence of serving one's own interests, but that's merely the effect—not the cause—of the choices one makes for living one's own life.

"The actions that will sustain or benefit life aren't arbitrary; they're determined by physical reality. They have nothing to do with 'political realities' that you spoke about. They aren't discovered by majority voting or produced by government threats. They're discovered by the rational identification of principles in physical cause-and-effect processes.

"It's the absolute, uncompromising nature of existence that makes knowledge possible. If water were H_2O today and some totally different chemical formula tomorrow, if acorns sometimes grew into oak trees and sometimes into pine trees or elephants or shrimp, there would be no way man's mind could know anything. Similarly, if human nature isn't the same today as it was yesterday, if a Constitution doesn't mean today what it meant yesterday, if laws can be made retroactive and arbitrary, if 'human rights' are whatever the government of the moment decides, then there's no way in which government can provide a political structure appropriate to the nature of man, in which human life can flourish.

"The only rational purpose of government is to protect the process of life, to allow people to live according to their nature, which means: by their minds and for their own interests without employing force or fraud against each other. In short, the purpose of government is to protect its citizens from criminals and invaders. The concept of 'rights' provides the framework for protecting every individual and delimiting criminal action by other individuals—or by government.

"Human rights aren't derived from government; they're derived from life. Government can recognize rights or deny them; it can protect them or violate them, but it can't invent or alter them because they depend on the physical process of cause and effect. They're as absolute and uncompromising as any other aspect of reality.

"The fundamental right is the right to life. Life is a process of action, and the right to life means a valid claim to one's own being and to the actions of living. It means that a human life is the purpose of its own existence. It means that the capability of self-generated action that is within it belongs to no one else, not to others or 'society' but entirely to the individual, and it is right for him to serve himself because it is right for him to live. If it weren't right for every man to serve himself, there could be no objection to slavery. The only argument would be over whom one should serve.

"Throughout history men were supposed to serve the pharaoh, the king, the feudal lord, the Church-state; but in America men were at last free to serve themselves. That famous phrase in the Declaration of Independence, the 'right to the pursuit of happiness,' means nothing if not an individual's right to live his life for its own sake. If that's being selfish, then the Declaration of Independence says everyone has an inherent right to be—and that, moreover, that right is 'unalienable.' It's 'unalienable' because intrinsic to life itself. Happiness is an internal, psychological process that can't be separated from the physical, biological processes of an individual's life; and the pursuit of happiness is the choices made by the individual's own mind.

"From the right to life, it's easy to derive man's other rights. If one has a right to his own life, then he must also have a right to his labor, for life is the source of labor. And he must also have a right to the products of his labor, that is, property—not because of the laws of government but because of the Law of Causality. The concept of property is the recognition of a physical effect of which life is the cause.

"It's similarly easy to derive the right to self defense. If everyone has a right to life, then obviously no one has a right to violate that right of others, and everyone must logically have a right to defend his life against any violator. The boundary that determines the violation of rights is the initiation of force—including the threat of force—against the life, liberty or property of another. Violence is justified only for self-defense, because its use for any other purpose necessarily violates the rights of others.

"Government, like everything else, is limited by its own nature. Government is force; that's its very nature. Everything it does involves either the threat of violence or its outright implementation. Since the only justification of violence is self-defense, the only justification of government is to protect and defend its citizens against those who would initiate force, that is, criminals and invaders. Any attempt to use government for any other purpose is to turn government into a criminal, into a violator of human rights instead of their protector.

"The beauty of a free market is that it allows people to act according to their nature and for their own self-interest. A buyer and a seller in an economic transaction each enters it for his own selfish gain. Because they both expect to gain, they participate voluntarily, as an exercise of that distinctive human capability of choice. That's the way it is—or should be—with all human relationships. Take romantic relationships as a model. If two people choose to marry or to engage in sexual activity, they both expect to gain—and they both must voluntarily agree to participate. No one has a right to force his desires or 'needs' on anyone else. Clearly, any use of force by one party—no matter how well-intentioned—necessarily violates the rights of the other person. The same principle applies to every transaction in society."

"Are you saying," asked the senator, "that any economic exchange in which the government plays a role constitutes economic 'rape'?"

"Why, yes, if you want to think of it that way," said Don. "It doesn't matter which side the government favors; if government interferes at all, it can't help but violate the rights of one side or the other—just as it would if it intervened to assist someone in satisfying his sexual needs with another person against that person's will. That's why government should have no role in economic matters. Those should be determined by the free choices of individuals throughout society. Why can't we have capitalism between consenting adults?"

"Because," said the senator, "sexual choice is a strictly personal matter. Economic choices have wider implications. I agree with most of what you say, but someone has to look out for the broader interests of society."

"Why?" asked Don. "If individuals look after their own interests, then society will automatically be taken care of, as a consequence. Besides, every economic decision is a personal choice. The food I buy and put into my mouth, the school I send my children to, the kind of automobile I buy, the kind of work I do for a living, where I work and who I hire are all *personal* decisions, which I and every other person attempts to make in his own self-interest. Every decision is a personal decision, because each is a decision of *my life*. No one else has a right to make them, because my life is my own. To live, really to live as a human being, means to live by making these kinds of choices for oneself. That's what a distinctively human existence means. To live merely by keeping ones biological processes functioning is to live as less than human, to half live. To half live is to fail utterly. That's why people are willing to die for freedom, to risk everything for the opportunity to live by making their own choices—even if their choices sometimes turn out to be wrong. It's the process of choice that is distinctively human and critical to a truly *human* existence. You politicians spend hundreds of millions of dollars of the taxpayers' money on preserving the natural environment for spotted owls, snail darters and other so-called endangered species; but you never seem to be aware that man has a specific nature and that that nature requires a specific environment for his species to flourish. That environment is freedom. It's the only environment in which man can be truly human, in which each individual can live by the uncoerced choices of his own mind and reach his full potential as a human being.

"The human mind is an adaptation for dealing with the physical diversity of this planet. There are a vast number of ways in which an individual can further or enhance his life, from the type of food or the way he obtains it to the kind of entertainment that gives him pleasure. Whether it's a decision about what to have for supper, or the job he needs in order to support himself, or which TV program he will watch, or how to plan for his retirement, he makes his choices selfishly for his own satisfaction—just the way a primitive man does when he hunts an animal for food or for its hide to clothe himself. Human nature hasn't changed. The motivation for human action hasn't changed, nor has the need for making choices. What has changed is the number of choices available to modern man because of the range of his knowledge. Mankind has come this far by expanding the choices available and by individuals exercising their ability to choose whenever they could—but you politicians think you can advance society by limiting choice! You're operating against human nature and the nature of progress. You're acting against man's mind.

"When a primitive man hunts, he constantly makes choices: this animal or that one?—which way does the trail turn?—should I release my arrow or spear now or try to get a little closer for a better shot? Each choice means foregoing the other one. Each choice is made for greater value, greater likelihood of success. He doesn't always make the right choice, but each choice is a matter of weighing not only relative values but risk against reward. These are the same kinds of choices that people are faced with in a complex economy. Should I buy this product or that one? Should I buy now or wait and hope to get a better price later? Which way should my career turn: should I take the new job and move to Atlanta or stay where I am? Each choice means foregoing the other one. Each choice is made for greater value and for one's own interests. The human mind operates the same way and for the same purpose in all of these examples. Reality provides natural rewards for correct choices and penalties for incorrect ones.

"The concept of rights provides the framework for economic choices in a free society. Every man has a right to trade his labor or property with anyone else willing to do so. They're his to do with as he wishes because they're his by reason of his life, which is his own. Each man is free to trade solely for his own interests *in the sole judgment of his own mind,* for no one—not government or others calling themselves 'society'—has dominion over his mind. No one, and no group of men, including government, has the right to determine how he should live or the right to force him into an economic exchange for others' benefit instead of his own. To do so is to deny his right to life and to force him to act against his own nature.

"Yesterday I visited many of the historic landmarks in your city, the way most tourists do. One of these was the Jefferson Memorial. There, on the base of the rotunda, were Jefferson's words that he had sworn 'eternal hostility to every form of tyranny over the mind of man.' Jefferson would turn over in his grave and vomit if he could see the kind of 'tyranny over the mind of man' that the federal government has established over the citizens of this country.

"The free market is the only economic system in which government exercises no tyranny over men's minds and instead allows people to live by their minds and for their own interests. That's why it's the only system consonant with the nature of man. That's simply a reality, just as two plus two equaling four is a reality. And there's no alternative to reality.

"In a free market everyone acts for greater value. In fact, he chooses the greatest value he can find. What makes it possible for two people to make an economic exchange to *mutual* advantage is that both place different values on the items exchanged. If a man sells his labor, it's because he'd rather have the money; it's of *greater* value to him. His employer has the *opposite* opinion; otherwise there would be no trade. If the laborer then spends the money he has earned, he exchanges it for something else that he would rather have, something once again of *greater* value to him. In fact, of all the things he could buy with his money, he chooses the greatest value he can find, foregoing all the others.

"Prices are always measurements of comparative worth. Government can't establish a 'fair' price for anything, because values are always relative. Some people are willing to pay more for a given item. In certain circumstances people are willing to pay more than they otherwise would. For example, if my car breaks down, I may be willing to pay more for a new one than I would if my old one were still usable. On a very hot day I may be willing to pay more for air conditioning. Or even a cold beer. People's needs and desires vary, as do their means—as well they should since some people are more industrious or talented than others. A free market allows people to sort all these things out and choose the greatest values for themselves according to their means. But they can achieve their desired values only in economic exchanges which offer other people the greatest values in return, in the judgment of *their* minds. The *cause* of every trade in a free market is the individual's self interest, but the *effect* is to benefit the other party in the transaction. The sum of these effects is a prosperous society. The prosperity results not from government coercion but from the mind-directed actions of millions of individuals fulfilling their own lives by acting constantly for greater values. People advance themselves—and as a consequence, society—voluntarily, by *un*forced actions, in their own self-interest, when they are not forced by others nor do they employ force against others. People don't need to be forced to act for their own advantage; they don't need to be forced to make a profit—they only need to be *free* to do so."

"Politicians attempt to improve society in exactly the opposite way: by taking away freedom and forcing economic losses on people. All your government giveaway programs, for example, whether they be welfare handouts, emergency relief for victims of floods or forest fires, or subsidies for business enterprises or products, such as ethanol, all create unavoidable losses elsewhere in the economic system. You make all these so-called worthy projects the cause of your laws that compel these economic transfers, and the *effect* you create in every case is a corresponding loss for all the citizens whose tax money funds your generosity without benefit to themselves. By contrast, everyone who benefits in a market transaction does so at a corresponding gain to others."

"What you're saying, then," interjected Billington, "is that every market transaction is a win-win situation, whereas every government redistribution of wealth is a win-lose situation."

"Exactly," said Don. "And you can't create prosperity when government forces more and more of the economic transactions in a society onto a win-lose basis instead of a win-win basis. That's why the more government intervenes in the economy, the more the losses pile up. And that's why complete government control of the economy must lead to economic collapse, as it did in the Marxist countries. The losses are simply the unavoidable consequence of trying to reverse cause and effect. Reality won't let you get away with it. You can't achieve what should be an effect, a prosperous society, by acting against what must be the cause, the individual's rights and self-interest."

"But is it fair to compare the programs of a democratic government with those of the failed Marxist regimes?" asked Billington. "Aren't democratic governments more benevolent, more sensitive to the citizens and administered with greater competence than was the case in the communist countries?"

"Well," said Don, "it's true that in a democracy the citizens can vote for new leadership to obtain more competent administration, but no level of competence or benevolence can make government economic intervention a win-win situation rather than a win-lose situation. Politicians, even democratic ones, rely on government's power to inflict losses—by laws threatening people with fines or jail sentences—for every economic benefit they try to confer. Nor is that surprising, for that's the nature of government. In a free market, however, people are motivated by the prospect of gains, not the fear of losses. Those motivations aren't interchangeable. The effects they produce aren't interchangeable. There's no way that government's power to distribute losses can manage an economy toward greater prosperity than one propelled by profits. Government doesn't create prosperity; people create prosperity for themselves by continually exercising their ability to choose greater values for themselves. You can't make society more prosperous by churning out an ever-increasing number of laws that threaten people with losses and reduce the choices available to them. In fact, if government's power to threaten or inflict losses on its citizens and reduce their choices were the means to prosperity, the Marxist governments, which had far greater powers in this regard, should have had a tremendous advantage. They should have been able to create extremely wealthy societies. Instead, the very opposite occurred, complete economic failure.

"Democracy can't make anything economic. The number of voters advocating any particular type of government intervention can't make it economic—any more than the number of voters advocating 5 as the answer to the problem of 2 plus 2 would make it correct. An economic loss is still a loss regardless of the political popularity of any policy or any democratically-elected government that produces it. The only difference a democracy makes is in the way that the losses are distributed. They will be allocated in response to the desires of the majority rather than those of a non-elected leader. Or, in the case of the United States they may be allocated according to the desires of the Supreme Court. But they will still be losses, enforced at the point of a gun if necessary.

"Furthermore, the kind of giveaway programs I just mentioned, welfare, disaster relief, etc., are blatant win-lose situations. Their very purpose is to give some people something at other people's expense, to dole out benefits without the recipients giving anything in return. Something for nothing. Those programs are inherently uneconomic. They're undisguised redistribution of wealth."

"That's right," said Billington. "Society—that is, the voting majority—has deemed it necessary for government to accomplish some of those things precisely because they wouldn't be accomplished in the free market. They're not economic, but they're needed. How do you answer the argument that government should be responsive to the needs of the people? Maybe the government has gone overboard in redistributing wealth, but isn't it a good thing that government is providing for the poor and unfortunate in society? You're a moral man, Mr. Emerson," said Billington with a teasing curiosity, "is it morally wrong for government to provide for the needy?"

"Absolutely!" said Don without hesitation, "because it can't do so without violating other people's rights. Government can't give to some without first taking from others through laws that threaten honest, hard-working, law-abiding people with guns—and *that* is morally wrong."

"But don't the needy have a right to life, too?"

"Of course they do. Just as much as anyone else."

"Then don't their needs take precedence over other people's right to wealth, their property rights?" asked Billington.

"Not in a moral society," said Don. "Government has a duty to protect everyone's rights, rich and poor alike. Everyone has equal rights to his own life and property and is entitled to equal protection of the law. But that doesn't mean everyone will have an equally long and equally healthy life or equal amounts of property. Those depend on the individuals' abilities. *A right doesn't give a man ability; only life can do that.* A right simply allows a man to utilize his ability and recognizes and protects the cause-and-effect relationships that result, namely labor and property. When government takes from some and gives to others, it is violating some people's rights instead of protecting everyone's rights. Then the concept of 'equal protection of the law' is meaningless."

"But government redistribution of wealth is considered noble, a moral duty," said Billington, probing to elicit his visitor's views rather than speaking from his own convictions.

"It's a criminal violation of human rights masquerading under a phony name of morality," said Don. "It's a 'substitute morality' just like your 'substitute economics' and 'substitute science.' The world needs to learn that it's more moral to see wealth distributed according to reason, liberty and the natural order of cause-and-effect than to see it redistributed more 'equally' by politicians threatening people with guns in the name of doing 'good' for society. Government redistribution is not justified or made less immoral by the fact those politicians are elected democratically by voters, a great many of whom hope to benefit from the government's confiscation of wealth rather than be victimized by it.

"The Founders of this country believed in equal rights among citizens, not equal distribution of wealth. When rights are equal, wealth will always be unequal—because *life* is unequal: some people are more industrious, more talented, more frugal, or live longer and are thus able to accumulate greater wealth. Madison observed that 'the possession of different degrees and kinds of property immediately results' from 'the diversity in the faculties of men' and that 'the protection of these faculties is the first object of government.' He warned of the need to guard against 'the leveling spirit.' Jefferson said, 'To take from one, because it is thought that his industry and that of his fathers has acquired too much, in order to spare to others, who, or whose fathers have not exercised equal industry and skill, is to violate arbitrarily the first principle of association, the guarantee to everyone of the free exercise of his industry *and the fruits acquired by it.*' Alexander Hamilton said on the floor of the Constitutional Convention, 'Inequality will exist as long as liberty exists. It unavoidably results from that very liberty itself.' Rufus King, a delegate to the Constitutional Convention from Massachusetts, said that the spirit of equality was 'the arch enemy of moral man.' And James Wilson, another important delegate at the Convention, wrote, 'When we say, that all men are equal; we mean not to apply this equality to their virtues, their talents, their dispositions, *or their acquirements.* In all these respects, there is, and it is fit for the great purposes of society that there should be, great inequality among men.'"

"How can that be?" asked the senator, puzzled. "I agree with your idea that wealth belongs to those who earn it, because of the cause-and-effect principle, but how can 'great inequality' fit the 'great purposes of society'?"

"I'll give you an example," Don answered. "Remember a few years ago when Congress passed a ten percent tax on yachts, luxury airplanes, jewelry, furs and expensive cars? The idea was to 'soak the rich'—in order to redistribute this tax money for 'worthier' purposes—but the effect was to deprive the working class of jobs and wages."

"You're right about that one," admitted the senator. "I'd forgotten about that. In the first year after we passed that law a third of all yacht-building companies in the U.S. stopped production and 20,000 American boat builders lost their jobs. Congress' Joint Economic Committee estimated that in just the first six months that luxury tax cost $159.6 million in lost wages. A typical million-dollar yacht requires 12,000 hours of labor, not counting all the manufactured parts obtained from other domestic industries, which also provide employment. Eventually we learned that that tax was costing the government more to administer than we were collecting in taxes, to say nothing of the losses we were creating throughout the economy, so we repealed it."

"My point," said Don, "is that if there weren't any really rich people, there wouldn't be any demand for luxury boats, planes, furs, jewelry or expensive cars. If no one could afford these luxury items, there would be no jobs in those industries or the related parts suppliers by which working-class people could earn wages to buy the bare necessities for themselves. Inequality of wealth creates jobs and opportunities that wouldn't otherwise exist. Once again, when people are free to make their own selfish desires—even for extravagant luxuries—the *cause* of their actions in the marketplace, the *effect* is beneficial for others and for society. Act against the cause, and you deprive others of those beneficial effects.

"Besides, the idea of equality among men in any sense except their natural rights is a fantasy, an absurd idea that can never have any correlation to the real world. Consider for a moment what it would mean to try to achieve equality of wealth throughout society. Suppose all the land in the United States were confiscated from its present owners and redistributed equally to everyone, so that everyone would have an equal-sized plot. Would that be 'equality'? Of course not, because some land parcels would be more fertile than others. Some would be in the desert, where no crops could be grown at all. Some parcels, even in the desert, would have mineral deposits, making them far more valuable than the best farmland. And urban land would be more valuable than rural land. Land with access to major highways or ports would likewise be more valuable than similar properties without these advantages. How would it be possible to redistribute the nation's wealth 'equally'? How could everyone possibly have 'equal opportunity' in a world of such natural physical diversity?

"If you tried to equalize wealth by redistributing the land on the basis of parcels of equal worth rather than equal size, you'd run into additional problems. To achieve equality with those people who might each receive hundreds of acres of desert, others might be given only a few square feet—or maybe only a few square inches—of valuable downtown real estate in a major city. Such small parcels would be completely impractical. So their value would decline drastically. Would you then redistribute the nation's property all over again to achieve a new equality? And what would you do if property values change for other reasons? Suppose oil is discovered under some people's property. Would you again redistribute everybody's property to restore equality? Or what if the price of copper or zinc soars, making those mining properties more valuable? Or what if the prices of certain agricultural commodities drop, lowering the value of the land that produces those products? Or suppose some stretches of farmland don't get their normal rainfall and consequently produce a smaller crop, or perhaps no crop. Those kinds of fluctuations in weather are entirely natural. But would you then penalize other people by again confiscating their property in order to redistribute it again to restore equality? Would that be *justice*? And how would you maintain equality with a growing population? Would you periodically confiscate everyone's property and redistribute it according to the latest population figure? We constantly hear the phrase 'the earth belongs to us all,' but how in the world could it ever be distributed 'equally'?

"Suppose instead an attempt is made to equalize wealth another way. Suppose some people receive cash to compensate for the value differences in the land parcels that are distributed. It's hard to imagine how this could be done to everyone's satisfaction. Millions of people would be complaining that they weren't getting their 'fair share,' that others were getting more than they. Nevertheless, assume for the sake of argument that this redistribution could somehow miraculously be achieved with widespread satisfaction. What then? Wealth would immediately begin to be redistributed unequally by the people themselves.

Some people would buy land from others. Some people would let their land lie fallow while others would toil to produce a crop, perhaps investing in machinery and fertilizers and even hiring others to aid the process. Some would dissipate their assets on booze or frivolous expenditures while others would save, and still others would build factories or make other investments that would multiply their wealth. Should government then use its police powers again and again to force a more equal redistribution of wealth as its citizens freely and continually produce an unequal distribution of it? Why should anyone think such a policy would be a moral solution or a moral ideal?

"Not only is equal distribution of wealth a fantasy that can never be achieved, but it can only be pursued by government acting against the minds of its citizens and against their efforts to live. A government that acts against the honest labors of its citizens and their rightful pursuit of happiness is not moral but immoral. It's not the protector of the process of life but its enemy. It's not the protector of human rights but their principal violator—regardless of how popular or democratic its actions are. The truly moral distribution of wealth is based on the *absence* of force, not the intervention of force by government; it's whatever results from people freely exercising their natural rights however unequal the outcome may be. All government can properly do is offer all citizens equal protection of their rights, that is, equal protection from force. That's what 'equal protection of the law' means, or should mean.

"If our government really did offer 'equal protection of the law,' it should be protecting everyone's property equally. Clearly that's not the case when it takes some people's wealth and gives it to others.

"I'm not in favor of taxation of any sort because it represents money taken by the threat of force. But you could make an argument for taxing everyone either the same amount or at the same percentage and still claim to be adhering to the principle of equal protection of the law. There's no way, however, that government can tax its citizens at different rates and still claim that the law is treating them equally. If someone earns three times as much money as someone else but has to pay six or ten times as much in taxes, his property rights aren't receiving equal protection. We need a Constitutional Amendment that states: In recognition of the equality of human rights and every person's right to equal protection of the law, every tax levied by the federal government shall be either at the same flat rate or at the same percentage for everyone; nor shall the federal government levy any tax upon any business, enterprise, activity or product except at the same flat rate or same percentage as it taxes every other business, enterprise, activity or product.

"That amendment would also have the desirable secondary effect of countering democracy's tendency to elect those who, in Cicero's words, 'curry favor with the people by promising them other men's property.' There would be no point in seeking votes by promising benefits at other people's expense when everyone would know that every such benefit would be as much at his own expense as at anyone else's."

"Then is there no place in government even for charity?" said Billington. He asked such questions partly to explore Don's views—so that he'd know what kind of society to promise him could be achieved through the telephone virus—but also because he wanted his visitor to think of him as a moral man who was concerned about these issues, someone who'd make a good president. He continued: "Isn't charity a moral virtue? Shouldn't the government provide at least some minimal level of benefits in the name of charity?"

"No," answered Don. "Government isn't a charitable institution. Its purpose isn't to dispense charity but to protect peoples' rights. The Declaration of Independence says that 'to secure these rights, governments are instituted among men.' It doesn't say that governments are instituted to provide charity."

"But can't government do both?"

"Of course not," said Don. "They're mutually exclusive. A government can't be protecting people's wealth while at the same time giving it away to others. Furthermore, the term 'government charity' is a contradiction in terms. Charity is voluntary giving; tax money taken by the government under the threat of guns can't be called charity, regardless of how it's disbursed or how benevolently it's intended. If people want to give to charity, they're free to give *their own money* to any charity they wish; but no one—or no group, even a democratic majority—has a right to use the guns of government to take *other people's money* and give it to charitable causes or any other 'worthy' purpose. Americans have always been a generous people, ready to help with voluntary contributions those truly in need. Private philanthropy in the United States is twice as large as government welfare."

"But isn't that unselfish? If people voluntarily give to private charities, doesn't that contradict your idea about selfishness in economic transactions?" asked the senator with surprise.

"Not at all," replied Don. "The voluntary nature speaks for itself.

If someone voluntarily decides to donate to a charity, what he 'buys' for himself is the satisfaction of helping someone else who represents values that are important to him. The size of his donation is in exact proportion to the amount of this satisfaction he's willing to buy. That's something that only the individual can decide for himself, based on his own needs, his means, and all the other things he could do with his money. And the system is far more effective and efficient than government welfare with all it's examples of fraud and waste. We rarely hear about fraud and waste in private charities.

"Furthermore, there's nothing in the Constitution that empowers the federal government to distribute charity. Throughout most of our history this was widely recognized. For example, when Davy Crockett was a member of the House of Representatives, a bill came up to appropriate money for a widow of a naval officer. Crockett told the assembly, 'Congress has no power to appropriate this money as an act of charity. Every member upon this floor knows it. We have the right, as individuals, to give away as much of our own money as we please to charity; but as members of Congress we have no right so to appropriate a dollar of the public money.' The bill, which was expected to pass unanimously, then was easily defeated, receiving only a few votes. The members knew they had no Constitutional authority for such an appropriation.

"In 1854 President Franklin Pierce, while stating that people had a duty to help those 'subject to want and to disease of body or mind,' nevertheless vetoed a bill to help such victims because 'I cannot find any authority in the Constitution for making the Federal Government the great almoner of public charity throughout the United States.'

"And President Grover Cleveland in 1887 refused to approve a mere $10,000 appropriation for free seeds for farmers in drought-stricken counties of Texas because he said, 'I can find no warrant for such an appropriation in the Constitution, and I do not believe that the power and duty of General Government ought to be extended to the relief of individual suffering.' It's hard to believe that was said by a popular president, of the Democratic Party, no less, which then as now proclaimed itself the party of the 'common man.' Even more surprising today is the fact that after he wrote it, the 'common' men of his time elected him to a second term. How times have changed!

"You know very well, senator, that the Constitution must rigidly be observed or it is meaningless. For if the powers of the government can be stretched for even a small charitable cause, then Congress can appropriate tax money for any cause it believes—or professes to believe—is a suitable charity; and it can appropriate any amount. Obviously, as Davy Crockett recognized, the door is then wide open for 'fraud, corruption and favoritism, on the one hand, and for robbing the people on the other.' And if government can stretch its powers beyond the limits of the Constitution in regard to funding charities, then it can do so for any other purpose it likewise proclaims worthy, such as education, the environment, the arts, health care, scientific research or anything else. Even its own election campaigns. Then there will be a stampede through the wide-open door for 'fraud, corruption and favoritism' as government exercises unlimited power for robbing the people."

"I'm impressed by your argument," said Billington, "but how do you answer those who say that government handouts, at least for certain basic needs, aren't charity but 'entitlements' to which every member of society has a *right?* They say society has a duty to provide the basics for all its members, not just those who can afford them, and that a *humane* society can provide no less."

Don replied, "That's not an alternative theory of rights but the rejection of rights. No one can claim to have a right to deprive other men of their natural rights, including their right to property, in order to satisfy someone else's needs.

"It's the purpose of life to satisfy its own needs. Every living being fulfills those needs in order to survive. Property rights are the means by which men can provide for their material needs by interacting with each other peacefully, without the use of force. It's to people's advantage to live in society, rather than as isolated hermits, because they can benefit from the specialization of labor and the exchange of goods and labor. In any society such items are either exchanged peacefully according to men's minds and in accordance with their natural rights, or they are exchanged by government acting against men's rights by violence or the threat of violence just as criminals do. It's either respect for rights or it's violence. You tell me which is the more humane society.

"The material values man needs for his life aren't obtained without effort. They're not plucked effortlessly from the air. They're produced by *life,* and they're not produced equally by all members of society. Therefore, they shouldn't be distributed equally; they should be distributed according to the cause-and-effect principle of nature, for that's the principle by which they're produced. Indeed, it's the principle of life itself, the means through which life is able to act to sustain itself; no life of any kind could exist in a world without consistent cause-and-effect relationships determined by absolute laws of nature. To claim that some people are 'entitled' to material benefits at the expense of other people's property rights is to claim they are 'entitled' to other people's lives, for lives are the source of those material benefits.

"No one can logically claim he is 'entitled' to another person's property, labor, or the energy of that person's life except by the cause-and-effect principle. Take children, for example; they are the effect of which their parents are the cause. Children, therefore, have a right to have their parents provide them with food, clothing, shelter and sufficient nurturing and education to enable them to provide for their own needs when they grow up.

"Another familiar example is that of automobile accidents. If two vehicles collide, the party at fault in the accident is the one who pays. The innocent party's right to collect damages is based on the physical cause-and-effect principle. People are responsible for their actions, whether those actions produce wealth or liability.

"By the same token, people can't logically be held responsible for effects they don't cause. While parents are responsible for providing for their children, the children aren't responsible for providing for their parents; to make them so is to try to reverse reality: to make the effect responsible for the cause. In most cases, where parents have provided more than the minimum for their children, the children will reciprocate with generosity because they value their parents. But if they do so, it's a matter of choice since they're not responsible for their parents' mistakes, misfortunes and failure to provide for their own old age. It's clearly an injustice to make an entire generation of children responsible for providing for their parents and grandparents as Social Security does. The children will have enough problems of their own without burdening them with obligations for which they have no causal responsibility.

"In the case of an automobile accident, if the guilty party can't be found or otherwise defaults on paying for the damages, those costs don't then become the responsibility of others who had nothing to do with the accident. Here again, making innocent people pay for something they didn't cause would clearly be an injustice to them. It would be even more of an injustice—and an even more grotesque inversion of the principle of cause and effect—to claim that the person who caused the damage should be fed, clothed, housed and rehabilitated at the expense of the innocent throughout society. But that's the way the criminal justice system works in this country. Innocent citizens are required to pay to feed, house, clothe and rehabilitate those who are incarcerated for violating other persons or their property not by accident but by deliberate intent. Why should the violation of other people's rights 'entitle' criminals to claims on the lives of the innocent? Why should innocent people have their wealth confiscated by their own government to support criminals in a lifestyle better than many taxpayers enjoy? Honest citizens must work to support themselves, but prisoners eat well without having to work."

"What would you do with them?—let them starve?" asked the puzzled senator.

"I think they should be required to work to earn their keep," answered Don. "Men have always had to work to feed themselves. Captain John Smith stated a simple requirement in accordance with the reality of life on earth when he said at Jamestown nearly 400 years ago that he who does not work shall not eat. Today's laws shouldn't exempt prisoners from the simple natural requirement that they provide for their own sustenance, just as everyone else does. If inmates choose not to work in prison, then let them not eat. If that's their choice, why should anyone worry about them? Other people aren't responsible for the crimes that put them in prison and shouldn't have to pay so that those violators can enjoy the luxury of not having to work for a living."

"Worse than that," chimed in the opportunistic Billington, seeing an chance to bolster Don's argument and show himself in agreement with his visitor's views. "At the Arthur Kill Correctional Institutional on Staten Island, N.Y., inmates are periodically treated to weekend theme parties at taxpayer expense. Furthermore, in addition to their basic needs, prisoners throughout the country enjoy a great many amenities. Almost every prison has a complete law library, extensive recreation facilities including basketball courts, air-conditioned weight rooms, snack bars, hobby and television rooms. And with plenty of time on their hands and law libraries on the premises, many prisoners file lawsuits at taxpayer expense. Some individuals have each filed literally hundreds of lawsuits over the most trivial issues. One that comes to mind is the individual who sued because he said the prison served him chunky peanut butter when he claimed he has a 'Constitutional right' to eat only creamy peanut butter. It costs the inmates nothing to file all these lawsuits; the taxpayers pay the millions of dollars it costs to process these suits through the judicial system even if the judges deny the prisoners' claims. In 1966 there were only 218 such lawsuits, but in 1994 there were almost 50,000."

"If prisoners had to earn their food and shelter—and also work to pay restitution to the victims of their crimes," said Don, "they'd be so busy and so tired they wouldn't have time to file all those ridiculous lawsuits. And they'd probably experience more rehabilitation from simply being required to work than from all the more expensive alternatives we've tried in our penal system—which certainly haven't worked, if you look at the numbers for repeat offenders.

"Anyway, the taxpayers shouldn't have to pay for all those lawsuits filed by inmates. The inmates should pay for them, either from money acquired before their incarceration or from money earned in prison or donated for that purpose. If they can't afford them, too bad. The taxpayers can't afford them either and, more important, they have no cause-and-effect responsibility to pay for them."

"But what about the Sixth Amendment, in the Bill of Rights, which says that an accused shall enjoy the right 'to have the assistance of counsel for his defense'?" asked Billington.

"As I said earlier," answered Don, "a right doesn't give a man ability. It only allows him to use the ability he has. The right to free speech doesn't mean that everyone has a right to a printing press or a radio station at the expense of the taxpayers. It means, among other things, that you can't be prevented from disseminating your speech through such media *if you have the ability to do so.* Properly speaking, the right to counsel should mean only that you can't be prevented from employing counsel *if you have the ability to do so*—not that innocent people will be required under the threat of guns to provide you with counsel at their expense. Besides, the Sixth Amendment pertains only to prosecutions. It says nothing about providing counsel after the prosecution is completed and the accused found guilty. It also says nothing about providing free counsel for the thousands of lawsuits inmates file having nothing to do with the trial procedure but rather conditions in the prison, such as the peanut butter case you mentioned."

"Most of the inmate lawsuits focus on the Eighth Amendment's prohibition on 'cruel and unusual punishment,'" said Billington. "Thanks to the Supreme Court's loose interpretation of that phrase, most state and federal prisons aren't designed and managed for the maximum number of inmates. Instead, they're structured to avoid accusations of 'cruel and unusual punishment.' Prisoners aren't required to do much because the Court might construe almost any work requirement as a violation of that Constitutional phrase. And a half million convicted felons are currently out on the streets courtesy of early release programs in order to avoid 'overcrowding,' which the Court considers 'cruel and unusual punishment.' Current practice is to house one or two inmates in a cell. Adding one more inmate to each cell would keep another quarter million felons behind bars to serve their full sentences, but that's not going to happen given the Court's viewpoint. Instead the taxpayers are spending billions on new prisons while living with the additional risk of all those convicted felons being loose."

"That's ridiculous!" said Don in disgust. "Clearly the Founders didn't consider almost any kind of prison a 'cruel and unusual punishment.' In their time, treatment of prisoners was far more harsh and prison conditions far worse than they are today. Petty criminals then were commonly put in irons or stocks in the town square, and flogging was not unknown. Prisons were miserable: dank, dark and cold in winter, hot in summer, and without flush toilets. Air conditioning hadn't even been invented. Food was terrible, little more than bread and a weak soup or stew. Criminals ought to be required to make do with what is less than ideal, just as the rest of society has to. If that means three to a cell or five to a cell, that's *their* problem, one they've brought upon themselves. Why should life in jail be easy, comfortable and risk free when it's not for those toiling on the outside? If inmates want better or more spacious accommodations, then *they* should provide them, not the innocents in society. New prisons should be built with convict labor and, as much as possible, with materials purchased by convict earnings in other forms of work.

"Nor were the Founders concerned that hard labor was 'cruel and unusual punishment.' In a letter to Edmund Pendleton, Jefferson wrote that anyone found guilty of burglary or housebreaking shall be condemned to hard labor for three years in the public works, as well as make reparations to the injured person. The Founders believed that prison should be punishment. We've tried the opposite direction, making prisons as nice as possible, and that hasn't worked. It's time to return to the idea that prison should be punishment, not just a means to get offenders off the streets and prevent them from committing further crimes. I'm not talking here about putting people in prison for dumping dirt on their own property—that shouldn't even be a crime; there shouldn't even be such laws—I'm talking about felons who violate the rights of other individuals.

"Since the Supreme Court's coddling of criminals is counter to the original intent of the Constitution and the Founding Fathers, we need a Constitutional Amendment that states: convicted criminals, having forfeited their rights by violating the rights of others, have no right to either legal assistance or cost-free living in prison at public expense; they shall be deemed responsible in principle for these expenses themselves, though the Legislature or the states may provide supplementary money for living costs. It shall not be considered cruel or unusual punishment for inmates to be required to work for their sustenance. 'Hard labor,' such as was known at the time of the Constitution, shall not be considered cruel or unusual punishment. In no case shall any federal court have any authority to declare imprisonment cruel or unusual in any prison where living conditions are better than was common in prisons in the United States when the Bill of Rights, with its prohibition on 'cruel and unusual punishment,' became part of the Constitution. In accordance with the fact that the Constitution vests the power of taxation in Congress, in no case shall any federal court require greater expenditure of tax money for prisons than that provided by the elected representatives of the people. Congress, through its powers of investigation and oversight, shall ensure that the federal prison system is the best available and best administered that can reasonably be obtained with the funds provided. Then if a court finds 'overcrowding' or other inadequacies in accommodations in the prison system, the inmates—not the rest of society—shall work harder to correct these inadequacies, but no inmate shall be released from prison because of any such deficiency. In no case shall tax money intended by Congress for prisons be used for the purchase of any amenities not commonly found in the homes of the lowest ten percent of the taxpayers.

"That last sentence should put an end to the law libraries and exercise equipment at taxpayer expense. If individuals or private organizations wish to donate such items to prisons, they should be free to do so.

"Whether the intent is to improve the living standards of criminals or the needy or to reward the producers of ethanol, the whole idea that government should determine how wealth is distributed is counter to even the simplest understanding of human action and the formation of material values. Government redistribution isn't based on the cause-

and-effect principle but on the rejection of it. It's not in accord with human nature but against it. It's not based on reality but on a theory divorced from reality: collectivism. I happen to be in the computer business. Computers are possible only because men are able to understand cause-and-effect even at the microscopic level. Today's computer technology is the result of a long chain of knowledge that goes at least as far back as men first grasping the cause-and-effect process of chipping stones to make crude tools or weapons. Every link in that chain throughout the centuries has been a process of understanding and utilizing physical cause-and-effect more precisely, more extensively, more minutely. It has meant learning to differentiate the effects of varying actions with increased precision. It's incredibly crude—and today inexcusably primitive—to ignore the varying effects produced by different individuals in society and to adhere to the collectivist view that wealth is produced collectively and belongs to 'society.' And just as collectivism doesn't regard individuals as being responsible for wealth, neither does it regard them as responsible for wrongdoing: 'society' is responsible for everything; the individual is responsible for nothing. If you fail, it's society's fault. Society will take care of everybody and every shortcoming because all the resources—money, talent, labor—belong to 'society.'

"Under collectivism what you earn isn't yours as a matter of right; 'society' decides how much you are allowed to keep—how much is your 'fair share'—and how much is others' 'fair share.' Your 'fair share' is determined not by physical reality but by 'political realities,' not by the moral principle of natural rights based on cause and effect but by the amoral principle of other people's opinions, not by the reality of your own existence and labor but by the 'needs' and 'good intentions' of others—as determined by the government. Democracy simply assures that the government that decides which 'needs' and 'good intentions' take precedence over your life and your natural rights will be a popular one. Democracy in America represents the 'triumph' of the collective 'will of the people' over individual rights, the physical reality of cause and effect, and the U.S. Constitution. Our government respects no Constitutional limits on seizing people's wealth and distributing it any way it wishes.

"Democracy has been presented to the world as the opposite of fascism, socialism or communism. It isn't. Democracy is another form of collectivism, in which power is held by the people *collectively*. The opposite of collectivism is not democracy but *individualism*. It was the Founding Fathers' orientation to individualism that led them to reject democracy as a form of government in the United States. And it's the trend toward collectivism in this country for most of this century that has led increasingly to democracy—and to the violation of individual rights.

"Under individualism everybody is responsible for his own life and actions. Under collectivism nobody is responsible for himself, but everyone is responsible for everyone else. Collective guilt. Everyone is 'responsible' for the criminals, the poor, the disabled, the incompetent, the racism of *other* people—even in previous generations or previous centuries—the education of *other* people's children, the lack of food in *other* countries, like Somalia, the lack of democracy in *other* countries, like Haiti; the list is endless. Government taxes everyone to pay for all these things; it places these 'needs' and 'good intentions' ahead of the lives of the people who pay the taxes. It forces taxpayers to serve the needs of others instead of their own needs as their nature requires. Farmers are taxed to pay for crime in the cities, for urban housing and urban recreation programs; meanwhile, urban dwellers are taxed to pay for farm price support programs, low-cost loans to farmers, and subsidizing the production of ethanol to benefit farmers. Everyone is taxed for everyone else's problems, so that government can promise to relieve everyone of the responsibility for his own actions and solving his own problems. Everyone's life is then at the direction of the government.

"How will government direct the lives of people to solve all the problems of society? Under collectivism government tries to force everyone's hands and feet to move for the benefit of society rather than the individual. Everyone must be forced to place the 'public interest' above selfish private interests. Choice cannot be left up to you, because you might choose *naturally:* you might act for yourself instead of for the needs of others and the good intentions of those in government. Mandates and regulations replace choice in directing human actions. A police state replaces a free society. The populace is led unwittingly to accept the collectivist premise that 'the more complicated the forms assumed by civilization, the more restricted the freedom of the individual must become.' Those are the words of Mussolini.

"America's greatness was achieved not by restricting freedom but by millions of individuals exercising it in the pursuit of happiness. But now the pursuit of happiness has been replaced by pursuit of the 'common good.' The political program adopted in Munich in 1920 that called for *'The Common Good Before the Individual Good'* sounds very familiar today. It proclaimed that 'the activities of the individual must not be allowed to clash with the interests of the community, but must take place within its confines and be for the good of all.' Those words are from the program of the National Socialist Workers Party of Germany—better known as the NAZI party. The individualism that was the core of the American system has been replaced with collectivism, and the switch is not only unquestioned but unquestionable because it has been accomplished through *democracy.*

"Of course, our government today doesn't display the brutality of the governments of Mussolini or Hitler—though we do put people in jail for harmlessly dumping dirt without a permit. For the most part, our government relies on the *threat* of force rather than violent displays of it as the Nazis, Italian Fascists and Communist governments did for achieving 'national goals.' It makes us seem so much more civilized and masks the fact that our government has adopted the same collectivist approach and has actually imposed even more laws and regulations on its people than those totalitarian regimes. Those regimes weren't cranking out 200 pages of new regulations per day restricting and threatening their own citizens as ours does. We have, as you've pointed out, laws regulating practically everything we do or have, everything we buy or sell. Government controls everything from the frontiers of science and medicine to the simplest aspects of our daily lives. It has established 'tyranny over the minds of men' in a million ways—even to the *intellectual processes* themselves: it governs our children's education and the *reasons* we didn't hire someone, promote him, give him a contract or grant him a loan.

"All these restrictions on freedom are presumed to be for the 'common good,' the betterment of society. That's a preposterous presumption! First of all, the reduction of freedom in itself degrades rather than improves the quality of life in any society, irrespective of any differences in material living standards; just being free is a more desirable condition in which to live than not being free. Second, the most rudimentary examination of human history shows that there's a cause-and-effect relationship between the degree of freedom in a society and the improvement in material living standards. To assert otherwise is, once again, to ignore cause and effect in the real world in favor of an ideology divorced from reality. There isn't a single example in any country in any century to support the belief that reducing freedom improves the lives of the general population.

"Furthermore, the advocates of redistributing wealth for the good of society ignore the cause-and-effect sequences resulting from their own policies. Those policies create effects that are contrary to the nature of life and to the good of society. When government gives money to those who don't earn it, it encourages indolence and discourages industriousness; it promotes dependency and deters self reliance; it rewards profligacy and punishes thrift. When government bestows tax money on unmarried mothers, it encourages illegitimacy and increases the number of children in society who aren't properly cared for, a condition that promotes rising crime. When government gives tax money to those whose homes are destroyed by floods, forest fires, hurricanes or other disasters, it removes the natural penalties for improper action—building homes in such places in the first place—and penalizes those taxpayers who used good judgment by not building in those dangerous locations. Government acts to reverse reality: to reward what nature penalizes and to penalize what nature rewards. It treats all of society in the same manner that led to the collapse of the savings and loan industry, the largest financial disaster in the history of the world: it protects those who make bad investments by forcing everyone else—the innocent—to pay for the resulting losses. It subsidizes error at the expense of correct action. That certainly isn't in the best interests of society."

"I agree," said Billington, "that people shouldn't build in dangerous locations, such as the flood plains of rivers, but isn't it a good thing, then, to have zoning or other restrictions to prevent people from building in such areas? Then nobody would have to pay for the rebuilding of those homes."

"That's the kind of argument that always leads to more and more restrictions," said Don. "It claims that the problem is too much freedom and that all we need to do is reduce freedom—just like Mussolini said. That approach means more and more regulations that threaten people with fines and jail sentences. But freedom provides its own solution: all that's needed is to allow people to be responsible for their own actions, to stop protecting them from the natural consequences of their own choices. Reality will let them know if they've chosen incorrectly, just as it will if they choose a wrong answer to the problem of two plus two. There's no reason for government to be involved at all in either case.

And the freedom solution saves society the cost of writing all the laws, the salaries of the regulatory bureaucracy and the enforcement personnel, and the costs of all the fines and litigation and of holding people in jail for things that shouldn't even be crimes, like dumping dirt or erecting a building on their own property. It's not just that those costs are greater than those of the damage the regulations are supposed to prevent—though that's usually the case—but in *all* cases those costs divert financial resources from being spent for things of *greater* value. Society is poorer, not richer, for all such laws. When the regulatory costs are spread, everyone's share seems small. So most people do not realize that the total is greater than the cost of the alternative damage, whose effects are concentrated on a few. And people never see the benefits that don't come into being because they've been pre-empted by required government expenditures; the people never see all the ways society would be better off if the billions of dollars that are consumed by the regulatory apparatus had instead been spent for things of greater value.

"Earlier in our conversation, senator, in listing the ways in which government operates differently than the private sector, you said, 'We spend other people's money; they can spend only their own.' Everyone knows, of course, that no one spends money as carefully or as wisely as he spends his own money. When an individual buys something, in his mind it's not only of greater value than the money he spends for it but of greater value than anything else he could buy with that money. If not, he would obviously buy something else. But when government spends other people's money, it has no way of knowing that what it buys is of greater value than its cost—let alone the greatest value that could be purchased with that money. It has no way of knowing how the people would prefer to spend that money themselves. Government 'buys'—or forces the citizens to buy—all sorts of things that are uneconomic because it has no way of judging comparative worth. Because it's other people's money."

"A good example of that," said Billington, trying to demonstrate that he was sympathetic to Don's views and thought like he did, "is a case that came to my attention awhile back. A company had cleaned up a polluted site to such a degree that children could eat the dirt for 70 days a year without harmful effect. The government, however, said that wasn't good enough. It said the dirt had to be clean enough to eat for 270 days a year and forced the company to spend an additional $9.3 million to achieve that standard. Obviously, it wasn't in society's best interest to have $9.3 million spent for such an insignificant benefit. The site was in a swamp where it was virtually inaccessible to children. Nobody gained from the dirt being so super clean. There were certainly thousands of other ways that that money could have been spent with greater benefit to society—or to the environment. The EPA's stated position is that defendants can't avoid cleanup costs on the ground they are 'unnecessary' or 'unreasonable.' So of course you're going to see spending that's unnecessary and unreasonable rather than economic."

"That dirt-cleaning example is one I'm not familiar with," said Don, "but it's a good one, and I'm sure there are lots of others like it. I know of a case only a few blocks from my home in Minneapolis where $130,000 was spent to clean up a spill of a mere *five gallons* of gasoline. Once again, the cost exceeded any possible benefit. That was a loss for the individuals involved, but society lost as well. It was a lose-lose situation."

Noting Don's approval of his example, Billington expanded on that line of thought: "The public has no idea how EPA has wasted money. A study by the Institute for Civil Justice found that in the late 1980s EPA spent more than $7 in overhead for every dollar spent on cleanup of the environment. The Office of Technology and Assessment found that between 50 and 70 percent of EPA's Superfund spending was 'inefficient and undermines the environmental mission of the program.' And a 1993 study by Washington's Center for Resource Economics, an independent environmental research group, found that only 20 percent of EPA's budget went for the most serious problems. The remaining 80 percent was closely aligned with popular notions about the environment that weren't really very serious problems."

"In other words," said Don. "Most of the money was spent according to political demands."

"Exactly."

"Everything a free man does," Don continued, "is a matter of selecting greater values instead of lesser ones in the diverse world he faces every day. When government intervenes economically, it forces people to accept lesser values, a less efficient way of doing things—or nothing at all in return for their money or effort. Otherwise it wouldn't be necessary to use threats of fines or jail sentences. Just reading government regulations, filling out forms and filing required reports are economic losses for people. They can gain nothing from the time and labor thus spent. The most they can hope for is to avoid losses, that is, fines or jail sentences, and avoiding a loss isn't the same as making a profit. Neither individuals nor society can advance simply by avoiding losses. Thus, in addition to the losses government regulations force through uneconomic exchanges of goods and services, government causes additional economic losses in just the paperwork that requires those exchanges. Society becomes less productive and more wasteful of human labor as its members must spend more time reading regulations. That, of course, pre-empts people from using that time for things of greater value in the same way that the government's regulatory spending pre-empts people from using that money for things of greater value. Once again, the alternative benefits to society are never seen or calculated because they're never allowed to come into existence. And the government never considers how extravagantly it spends other people's time and labor, just like it never considers how extravagantly it spends their money. Because it *is* other people's."

"You're right," said Billington, going along with the argument, "that government doesn't consider the time and effort involved in reading regulations. Recently I learned that the mayor of Columbus, Ohio requested copies of the latest changes in federal regulations affecting municipal governments. The *Federal Register* publishes an index of such changes every six months. The mayor had requested the 524 rules listed in the latest index. He received just 207 of these—and they consisted of over 7,000 pages of rules and 9,500 pages of supporting documents! Keep in mind that these are just the *changes* for the last six months—and only 207 of them instead of the total 524. Yet every city and village in the country is supposed to read all these and figure out how to apply them. No municipality I know of has a staff adequate to keep abreast of all the required federal regulations. And don't even ask me what the Constitutional authority is for all those regulations, because we both know the Constitution gives the federal government no power at all to regulate local governments. That field should belong entirely to the states.

"Of course, there are even more federal regulations over private businesses and individuals than over municipalities. The federal regulations on just the disposal of cleaning rags make a stack more than six feet high. Between a thousand and two thousand business regulations change every month. How can private companies possibly keep up? They don't have the staff, and anyone can see it would be an uneconomic use of society's resources even if they did.

"There are hundreds of pages of regulations governing ladders. A ladder is one of the simplest devices you can think of. It has been used for centuries even by illiterates who had no trouble understanding it. Its operation is so self-evident that I don't know anyone who doesn't know how to use one. But the regulations include such gems of wisdom as the rule stating one must always face the ladder when walking up or down it—as though that would never occur to someone."

"That's certainly something that people ought to be able to figure out for themselves," said Don. "That's what people's minds are for, solving day-to-day problems, most of which are far more difficult than that. And if someone wants to walk up or down a ladder backwards, why should anyone want to prevent him from doing so? He'll learn more from the experience than from any regulation. Such regulations seem intended to make thinking unnecessary, to make the world safe for stupidity. But anyone who is too stupid to figure out something as simple as that ladder rule will almost certainly be unable to understand the regulations or even figure out how to get a copy of them. So the regulation benefits no one, but it costs something to produce. Government employees are paid for doing something of no value, which is worse than nothing; it's a drain on society. It's a drain to produce, it's a drain of people's time and effort to read, and it pre-empts them from devoting that time and effort to things of greater value. It's a lose-lose-lose situation.

"The collectivist premise is that government can allocate resources for the 'common good' or 'public interest' more wisely than the sum of individual choices of a free society. Just the opposite. Government can only make economic decisions *less* profitable for society; that's the effect that's caused by making them less profitable for individuals. For example, earlier you mentioned how federal mandates force states and municipalities to spend money for things that are of less value to them than other ways they could spend the money. You mentioned that all fifty states are required to spend money testing water supplies for a pesticide used only on pineapples in Hawaii. Clearly, there are other things, such as hiring more police officers, which would be of greater benefit to society. Well, the same thing happens with every government mandate on economic activity, whether it's consumer products or public education or anything else. Every government requirement forces people to spend money on something, meaning they must forego every possible better way of spending that money. Is every dollar that people are forced to spend on public education the very best way that dollar could be spent for education or anything else? Is every safety feature the public is forced to buy, every political campaign they are forced to finance, every pork barrel project they are forced to pay for, the greatest value they could receive for their money? It's true that, if given a choice, not everyone would spend his dollars more wisely than for these purposes—but government mandates guarantee that *nobody* will. So society is worse off.

"Given the diversity of human needs and circumstances, there's simply no way the government can know that a particular expenditure is the single best choice for everyone affected. Some people, for example, have greater needs than health insurance. Young people, for instance, may have less need for health insurance and may prefer instead to spend the money on a college education. Government directives simply aren't an adequate substitute for the individual's ability to choose in his unique circumstances what will best advance his own interests. Moreover, it's the *differences* in value that people place on various goods and services that make it possible for people to exchange them to mutual benefit. Everything can't possibly be of the same value to everyone; if that were the case, the economy would grind to a halt because there would be no purpose in any economic exchange. Yet government assumes values are uniform throughout society and believes society can be advanced by mandating uniform solutions. It spends a great deal of other people's money and deprives them of much of their freedom in its efforts to achieve a uniformity that would be self-defeating if attainable."

"Basically, I agree with you," said Billington. "But aren't there some good things that result from government mandates, which we wouldn't have otherwise? You may be right that not everyone has an equal need for health insurance, but how about food? Everyone has to eat. A few years ago we passed the Food Nutrition and Labeling Act, which requires that all food containers specify nutritional information. It cost the industry between two and four billion dollars. It's not the labels themselves that were so expensive but all the laboratory testing to determine percentage of fat, the amount of sodium, total calories, etc. that must be on the labels. That's something that wouldn't have been done if it wasn't required by law. Wasn't that a good thing?"

Don replied: "Nutrition labeling information isn't bad in itself, but is it worth the cost to the consumer? All values are comparative. The billions in added costs to industry were simply passed on to the consumers in the form of higher food prices. Would consumers rather pay more for every can of food they buy at the supermarket and get a label most never bother to read anyway—or would they rather spend the money some other way? Government has simply forced people to forego all the possible better things they could do with that money, including buying more food or better food. For poor people especially, wouldn't having more money available for food itself be of greater value than buying the new labels? If people could see in a super market two cans of food with identical contents but with one costing more and having a nutritional label, which one do you think most people would buy? Of course, government doesn't allow people that choice. By requiring *all* labels to have nutritional information, it doesn't allow consumers to see that the benefit government has given them isn't worth the cost and to realize that the money involved could've been spent for things of greater value. To see how little benefit the expensive labeling requirement has actually produced, just look at the results of surveys showing that it's had no significant effect on the diet of Americans. It turns out that such factors as taste, familiarity and convenience are far more important in the consumers' selection of foods than the nutritional information they're now forced to pay for on the labels. Government has simply forced people to spend billions of dollars on something which sounds good but which is of so little value to them that it's impact on their food-buying behavior is statistically insignificant.

"Every time an individual considers a transaction, he measures the benefit against the cost and acts for greater value. But the fact that government has no economic way of measuring whether the cost will be greater than the benefit all but guarantees that it will be. The government's measurement of the worth of its laws is not economic but political: whether it is likely to gain a greater number of votes than it will lose. So government passes more and more laws to gain votes by measures that are more and more uneconomic, which force people to 'buy' things that pre-empt them from buying other things of greater value to them. Society becomes poorer, not richer. It's more than a coincidence that as government has assumed more and more control over the economy and people's lives, the United States has gotten relatively poorer. The per capita income of the American worker has actually fallen in terms of constant dollars. Our standard of living, once the highest in the world, is being surpassed by a growing number of countries—eleven at the last count I saw. And our government went from the world's largest creditor to the largest debtor in history as it has had to borrow ever-larger amounts for its economic and social programs that represent a net loss to society.

"This country became the greatest on earth because of government protection of individual rights and individuals exercising those rights in their pursuit of happiness. If government could create an even better society by the collectivist policy of placing the 'common good' or 'public interest' ahead of individual rights, then that should have been apparent in recent decades. The United States should have gotten richer instead of plunging abysmally into debt; our social problems should have diminished rather than grown; our educational system should have gotten better instead of worse; and our productivity should have outpaced that of other countries instead of falling behind. In 1960 the United States produced 60 percent of the world's gross national product. Today it produces 20 percent.

"It's individual rights that are the basis for the betterment of society. No government can hope to benefit society by acting against those rights. But more important than the practical results—failures—of collectivist policies is the underlying assumption that makes collectivism possible. It's this: that the individual belongs to society rather than to himself, that a man's life is not his own but the property of the collective, to do with as it chooses. It follows, then, that he has no inherent rights, no *natural* rights, but only such 'rights' as are granted by the collective; in fact, he has no rights at all: he lives and labors only by *permission* of the collective, obtained through an elaborate system of permits and regulations for everything he does. This procedure is necessary to ensure that every individual serves the collective—the 'common good' or 'public interest'—ahead of his own life, usually defined as 'selfish private interests.'

"Earlier, senator, you mentioned Socrates. Most people know that he died by being forced to drink hemlock. Few people, however, know that he was given the opportunity to escape but chose not to. Friends in just the right places told him they could arrange his escape, but he refused because he believed his life belonged to the collective, to society, rather than to himself. He believed society had a right to act against his life in seeking the greater good of the community. When he was condemned—by democratic vote, no less—to drink the hemlock, he believed he had no right to evade that decision. He accepted the cup without complaint and drank.

"Of course, we still hold the vision of everyone in the United States having a right to his life. But that's a false image, a mask that disguises the reality that people no longer control their own lives. Ownership—true ownership—means control, but our lives are controlled by society, the collective. The fascist principle of private ownership under government control has been applied to life as well as to property. The Italian government under Mussolini preserved the fiction of private property by allowing ownership of industry to remain nominally in private hands while it exercised complete control. In that same way, our government preserves the fiction that people's lives are their own while it exercises virtually complete control over them, just as it does over their property. This is what the loss of freedom really means; it means your life is no longer really yours.

"What's the difference whether a man's life is owned by a slaveholder or by the mass of men under the name of 'society'? To the individual, it only matters whether he is free or not—not whether his master is one or many.

"We're often told that government must strike a balance between the rights of the individual and the 'rights' of the public or of society. But there are no 'public rights' or 'rights of society' except as individuals. Rights are the result of life, and neither society nor the public has any life except for its individuals. 'Society' is merely a term for classifying a certain number of individuals. A person neither gains nor loses rights depending on the number of other people, for his rights depend upon his own life, not theirs. That's why, as the Declaration of Independence states, a man's rights are 'unalienable.' They can't be voted away by democracy or repudiated by any government in the name of the 'public interest' or the greater good of society.

"If a man has an 'unalienable' right to his own life, then nobody is 'entitled' to anyone else's. Then there can be no 'entitlements' by other members of society to anyone's labor or property except as a consequence of his own actions. No group of people, however large—even all of society—can claim they're 'entitled' to someone else's earnings, for his life doesn't belong to them. The Declaration of Independence says everyone has an 'unalienable' right to life liberty and the pursuit of happiness. It doesn't say 'unalienable unless the environment is threatened' or..."

"That's not fair," interrupted Billington. "The environment wasn't an issue in those days. It has only become an issue because of the advances of science and technology, which couldn't have been foreseen 200 years ago."

"All right," said Don. "It doesn't say 'unalienable unless other people are starving, or orphaned, or homeless, or elderly and destitute, or disabled or their children need an education.' The Founders were very familiar with all such needs. There was more poverty and illiteracy then than there is now. Washington and Jefferson in particular were very outspoken about the need for education. Yet neither they nor the other Founders proposed that the federal government use tax money for any of these purposes. They believed that everyone had a basic, unalienable right to employ his labor and earnings for the pursuit of his own happiness rather than the needs of others. They believed that every man's life and property were his own and that the needs of strangers did not 'entitle' them to either. Moreover, they believed that everyone's needs were his own responsibility and could best be provided for through his own liberty and labor. The Founders weren't hardhearted or cruel. They were realistic men who were wise enough to know that government *by its very nature* was incapable of performing the functions we now demand of it. And they knew that government could attempt such functions only by destroying the liberty that they fought so hard for. They deliberately and severely limited the role of government *on principle* because they recognized that government itself is the greatest danger to the rights of man.

"By putting individual rights above all else, the Founders created a political structure from which undreamed-of benefits flowed *as a consequence:* the unprecedented production of wealth, the proliferation of labor-saving inventions, magnificent cities with the greatest skyscrapers in the world, the best-fed populace in history, the conquest of diseases and the dramatic extension of human life. For in a society where individual rights were paramount, people were free to choose the greatest values for themselves and the most efficient ways of doing things. They had the incentive to do so because they themselves would benefit. As a consequence, therefore, capital was channeled to the most productive uses. And human labor and ingenuity were voluntarily drawn to provide goods and services in proportion to other people's placing *greater* value on them than their cost. So society became richer.

"Richer in every respect. There was more food available for everyone, and it was cheaper. The same was true of other products. The 'common man' could own radios, television sets, refrigerators, even automobiles—luxuries beyond the grasp of the richest rulers of earlier times. Even the environment got better in the process. The greatest environmental destruction occurred not in the United States—where environmental conditions were actually improving—but in countries where individual rights weren't recognized, most notably the communist countries but also in some Third World countries. There one could see open sewers or no sewers at all, massive soil erosion from crude agricultural practices, and pollution from the kinds of primitive manufacturing operations we haven't seen since the 19th century. Those countries lacked the technology and the wealth to provide even basic sanitation, let alone clean industrial processes."

"You've made some good points, and I agree with them," said Billington. "But how do you answer the argument that there are some needs of society, such as public education, that have to be provided by government even if that means collectivism?"

"Education is no different than other goods and services in society," said Don. "It could be produced better, more efficiently and cheaper by private enterprise than by the present collectivist system. But the fundamental point is that forcing some people to pay for educating other people's children violates their rights. Anyone's right to his life is violated when he is forced to serve others' needs. It's not in his pursuit of happiness to pay for other children's education, nor are those children his responsibility. He didn't cause them to be born. Public education is a good example of trying to provide for human needs by violating individual rights rather than by means of individual rights. And look what the results have been. We have an educational system that is costly, corrupt, inefficient and failing in its basic mission. Our schools turn out functional illiterates at an ever-increasing rate, and the scholastic results of even our brightest students are in a long-term decline that shows no sign of stopping. And the ideological content of public education is disgustingly warped. Children don't get a real education any more. They get 'substitute education.'"

"But if it weren't for tax-supported education," Billington persisted, "some people couldn't afford to send their children to school. How could free enterprise possibly make education affordable for all?"

"Senator," said Don, "You could've asked the same question about food: 'If government doesn't provide food, if only private farms and private food processors provide food, some people wouldn't be able to afford it. How can free enterprise possibly make food affordable for all?' That kind of thinking led the Soviet Union to try to feed its people through collectivism, and the results are well known. With some of the best agricultural land in the world and cultivating three times the wheat acreage of the United States, it became the largest importer of food in history—most of it coming from private farms in the United States. The policy of putting people's need for food ahead of individual rights was a disaster for the Soviet Union. But people still use the same argument for putting people's need for education ahead of individual rights in the United States. The result: we have an educational disaster just like the Soviets had an agricultural disaster.

"The idea that government can be the answer to the problem of education just because democracy votes that way is ridiculous. It's just like what you said about the 'correct' answer to the problem of two plus two being three or eight or 26 million or whatever the people vote for. Reality won't let you get away with it. Individual rights *have to* come first. If they do, then an abundance of food, quality education and material goods, even an improved environment will follow *as a consequence.* But you can't reverse reality; you can't put these things ahead of individual rights and expect to achieve the effects that come from putting individual rights first. The effects of freedom won't be achieved by threatening people with fines and jail sentences to force them to surrender their earnings and prevent them from using their minds and their earnings for their own interests.

"If you had asked anyone early in this century how private enterprise in America could possibly provide the common man with such things as telephones and automobiles—or even such a basic item as shoes—he wouldn't have been able to tell you. Yet these things became so commonplace that today we take them for granted. They became abundant and affordable simply as the result of freedom. Freedom means the primacy of individual rights. At one point—before the federal government started limiting freedom by regulating manufacturing—the United States with about seven percent of the world's population had half of the world's telephones and two-thirds of its passenger automobiles. Governments elsewhere that produced these things turned out vastly inferior products and did a pitiful job of making them abundant and affordable. In recent years governments all over the world have been privatizing their phone companies and other government-owned industries. It's time to privatize education in America.

"The first step should be to get the federal government out of education entirely. The Constitutional amendment I suggested earlier about restricting the federal government to the powers enumerated in the

Constitution should accomplish that. Then the states would be free to experiment with privatization.

"When I send my kids to school, my only purpose will be to see that they get a good education. That's the intent of parents all over America. Surely our choices for schools would result in better education for our children than the decisions of judges in Washington for whom the education of our children is *secondary* to social policy. If parents all over America were free to select the schools for their children, the quality of education would improve, just as the quality of other goods and services improves through competition and consumer choice. Bad schools would have to improve, by adopting the methods of successful schools, or they would have no pupils; they would go out of business the way every other incompetent enterprise does in the marketplace, and better ones would take their place.

"At the core of the issue of education is the fundamental question: to whom do our children's lives belong? If their lives really belong to them, they should have a right to be educated for their own sake, to serve their own interests—not to be bussed in order to provide a better learning environment for *others* or to implement national social plans. But if their lives belong to the State, then it follows that the government can force them to serve *its* interests rather than their own; the educational system is merely a tool by which the government manipulates a national resource—children's lives—to serve national ends. The government, not the parents, will decide what children should be taught and by whom. All in the name of the greater good of society.

"The government attempts to manipulate all our lives the way it does those of our children, and for the same reason: our lives are not really our own. Government 'manages' them—through regulations—to serve *its* purposes. Our earnings do not belong to us but to 'society,' to be distributed by government as *it* sees fit for the collective good. Our property is not really 'ours'; we are mere caretakers for society, which collectively determines how we may use it in keeping with national goals.

"There have always been men who have dreamed of all the 'good' they could do if only other people's lives were theirs to command. Some achieved those dreams. Slave labor was used to build pyramids, palaces, temples and, in our own country, to pick cotton. Now the dreams of government leaders are not physical monuments or products but national social and economic programs, such as social security, affirmative action, public education, universal health care, and even environmental causes, such as saving spotted owls and other so-called endangered species. All these items have been placed ahead of the individual's right to his own life, and we are all forced to serve them…"

"But," interrupted the senator, "how could the spotted owls you just mentioned ever be preserved if it weren't for government policy to protect endangered species? How would you answer those who say that there is no other way to accomplish this worthy objective except by placing it above individual rights?"

"Suppose," said Don, "the question were: how could all that cotton in the South ever get picked if it weren't for government policy to protect slavery? How would you answer those who say there is no other way to accomplish the 'worthy objective' of getting the cotton picked except by placing it above individual rights? The issue is not which 'worthy objectives' should be placed ahead of individual rights. It is that *no* objective is worthy to be placed ahead of them, and no government has any legitimate authority to do so because people's lives are not its to command. That is the meaning of individuals having a right to their own lives and that right being 'unalienable.' If picking cotton or saving owls can't be accomplished *through* individual rights, instead of by violating them, then it shouldn't be done at all."

"I don't disagree with what you say," said Billington, "but your view is certainly opposite to that of the Supreme Court. The Court has stated that preserving endangered species is the 'highest of priorities' and should be pursued 'whatever the costs.'"

"That," said Don, "is a perfect example of how the Court has its priorities backward and why this country is so screwed up. If one 'good cause'—even a single species such as the spotted owl—can be placed above individual rights, there is no limit to the number of causes—or owls—that will receive such priority. In 1986 a National Audubon Society committee of owl experts said a minimum of 1500 breeding pairs of spotted owls was needed to preserve the species. Four years later the government said 2,320 pairs were needed. By 1993 the government said there were 3,500 breeding pairs *on public land alone* and at least 9,000 individual owls. But that still isn't enough for the federal government, which regularly prohibits timber harvesting on private property within 10,000 acres of owl nests. A government that believes its 'highest priority' is preserving other species will search for more and more specimens to which it can sacrifice individual rights. It will protect not only owls but 1,363 other species as well, and it will do so 'whatever the costs.'

"The Constitution says that no one may be forced to quarter soldiers on his property in time of peace without his consent. Current federal regulations, however, require landowners to quarter a variety of species without consent or compensation though the cost of doing so runs into millions of dollars for some individuals who are prevented from using their land for other purposes. The only reason I don't say we need a Constitutional amendment requiring payment of compensation for such a 'taking' of private property for public purpose is that the federal government has no legitimate authority here *period*. I would hope my amendment restricting the authority of the federal government to its enumerated powers would eliminate the role of the federal government in this area. Our government, as Jefferson said, was instituted to secure the rights of man, not to sacrifice them to animals."

"So spotted owls would just become extinct?" asked Billington.

"I'm more concerned about protecting individual rights from becoming extinct—and *that* should be the Supreme Court's 'highest priority.' But those owls could be saved *through* individual rights rather than by violating them."

"How could that be?" asked a puzzled Senator Billington. "I don't see how that could happen."

Don replied: "The fact that people can't foresee how something could happen in the free market doesn't mean it won't happen. Over the years the advocates of all sorts of causes have clamored for federal intervention because they couldn't see how their objectives could be achieved otherwise, but their shortsightedness shouldn't be the basis of national policy. A lot of good things happen in a free market that no one could foresee. If you had asked anyone early in this century how the system of individual rights could save millions of acres of wetlands for waterfowl habitat, he would have been unable to tell you—just like he would have been unable to tell you how such a system would produce an abundance of shoes, automobiles and all the other goods we enjoy. But a single private organization, Ducks Unlimited, has preserved more wetlands than the federal government. It has done so without putting a single person in jail for filling a wetland or failing to obtain a permit. And it has done so without government's power to obtain tax money by threatening people with fines or jail sentences in order to fund its endeavors. Owl habitat could be purchased in the same way. Furthermore, the wood duck, which was an endangered species early in this century, now thrives because of boxes built voluntarily for their nesting on private property. But there is no incentive to help the owls in a similar manner now because, thanks to the Endangered Species Act, attracting owls to one's property will result in a loss of property rights that can mean very substantial financial losses."

"Maybe what you say is true for ducks and owls, but do you mean to tell me that all species would be preserved through private property and individual rights?" asked the senator.

"Perhaps not," answered Don. "I don't know how people would use their rights. That would be up to them. They will act voluntarily to preserve species that are important to them. I doubt they would want to protect some species of insects. But let's keep things in perspective. There is probably nothing that can be done to preserve every species on earth. Ninety-nine percent of all the species that have ever existed are already extinct, and almost all of them vanished before the human race even came into existence. It makes no sense to talk about 'saving nature' by acting against man's nature—sacrificing his natural rights—to try to arrest a natural process that has been going on since life began on this planet. That policy is not in harmony with nature but against nature. Why should it be considered wrong for man to live according to his nature but right for every other organism to do so?

"The spotted owl—if it really were endangered—could be saved through voluntary measures just as was done in the case of ducks. That, of course, would mean the advocates would have to use *their own money*. The real attraction of employing the federal government in protecting species is the same as for the federal role in education, welfare or 'charity,' or any other government economic program: you get to use *other people's money*. Here is just one more way of doing 'good' by threatening people with guns in order to redistribute their wealth for 'higher' purposes.

"By using government to confiscate other people's earnings, voters can use the lives of others for 'higher' purposes the way ancient tyrants used slave labor to build pyramids, palaces and monuments. Democracy gives every man a chance to be a tyrant, to command the labor of others for his 'good' purposes if he can get enough votes. And today's politicians are the slave traders, who exchange other people's labor—in the form of their earnings—for votes. They have even sold our children and grandchildren into the bondage of debt.

"The slaves were freed in this country well over a century ago. They were told that henceforth their lives were their own and that they would no longer be forced to serve others. But now we are all being forced to serve others. Our lives and interests are made subservient not only to other people but even to owls. We're not forced to pick cotton, but we're forced nonetheless to labor for others' purposes when our earnings are taken from us. Feudal serfs were said to be unfree because one-third of their labor went to the feudal lord, who was the government. Now the average taxpayer labors about half the year for all levels of government. And, based on current trends, it has been calculated that children born in 1994 and later will pay 82 percent of their lifetime earnings to the government, because of all the 'good' purposes—'entitlements'—that democracy in our time has placed above their lives and decided that they should pay for.

"We're no longer free. We're slaves to those who take our earnings to build their dreams rather than allow us to build our own or allow our children the freedom to build theirs. Democracy forces us to serve others because they are *'entitled'* to our lives, our earnings; they're even *'entitled'* to the lives and earnings of the unborn because, after all, that's the judgment of democratically-elected government. That's 'truth' as determined by the democratic process. Thus has the doctrine of collectivism turned government—which should be the guarantor of individual rights—into the greatest violator of them through democracy. The American dream of freedom has been killed just like Socrates was, by ignorant men with the best of intentions pursuing the collective good of society at the expense of the individual.

"And the American people are expected to behave like Socrates. They don't have to drink the fatal cup all at once as he did, but they're expected to drink the poison of collectivism a spoonful at a time without complaint because that's what democracy demands. They're expected to swallow every government prescription for terminating not their lives but portions of their liberty or their property rights because these 'medicines,' though poisonous to the individual, are alleged to cure the illnesses of society."

"You put that rather well," complimented Billington, "but you didn't go far enough. The situation is much worse than you realize. The government is acting not only against people's liberty and their property rights, as you point out, but against their very lives. It's endangering their health as a matter of public policy. I can tell you all about this issue because I'm on the Senate Health Improvements Committee. The first step in the policy of sacrificing some people's health to newly-invented 'civil rights' of others was a 1987 Supreme Court decision that a teacher with tuberculosis was wrongfully fired.

"Now, under the Americans with Disabilities Act, discriminating against people with contagious diseases can be a federal crime. Employers must hire people with contagious diseases unless they can prove a 'high probability of substantial harm' to other workers or employees. The burden of proof is on the employer. The National Council of Chain Restaurants was told 'in no uncertain terms' that the government was going to use the restaurant industry to change public attitudes about AIDS. Of course, it's unlikely that any restaurant patron would acquire AIDS from a restaurant employee, but AIDS-infected people are very susceptible to contagious diseases such as tuberculosis. A Connecticut restaurant was sued by the government after it failed to rehire an AIDS-infected worker following a bout of double pneumonia. That the individual was 'sluggish and weak' and that 'his hands shook so much that he couldn't carry cocktail trays' did not prevent the government from charging the restaurant with 'discrimination.'

"Here in the District of Columbia federal judge Joyce Hens Green ruled that the fire department violated the civil rights of a firefighter infected with hepatitis B by specifically prohibiting him from mouth-to-mouth resuscitation. Hepatitis B is an infectious disease that attacks 300,000 people and results in 7,000 deaths every year in this country.

"An article in *The New York Times* noted that a hospital's decision to allow a UCLA surgeon with hepatitis B to continue to operate and to do so without any warning to his patients was 'in compliance with federal guidelines.' His disease was spread to 18 of his heart surgery patients in 1991-92, apparently through tiny holes in surgical gloves.

"A hospital in Westchester, New York, was penalized by the federal Department of Health and Human Services for preventing an HIV-positive pharmacist from preparing intravenous solutions. The hospital argued that pharmacists often stick themselves accidentally with needles and must break glass vials in preparing IV solutions. Thus it wasn't inconceivable that a patient could become infected through an IV solution. Nevertheless, the government ruled the pharmacist's 'civil rights' had been violated and ordered the hospital to pay him $330,000.

"At least 120 health care workers have become infected with AIDS/HIV from patients, and 200 more die every year from patient-transmitted hepatitis. Yet, thanks to the Disabilities Act, health care workers are now restricted in how they can protect themselves. The official publication of the American Dental Association, for example, has warned dentists that they could be charged with discrimination for using 'extra precautions' while treating AIDS patients."

"Senator," said Don, "I couldn't have made up more outrageous examples than you have just given of government denying people's right to their own lives and their pursuit of happiness. But forcing people to subject themselves to health risks that could kill them is the logical outcome of the doctrine that individual rights must be sacrificed to the collective. A government that can manipulate children's lives in the name of so-called 'civil rights' for others can force anyone to risk his health and even his life for the same purpose. Government shouldn't have such power."

"You keep mentioning the pursuit of happiness," said Billington, "but that phrase is from the Declaration of Independence. It's not part of the Constitution."

"I know," said Don, "but it should be. We hear a lot of lip service to the idea that everyone has a right to life, liberty and the pursuit of happiness, but your examples show how hollow those words have become. Because the federal government now acts to deny us those basic rights, it's time to incorporate those principles of the Declaration of Independence into the Constitution. We need a Constitutional amendment that states: Every freeman having an unalienable right to life, liberty and the pursuit of happiness, the government shall not violate his right to freedom of association in the pursuit of happiness or the well-being of his life. No person except those convicted of a crime or lawfully detained in the prosecution of a crime shall be required to make any association or transaction with any other person or persons if in his sole judgment such association or transaction would be counter to his life, his interests or his pursuit of happiness except as a consequence of his own actions in cases of contract or liability. Furthermore, recognizing that man's other rights cannot be implemented fully without the right to property, the federal government shall not restrict or deny any free citizen's right to use his property for his pursuit of happiness in any manner that does not infringe upon other persons' equal rights to their lives and properties; nor shall it tax property for the purpose of redistributing wealth to others, such redistribution being an inherent violation of the pursuit of happiness of those from whom the wealth is taken."

"Well, that last provision would certainly put an end to welfare," said Billington, "but I'm not surprised because a lot of people besides yourself are concerned about the pernicious effects of welfare on the recipients as well as on society in general, not to mention the enormous amounts of money it wastes. But what you've proposed would also end federally-imposed affirmative action."

"I intend that it should," Don replied. "Affirmative action is a form of racism; it's racism in reverse, and it's sheer hypocrisy for the government to practice racism itself, or require anyone to practice racism, in the name of correcting racism by others. Economic decisions shouldn't be made on the basis of race—either for or against—but the real issue is that people should be free to make decisions on the basis of their right to act for themselves, that is, for their own lives and their pursuit of happiness.

"To prohibit racism by the federal government, we need a Constitutional amendment that states: No branch or agency of the federal government shall use race, sex, color, age, ethnicity or national origin as a criterion for either discriminating against, or granting preferential treatment to, any individual or group in employment, public contracting or the receipt of public services, nor shall it require any state or its political subdivisions, any private corporation, organization or individual to do so or to collect or furnish to the federal government any data which could be used for that purpose.

"The government should be 'colorblind.' I would like to propose a similar amendment to prohibit states from imposing affirmative-action programs, but that's a matter for the states themselves, not the federal government."

"Actually," said Billington, "the Civil Rights Act of 1964 declared explicitly that no employer shall be required to grant preferential treatment on the basis of race, sex, ethnicity or national origin, but that's not the way it has worked out.

"However, your previous amendment proposal, your 'Declaration of Independence Amendment,' if I may call it that, the one that incorporates the right to the pursuit of happiness, would nullify Titles II and VII of the 1964 Civil Rights Act. Those are the sections that deal with discrimination in private employment and 'public accommodations,' such as privately-owned restaurants and hotels. I gather from what you just said that you also intend that effect."

"I do. I'm unalterably opposed to racial discrimination," said Don, "but no one has a right to dictate the private decisions of anyone's life—not if people really have a right to their own lives. If a law conflicts with a person's right to the pursuit of happiness, then the law must go. No one has a right to any association or transaction with another individual without that person's freely-given consent. It's like the issue of rape I mentioned earlier. No one has a right to satisfy his needs by means of another person against that person's will. Every association or transaction must be by mutual consent. Otherwise you've got the situation where some people are forced to serve others—just like some people being forced to pick cotton for others or build pyramids. *No man can be said to be free who is forced to serve another. No man truly has a right to his own life if he is not free to act for himself, to pursue his own happiness."*

"And what do you say," asked Billington, "to those who claim that after two hundred years we need to adapt to the times? They say the complexities of modern civilization demand a new and expanded role for government not limited by archaic Constitutional provisions and that necessitates less freedom for the individual."

"That sounds like the Mussolini statement I quoted earlier," replied Don, "that 'the more complicated the forms assumed by civilization, the more restricted the freedom of the individual must become.' But it's important to know why that idea is as incorrect now as it was in Mussolini's time or will be at any time in man's future. The Declaration of Independence is timeless. The rights of man that it speaks of apply to all men everywhere, at any time. They are *universal principles.*"

"Just like two plus two equaling four?" asked Billington.

"That's right. Human rights don't change because human nature doesn't change, not any more than the answer to two plus two changes. Earlier I explained how man's mind functions even today in the same basic manner as in primitive times. Man's rights do not vary as society becomes more complicated, because they depend upon himself, on the fact of his own existence and the nature of his own being.

"The Constitution was beneficial to human life and lasted as long as it did because it was consonant with the universal principles of the Declaration of Independence. When Constitutional principles were no longer observed—when 'good' purposes could be placed above the 'archaic' language and intent of the Constitution—then 'good' purposes of the Supreme Court and democratically-elected officials could be placed above man's natural rights, which the Declaration of Independence said were the reason for our government. Thus government undermined the reason for its very existence."

"I guess it shouldn't be surprising," said Billington, "that a government that could ignore the Constitution's enumeration of powers, its prohibition on retroactive laws, and the true meaning of its 'commerce clause' would also ignore the precedents of previous Supreme Court decisions and the Constitution's amendment procedure in its haste to achieve the 'good' purpose of 'civil rights.' There were people who opposed the Civil Rights Act of 1964 on Constitutional grounds, but they were shouted down with charges of being 'obstructionists,' or 'racists,' or worse epithets.

"One of those was Senator Barry Goldwater. He certainly was no racist; he had voted for civil rights bills in 1957 and 1960 and had repeatedly introduced amendments to labor bills to end racial discrimination in unions. Nevertheless, he was denounced as a 'racist' by many for saying that he could find no Constitutional authority for Titles II and VII of the 1964 bill. He said that instead of doing something unconstitutional, the government should first obtain a Constitutional amendment giving it the required power. In this he was perfectly correct. For, as you pointed out regarding charities, once an exception is made to strict adherence to the Constitution, the door is wide open for unlimited abuse. In 1883 the Supreme Court with a single dissenting vote struck down an 1875 Civil Rights Act with 'public accommodations' provisions that were virtually the same as those in the 1964 act. The Court said it was beyond the power of Congress to enact 'law regulative of all private rights between man and man in society.' Members of Congress, sworn to uphold the Constitution, should not have enacted a law in 1964 that was beyond their Constitutional power as defined by the Supreme Court and the Constitution itself. And Goldwater warned that the unconstitutional provisions of that law would 'require for their effective execution the creation of a police state.'

"Another person with a similar view was the distinguished lawyer John Creighton Satterfield, who had been president of the American Bar Association. Because of his thoughtful Constitutional objections to the 1964 Civil Rights Act, he was subjected to a *slanderous* attack by Attorney General Robert Kennedy. Satterfield warned that 'government by intimidation' was beginning, that its first step was 'public castigation, threats of financial reprisals against public bodies and individuals, and the misuse of the power of the federal executive branch to command the attention of the public press.' He said the next step would include 'federal control over individuals, businesses and state and local governments far beyond that provided in the Constitution.' Finally, he said, that the vast financial power of the federal government and threats of the imposition of federal fines and imprisonment would be used to strangle every business and professional establishment and every individual who disagreed with the wishes of government.

"His predictions now seem prophetic, but few in Congress at that time were concerned about the eventual consequences. Few were aware, like Senator Goldwater, that the legislation produced in response to cries of 'Freedom!' would actually take away freedom in the coming years and move us toward a police state. It should have been obvious that the 1964 act was taking away a basic civil right, the right to freedom of association; but most politicians didn't want to be seen as voting against 'civil rights' any more than they wanted to be seen as voting against 'clean air' or 'clean water.'

"Nor did the Supreme Court want to vote against the 1964 Civil Rights Act. It was willing to stretch the meaning of the Constitution to accommodate what it regarded as a 'good' purpose. It provided the *image* of Constitutionality by upholding that 1964 act on the grounds of Congress' power to regulate interstate commerce.

"I think part of the problem was that people couldn't foresee how racial barriers could be overcome without federal intervention, just like they couldn't see how wetlands or spotted owls could be preserved any other way."

"The biggest problem, of course," said Don, "was government itself: various governments in the South had imposed racial discrimination as a matter of law, through the infamous Jim Crow laws. Remember that the drive for civil rights started in response to discrimination in municipal bus service in Birmingham, Alabama. Blacks had every right to object to such discrimination because every level of government, from the smallest municipality to the federal government, should treat every citizen equally. That's why we need the amendment I suggested to prohibit racial favoritism by the federal government. The government belongs to all its citizens, and its purpose is to serve its citizens. People's lives, however, belong to themselves, and their purpose is to serve themselves. People's lives don't belong to them *collectively* but *individually,* each man having a right to his own life. And it's each man's purpose to act for himself—his very existence requires it—and to pursue his own happiness. There's no such thing as 'collective happiness.' There's no 'public happiness' or 'national happiness.' Happiness is an individual phenomenon; it can be experienced only inside the brain of an individual.

"Life itself is an individual phenomenon. So are rights. There are no 'collective rights.' There are no group rights. No one can acquire rights by being a member of a group that he doesn't already possess as an individual. There are no rights of blacks or whites or employees or employers or disabled people; there are only *individual rights,* which are the same for all people. When government attempts to grant additional rights to special groups—in order to achieve 'equality'—it can only do so by depriving others of their natural rights. Every attempt to grant special rights to those who are disadvantaged or disabled is an attempt to make *life* 'equal' by making *rights unequal.* It therefore defeats the promise of equal rights, the only equality to which everyone is entitled and which government is supposed to protect."

"What about 'equal opportunity'?" asked Billington.

"That's another case where the Supreme Court invented something and 'interpreted' it into the Constitution," said Don. "As you probably know, the word 'opportunity' doesn't even appear in the Constitution. Clearly the Founders had no intention of trying to create equal opportunity, and with good reason. It's no more possible to equalize opportunity than it is to equalize wealth. The physical diversity of the earth, which I described earlier, makes the concept of equal opportunity completely unrealistic. To this natural diversity of the planet, the natural diversity of human ability and enterprise adds further disparity. Hamilton pointed out that inequality will exist as long as liberty exists and, in fact, results from liberty. The Founders clearly preferred liberty to equality or 'equal opportunity,' but the Supreme Court has decided just the reverse. It sacrifices our liberty in the pursuit of equality of opportunity—which is a cover for the redistribution of wealth and for making rights *unequal.*"

"But how do you answer those who say racial discrimination would never end without government intervention?" asked Billington.

Don replied: "When there are no Jim Crow laws requiring racial discrimination, the free market works to eliminate race and other irrational criteria from economic decisions. The profit motive makes racial discrimination uneconomic. For example, there was not a single black basketball player in the National Basketball Association before 1950, but professional basketball was desegregated voluntarily by the owners because doing so was in their self-interest. The economic incentive to hire the many talented black basketball players was too great to pass up. Similarly, the official baseball rule book once stated that baseball was 'a game for caucasian gentlemen,' but organized baseball was desegregated well before the arrival of civil rights legislation. The integration of professional sports came about because of people exercising their freedom of association and acting for what they perceived as their own interests. That's just the opposite of what the civil rights legislation attempted: denying people freedom of association and forcing them to act against what they perceive to be their own interests. Once again government has tried to reverse the natural order of things."

"But what if some people still wanted to discriminate in the marketplace and were willing to pay the economic price?" asked Billington.

"That's their right," answered Don. "No one should be deprived of his rights because certain other people don't like how he exercises them. No one should be deprived of his right to free speech or religion because certain other people don't like how he exercises those rights. The same should be true of freedom of association. If other people can dictate how you will use your 'rights,' then you don't have any rights. In a free society everyone has to accept the fact that others may not always use their rights the way you or I or anyone else would like them to. That's their right, even if they make a mistake. If a man wants to have sex with a woman and she turns him down, she may be making a mistake—but that's her right. It's her life. It doesn't matter why she 'discriminated' against him. She has every right to for any reason she wishes. It doesn't matter that the man has suffered a 'loss' by her refusal, because he had no right to what he might gain from her life or anyone else's. That's the way it is if rights mean anything. I can't claim I have a right to make my employees work for me against their wishes because I have no claims on their lives, nor they on mine. My needs aren't superior to their rights, nor are their needs superior to my rights.

"In a free society people would have a right to make their pursuit of happiness the standard for all their decisions in the exercise of their rights. The individual, not the government, would be the sole judge of that standard, and there would be no appeal beyond the voluntary consent of other people's minds. There would be none of the litigation we now see concerning the basis of one's choices, litigation that has stretched out for twenty years or more in some cases. There would be none of the 'tyranny over the minds of men' that we have by the federal government overseeing all our economic decisions and threatening us with fines or jail sentences to enforce that tyranny. There would be none of the endless record keeping and reporting requirements that the government demands in order to determine whether we have acted as *it* wants us to for what *it* regards as the collective good of society, the 'public interest.' The individual doesn't need all that record keeping to decide how to pursue his happiness, and he shouldn't have to waste his time documenting his life for the government so that it can establish tyranny over him. He has a right to make all economic choices without *any* government interference because it's *his* life."

"But," asked the senator, "what about those who aren't able to make correct choices?"

"Their lives are still their own," replied Don. "They're not yours to decide how they should live." As he spoke, Don thought about his mother, Helen, and about how living to her meant directing her own affairs, even into her old age with its reduction of abilities. He thought about how depriving her of the personal choices in her life would diminish that life.

"But," insisted the senator, "What about the people who lack ability? Don't we have to enact laws to protect them from their own bad decisions, *just as a precaution?"*

Don answered, "Jefferson said: 'The legitimate powers of government extend to such acts only as are injurious to others.' It's not the purpose of government to protect people from actions injurious to themselves. When you try to protect people from their own bad decisions, you're 'protecting' them from life itself. You're depriving them of the right to live by their own minds. You're depriving them of their right to the pursuit of happiness. You're condemning them to a less than human existence on the grounds that they're incompetent to live a truly human one. Again, you arrogate to yourselves the decision as to how other people should live—as though their lives were your property to dispose of as you see fit. You treat the citizens of this country as though they're all hopelessly senile or as children who can never be regarded as grown up enough to make decisions for themselves and be responsible for them. Government regulations have become like a life-support system that keeps people alive in a vegetative state while denying them a truly human existence *just as a precaution.* Every law either prohibits action or requires it. In either case it deprives people of their natural choices, which are the essence of human existence.

"Sure, there are risks in making choices, in using one's mind. Life is not without risks. Freedom is not for the timid. It's for those who want to really live.

"We need a Constitutional amendment stating: The purpose of government is to protect the individual from violation of his rights by others; therefore, government shall make no law to protect the individual from himself, such law being itself a violation of the individual's rights to life, liberty and the pursuit of happiness."

"I agree that government regulation has gone too far," said Billington, "but don't we need *some* regulation, some consumer protection laws, for example? How would people know which products to buy, which were safe?"

Don replied: "It's ridiculous that you politicians should argue that people are incapable of making the correct choice about products they buy, even the smallest items they may put into their mouths—from pills to balloons—and yet argue that these same people have the wisdom to select a president to rule the entire nation, complex as that job is. People who are too stupid to govern the simplest of their own affairs are somehow smart enough to decide who should govern the country? Democracy seems to be predicated on the absurd idea that if enough stupid opinions can be aggregated, then wisdom will result—and the more stupid and uninformed voters who can be encouraged to participate, the wiser will be the result. How ridiculous! If you aggregate stupidity, you will arrive at stupidity, not wisdom.

"Furthermore, how did safe and continually better products come on the market before there were any consumer protection laws? Those kinds of laws are relatively new in our history. People bought balloons and marbles—not to mention food—for a very long time in this country without federal regulation of those items.

"And just how effective is government regulation of foods anyway? In spite of the billions of dollars we spend for government food inspection, the Centers for Disease Control said in its letter to me that there are 6.5 million cases of food-borne illnesses resulting in 9,000 deaths every year in the United States.

"Remember in 1993 when the Jack-in-the-Box fast food chain was found to have served hamburgers with dangerous bacteria that killed four children and made hundreds more sick? There were cries that government should've prevented this disaster and that we need 'greater regulation.' But the restaurants were in compliance with all regulations. The fact is that the U.S. government, far from protecting the public, *prevented* them from being protected by a technology that would have made the hamburgers completely safe. Irradiation of food kills all bacteria, has been approved by the World Health Organization and other international health agencies, and is used in 37 countries with no adverse effects whatever, yet it was illegal to use on those hamburgers in the U.S. Irradiated foods have been used in France, Israel and Japan for over thirty years, and NASA has supplied them to our astronauts for over twenty years."

"How do you know so much about radiation?" asked the senator with surprise.

"I used to work for a company that made scientific instruments, including instruments for radiation detection," answered Don. "So I know quite a bit about the technology.

"While government has 'protected' the public from obtaining truly safe meat, its highly-touted inspection system has failed dismally. In 1994 the CBS program *48 Hours* showed that four federal meat inspectors in a single meat-processing plant in South Dakota failed to prevent unsanitary practices. CBS staff members bought 30 packages of 'U.S. Inspected' ground beef in various cities across the nation and found 10 contaminated with harmful bacteria. They also bought 30 government-inspected chickens and found 25 were contaminated with either salmonella or listeria, two harmful bacteria. Even the U.S. Department of Agriculture, the agency responsible for meat and poultry inspection, has estimated that 35 percent of the chickens sold with the 'U.S. Inspected' stamp are contaminated with salmonella. Statistically, you're more likely to get sick from U.S. government-inspected chickens than from fish and seafood, which do not receive USDA inspection. Government inspection doesn't protect the consumers; it provides only the *image* of protection— 'substitute protection'—because bacteria can't be seen by the inspectors. Instead of protecting the public, government inspection has led buyers to be less cautious than they otherwise would be, made it unnecessary for industry to demonstrate to the public the cleanliness of their products, and prevented the industry from employing safer technologies.

"And how did aspirin come into widespread use many years before the U.S. Food and Drug Administration even existed? It came into use gradually as people decided it was in their interests to try it because it was being used successfully by more and more people. They didn't have to wait for—or need—FDA approval.

"And how about the first vaccines? They came into use not because of government approval but because people considered them less risky than the likelihood of contracting the disease. As always, people weighed the risks and benefits and made a choice about what they selfishly thought was best for their own lives. Nature—not government—determined whether their choices were correct. There was no need for laws or regulations threatening people with fines or jail sentences. The fact that the trend toward longer and healthier lives began before the government began to regulate foods and medicines proves the efficacy of free choice."

"Yes," said the senator, "but the regulations requiring FDA approval have prevented many unsafe drugs from coming on the market."

"True, but they also delayed or prevented many safe drugs from coming on the market," said Don. "The benefits have been more than outweighed by the losses. It often takes several years to obtain FDA approval of a new drug, and countless deaths result from these delays. It has been estimated that more lives have been lost by delays in FDA approval of drugs than in all the wars this country has fought in since the Civil War."

"Hmm. I never thought about it from that perspective," mused the senator. "But it doesn't matter anyway. Politicians do what the people want, what the majority believes is good for them. That's what the political system demands."

"But it *does* matter," insisted Don. "Majority votes and political popularity can't alter the physical realities that determine whether people live or die. It *does* matter that laws you pass in the name of saving lives are instead killing people."

"Well," said the senator. "You mentioned aspirin. Don't you think it's a good thing the government requires child-proof safety caps for aspirin bottles? Hasn't that prevented at least some accidental child-poisoning deaths from aspirin?"

"No," said Don. "There has actually been an *increase* in such deaths since the safety-cap requirement, according to a study by Kip Viscusi of Duke University. Apparently those caps are so frustrating to adults that many simply leave the caps off. Either that or they feel so protected by the government regulation that they don't exercise the same caution in the storage and handling of those bottles that they otherwise would. Or perhaps they transfer the medicine to other, improperly labeled bottles because the original ones are too hard to open. Whatever the reason, accidental child-poisoning deaths from aspirin have increased since the government required child-proof safely bottles. The point is that there's no alternative to free choice as a mechanism for human advancement. That's the nature of reality."

"Well, what about auto safety laws?" asked Billington. "Didn't we need them to prevent auto companies from selling unsafe cars to the public? Haven't those regulations been a good thing? Haven't they saved lives?"

"Actually, no," said Don, to the senator's surprise. "The number of traffic accidents dropped steadily decade after decade since records were first kept—until the advent of federal safety regulations. The decade of the 1960s, when those regulations were introduced, became the first decade in history in which traffic accidents—measured either in terms of passenger miles or the number of registered vehicles—*failed* to decrease. All that was needed for product improvement in automobiles, as with everything else, was for people to be allowed to make decisions for themselves in the marketplace. Government regulation has been *less* effective in achieving automobile safety. Furthermore, the federal government's fuel efficiency standards have made cars lighter and inherently less safe, resulting in 3,900 additional traffic fatalities over a ten year period and 11,000 to 19,500 additional serious injuries."

"I don't know the statistics about auto accidents," said the senator, "but how about industrial accidents? Don't we need regulations to protect people in the workplace?"

"Of course not," replied Don. "Like auto accidents, the number of industrial accidents dropped steadily from the time records were first kept, in 1912, until the advent of federal regulation. The Occupational Safety and Health Act of 1971 brought an *increase* in workplace accidents. Better and safer ways of working, just like better and safer products, are *consequences* of freedom in the marketplace. They are *effects* of which individuals acting for their own self-interests are the *cause*. Freedom is more successful in achieving safety as an effect than are laws that try to *cause* safety by reducing freedom. The *effect* of such laws is more accidents. A study in 1992 by the U.S. Labor Department showed that while industrial accidents have increased in this country, they have plummeted in Japan—a country that does not have intrusive and punitive workplace regulations as we do. The overall injury and illness rate for workers in the U.S. was seven times that of workers in Japan, and for manufacturing the rate was eleven times higher."

"Where the hell are all your facts and statistics coming from?" asked the senator, somewhat peeved.

"From Edmund Contoski's book *Makers and Takers*," said Don. "You can check them out for yourself."

"I'll take your word for it," said the senator. "The actual results don't matter anyway as long as people approve of the method. Look at public education. If people were really concerned about results, don't you think they'd have done away with public schools a long time ago? It's not the results but the *method* that the majority of people approve of. So they stick with the system in spite of its failing results. Any talk of 'reform' is simply a matter of tinkering with the system, not throwing it out. The method that the public won't abandon is that of obtaining something through government's power to threaten people with guns. As I told you before, that's the power that people believe in and vote for. They don't believe in freedom any more in the sense that they don't think it can give them what they want. Or, at the very least, they think it's easier to obtain it by pointing a gun at others."

"But you're the same way, senator," said Don "when you talk of needing the federal government for auto safety laws, industrial safety and meat inspection. Don't you believe that freedom can accomplish these things?"

Billington felt himself in an uncomfortable position. He wanted Don to think that they shared common political views in order to make it credible that the senator would use the telephone virus to achieve Don's objectives. Of course, Billington had no intention of doing so. Although everything he had said was true, he had simply been feeding Don what he thought his visitor wanted to hear, in order to gain his cooperation. Once he became president, the senator had no intention of cutting back the role of the federal government and reducing his own power. Far from it. For him the greatest attraction of becoming president was the power to indulge in favoritism and manipulate people on a even grander scale than was possible from his position in the Senate. But now he had allowed himself to be carried away by the drift of the conversation and to display a view of the federal government's role different from Don's. So, as an adroit politician, he simply reversed his position: "Well, you've brought up some interesting facts and statistics that I was unaware of. And in view of what you've just said, I think you're absolutely right that the federal government should have no role in such things as meat inspection or auto safety any more than it should in education or the other subjects we already agree on.

"Please understand, Mr. Emerson, that in the course of our conversation it has sometimes been necessary for me to play the devil's advocate to get you to tell me about your views, so that I could be sure they're in agreement with my own. I hope some of my questions haven't misled you into thinking my views are different from yours. These last issues that you raised are the only ones on which we've had any difference of opinion; and now that you've enlightened me on them, I'm happy to see that we're in agreement on everything. I must say that you certainly surprised me with some of the Constitutional amendments you proposed, but I fully agree with all of them." That was an outright lie, but like most successful politicians, Billington was adept at sounding sincere even when he wasn't.

He smiled as he spoke, but he was becoming increasingly annoyed with his visitor. Initially, he had been pleasantly surprised by Don's knowledge of history and enjoyed the intellectual character of the conversation. But as Don kept coming up with more and more Constitutional amendments, the senator's attitude changed. He had thought this Emerson fellow would probably be satisfied with an amendment to balance the budget, perhaps another on term limits. These were the sorts of things everyone was talking about, and they would probably come to pass even without help from the telephone virus. But the senator would then claim he had brought them about, had fulfilled his end of the bargain, and Don would have to continue to keep his mouth shut as his part of the bargain. Now, however, with all the novel amendments Don was coming up with, there would be a problem getting him to continue keeping his mouth shut unless the senator actually delivered on passage of those amendments, which he certainly had no intention of doing.

"Do you have any other interesting amendments to propose?" asked Billington as he pondered the new problem these amendments were causing him.

"Yes," said Don, "but first tell me a little more about Congressional salaries and the retirement program that you said was the most generous in the world."

"Well, the last time we voted to raise our salaries, in 1989, we got a lot of heat from the public and the media. They were incensed that at a time when federal spending was ballooning out of control we would vote ourselves a whopping raise from $89,500 to $125,000 a year. Knowing it would be a long time before we could vote ourselves another raise, we put an automatic escalator clause in the same bill with that raise. Consequently, we now get an automatic pay raise every year until the end of time without the political embarrassment of ever again having to vote ourselves more money. That provision pushed our salaries to $133,600 by 1993.

"In 1989 the old Congressional salary of $89,500 was about five times U.S. per capita personal income. Today our salary is about six and one-half times that amount. In 1989 we already were receiving a larger income than 90 percent of American families—not individuals but *families*—and by 1993 our income was larger than 95 percent of American families. Thus we've been getting richer and richer than the people we represent, and we'll continue to do so indefinitely."

"So while the government talks piously about the need to narrow the gap between the rich and the poor," said Don, "and while it redistributes *other* people's wealth in pursuit of such 'equality,' Congress hypocritically makes itself richer and richer than the rest of the American people."

"Certainly. I already told you we're an elite," said Billington. "But salaries aren't the whole story. In fact, they're not even the biggest part of it. The biggest part is the retirement benefits. When Tom Foley, former Speaker of the House, left office after being defeated in the 1994 election, he started drawing a pension of about $124,000 per year. When Bob Dole resigned from the Senate in 1996 to run for the presidency, his pension started at around $126,00. And those pensions will keep on increasing for the rest of those gentlemen's lives. Pension benefits in the private sector typically amount to 25 percent or less of a worker's salary, and 99 percent of business pensions aren't adjusted annually for inflation. But Congressional pensions are adjusted so lavishly for cost-of-living increases every year that retirees frequently receive annual benefits greater than their salaries when they were in office. J. Caleb Boggs from Delaware retired in 1973 after two terms in the Senate and three in the House. Seventeen years later he was drawing an annual pension more than double his last salary as an elected official. Frank Karsten from St. Louis, who spent 22 year in the House, was drawing a Congressional pension in 1990 that was 276 percent of his last House salary. For George Smathers, the retired senator from Florida, his annual pension in 1995 was 260 percent of his last Senate salary.

"Of the 100 senators in office in 1994, nearly three-fourths—72 to be exact—stood to collect pension benefits of one million dollars or more. For long-time office holders such as Bob Dole or Tom Foley, their pension benefits could total two to three million dollars each. Of the 435 member of the House, 231 were future 'pension millionaires'..."

"Let's see," Don interrupted, "Congress creates budget deficits that the Federal Reserve has to 'monetize.' As you explained earlier, that causes inflation, because it increases the money supply. But Congress protects itself—in fact, *more* than protects itself—against the effects of the inflation it has caused. Meanwhile, private citizens lose steadily because they have no such protection. Private pensions and salaries aren't constantly boosted to stay ahead of inflation the way Congressional pensions are."

"Right," said Billington.

"So because Congress has protected its members' incomes against inflation, it has no incentive to balance the budget and maintain a stable dollar, which everyone else depends on for the value of their savings, pensions and life insurance," said Don.

"You catch on quickly," said Billington.

"In fact," Don continued, "Congress even has an incentive for deficit spending because its members will become even wealthier in comparison to the rest of the populace, who are not so fortunate as to be automatically protected against the inflation Congress causes."

"Right," said Billington. "And the protection that Congress has built in for itself, as well as for other federal workers, will be at the expense of future generations."

"Just like Social Security."

"Right again," said Billington. "Congressional pensions are part of the $65 billion-a-year federal retirement system, which like Social Security, is creating a huge unfunded liability for coming generations. The cost-of-living adjustments for Social Security, military and civil service retirement programs exceed the private sector wage index. To put it bluntly, government retirement benefits are growing faster than workers' wages.

"The case of former Massachusetts Congressman Hastings Keith illustrates just how unfair the generosity of Congressional pensions is to future generations. By 1994 he had already received $1.2 million in federal pension income and, according to actuarial tables, he could expect to live another eight years. If he does, he'll collect another million dollars. Yet he paid less than $50,000 toward his federal pension.

"Mr. Keith's case points out something else, 'double dipping.' He can count years of military service for both his civil service pension, that is, his Congressional pension, and for his military pension. To his credit, he has been actively lobbying—without much success—to reduce cost-of-living adjustments for federal pensioners such as himself out of a sense of fairness to future generations.

"While Congressional pensions come under civil service, they're far higher than those of most other federal workers. This is because lawmakers get a high 'accrual rate.' That's the number that's multiplied by years of service to determine pension size. Congressmen get the same high accrual rate as those performing hazardous duty, such as firefighters and law-enforcement officers. Congress changed its accrual rate in 1984, but today its members still get an advantage of 55 to 70 percent over other federal workers for the first 20 years of service."

"Congress certainly takes care of its own," said Don.

"In more ways than you realize," said the senator. "Congress has even guaranteed the pensions of its convicted felons. In 1979 Frank Clark, a former Pennsylvania Congressman, was sentenced to two years in prison for mail fraud and income tax evasion. In 1990 he was collecting a pension equal to 151 percent of his old Congressional salary. John Dowdy, a Democratic Congressman from Texas, went to prison in 1974 for perjury and bribery. In 1990 he was collecting 157 percent of his last salary as an elected official. Arch Moore, a former Republican Congressman who was also a three-term governor of West Virginia, was sentenced in 1990 to five years in prison for tax fraud, mail fraud, extortion, and obstruction of justice. He continued to receive his Congressional pension while in prison. He didn't get his state pension of more than $20,000 annually as an ex-governor because West Virginia, like a few other states, terminates pension benefits for public officials convicted of crimes. More recently, former Congressman Dan Rostenkowski was sentenced in 1996 to seventeen months in prison, but he continued to receive federal pension checks totaling over $96,000 annually, even while incarcerated. As of 1996 more than $10 million in federal pension money in the previous 25 years had gone to former members of Congress while in prison."

"I didn't realize things were that bad," said Don. "We've heard a lot of talk about limiting the number of terms a congressman could serve, but that won't solve the problem. It's typical, however, that those who believe all problems can be solved by somehow limiting the choices of the people favor that idea. What we need isn't to limit people's choices of whom they can vote for but to limit Congress' choices of how it can put our money in its own members' pockets. We need to remove the incentive for elected officials to gain at our expense. We need to take away Congress' ability to inflate its salaries and pensions to escape the effects of inflation, which it causes. Congress should have an economic incentive to maintain a stable dollar and avoid inflation, from which it benefits while the rest of the country suffers. Congress should have no automatic raises in salary, nor should it have any cost-of-living adjustments in its pensions. If it maintained a balanced budget and a stable dollar, there would be no need for cost-of-living adjustments. If Congress is going to engage in irresponsible spending that reduces the purchasing power of the dollar—as it has been doing for decades—then it should feel that pinch in its own salaries and pensions.

"As the system is now, there's great incentive for members of Congress to pass laws that redistribute our wealth to others in return for the votes that will give them financial security for the rest of their lives. There's the same incentive to bargain away our freedom for votes. All that ought to be stopped.

"Obviously, in view of its past performance Congress itself can no longer be trusted to set its own salaries. We need a Constitutional amendment that gives the state legislatures the power to set salaries of the U.S. Congress, and those salaries would be paid out of the state budgets, not out of the federal treasury. In effect, this arrangement would be like an unfunded mandate in reverse. Instead of the Congress specifying all sorts of things that the states and the people must spend unlimited amounts of money on, the states and the people will be specifying to Congress: this is *all* we are going to spend on *you!*

"There are at least three advantages to be gained from paying U.S. Congressional salaries from state budgets. First, of course, it'll eliminate the abuses we've experienced when Congress sets its own salaries.

"Second, it'll aid in redressing the balance of power between the states and the federal government. When the states can exercise some measure of control over the federal government, Congress will no longer be able to totally ignore the states and thrust all sorts of programs down their throats—and the throats of the people—as it does now. The states could once again become more equal partners in the federal relationship and could help to protect their people against the tyranny of the federal government.

"Third, the states don't have the power to make future generations pay for their extravagance the way the federal government does because they don't have the power of inflation and unlimited deficits. The

Constitution prohibits any state from making anything but gold or silver legal tender, as we discussed earlier."

Billington was only half listening. He was preoccupied with the problem of how to make sure Emerson would keep his mouth shut. Maybe, he thought, Malcolm Steiner was right after all. Maybe the "Markowitz solution" really was the answer. Billington wasn't against murder as a matter of principle. He didn't have any principles. He was against murder for the very practical reason that he was afraid of getting caught. But if Steiner's hit men had enough time, if they had a few months to go out to Minneapolis and plan everything as carefully as they did with Markowitz…

"This Constitutional amendment," continued Don, "should say that each state legislature as part of its budget shall set the salaries of the representatives from its state to the U.S. Senate and U.S. House of Representatives until the state's next budget. In the event a state fails to set these salaries, the salaries for its members of the U.S. Senate and U.S. House of Representatives shall be the same as for corresponding members of its state legislature. Each state shall provide for travel allowances and other expenses for its U.S. Congressmen as it deems appropriate."

Billington was barely listening, but he was alert enough to catch the gist of what Don was saying and to ask: "So Congress would have as many different salaries as there are states?"

He would have to be sure, he thought, that Steiner's men would have enough time and that Emerson could be kept quiet meanwhile. Still, how could he be sure they would do as perfect a job on Emerson as they did on Markowitz?…

"Not necessarily," answered Don, "though there would be nothing wrong with that and, in fact, several advantages. Not every doctor, lawyer, plumber or laborer of any kind earns the same amount as every other though they may perform identical services. Nor are living costs or the prices of commodities uniform throughout the country. Nor are the people of every state as wealthy as those of every other and as able to pay the costs of government and its programs. Different salaries for members of Congress from the different states would be a useful and constant reminder of the diversity of the people they represent and the fact that uniform solutions out of Washington for every problem don't fit reality and can't possibly meet everyone's needs.

"However, if Congress wanted its members to all have the same salary, it could redistribute their earnings to achieve that equality. It would be interesting to see how those in Congress would react to redistributing their own money instead of everyone else's. The amendment would state that to equalize the salaries in each house would require a two-thirds vote—the same proportion as required for a Constitutional amendment—in that house. Each house of Congress would vote on this matter at the beginning of each Congress. That is, no Congress could bind future Congresses by its vote."

Billington knew he would have to find some way to be sure the 'Markowitz solution' would be successful. It would have to be what every criminal dreams of, the perfect crime.

"As for pensions," Don went on, "I read recently that the premier of the Canadian province of Alberta has abolished all pensions for members of parliament. That's not a bad idea. But if the states wished they could give members of the U.S. Congress the same pensions as they give state legislators or other state employees; however, no member of Congress should ever have a cost-of-living adjustment in his government pension, for the reason I gave earlier. An alternative idea would be to give each U.S. Congressman the cash equivalent of the amount of money that would be invested every year in his state's pension plan and let him invest the money himself in a private annuity or retirement fund. That would make members of Congress responsible for themselves, which is as it should be, and also give them a stake in the private sector and its economic health. They would no longer be completely isolated and insulated from the real world by government pensions.

"Of course, there would be no provision for equalizing pensions of members of the U.S. Congress. The absence of such a provision would be a deliberate and permanent reminder that they're representatives of the people of their states, who pay their salary, and those states aren't all economically equal. Members of state legislatures don't receive the same salaries and pensions as their counterparts in others states. The new amendment would simply extend this principle to the U.S. Congress, whose members would henceforth be state employees.

"Obviously, members of Congress wouldn't receive such lavish pensions from the states as are currently dispensed by the federal government. That's as it should be. Then they won't have the incentive, as they currently do, to vote away other people's property and freedom in return for their own lifetime financial security. In many other countries members of the legislature do not even rely on government salaries to support themselves *while in office,* let alone for the rest of their lives. In Switzerland, for example, the legislators *all* have careers elsewhere; being in the legislature is only a part-time job."

"But if that were the case in this country," said Billington, "we wouldn't have enough time to do our jobs as legislators. Even now we're so overloaded with work that we often pass legislation without even reading it. I know of only one member of Congress who even claimed to have read all the 1300-plus pages of the president's 1993 health care bill, and that was a bill that would have affected one-seventh of the nation's economy. And there are plenty of cases of legislation being passed that *none* of us has actually read. I know this happens because I know of cases when no draft of a bill has been available in time for any of us to read it before we had to vote on it. On those occasions, bills were cobbled together at the last minute by staff members of committees and subcommittees."

"It's absolutely outrageous," exclaimed Don, "that you people should be passing laws that spend the taxpayers' money, take away their freedom and threaten them with fines and jail sentences without even reading the laws that you are passing! If that's the way you operate, then Congress doesn't even deserve full-time salaries, let alone lifetime pensions. I would say there should be a requirement that every member of Congress read every word of every bill that he votes for if I could think of a way to enforce that requirement. Instead, Congress should simply reduce its workload and leave more issues to the states or to the people. Clearly you are dealing with too many laws. That's why we need the amendment I suggested earlier to limit the role of the federal government to the powers enumerated in the Constitution. Your workload must be cut back—and eliminating your lifetime financial security for being a legislator will give you people an incentive to make the necessary cutbacks and find other employment—in the *real* world—for your financial survival. Besides, it would be extremely beneficial to the country if members of Congress had to support themselves at least in part in the business world where your regulations make it so difficult for everyone else to function."

"You wouldn't propose to cut back the pensions of those currently in office, would you?" asked Billington. He really didn't care what Don's answer to that question would be, for he had no intention of seeing such an amendment carried out. He asked the question simply because he thought it would indicate an authentic concern from someone in his position and thus give the illusion of sincerity on his part.

"I guess in fairness to what those in office have already been promised," replied Don, "an exception would have to be made for pension benefits they've already accumulated."

"I'm glad you made that exception," said Billington, smiling. "Otherwise I couldn't have supported your amendment." He would have supported anything Don would have said, just to get his cooperation, but Billington knew his last comment would make his support seem more genuine.

"You mentioned the need to reduce the workload of Congress," the senator continued. "The idea of 'block grants' to the states has attracted a lot of attention. Under this concept the federal government gives financial grants to the states for certain purposes but allows the states the flexibility to run the programs and determine how the money is actually spent. Allowing the states to handle the details certainly reduces the federal workload. What do you think of that idea?"

"Block grants are a terrible idea for three reasons," said Don. "First, the concept concedes to the federal government a role where it has no Constitutional authority. It endorses federal supervision of the states in areas that should be the prerogative of the states, where the federal government should have no role at all. In doing so, it makes the states responsible to the federal government instead of to their people—which is a horrible development. The voters of the states—not the federal government—should judge the performance of state governments. Instead of federal block grants for purposes not covered by the enumeration of powers in the Constitution, the states should be left to handle such issues entirely on their own. My earlier proposed amendment to limit the federal government to those enumerated powers would accomplish that.

"Second, even without federal supervision, giving federal money to the states would decrease accountability to the voters. If the states instead had to raise the money through their own taxes, they would be held accountable by the voters and would be less likely to be irresponsible in their spending.

"Third, block grants will lead to overspending because the true costs of programs will be hidden through inflation and cost-shifting to future generations. Because the states don't have the power of unlimited deficits or of creating paper money as the federal government does, the states have a built-in discipline to keep spending in line with tax revenues. That's one more reason the states should pay for their own programs through state taxes, not block grants from the federal government."

While Don had been talking, the senator was puzzling over how he could be sure that Emerson could be disposed of safely. Then the idea hit him. It was so obvious he wondered why he hadn't thought of it earlier: the telephone virus. If it could be used to make people vote for him, or to make members of Congress vote for Constitutional amendments, why couldn't it be used to control how a jury would vote? That would be a last resort, of course, because it could first be used to control any police investigation of the deaths of Emerson, his wife, and that guy from the phone company. It could be used to lead investigators in false directions, perhaps cause them to destroy evidence, or to close the investigation before anything meaningful could be uncovered.

"Back on the subject of pensions," said Don, "we need to do something about the rest of the federal pension system. What I've already suggested would take care of congressional pensions, and I'm not worried about military pensions though I do think that military service shouldn't count toward *both* military and civilian pensions. What needs to be corrected is the federal civil service pension system. It shouldn't be a means for redistributing wealth from future generations to today's federal employees. That's completely immoral. Since only the federal government has such immoral power, it shouldn't be administering the civil service pension system. The system should be privatized. That's the only way I can see to be sure that employees' pensions will be based on their own contributions rather than on robbing the unborn. A private insurance company would have no incentive to pay recipients more than the fair investment value resulting from their own contributions, and it wouldn't have the legal ability to steal from others and redistribute their money. It would be illegal for any insurance company to operate a pension fund as the federal government does. And turning such a service over to the private sector is not without precedent. Michigan, for example, has announced it is getting out of the insurance business and has privatized its workers' compensation fund."

How, wondered Billington, could he be sure the telephone virus would work as he intended? Even if he were elected president, how could he be sure that that was due to the virus and not just to his own popularity, the powerful political machine he had developed, and the immense campaign financing he knew he could command?

"There would almost certainly be a considerable gain in efficiency, too, by having the pension system administered by a private insurance company," said Don.

Just then it occurred to the senator that he could test the effectiveness of the telephone virus—once Steiner had perfected it—by trying it out on a few unimportant bills in the Senate. He always knew well beforehand how every senator intended to vote. So it would be easy to tell if anyone's vote was changed by the telephone virus. He could make as many of these tests as he wished in order to be *sure* the virus would work before Emerson and the others were bumped off. All that was needed was to buy enough time to allow Steiner to complete his work and to test it in the Senate. He would agree to anything this Emerson fellow proposed just to buy the necessary time.

There was a momentary lapse in the conversation after Don's last sentence. The senator broke the silence by asking, "Is there anything else?"

"No."

"You mean this is it?" asked the senator sarcastically. "Just these few things? You can't think of anything else?"

"No. That's it."

"All right, then. Here's the deal," said Billington, rubbing his hands together. "You agree to cooperate with us, and once I'm president I'll use the telephone virus to get every single one of your proposed Constitutional amendments approved by both houses of Congress and ratified by the states."

"No deal," said Don without hesitation.

"What?!" exclaimed Billington in disbelief as he jumped to his feet and threw his hands in the air in exasperation. "I'm offering you everything you want. What more could you ask for? If you weren't going to go along with me, why have you been stringing me along for the last couple of hours?"

"I wasn't stringing you along, Senator. You asked me what was needed to get this country back on the right track. So I told you. I never said I'd go along with using the telephone virus for that purpose."

"No, I guess you didn't," said the senator. "But do you mean to tell me you're just going to let the country continue to go to pot when you've got a chance to do something about it? You know how bad things are. Don't you think you've got a responsibility to your country to do what you can to correct the situation?"

"Did I *cause* the mess this country is in?" asked Don.

"No."

"Then I'm not responsible for it, am I?" replied Don. "A man is responsible only for his own actions. I'm not responsible for effects that have been caused by others."

"Don't give me that cause-and-effect crap again," said Billington.

"It's not crap," said Don. "It happens to be the way the world works."

"All right. It's not crap. I shouldn't have said that. But we have a chance to save the country. The country *needs* you."

"Other people's needs aren't a claim on my life. I'm not responsible for other people's needs that aren't consequences of my own actions," said Don.

"But who is going to save the country, if you're not willing to do your part?" asked Billington.

"Millions of people are responsible for the mess in this country. Millions are going to have to save it—and save themselves. They can't expect me to be their savior. There have already been too many 'saviors' trying to do what other people should be doing for themselves," said Don.

"Look," said the senator with dismay, "Don't you think you're carrying this individual responsibility stuff too far? It's a beautiful idea. You did a beautiful job of explaining your philosophy, all that stuff about causality and responsibility, but we have to be realistic."

"I am being realistic. That's what philosophy is, a way of understanding reality so that we can deal with it appropriately," said Don.

Billington was exasperated. He sat down again and tried to compose himself. He sank back in his chair. But he rocked forward again almost immediately to make another effort. He sat upright, placed his forearms on the desk and said, "Look. Maybe it's my fault. Maybe I didn't impress upon you sufficiently just how critical the situation has become in this country. Did you watch the television hearings for Judge Clarence Thomas' nomination to the Supreme Court?"

"I caught some of it, but I didn't watch the whole thing."

"Well, did you see that part where Senator Joe Biden was badgering and browbeating Judge Thomas and asked, 'Are you now, or have you ever been, a member of this cult that believes in the sanctity of individual rights? Do you believe that natural rights should underlay the Constitution and our legal system?'"

"No, I didn't see that part, and I'm shocked by what you're saying about it."

"Well, you can judge for yourself what kind of future individual rights have in this country when members of the Senate—who were supposed to be guardians of individual rights—have that kind of attitude.

"Here's something else to consider. If you think we have too many government regulations now and too much government infringement of property rights, wait till you see what happens if we have a real economic emergency. The laws are *already on the books* to turn this country into a *total* police state. The International Economic Emergency Powers Act, for example, authorizes the administration: to issue any instruction or require licenses for any activity; to require anyone to keep and furnish records; and to 'investigate, regulate, prohibit, direct, compel, nullify, void, prevent, or prohibit any transaction, acquisition, holding, use, transfer, withdrawal, transportation, importation or exportation, dealing, or exercising any right, power, or privilege with respect to any property.' And if that's not enough, there are hundreds of other sweeping emergency controls embodied in current laws, agency powers, and executive orders. Sooner or later the ever-growing mountain of national debt, which is a consequence of our budget deficits, will precipitate an economic crisis that will become the excuse for exercising all those standby powers. The last vestiges of freedom will be exterminated, and it will all have been done through perfectly legal means by democratically-elected government.

"Now, I'm not asking you to participate in what Dr. Steiner and I are doing. We'll take all the risk and assume all the responsibility for that. We'll do all the actual work. All we're asking you to do is *just keep quiet*. That's not asking too much, is it?—when it's a matter of saving the country?"

"It is when what you're doing is immoral. My silence would be condoning it."

"C'mon, now. We've got to be practical..."

"Like most people," said Don, "you seem to think the moral and the practical are opposites. They're not if one's morality is based on reality. In that case the moral *is* the practical. The only 'practical' way to save this country is by moral means."

"Don't play word games with me. I agree that it would be ideal if we could do everything in a perfectly proper, idealistic, completely Constitutional, totally moral manner. The fact is that *this is the only way to achieve our goal...*"

"But," interrupted Don, "that's the same argument that's used for government intervention to save wetlands or spotted owls or regulate the sizes of peaches and nectarines."

"Oh, for Chrissake! We're not talking about swamps or owls or peaches. We're talking about saving the country!"

"The same principle applies. That's the thing about *universal principles*. They apply to everything."

"Do you have to have such a rigid adherence to principle? Can't you make an exception for a moral cause? Saving the country is a *good purpose*."

"Wetlands, owls, peaches, affirmative action, the education of other people's children, caring for 'crack' cocaine babies, feeding starving orphans, cleaning up the environment, they're all 'good' purposes," said Don. "The appeal of 'good' purposes makes it easy to succumb to the idea of using any means available in order to achieve them. I admit that I myself have been tempted in this regard." He was thinking about how he was tempted to apply for a government research grant for studying the telephone virus.

"Every violation of Constitutional principles," he continued, "whether by judges or Congress or the president, has always been for a 'good' purpose. No one undertakes to violate the Constitution for a bad purpose. Yet every exception to Constitutional principles has led inevitably to greater evil than the good it was supposed to achieve. That's what happens when people put the expediency of achieving a 'good' purpose ahead of principle in obtaining it."

"But there simply is no other way to save this country," insisted Billington. "Think about your children. What kind of life will they have in this country if Dr. Steiner and I don't succeed with our reform? Are your principles more important than your children? Won't you make an exception to your principles for the sake of your children? Think about your children, Emerson. Think about your children."

"I am thinking about them," said Don. "I don't like to think of them being yoked together with their contemporaries like beasts of burden pulling a $5 trillion debt down the highway of life—the load of other people's 'good' purposes. I'd like to think of them growing up in a country where they would be free to fulfill their own dreams, where they could pursue their own happiness instead of being shackled to pull the collective load of everyone else's shortcomings, failures, mistakes, inabilities, 'needs' and 'inequalities.' It used to be said that this was a country where people could rise as high as their abilities would take them. We never hear that any more. That was the America where individual rights—man's natural rights—were paramount, where people were free to use their abilities for themselves. They were free to be unequal. Now we hear only about everything that's wrong and 'unequal' in society and how government must take away more and more of everyone's money and freedom for collective solutions—in the 'public interest'—in order to *level* society rather than allow people to reach heights. This is the America where government has invented phony 'rights' to displace man's natural rights, where 'rights' are made deliberately unequal in order to try to *level life*. It's a nation where people are now forced to serve others instead of being free to serve themselves, because their abilities, their property, their very lives belong to 'society' and must serve government-decreed 'equality' and collective needs.

"What made this country different from any other—and the reason it was more successful than any other—is that people found it was practical to solve their problems through moral means, namely, individual rights. If this country has now become so twisted that it's no longer possible to save it except by immoral means, as you and Dr. Steiner are trying to do, then this country isn't worth saving and the life my children would have here wouldn't be worth living. Moral living will no longer be possible. If America has become a country where one's life depends either on immoral choices or on living in a society where one can't make meaningful choices at all—a society without freedom—what future does anyone have?"

"Then you won't agree to keep quiet?" asked the senator.

"Of course not. As soon as I leave this office, I'll tell anyone who'll listen to me."

"Do you think you can stop us?" cried Billington. "You're one individual. What the hell do you think one person with his individual rights can do compared to the power and government resources that Steiner and I control? We will not be stopped!!" he bellowed as he slammed his fist down on the desk. He was bluffing, but Don didn't know it.

"The people who founded this country," said Don quietly, "risked everything, including the lives of their families, in the cause of freedom. They knew that a life without freedom wasn't worth living. I now make the same choice not only for myself but for my wife and children. I'll risk everything for a moral solution to the mess this country is in. But if no moral solution is possible, if I can't stop you by the moral action of speaking the truth, and if because I speak out against the immorality of your solution, you choose to wipe us out as you did Markowitz, then so be it. We shall all have died in the cause of freedom. We shall have died for the only principles that make a truly human existence possible, because I refuse to accept anything less for myself or my family. Everything else is not really living; it's just 'substitute living.'" He wasn't bluffing, and Billington knew it.

"Dammit! I told you I had nothing to do with Markowitz. The police said it was a random shooting. How many times do I have to tell you that?

"And when I said Dr. Steiner and I would not be stopped, I didn't mean to imply any threat to you or your children. I was merely expressing my determination to succeed, to follow through with our project for the good of the country." That, of course, was a lie. Billington had simply seen that his bluff hadn't worked, so he backed off.

Don continued almost as though he hadn't heard what Billington had said. "It may well be that I can't stop you, but no one can foresee all the good consequences of individuals utilizing their liberty. I pointed out that early in this century no one could've foreseen the immense rise in material wealth in this country, the great cities, the technological advances, the abundance of automobiles, telephones, even shoes, that occurred simply because people acted within their rights. And no one could've foreseen that more wetlands would be preserved by people exercising their individual rights than by government coercion. It simply turns out best in the long run if everyone acts within his rights even if all the consequences can't be predicted. That's why freedom 'works.' Better solutions always can be found within the context of individual rights than through the immorality of government violating those rights or by the kind of scheme you're attempting. All of which is another way of saying that the moral solution is the practical solution."

"Look," said Billington, "if there were a better way, a perfectly moral way, I'd be for it. But there just isn't any other way. You know yourself that Congress would never pass the Constitutional amendments you've proposed. You admitted this early in our conversation in discussing one of your amendments; and since then, you've added other amendments that Congress would be even less likely to approve. You know that. So, c'mon, now. Admit there's no other way than what Dr. Steiner and I propose, and let's all work together—as a team—to save this country. What better purpose could we dedicate ourselves to?"

"Even if there were no other way, senator," said Don, "I still couldn't be a party to your scheme. It's not that you aren't pursuing a good purpose. It's that the most noble, the most moral purpose must still be achieved by moral means. No code of morality in history has ever been able to defend the doctrine that the end justifies the means. It's no less immoral to pursue a moral end by immoral means than to pursue an immoral end. *Both* ends and means must be moral. What has gotten this country into so much trouble are the attempts to achieve all sorts of 'good' purposes through immoral means, namely, government's power to threaten people with guns. People have been deluded by the idea that the actions of democratic government are moral because they're democratic. But democracy can't determine morality any more than it can determine truth. Neither the morality of an action nor the truth of an idea can be determined by voting or any political process.

"If I agreed to cooperate with you, I would be guilty of the same immoral the-end-justifies-the-means approach that has led to all the governmental abuses and problems we've been talking about all afternoon. And there's no telling what further abuses and problems would result from my action. For just as people acting within their individual rights ultimately benefit society in unexpected ways, government actions against individual rights—no matter how 'good' the intended purpose—are ultimately harmful to society in unexpected ways. That's why socialism doesn't work and why every government policy is detrimental to society in proportion as it violates individual rights. Every unwarranted and immoral government intervention, even with the best of intentions, leads inexorably to greater abuses and violations of individual rights. That's the history of the expansion of federal power. It begins with the 'good' purpose of regulating the price of wheat in interstate commerce and ends up regulating practically every transaction between man and man in society; it forces some people to serve others, destroys everyone's right to freedom of association, and obliterates one of the founding principles of this nation: everyone's right to the pursuit of happiness. Similarly, the good purpose of clean water at the expense of property rights has led ultimately to people being thrown in jail for not having a permit to dump dirt on dirt—clean, unpolluted dirt on privately-owned dry land.

"It's true that Congress would never approve the Constitutional amendments that I proposed. I wasn't thinking about Congress when I suggested them. The U.S. Congress is totally worthless as a means for achieving the kind of reforms that are necessary in this country. In fact, it has done more to create the mess this country is in than anything else I can think of, although the executive and judicial branches certainly deserve a share of the blame, too. It's hard to think of a problem in contemporary America that, if not caused by Congress, has at least been significantly exacerbated by it. From the decline of the dollar to the decline of American education, we can clearly see the effects Congress has wrought; it's the root cause of inflation and the major reason behind the nation's educational disaster. From the fraud and waste of government welfare to its subsidization of the breakdown of the family and the rising crime that follows, we can clearly see the causative role of Congress. For the waste and misallocation of resources in everything from government mandates to fraudulent research programs, from the $180 billion annual waste in just the administration of federal agencies to the subsidization of synthetic fuels and ethanol, Congress is clearly to blame. For the multi-trillion dollar national debt that must result in either national bankruptcy and the complete destruction of the dollar or a crushing debt burden for generations as far as we can imagine, there is no one to blame but Congress. For the world's largest Ponzi scheme—Social Security—and for its ultimate collapse, for the most asinine and irksome regulations we have to put up with in our daily lives, for regulations that endanger our health and safety, and for laws that take away our precious liberty in return for votes that buy lifetime financial security for members of Congress, there is no one to blame but Congress.

"Even when Congress has accomplished something of value, it invariably has done so at a net loss. Everything an individual does is a matter of trading his time, effort or material resources for something of *greater* value. But everything of any value that Congress has accomplished has been by forcing taxpayers or future generations to pay more than its worth—which, of course, is why they must be forced. This is as true of Social Security as it is of environmental cleanup costs, many of which even EPA has admitted to be 'unreasonable' and 'uneconomic.' Congress seems to believe that it can determine 'worth' independent of economic reality—by substituting 'political realities' for economic reality. But Congress, despite being anointed by the sacred process of democratic election, has no divine power to determine worth any more than to determine truth or morality.

"No, senator, I wouldn't depend on Congress for the necessary reforms when Congress is the biggest part of the problem. Those reforms can only be achieved by circumventing Congress. As you know, there's another Constitutional procedure for initiating Constitutional amendments besides having Congress do so."

Billington was startled. "You mean have the legislatures of the states call another Constitutional Convention?"

"Exactly," said Don. "That would leave the U.S. Congress out of the amendment process entirely."

"But that's never been done in over two hundred years, " said a flustered Senator Billington. "It's not practical."

"Don't give me that 'practical' crap," said Don.

"But we've had almost thirty amendments to the Constitution," Billington insisted, "and they've all been initiated by Congress. The other method has never been used. There hasn't been a Constitutional Convention since the one that founded this nation."

"So what? The mechanism has been right there in the Constitution all the time. There's no reason it couldn't be used. Now is the time to use it."

"But the people won't use it," insisted Billington. "They've never used it before, and they won't use it now. Certainly it's within people's rights to do what you say, but they won't do it. That's why we need to use the telephone virus."

"Whether its saving owls or wetlands or saving the nation," said Don, "if it can't be done within the context of man's rights, it shouldn't be done at all. You can't act against people's rights just because you don't like their choice of exercising those rights. The people have the moral, Constitutional means to reform their government without Congress—even in spite of Congress. But whether or not the people choose to do so is up to them.

"You may very well be correct that the people won't demand another Constitutional Convention in order to amend the Constitution. They've certainly had ample cause long before now and yet have never done so. They could've done so even for far more limited objectives than I've raised, yet they didn't. They could have, for example, used this procedure to end federal meddling in education or, more modestly, simply to end school bussing—something that's widely opposed by both blacks and whites. After decades of mandatory bussing, public schools are still seventy percent segregated. So what has bussing accomplished? It certainly hasn't improved academic results. Yet the American people, despite constant grumbling, for decades have chosen to do nothing about this issue. They could've used this amendment procedure to achieve a balanced budget; several attempts were made but for decades too few people cared enough to support them. Again, most people chose to do nothing. They could've used this procedure to establish sound money, to correct the Supreme Court's interpretation of the 'commerce clause,' to eliminate Congress exempting itself from its own laws, to confine the federal government to its enumerated powers in the Constitution, or to reassert the right of everyone to the pursuit of happiness. They could've stopped the 200 pages per day of new regulations the federal government is spewing out. Instead for decades the people chose to do nothing. They simply resigned themselves to accepting whatever the government forced upon them.

"If the people don't care enough to use the legitimate means available to save themselves from the tyranny of the federal government, why should I or anyone else worry about saving them? If the people have become 'so debased,' to use Madison's phrase, that they will 'tolerate anything but liberty,' then the nation can't be saved and isn't worth saving. Whichever choice the people make, they'll get what they deserve. The choice is theirs to make; it's not up to me or you or Dr. Steiner. *It's their responsibility.*"

Billington didn't reply. Instead he swiveled his chair so that he was sideways to Don and looking out the window. There was what seemed like a long silence, but which actually was only a minute or so, perhaps even less. Finally, without averting his gaze from the window, he said, almost feebly, "You won't help us then." It was a statement, not a question.

Don didn't respond immediately. He waited to see the senator's face turn toward him for his reply. But the senator's head never moved. Finally, Don said quietly but firmly, "No."

There was another long pause, longer than the first one, in which neither man spoke or moved. They were like two prize fighters who had punched themselves out, who had thrown everything they had at each other and were now too exhausted to continue. Neither had anything more to say.

Then Don slowly got to his feet and said, "Well, I guess I should be going." He thought maybe the senator would want to shake hands or that he should thank the senator for inviting him to his office and listening to all his ideas. But the senator was motionless. Don knew he wasn't asleep because he could see his eyes were open and occasionally blinked. Then the senator made a short wave with his open hand toward to door, signaling Don to leave.

Don walked to the door and opened it. He paused and looked back thinking perhaps he should at least say good-bye. But the senator was still gazing out the window, his back now toward Don. Neither man spoke. The next sound was that of Don closing the door behind him.

Chapter Twelve

Once outside the building, Don got a taxi and headed back to his hotel. But after going only a few blocks, he told the driver to take him to the nearest pay phone first.

He called Jan and said, "Listen, dear, this is very important. There's an enormous plot to use the telephone virus to take over the government of the United States. I'm calling you from a pay phone because I've been under surveillance here and my phone in the hotel may be bugged. But be careful what you say because the phone you're on may be bugged too.

"I was going to wait until I got back to Minneapolis to tell you all the details, but the situation is too urgent. If anything happens to me and I don't make it back to Minneapolis, I'm depending on you to get this information to Bobby. I don't want to say his last name over the phone, and I don't want you to, but you know who I mean."

"Yes, of course."

"Do you know how to spell his last name?"

"Yes. I think so."

"Good. You'll have to find the address of his parents from the phone book. His father's name is William. Go over there…no, you might be followed. Better yet, get the phone number and then go to a pay phone. But don't write down the address or the phone number; memorize the phone number. If anything happens to you, I don't want anyone to discover anything that would lead them to Bobby. Call Bobby, tell him what's at stake, and tell him what I'm going to tell you. It may be vital to his research."

"I'll try," she said, taking a deep breath, "but I don't have your phenomenal memory."

Don began to tell her what he had learned from his meeting with Dr. Steiner and from the tour Monica had given him of the research facility. Though he remembered virtually everything, he didn't try to tell it all to Jan. He didn't want to confuse her with unnecessary details and make it more difficult for her to remember the really important things, and there wasn't time to tell her everything anyway. He tried to tell her only what he thought would be significant to Bobby.

When he finished, Jan said, "Boy, that's a lot to remember, but I think I've got the main ideas. I just hope I don't forget anything. But, honey, I'm so worried!!"

"I'm worried, too," he said, "but we've got to keep clear heads and do what we have to do. I'm depending on you."

"I know. I'll do my best."

"I know you will. I'm depending on Bobby, too, and I know he'll do his best. Tell him it's like the days we used to play tennis together. There were many times when he saved us with that big serve of his. Tell him it's his serve now and match point. It's all up to him. If I ever needed a big serve from him, it's now. Tell him we need an 'ace.'"

"If anything happens to you," said Jan, "even if Bobby succeeds in his research, will he know what to do with his results?"

"Yes. I told him what my plan is."

Don looked at his watch. "It's 5:20 here in Washington. That means it's only 4:20 in Minneapolis. You should still have time to contact that guy from the phone company. I don't want to mention his name either, but do you know who I mean?"

"I know who you mean, but at the moment his name escapes me!" she said with consternation. "Darn! I know it will come to me…Wait a minute…Yes! I've got it!"

"You're sure?"

"Uh, huh."

"Fine. Either call him from a pay phone or go over to the phone company. If you call him, don't use the same pay phone you're going to use to call Bobby unless you can call one right after the other. Whatever you do, you've got to protect Bobby. If the phone at our house is bugged, whoever is listening will know you're going to contact the phone company, but they won't know who you're going to contact. Of course, it's not as important to protect his identity as it is that of Bobby, but let's not give out any more information than we have to. Tell the guy from the phone company what's at stake and ask him to come out to the house and check to see if the phone is bugged."

"Anything else?"

"No, that's it for now. With luck I should be back in Minneapolis tomorrow, but don't plan on picking me up at the airport. I think you'll be safer staying at home. I'll just take a cab. The scope of this plot is so tremendous there's no telling what might happen next or where. And if anything does happen to me, remember always that I loved you, and tell the children I loved them, too."

Jan started to cry. "I love you, my darling, and I'll tell the children." Then she quickly hung up so Don wouldn't hear her crying.

Once at his hotel, Don locked himself in his room. He decided he would remain there until the next morning when he would check out to go to the airport. He had his evening meal sent to his room.

He knew that if Steiner and Billington had agents in the hotel who took that picture of him and Monica, there were probably agents right now in the hotel watching for him—and that they would be prepared to act. After all, he had told Billington he would tell anyone about the plot as soon as he left his office. It was inconceivable that Billington would not make an effort to keep him quiet. And certainly the plotters were not above killing him if they had already murdered Markowitz for the same reason.

As he ate his dinner alone in his room, he thought about Jan and the children eating without him. He wondered if he would ever see them again. He wondered if Jan was thinking the same thing.

The food was good, but he didn't seem to have much of an appetite. He ate as much as he could, then turned on the TV to try to take his mind off his family and his own predicament. He made the rounds of all the channels, found nothing of interest and turned off the TV set.

He wanted to call his wife, to hear her voice one more time, perhaps hear his children's voices one last time, too. But he thought perhaps it would be best if he didn't call, perhaps it was best not to run the risk that he or Jan would accidentally say something that might give an advantage to their enemies. He'd already said everything that needed to be said when he called from the pay phone before returning to the hotel. Maybe it was best to leave things as they were. Still, he wanted to hear Jan's voice again. As he was trying to decide whether or not to call, he began to pace back and forth in the room.

Finally, after much pacing and much thought, he decided that maybe he should call. Jan would be wondering if he was still all right, and maybe he should call just to let her know that he was. He would keep the conversation short, not risk saying anything he shouldn't.

Just then the phone rang. It was Jan. Her thoughts had paralleled his own.

"Thought I'd call just to see how you are," she said as matter-of-factly as possible.

"I'm fine," he replied. "How are you and the children?"

"We're fine," she said. "I gave the children the new toys this evening that you wanted me to give them. They're occupied with them, because there are no distractions here; everything is quiet. The TV is off."

That was clever of her, he thought. There were no 'new toys' that he wanted her to give the children. What he wanted her to give was the information to Bobby and Eilers. Clearly, she was using the word 'children' to refer to those two men and to tell him that she had accomplished what he had asked. Her comment that they were 'occupied' with the 'new toys' meant that the men were acting on the information she had passed them. Her comment that 'there are no distractions here; everything is quiet' meant that there had been no attempt to stop her or to interfere with Bobby or Walt. The comment that the TV was off was merely to make the rest of her comments seem relevant to the home scene.

"That's fine," he said. He would like to have heard the children's voices one more time. But after Jan's comments, he couldn't talk to them about the 'new toys,' and not mentioning them would seem unnatural and make her comments suspicious to anyone overhearing the conversation. So he said, "Well, there's really nothing more to say. There's no point in running up a phone bill. I'll see you tomorrow."

"I love you. Good-bye," she said.

"I love you, too. Good-bye"

He felt good that Jan had called. He was not only glad to hear her voice but delighted with the loaded message she had conveyed.

Now he had to worry about how to get out of the hotel alive in the morning. As he pondered the question, he thought about calling the front desk, or even the hotel manager, in the morning and asking the hotel security staff to provide an escort from his room to the front desk. But that might make matters worse. Why, the hotel would wonder, does he need such an escort? If he was carrying a large amount of cash, why didn't he deposit it in the hotel safe? If he was unafraid to carry a large amount of cash to his room, why would he be afraid to leave with it now? The obvious question then would be whether he did not enter the hotel with such a large sum of money as he now planned to exit with; had he, in fact, used the hotel room to collect drug money or payoffs for other illicit purposes? If the hotel was suspicious, it might notify the police. Remembering Monica's comment that Billington and Steiner controlled the police in this city, he didn't want to give their people an excuse to arrive on the scene.

He thought about simply calling the front desk in the morning to ask for a porter to carry his luggage down. He only had one small suitcase, which he could easily carry himself. But with this plan there would at least be another person, perhaps someone to help him ward off an attacker, or at least be a potential witness, someone, moreover, who would be missed rather quickly by the hotel if anything happened to him. Also, his own hands would be free to grapple with an assailant, and he could run faster if unencumbered by his suitcase.

At first he liked this idea, but the more he thought about it, the less satisfactory it became. How would he know that the hotel wasn't collaborating with the agents he feared? How would he know that the person the hotel might send to help him with his luggage wasn't one of them? Besides, if his phone was bugged, just calling the front desk to ask for help with his luggage would alert his enemies to the exact time of his departure. The one thing in his favor was that they didn't know exactly when he would leave. He was reluctant to give up that one small advantage.

He finally decided he would carry his own suitcase and make a dash for it in the morning. If he saw anyone suspicious, he would return to his hotel room and try again later. If he then saw the same suspicious person or persons again, he would call the front desk, ask for a security escort, and say the reason was the suspicious person or persons he had seen in the hall. Of course, that wouldn't work either if the hotel was collaborating with the agents, but at that point there would be nothing more he could do anyway.

Then there was the matter of the elevator. If he were only two or three floors up, he would've considered taking the stairs, figuring that he would've been expected to take the elevator. But he was on the eighth floor. It's not that he wasn't in good enough shape to run down eight flights of steps. That didn't bother him. What concerned him was that it would take too long for him to do so—long enough for his enemies to realize what he had done and to ambush him. Hotel stairwells were usually deserted, used mostly for emergencies. They would be a lonely place—entirely the wrong place—to meet a potential assassin. He would have to take the elevator.

The ideal situation would be either an empty elevator or a nearly full one, where there would be many potential witnesses. The worst situation would be an elevator with two or three husky men and no one else. In that case, he would return to his room and try again later.

Such thoughts, interspersed with those of his wife and his children, occupied the mind of Don Emerson all evening and through most of the night, the night he thought might be the last of his life. He lay in bed trying to sleep, but the thoughts kept coming back and kept him awake. Finally, he made one last addition to his plan. In the morning he would call the front desk and ask for a porter to help him with his luggage a half hour *later* than the time he really intended to leave. Then he would take his own suitcase and leave before his enemies, thinking they knew the time of his departure, would expect him. He knew his plan might not work, but it was the best he could come up with. Knowing that, he was at last able to fall asleep.

Senator Billington sat gazing out the window for more than half an hour after Don left. An observer might have thought he was daydreaming. But the faraway look in his eyes masked a mind that was working at high speed to find a way to save the Trojan Project. He went over every scenario he could think of. He tried to think of every possible way that he and Dr. Steiner could utilize the vast resources at their disposal to bring about the desired result. Finally, he did the inevitable. He bent over the desk, picked up the phone and dialed. When Steiner answered, Billington said, "Shred everything."

"You couldn't get him to go along, huh?" asked Steiner.

"No," answered Billington wearily. "I spent all afternoon with that son-of-a-bitch. I tried arguing with him, agreeing with him, bluffing, threatening, everything—even a moral appeal for the good of the country. Nothing worked. It turns out he's one of those goddam idealists who won't compromise his principles. There's no way to deal with such people. They won't listen to reason. They won't be practical. That's what's the most frustrating aspect of the whole thing. We handle all the practical problems of setting up and running this gigantic program, funding it, doing the complex scientific stuff—and then we get defeated by some goddam idealist with his stupid 'principles.' But that's the way it is. So now you know what you've got to do. Get that shredder going."

"Okay," said Steiner. "I'll start right away and work through the evening."

Shortly after Billington arrived at his office the next morning, he had a phone call. It was Steiner. "Did you take care of everything the way you were supposed to?" asked the senator.

"Almost," said Steiner. "I got rid of any reference to you or anything that could implicate you. So you've nothing to worry about. I've gotten rid of most of the research data already, too, but I've been trying to scan everything before I destroy it. That's why it's taking me so long. I was up all night on this. And in going over all this stuff before I feed it through the shredder and it's gone forever, I've seen some correlations I didn't notice before. I've seen what could be the breakthrough we've been looking for all along. The reason I'm calling you now is to see if I can't have another month to check this out before I shred the rest of this stuff, the core material that may hold the breakthrough."

"No," said Billington decisively.

"Well, then, how about a couple of weeks? I might be able to do it in a couple of weeks, maybe less. Can't you give me even another couple of weeks?"

"No," said Billington even more decisively. "It's over, Mal. We've got to cover our tracks, forget about the Trojan Project, and hope for another opportunity somewhere else."

"But," pleaded Steiner, "we'll never have another opportunity like this. I'm 59 years old. I'll never get another chance like this. Can't you give me even another couple of weeks?"

"You know I would if I could," said Billington. "I'm older than you are. I'll probably never get another opportunity like this either, but we've both got good-paying jobs and can look forward to generous pensions. There's no point in blowing everything we've got for Trojan now that the odds have turned against us. This guy Emerson said that as soon as he left my office he'd tell anyone who'd listen to him. So we simply don't have any more time, Mal. Not two weeks. Not even two days."

"But did you try the IRS?" Steiner persisted. "Maybe you could use the IRS to intimidate him. Everybody is afraid of the IRS and what it might do to them."

"I'd already have done so if I thought it would work," said Billington. "But, first of all, there isn't time. Second, I don't think it would work anyway. If this guy Emerson is willing to risk even the lives of his children, he's not going to be intimidated by threats of the IRS."

"No, I suppose not," said Steiner dejectedly.

"All right, then. Be a good boy and get back to your shredder," said Billington.

"Okay, but you're sure you couldn't give me even a week?"

"Positive."

"Well, okay."

At the hotel Don awoke to a beautiful day. He looked out the window and thought wryly that if this was indeed the last day of his life, at least the weather was going to be nice.

He looked over the room service menu to see what to order for breakfast. He wasn't very hungry despite not eating much the evening before. He thought he would just order coffee and a roll and perhaps a glass of orange juice. But what the hell, he thought, this just might be the last meal he would ever eat. He might as well order the eggs benedict. He even thought of ordering a bottle of champagne but decided he'd better keep a clear head for the ordeal he knew was awaiting him. He placed his order, then shaved, got dressed and packed his suitcase.

When his breakfast arrived, Don peered cautiously through the peephole in the door. There was no one else in the hallway, just the deliveryman with the food cart. He opened the door. The cart was wheeled in. He quickly tipped the man, who then left, and locked the door again. Well, he thought, at least he had managed to get breakfast without any problem. The real problem—how to get out of the hotel—still lay ahead.

He started eating and was surprised how much he was enjoying the food. He told himself he must be hungry from not eating much the night before. It had been quite awhile since he had had eggs benedict, and he was really enjoying them.

But then, he thought, *what if the food is poisoned?* Suddenly he wasn't hungry any more. He tried to tell himself that it was ridiculous to think his food could be poisoned and that he should just try to enjoy it, because even if it had been poisoned, he'd probably already eaten enough to kill him anyway. He forced himself to take a few more bites, but he no longer had an appetite. He pushed the plate away.

He still had a lot of time to kill before he would try to leave or even until he would call the hotel desk and give the phony time for picking up his luggage. He began to pace back and forth in the room, periodically glancing at his watch. Finally, it was time to make that call. Having done that, he resumed his pacing while going over in his mind every possible difficulty he might encounter in his effort to get to the lobby.

The time was fast approaching for him to leave for the lobby when the phone rang. Who could this be, he wondered? Was it Jan? Did she have something new to tell him? He thought she wouldn't call again unless there was some new development. Was it an 'agent?' Maybe he shouldn't answer. But curiosity wouldn't allow him to let the ringing continue unanswered. He picked up the phone with trepidation.

"Hello, Mr. Emerson. I'm glad I got a hold of you. I was afraid you had already checked out of your hotel."

"Monica!"

"I had to call you," she continued. "Dr. Steiner is dead."

"What?!" he asked in disbelief. "How did it happen?"

"When I arrived at work this morning, Dr. Steiner looked very tired and drawn. I think he was up all night. A little while ago I found him slumped over his desk beside a huge pile of shredded paper. The secret filing cabinet was open but about 90 percent empty. He must have been shredding those papers all night. I tried to awaken him by shaking him. He seemed to come to, said a few words in obvious pain as he clutched his chest, and then slumped over the desk again. I called 911, but he was already dead when the ambulance arrived. The ambulance personnel said he probably had a heart attack. I suppose they'll do an autopsy, but I don't know that the real cause of his death will appear on the death certificate."

"Why do you say that?"

"Because I don't think any coroner is going to put 'killed by his VCI' as the cause of death on a death certificate. A few minutes before I discovered Dr. Steiner slumped over his desk, I had seen him down the hall—or what I thought was him. We even exchanged a few words. But when a few minutes later I found him slumped over his desk, I realized that I must have been talking to his VCI in the hallway, because there was no way he could have gotten past me to get back in his office without me seeing him. I think Dr. Steiner was so tired from staying up all night that he put his head down on his arms on the desk to rest, perhaps even intending to nap briefly. Then, being so terribly tired, he quickly fell into a deep sleep, deep enough—at least in his fatigued state—for his VCI to get loose."

"So you think," said Don, "that when you tried to awaken him, the sleeping host perished instead of the VCI? I worried that that might happen when I thought of awakening my mother in her house that time my wife saw her VCI. I didn't know if that could actually happen, but I'm certainly glad I didn't try to awaken my mother. I told you and Dr. Steiner about that incident, but I don't know if you remember it."

"Yes, I remember it," said Monica, "but it's not the same thing. We've awakened all sorts of subjects in our laboratory experiments, and it's always the VCI that perishes, not the sleeping host. There's a crucial difference in the case of Dr. Steiner. Do you remember when Dr. Steiner was explaining how a VCI acts? He said it will use the abilities of the host and act exactly as the host would in any situation—and, therefore, it cannot commit a crime *unless the host already has a criminal mind.*"

"Of course, I remember. I have a very good memory," said Don. "So because Steiner was capable of murder in the case of Paul Markowitz, his VCI would also have been capable of murder. If Steiner would've murdered in the situation in which his VCI found itself, then the VCI would also commit murder."

"Exactly."

"Then do we need to worry about his VCI still roaming around out there?"

"No," she replied. "That's the good thing about me being able to awaken Dr. Steiner before he died. His becoming conscious would destroy the VCI. I'm positive of that. If he died without awakening, then we might have a problem. I don't really know what would've happened then, and I don't know that anyone ever will know. At any rate, they're both dead now. I think they killed each other, but it's certainly possible that Dr. Steiner really did have a heart attack independently. I know he's been under a lot of stress and working very hard on what amounts to two jobs. When I awakened him, he had great difficulty trying to speak, but his words sounded like, 'It's killing me.' Did the 'it' refer to the VCI or to the pain of a heart attack? We'll never know. And if the VCI did kill him, how did it do it? By somehow inducing a heart attack? By some other mechanism? Again, we'll never know."

"You said that the secret filing cabinet was open but that 90 percent of its contents has already been shredded," said Don. "I'm wondering if what's left is enough to prove the existence of the telephone virus."

"Oh, sure," Monica replied, "more than enough even to show a government program to research it. There are 15 or 20 pages right on the top of Dr. Steiner's desk that would prove that much. I know because I scanned them while waiting for the ambulance to arrive. I didn't see anything to prove the existence of the second, more secret program—the one to try to manipulate the virus in order to take over the country—but, of course, I haven't looked at what's left of the papers in the cabinet. I doubt, however, that I'd find anything on that there because I think those would be the first papers Dr. Steiner would've shredded."

"I'd like to ask you to do something, Monica, to foil this whole plot, but it may involve considerable risk for you. So if you don't want to, just say so, and that'll be okay. You're probably at some risk even to be talking to me about all this."

"I thought about that before I called," she said, "but I'm calling on the phone in Dr. Steiner's office. I've been cautious for a long time about what I say over the phone in my office or even the one in my apartment because I think those lines are probably tapped. That's why I had to come to your hotel that night. But I doubt that Dr. Steiner would've put a tap on his own phone. So I think I'm all right here."

"But you're not considering the fact that the phone in my hotel may be bugged," he said. "I'll bet you didn't know that agents were watching when you came over here. They even took a picture of the two of us in the doorway of my hotel room."

"That 'drunken' couple that came by as I was leaving!" she said.

"Yes," he said. "So if we were under surveillance here, it's not too far-fetched to think the phone here may also be bugged."

"You're right."

"So if you want to go along with trying to foil this plot, you'd better be prepared to get out of town as quickly as possible."

"I suppose you're right," she said. "I really don't think there's much danger now that Dr. Steiner is dead. I think the whole plot will just collapse, because I don't think there's anyone to take over what he was doing. But I really don't know for sure. This program has so many tentacles stretching out over the whole country that I really don't know who else might be involved in all this. There are still a lot of things I don't know about how Dr. Steiner was handling the program. So you're right. I'd better get out of town because if there is someone listening to us, I could be in big trouble."

"But do you want to go ahead, then, in spite of the risk?"

"Yes. I'm tired of living in fear. I'm not going to go on living the way I've been for the last five months. And if the Trojan Project succeeds, this country will be a nightmare for me as well as for everyone else. Besides, I've got a score to settle for Paul's murder."

"All right," he said. "I assume you have access to a copy machine nearby. Right?"

"Yes."

"Okay. Make copies of those 15 or 20 pages you just mentioned, put them in an envelope and mail them to Jim Phillips, science editor at the *Minneapolis Journal American*. The address is 1021 Eighth Street South, Minneapolis, Minnesota." Don was glad he had bothered to notice the numbers above the doorway on the building when he visited Phillips. "Then you have to get out of town because even if this phone isn't bugged, you could be in big trouble if Phillips puts this information in the newspaper."

"You're right. Anyone involved in the Trojan Project will know this information had to have come from me. But I don't know where to go. Obviously, I can't go to any of my friends or relatives," she said.

"Obviously," he replied. "Those are the first places anyone would look. If Steiner's agents have been watching you, they know all about those people. You have to go somewhere nobody would think of looking." As he spoke he tried to think of where that might be, and an answer came almost immediately: Aunt Cess. No one would ever think of looking for Monica there, in the home of an elderly unrelated woman living alone in a modest home in Minneapolis. Furthermore, he knew that Aunt Cess would not only go along with the idea but would be downright delighted by it. He knew exactly what she would say: "Oh, Kiddo! That would be wonnnnderful!!' She always called everyone 'Kiddo,' and everything was always 'wonnnnderful!' Despite her advancing age she had retained an adventurous spirit, a youthful enthusiasm for new experiences and meeting new people, especially younger people. They were all 'wonnnnderful!' She was a generous person always willing to share her home and whatever else she had. She would certainly be more than happy to have someone as intelligent and vivacious as Monica as a companion in her home for a few days or a few weeks or however long was necessary.

There was even a bonus to this location. Aunt Cess could serve as a go-between for passing information between himself on Monica through Cess' many visits to his mother's house. Communication could thus be carried on without worrying about the telephones being tapped. And Aunt Cess would be delighted by the adventure of playing such an important and secretive role.

"Look," he said, "I've got the perfect spot for you to go to, but obviously I shouldn't give the address over the phone. Have you got a credit card in your purse that you could use to pay for an airline ticket and whatever else you might need?"

"Yes, I've got credit cards and my checkbook, too, in case I need that."

"Good. I was going to tell you first to mail that envelope to Jim Phillips, but you can actually do that at the airport. So, after making the copies we talked about, go directly to the airport. Don't go back to your apartment for any reason, not for clothes or a toothbrush or anything else. Don't even take your own car to the airport. If anyone is listening to this conversation, there could be someone waiting for you at your car. Take a taxi right from your office to the airport. Buy a ticket there for the first flight to Minneapolis. I know you won't make the flight I'm on. You've got further to go to the airport than I do, and I don't have much time to spare in making that flight myself. I don't know when the next flight is, but take it. When you get to Minneapolis, call me from the airport, and I'll then call you back from a pay phone and tell you the address where you should go. You'll find my number listed in the directory.

"I've really got to be going now. Any questions?"

"No."

As they said good-bye, Don looked at his watch. He was shocked to see that most of the half-hour security period he had so carefully planned for his departure had already disappeared. He would have to hustle even to be on time for his plane. He hastily grabbed his suitcase and bolted for the door.

But before he got there, the phone rang again. He was sure it must be Monica again, either with a question or some other news.

"Hello, darling, I've got good news for you." It was Jan. "I really can't tell you everything now, but Bobby said I should just give you this short message: 'Game, set and match to the team of Emerson and Bednarz!'"

"Really? I'm amazed. I don't know what's happened, but I didn't want you to use Bobby's last name over the phone," said Don. "There's still the likelihood that our phones are bugged."

"The guy from the phone company checked our phone last night after work and again this morning, just to make sure nothing changed during the night. He said our phone has not been bugged. As for your phone at the hotel, Bobby said it doesn't make any difference. It's too late for them to stop you. It's over! You've won!!"

Don was stunned. "How can that be?"

"The story of the telephone virus is all over the front page of this morning's *Journal American*. There must be hundreds of thousands of copies of that newspaper already in the hands of people. The word is out. It's too late to try to cover it up any more. Jim Phillips, the guy you met down at the newspaper office, wrote the article."

"But how could he?" asked Don, more stunned than ever. "The information I arranged to have sent to him hasn't even been mailed yet."

"Aided by the information you asked me to give Bobby," said Jan, "he solved the mystery of the telephone virus last night. Even though it was late, he called the newspaper and found Jim Phillips in his office working. Evidently he's a night owl. Bobby called Walt Eilers, and the two of them went to Phillips' office. When they were able to convince him that the telephone virus really exists, he wrote a quick story in time to get it in the morning paper."

"That's great! But listen, dear, I've got to get out of this hotel. I'll hear the rest of the details later."

"I know you've got to leave," she said. "Bobby wants to tell you all the details himself. He asked what time your plane arrives and said he'll come over to the house."

"Fine, dear. Good-bye. I've got to run."

He opened the door to the hall and looked out. No one was in sight. He walked quickly toward the elevators. As he turned a corner, he could see a couple with two children, several years older than his own, waiting for an elevator. Surely, he thought, with children like that they couldn't be agents. Standing a little to one side was a very refined-looking woman about his age, smartly dressed in a conservative suit. He thought she was probably just what she looked like, a successful businesswoman. He didn't think he had anything to fear from her unless she pulled a gun, which he thought unlikely with four pairs of eyes present as potential witnesses.

An elevator arrived, but it was going up, not down. No one got on or off.

The next elevator was going down. It contained only a very elderly couple—clearly far too old to be any sort of sinister agents. He looked down the hall in both directions. No one else was coming. This was it. The other five people were getting on the elevator. With him that would make a total of eight. That was certainly a safe number, and he couldn't have hoped for a more innocuous-looking group of people. The last to board the elevator, he positioned himself as far away as he could from the 'businesswoman.' The doors closed, and the elevator began its descent. A moment later he was standing in the lobby with people milling about. He could scarcely believe it.

He walked quickly to the front desk and checked out. Then he walked out the front door of the hotel, where he found a waiting cab that took him to the airport. He arrived there safely and just in time to board the plane, which he did without incident. Airport security being as tight as it is these days, he now felt secure for the first time in days. The worst was behind him now. In a few hours he would be back home.

Upon arriving in Minneapolis, he immediately got a cab for the final leg of his journey. Several times along the way he looked around to see if he was being followed, but he saw no sign of that. He reached home with no problem.

Jan ran out to the curb to meet him, kissed him and gave him the longest, hardest hug since they were married. When she finally let him go, Kathie, who along with Jason had followed Jan out of the house, asked, "Why are you crying, Mommy?"

"I'm just so happy to see Daddy again," she answered wiping away the tears.

As they walked to the house, Jan said, "I don't suppose you've heard the news, have you?"

"No," he replied. "I haven't had a chance to get near a radio or TV."

"Well, it seems the article in this morning's Minneapolis newspaper has attracted national attention. The president has called a news conference for this afternoon to make an announcement on the subject," she said. "That'll be in about two hours."

"What a change!" said Don. "It wasn't long ago that I couldn't get anyone to take me seriously, to believe the telephone virus even existed, and now the president of the United States is making public announcements about it!

"I think I'm getting my appetite back. In fact, I'm starved. I haven't eaten much lately. Is there anything to eat in this house?"

"Of course, my darling. I'll be glad to fix you anything you want," she said. "But there's someone coming up the front walk. Is that Bobby?"

Don looked out the window. "Sure. I'd forgotten for a moment that you two have never met."

He had the door open before Bobby got that far.

"Geez! It's good to see you!" said Bobby seeing Don standing in the doorway. "For awhile you had me pretty worried."

"For awhile," Don responded, "I had myself pretty worried. But I knew you'd come through for me somehow. You always have." Then he introduced Bobby to Jan and said, "We were just going to have some lunch. Come into the kitchen with us and have a bite to eat or a beer or whatever and tell me what happened."

They were all smiles and laughter as they went into the kitchen. Bobby pulled up a chair, opened the beer that was handed him, took a long draft and began: "It was strange the way things worked out. I'd been pursuing several ideas that seemed to be leading me in diverging directions. I couldn't find the unifying principle to bring everything together. When Jan called with the information you wanted her to give me, it helped fill in some of the blanks, but I still couldn't put it all together.

"Did you ever notice how when you're working on a problem for a long time, sometimes the answer comes to you suddenly when you're not looking for it, when you're doing something else? When you're studying a problem, you're loading data into your subconscious. But when you can't find the answer, it's often because your conscious effort is an incorrect thought process that becomes a mental block to discovering the answer. Then, when you're no longer thinking about the problem, that mental block is no longer there; your subconscious—which has continued to work on the problem—comes up with the answer and alerts the conscious part of your mind. Suddenly, you become aware of the answer. Einstein said some of his best ideas came to him not while he was consciously working but while out for relaxing walks. His subconscious, of course, was continuing to work in just the manner I described.

"Playing the piano does for me what walking in the park did for Einstein. It's a relaxation that diverts my conscious mind from the scientific problems I've been working on. The music totally occupies my consciousness, leaving my subconscious to solve problems without the limitations imposed by conscious directions of thought. And in this case the music itself seems to have provided a missing element, some additional input that my subconscious integrated with all the information it had stored relating to the telephone virus.

"I'd been working long hours on the telephone virus for several days before Jan called. My subconscious was already teeming with data on the subject. Just like when I was a student living at home, I still find it relaxing to play the piano after work. So I've often done so during my current stay with my parents.

"Yesterday evening, however, I was just too tired to play. So instead I relaxed by listening to an old audiotape cassette of piano music that I'd made a long time ago from your mother's old phonograph records. I must have left it behind when I moved out of my parents' house years ago. You know, Don, how absentminded I can be sometimes. I'm always losing things or mislaying them. This particular cassette, lost for many years, I discovered a few days ago in going through a box of old stuff in my parents' basement.

"I started playing the cassette and stretched out on the davenport. The first few pieces were interesting and relaxing but of no special relevance. Then came a recording of a Chopin etude. It was the opus 25, number 6."

"The study in thirds," said Don. "I remember working on that piece in my student years. It's a very difficult one."

"That's the one," said Bobby. "As you know, it begins with 32 pairs of alternating notes for the right hand. Those pairs of notes, at harmonic thirds, go back and forth, back and forth, very rapidly. The tones seem to be oscillating—or *vibrating* between those two pairs of notes. Then the left hand adds an undulating rhythm in the base. The amplitude of the original 'vibration' in the right hand increases and then runs out of its range—only to return with a *periodicity* of its own. The whole thing is a study in tonal oscillation, a complex musical creation that ingeniously reflects the physical nature of acoustic vibration in multiple ways.

"The artist on that old recording was the romantic Paderewski. Under the spell of his rich, warm tone and the sensuous musical lines he wove, I may have dozed off. Maybe I was sort of half awake. I don't really know. The next thing I remember was the same piece being played further along on the tape, this time by Moritz Rosenthal. He was playing the same 'vibrations' with the perfect precision of one of the greatest techniques in piano history. Perhaps it was a cumulative effect of hearing those two old masters playing the same piece at just the time when my mind was receptive and my subconscious loaded with information about vibration. At any rate, my subconscious somehow put everything together and alerted my consciousness. Suddenly I was not only wide awake; I was instantly aware that I now understood Gann's long-lost Law of Vibration and could see how it provided a theoretical explanation for the telephone virus."

"That's what makes you a genius, Bobby, the ability to make mental connections that none of the rest of us can make," said Don.

"With that knowledge," Bobby continued, "I knew I had the basis for a way to destroy the telephone virus. It took me only several minutes more to consciously carry the basic idea through to its logical conclusion. What I came up with was a concept for a small device that can be inserted at intervals into the phone network to purge the virus from the lines.

"I was sure I had the answer, but I dashed over to Professor Sorenson's lab to make a couple of simple experiments to prove it. Everything checked out perfectly.

"So then I tried to call Jim Phillips at home. I didn't think he'd be at his office at that hour. But his wife said he often works late into the night and that I should call him at the office. She even gave me the number.

"When he answered, I gave him a few lines on my credentials so he'd take me seriously. I think some of the scientific honors and awards I mentioned almost blew him away. Then I told him this was the biggest story he was ever going to write, one of historic national significance. I said that if he would allow me, I would come down to his office immediately and lay out the scientific proof before him. I also said I would try to get one of the top-ranking technical people from the phone company to come down with me. Phillips invited me to come right down. Then I called Walt Eilers, and he said he'd meet me there.

"Of course, I didn't expect Phillips to follow my scientific proof. I knew it would be way over his head, and I thought it would be over Walt Eiler's head, too. That's where I got a pleasant surprise. Eilers followed everything I was saying.

"When I finished my scientific explanation, I told Phillips that you were in Washington and had discovered that the Pentagon already knew about the telephone virus. I told him there was a colossal supersecret program going on there not to counteract the virus but to try to manipulate it in order to gain control of the country.

"At that point Eilers jumped into the discussion. He said that since he learned of the virus from you, he has been researching it in the laboratory at the phone company. While that research hasn't uncovered much, he said it does prove that the virus at least exists. He also said he's had some personal experiences very similar to your own, which have convinced him of the accuracy of your claims. Then he said that the proof that I had just laid out was fully consistent with his research and his own personal experiences—and then he took some of the things I'd just said and restated them in layman's language that even Phillips could understand! I tell you I was really impressed with that Walt Eilers.

"I don't know that Phillips really grasped everything that Eilers was telling him, but he got enough of it to be convinced. He said he would write an article right away, in time to get it in the morning paper.

"As we were ready to leave Phillips' office, Eilers volunteered to make a few of the little virus-killer devices I had described. He said it wouldn't take more than a few hours to do so in the phone company lab this morning. Then he was going to install them—starting first with your own neighborhood. Every switching station and relay station of every phone company in the country will eventually have to have one of those. That will mean tens of thousands of units of my little invention. I figure they can be made for less than one hundred dollars, but I will sell them for two hundred dollars. Even with that big markup, it's still an inexpensive device. The money involved will be peanuts to a phone company, but it will add up to a very nice profit for me.

"While Walt Eilers was working on making those devices this morning, I was meeting with a patent attorney in order to protect my invention. That's where I was before coming over here," Bobby said. He continued his explanation until Jan finally said, "Listen, as long as we're all through eating, why don't we move this discussion into the living room. The chairs are a lot more comfortable in there, and the president will be speaking in a little while. Let's watch him from in there." They adjourned to the living room as Jan suggested, and the discussion continued.

When there was still about ten minutes until the president's speech, Jan said, "There's someone coming up the front walk." Don looked and then moved quickly to the front door. He opened it, and the visitor stepped quickly inside.

"How come you came here?" he asked in bewilderment. "I thought you were going to call."

"I tried to," Monica replied, "but your line was out of order. The operator told me that all the lines in your whole neighborhood were temporarily out of service due to some work that's being done by the phone company. She couldn't tell me how long it would be until service was restored…"

"That was Eilers installing my little devices," interrupted Bobby. "It wouldn't have taken more than a few minutes, but the operator didn't know that."

"Well, I couldn't stand around the airport for any length of time, could I?" Monica asked. "If any of those agents who were following us in Washington decided to take a plane to Minneapolis, it would be pretty stupid of me to be just standing around the airport waiting for one of them to find me. I had to go someplace. I wouldn't have come here if I thought I was endangering you or your family, but obviously our enemies already know where you live. If not, they could find you in the phone book just like I did. So it's not like I'm giving away any big secret.

"Besides, I'm sure I wasn't followed. I told the cab driver we might be followed, and he took a devious route—and also pulled some slick moves—in order to be sure no one could follow us. And now if you'll just tell me where I'm to go, I'll be very glad to leave."

"Actually, you can't go anywhere yet," said Don, "because I haven't gotten around to asking the person I want you to stay with if it's okay. I'm *absolutely sure* it will be, but I have to ask. I thought I would have plenty of time to do that, because I was expecting you to call from the airport. Then I got engrossed in Bobby's explanation, and time just whizzed by. Now you're here. So come in and meet my wife and my friend Bobby, and I'll call my aunt. She's the one I thought you could stay with."

Monica exchanged greetings with Jan and Bobby. Then Don said, "Bobby, I know you probably think I'm just like my mother, always trying to fix you up; but I assure you this situation was totally unplanned. It's all just a coincidence. Now if you'll excuse me for a moment, I'll try to make that phone call from the next room. Meanwhile, I hope you and Jan will get acquainted with our visitor and make her feel welcome."

Don quickly returned from the kitchen to find Bobby explaining some scientific detail about the telephone virus to a very attentive Monica. He wondered if he had looked as bug-eyed the first time he met Monica as Bobby now did.

"I can't get a hold of Aunt Cess," Don said. "I tried several times, but her line is busy. She's probably talking to my mother. Those two can talk for an hour or two at a time. So, sit down, Monica, and make yourself comfortable. We were just going to watch President Clarkson's news conference on television. He's going to say something about the telephone virus. I'll try to call my aunt again later."

A moment later President Clarkson appeared on the television screen, and an announcer's voice intoned, "Ladies and gentlemen, the president of the United States."

"My fellow Americans," the president began, "I'm speaking to you today because of news stories that have been floating around since early this morning about a computer virus that can affect people and is spread through the nation's telephone network. I want to put your minds at ease by telling you there is no cause for concern. The virus is harmless, and an apparent cure for it has already been found. And I want you to know that my administration—as always—is doing everything it can to safeguard the public interest.

"According to the story, which broke this morning in the *Minneapolis Journal American,* there was some sort of plot to use this virus to take over the government of the United States. I don't know who dreams up this stuff," he said ridiculing the idea with a few chuckles, "but that's what the paper said." He paused to laugh again, and some of the members of the press corps began to laugh with him. "Investigators who have been looking into the matter since we first heard about it early this morning have found no evidence of any such plot. None whatsoever. What they have found is a secret program run by the Defense Department to protect the public by researching ways to cure or eliminate the virus.

"While I never condoned the secrecy of this program—in fact, never even knew about it—I can appreciate that those responsible for the program felt a need for secrecy in order not to panic the public. They felt that to make this issue public would be equivalent to shouting 'Fire' in a crowded theater. That would've been irresponsible. That would not have been in the public interest. There are a lot of programs in the Pentagon that require secrecy. It's a grave disservice to those who were administering this particular program for the good of the country to accuse them of some sort of plot to take over the government when there's not one shred of evidence to that effect. I repeat," he said with great emphasis, "there's not a single shred of evidence of any sort of sinister plot to take over the government. There's not a single shred of evidence that this program was operated for any purpose other than to serve the public welfare by eliminating the virus. And in order to assure the public of this, I'm pleased to announce that Senator Billington will head an investigation into this whole affair. I can think of no one who is better qualified for such a job. I'm sure that in his capable hands the investigation will bring forth the truth for everyone to see. My administration will cooperate with the investigation fully in every respect. We have nothing to hide. As you know, my administration has always been open and honest with the American people."

Monica and Don looked at each other in amazement on hearing that Senator Billington would head the investigation. "What a cover-up!" she said incredulously.

"This morning," the president continued, "the chief scientist responsible for the anti-virus research program, Dr. Malcolm Steiner was found dead in his office. Although the exact cause of death hasn't yet been determined, there's no evidence whatever of any foul play. There's every indication he died of natural causes. While we have not yet received the autopsy report, the preliminary opinion of the medical personnel involved is that he probably died of a heart attack.

"Dr. Malcolm Steiner was a brilliant scientist with a long and distinguished career of service to his country in this nation's Defense Department. His name was never a household word because of the necessary secrecy surrounding his work, but we're all indebted to him. Never once in his long and honorable career has there been any shadow of doubt about his integrity or his dedication to the country. It's a great disservice to the memory of this dedicated public servant now to try to connect him with some sort of fictitious plot to overthrow the government *without one shred of evidence to that effect.* The nation owes him a debt of gratitude for many years of public service. This good and great man died quietly in his office this morning while at work as usual. He died literally with his boots on in the service of his country.

"While a public servant such as Dr. Steiner was working so hard on this issue for the good of the country that he actually worked himself to death, what were the nation's telephone companies doing about the telephone virus? Not a single thing. Not one blessed thing! Were they concerned about the public welfare? Of course not! We all know what they were concerned about. Their own selfish profits! That's all they care about! Their own *unconscionable profits!!* The nation's phone companies in all the years they've been in business have never spent one penny to protect the public from this kind of virus. Not one penny! Millions, even billions of dollars for selfish private profits, and not one penny to protect the public!" He paused briefly to let his words sink in.

"I believe in private enterprise," he resumed. "You all know that. Private enterprise has its place." Then bending over closer to the microphones and lowering his voice slightly, he said slowly and very distinctly, "But we need *greater regulation of the phone industry."* He paused again for effect and then resumed his normal delivery: "There's no other way to achieve our objective of protecting the public. The modern solution is a partnership of business and government, where business creates goods and services and the government regulates everything.

"Therefore, I propose to rejuvenate the Interstate Commerce Commission and give it the new mission of regulating the telephone industry, including telecommunications of the new Information Superhighway. This will ensure that the nation's phone lines are free of any sort of computer virus or telephone virus. I'm asking Congress to pass legislation to this effect, to be called the Clean Telephone Act. Senator Billington has assured me of his cooperation and that there will be no problem in passage of such a bill in the Senate. And I've talked with various members of the House who have assured me of their support and that such a measure will likely pass there, too.

"I'm also asking Congress to pass a Consumer Telephone Protection Act, which will require a five-day waiting period in order to purchase a telephone in this country. This will be very similar to the five-day waiting period in order to purchase a handgun. In the case of handguns, the waiting period is used to run checks on the buyers. In the case of telephones, the waiting period will be used to run checks on the products being sold. The principle is the same; we're just applying it to the other end of the transaction. The waiting period will give the government the opportunity to know what brand and model of phone the prospective buyer intends to purchase in case there are any problems with that particular phone. Phones these days are made all over the world; therefore, a prospective buyer can't possibly know whether the phone he wants to buy is safe or whether it contains some sort of virus like the one that's the subject of all these news stories today. Phones are just like other consumer products. There's simply no way for people to know whether a telephone or anything else is good for them unless the government tells them.

"How would people know what's safe to put into their mouths if we didn't have federal meat inspection and federal regulation of pharmaceuticals and balloons and other children's toys? If people knew what was good for them without the government telling them, there would be no need for such programs. But everyone recognizes that such programs are necessary. Who knows what people would be putting in their mouths if we didn't have these regulations? Well, I say to you here and now that what people put into their ears is just as important as what they put into their mouths. Government has to tell people what's safe to put into their ears just like it tells them what's safe to put into their mouths. People have to be told what's good for them. How else will they know? How would people know which doctors were safe to go to without government licensing? How would people know what their children should be taught in school—or even which school to go to—unless the government tells them?

"I know the idea of a five-day waiting period to buy a telephone will meet with some opposition initially. Remember what a long battle it was to get a five-day waiting period on handguns. Yet now everyone just accepts it. Progressive measures are always ahead of their time. It takes awhile for the public to get used to them and to accept them. In the end it's all for the common good.

"In the case of telephones there's even more justification for the five-day waiting period than in the case of handguns. We all know that the vast majority of handguns are never used in the commission of a crime, and even a deranged individual with a gun can endanger only a very limited number of other individuals. But in the case of a telephone virus, a single phone can contaminate the entire network even though the user is not deranged or intending to harm anyone, and millions of people throughout the country can be infected. Every time a phone call is made from a contaminated phone, the virus is spread to another phone, which can then spread it to still other phones. So there's much greater need for regulation in this area in order to protect the public.

"Furthermore, while the pro-gun lobby has made an issue of the Constitutional right to bear arms, there's no Constitutional right to own a telephone. So there are no Constitutional barriers to greater regulation of the phone industry or to requiring a permit for anyone to own a telephone.

"When a person applies for a permit to buy a telephone, there would, of course, be a modest fee to cover the cost of administering the program. Granted, there will be some delay in processing the application before a person will be able to purchase the telephone he wishes, if his application is approved. But that will be a small price to pay for assurance that the nation's phone network is safe. There are delays now in the regulatory approval of new pharmaceuticals and medical devices. And while those delays should be minimized as much as possible—and my administration is striving to do just that—no sensible person believes we can get along without such regulations. No sensible person believes that those delays aren't a worthwhile price to pay for the benefits we enjoy from those regulations.

"I wish as much as anyone else that regulation was unnecessary, but that's simply not realistic in this day and age. As I said in my State of the Union address, 'We cannot go back to the time when our citizens were left to fend for themselves.' We simply can't have unrestricted freedom the way we did in frontier days. We need modern solutions for modern problems. We all have to accept the fact that the more complicated the forms assumed by civilization, the more restricted the freedom of the individual must become. That's just common sense. We can't turn the clock back, as some people would like to do. We must go forward to a better future for America, a brighter future for everyone regardless of race, creed, national origin, gender or sexual preference, a future where everyone will know his or her phone is safe from any sort of computer virus or telephone virus. We look forward to a vision of the future where everyone will have a *right* to a virus-free telephone.

"Throughout our history our government has constantly made people's lives better by creating new rights for them. This country started with the basic *political* rights to life, labor and property, so-called 'natural' rights. Then, under Franklin Roosevelt, we added *economic* rights. Later we added *social* rights, such as 'equal opportunity' and integration, and *special* rights for the disadvantaged and other select groups. We added *health* rights, such as Medicare and Medicaid; and to this I hope we will add universal health care insurance. Now I propose a new class of rights, *technology* rights. Everyone should have a *right* to the latest technology, a right not only to virus-free telephones but to the very latest of every kind of technology. Government should see to it that everyone has the best of everything as a matter of *right*. Democracy demands nothing less. Anything less would be discrimination. It would be denying some people 'equal opportunity.'

"In order to achieve this new goal, government must hold down the costs of technology just like it must hold down the costs of medical care. We can't have the inventors of new technology ripping off the public and making *unconscionable profits* any more than we can afford to allow the doctors and drug companies to do so. That's why we have *inflation*. That's why prices are too high. That's why technology keeps getting more expensive all the time just like health care does. There is simply too much selfish greed for *unconscionable profits,* and that causes prices to spiral upward. Inventors and scientists must serve the public—just as health care professionals must—rather than their own selfish private interests.

"I realize that in regard to the telephone virus, where some inventor apparently already has devised a solution, it's too late to prevent that individual from making unconscionable profits on his invention. But my administration intends to take action to prevent this sort of thing from happening in the future in order to hold down the costs of technology in the public interest."

"But for me serving my own interests," said Bobby quietly and bitterly, "there would be no solution. And what I'll receive will be a small fraction of what the government already spent on the telephone virus—and a still smaller fraction of what it would have to spend to find a solution."

"That's the end of my prepared statement," said the president. "Now I'll take a few questions."

The first question was from Rosalie Buttonworth of ATS, the American Television System. She asked, "Mr. President, in view of the recent backlash against excessive government regulation, how can you be so sure that Congress will pass your Clean Telephone Act?"

"That's easy, Rosalie," answered the president. "The people of this country want clean telephones just like they want clean air and clean water. Members of Congress won't want to be known as champions of 'dirty' phones anymore than of dirty water or dirty air. Next question…over here…Eric."

Eric Dahlgren of the Times-Sentinel newspaper chain asked, "Mr. President, if there's no truth to the story about a plot to take over the government, why do you think that story was printed?"

"Cheap, partisan politics," replied the president. "I hate to say this, but some people will stoop to anything to try to embarrass my administration for their own partisan political advantage. Next question…in the back…Ralph."

Ralph Stubbins, editor of a small bimonthly journal, *The Philosophic Conservative,* and known as "stubborn Stubbins" for his unrelenting defense of individual rights, asked, "Mr. President, aren't you confusing 'rights' with 'abilities'? And when you talk about the federal government 'creating' rights, such as 'economic rights,' 'social rights,' and now your 'technology rights,' isn't it true that all these so-called rights are at the expense of people's natural rights to life, liberty and property? How do you answer the argument that there aren't any rights except political rights—'rights' itself being a political concept—that the natural political rights to life, liberty and property encompass *all* of man's rights, and that, therefore, government is not actually creating rights but destroying them?"

"To begin with, I think you're living in the wrong century, Ralph," said the president to titters of amusement from the rest of the press corps. "But to answer your questions, the term 'ability' in modern political context means 'political ability.' It's the ability to obtain whatever rights can legitimately be obtained through the democratic process. Your definition of 'rights' may have been true a hundred years ago or two hundred years ago, but it's not true today. We have to change with the times. We've progressed far beyond that primitive beginning. In a democracy we're no longer limited by *natural* rights; 'rights' are whatever democracy decides they are. If voters don't approve of the rights we in government are giving them, they'll vote for those who'll give them some other rights. That's the way democracy works. Next question…over on the side."

Nelson Palmer of World Compu-News said, "Mr. President, the average salary of major-league baseball players is $1.2 million per year. That's far more than almost all doctors or inventors make. Yet you've criticized doctors and inventors for making 'unconscionable profits' while saying nothing about professional athletes, rock musicians and film stars, who make far more money for far less essential services. Do doctors and inventors, who provide more essential services, have fewer rights than sports and entertainment figures?"

"In a sense that's true," conceded the president candidly. "Society must provide for the needs of its members. Society has a collective responsibility to do so. It must allocate its collective resources—both financial and human—to meet those needs. A democracy 'redistributes' human ability and effort according to the needs of society in the same way that it redistributes wealth and for the same reason. In fact, the redistribution of wealth is itself a redistribution of human ability and effort. Either way, the process requires 'redistributing' rights according to the needs of others. It gives more rights to those who need them and fewer rights to others, who don't need them so much, in order to serve the greater good of society. Democracy sorts out who gets what. Where necessary, it sacrifices the interests of a few for the good of many in this pursuit of the collective good, the public interest. The broader interests of society must come before the interests of individuals or particular groups of individuals. And in our case democracy has decided that the public interest is best served by sacrificing the selfish interests of doctors and inventors rather than athletes, rock musicians and film stars. You can't fault democracy for doing what it thinks is best for the overall good of society. In the long run that probably is what's best. Athletes, rock musicians and film stars may make a great deal of money—and they should pay their fair share in taxes toward the redistribution of wealth in society—but at least their fortunes aren't at the expense of other people's basic needs. That's what makes profits 'unconscionable.'"

"Spoken like a true collectivist," said Don in disgust, "and an economic primitive as well. He might as well have said, 'From each according to his ability, to each according to his need,' just as Karl Marx said."

There were a few more questions from reporters, but Don wasn't interested in hearing any more. He looked around and saw that the others were no longer interested in the press conference either. Nobody was watching the TV. Bobby and Monica were sitting very close to one another, smiling and gazing into each others' eyes like a couple of moonstruck teenagers, oblivious to anything else. If ever there was a case of love at first sight, this was it. Jan was watching the two of them with a smile of amusement.

Don broke into a broad grin. He was delighted that these two beautiful and brilliant people were finding such joy in each other and felt deep satisfaction for having been instrumental in bringing them together. Speaking softly as an aside to Jan, he said, "Well, we can't expect any more from those two. They're in a world of their own." After a moment's pause, he added, "But they've done enough."

"So have you," she replied.

"The rest," he said, "is up to the American people."

MAKERS AND TAKERS
How Wealth and Progress are Made
and
How They are Taken Away or Prevented

by
EDMUND CONTOSKI

with a Foreword by
John Chamberlain

MAKERS AND TAKERS shows how the free market works—and why government intervention doesn't. It examines various forms of economic intervention (taxation, regulation, monetary policy) and their effects on consumer products and services, the health and lives of Americans, and the nation's economic well-being.

The book also explores a broad range of environmental issues. Scientific subjects such as pollution, acid rain and global warming are explained in clear, nontechnical language—and some surprising facts here discredit popular beliefs and current government policies.

Finally, the author explains the development of the original American political system and how that system fostered an unprecedented society of "makers"—the greatest production of wealth and scientific advancement in history. He points out the subtle alterations in our political orientation that now favor the taking of wealth rather than the making of it. We have even taken it from our children and grandchildren in the form of a multi-trillion dollar debt, which they are going to have to pay. Here is a book that explains what made America great, what went wrong, and what has to be done for the future.

"Ludwig von Mises [the man often considered the greatest economist who ever lived] has made the classic case against government interventionism. He did it in terms of logic. But never, till now in Edmund Contoski's MAKERS AND TAKERS has there been a book to document the Mises' points with examples that span the entire gamut of State interference as it has affected the lives of creative individuals." —John Chamberlain, formerly the book review editor for *The New York Times,* in his foreword to this book.

480 pages, includes extensive references, bibliography and index.
6 by 9 inches. Quality paperback. Price: $24.95
To order this book, see back of this page.

Books by Edmund Contoski available from American Liberty Publishers:

THE TROJAN PROJECT $17.95

MAKERS AND TAKERS
  How Wealth and Progress are Made and
  How They are Taken Away or Prevented $24.95
    (See description on previous page)

What others have said about MAKERS AND TAKERS:

"In my opinion the kind of intellectual treasure that finds its way into print during few generations.... I consider your work to be timeless to a large extent.... I'm particularly impressed with your ability to express things so clearly."
—Mr. Sherrill Edwards, President of The Fisher Institute.

"Very interesting and most clearly and capably written... really a stunning job of analysis..." —Scott Meredith, President Scott Meredith Literary Agency

"The [principal] metaphor is nicely sustained throughout, you have made wonderful use of quoted material, and your writing is clean and flows well." —Beth Hoffman, Senior Editor, The Foundation for Economic Education

"A vigorous and sustained argument for free enterprise, this book marshals such overwhelming evidence as to devastate any rational opposition.... Quite riveting." —John Hospers, Ph.D., Professor Emeritus of Philosophy, University of Southern California

Add $2.95 shipping and handling for each book.

```
Please send me:                                           Total
_____ copy (copies) of MAKERS AND TAKERS @ $24.95 _____
_____ copy (copies) of THE TROJAN PROJECT @ $17.95 _____
           Minnesota residents add 6.5 percent sales tax _____
                     Shipping and handling @ $2.95 each _____
                  Check or money order enclosed for $ _____

Name_____
Address_____
City _____State_____Zip_____
```

Make check to: American Liberty Publishers
Mail to: American Liberty Publishers, Box 18296, Minneapolis MN 55418

This page may be photocopied